THE COVENANT

Christopher Kerr

The Book Guild Ltd

First published in Great Britain in 2021 by
The Book Guild Ltd
9 Priory Business Park
Wistow Road, Kibworth
Leicestershire, LE8 0RX
Freephone: 0800 999 2982
www.bookguild.co.uk
Email: info@bookguild.co.uk
Twitter: @bookguild

Typeset in 11pt Minion Pro

Printed on FSC accredited paper
Printed and bound in Great Britain by 4edge Limited

ISBN 978 1913913 243

British Library Cataloguing in Publication Data.
A catalogue record for this book is available from the British Library.

To my beloved wife, Sheila, who gave me the inspiration to write this, but sadly did not live to see publication Forever in my thoughts — We lived the dream

Prologue

"Round like a circle in a spiral, like a wheel within a wheel
Never ending or beginning on an ever spinning reel"

The Windmills of your Mind –
Sung by Noel Harrison 1968

Monday 18th June 2018, 7am
Hôtel Plage des Rêves, Port Grimaud,
Côte d'Azur, Southern France

The balcony has a stunning view across the beautiful bay of St-Tropez. The soft, warm wind, heavy with the scent of mimosas and summer pine, lazily wafts the curtains; the gentle splash of glistening waves can be heard lapping at the water's edge, fringed by pine trees, only fifty metres away. From the right, white-sailed boats glide over sun-kissed waters out of Port Cogolin; whilst across the calm blue water, St-Tropez Port, the idyllic harbour village of their dreams, peeps through the shimmering haze. Memories of fifty years ago become as now.

Back then, in 'Haven's Reach', as they called it, fishing boats and small smacks, rowing boats and tenders vied for a position with the luxury yachts of the emerging rich-and-famous 'jet set' at what had once been a small quay. That was alongside the seafront walks they had shared long, long ago, hand in hand, so aware of one another. There, they had loved strolling slowly along the harbour and around the shore to the beaches beyond, taking in the evocative old life openly embracing the new. They had revelled in the exciting, heady atmosphere of 1969, when ideas were openly expressed and explored in poetry, art, theatre, film, literature, sexuality, fashion and, above all, music. They had embraced the mantra of 'Love and peace' which was celebrated everywhere whilst flower power challenged authority. This was their time, this was where it was all happening, and this was their generation.

He smiled, recalling the giddy summer of carefree days and nights; the blissful dawns opening to days of playful fun filled with laughter and suffused with music. This was where they had celebrated their Summer of Love. He warmed, remembering the lamplit evenings on the beach where, naked to the waist, he would play the chords of well-known songs on his guitar, whilst she, clad in a kaftan, sang softly, joining in with the words they both knew so well. His thoughts drifted to sharing long campfire chats with others on how they were going to 'make it all happen'. Music floated through to them from Woodstock, the New York State rock festival of the year that seemed to celebrate their new generation, and they wished they had been there. They swayed to the music of Steppenwolf, the Beatles, Jimi Hendrix, the Byrds and so many others, rejoicing in the expression of the emerging culture of love. They joined others who flocked to see *Easy Rider*, the movie sensation which, like so much at that time, kind of puzzled and delighted them in equal measure; but it was all, in the words of the day, 'so outta sight and cool, man'.

To the left of the balcony stretches Port Grimaud beach, the horseshoe curve of sand bordering the Mediterranean, upon which, so long, long ago, they made their Covenant.

He now recalled that event which had become a beacon that lit up the darkest places, and had been the guide that drew them back to this moment; this moment where time took forever to create a present they embraced from a joyful commitment that, once upon a time, they had made to one another.

Looking down from the balcony towards the Grand Rue, a vision from the past emerges as he sees their favourite cafe, the shutters now closed on the window that was open to the world and beyond that magical night half a century ago. Struck by the vivid recollection of the past, but so aware of their presence now, he turns – "*Un peu plus de champagne, chérie?*" – his words almost a whisper.

"*Mais oui,*" comes the sleepy murmured reply, with a giggle; the voice made more gentle from their shared sleep and the evening's past intimacy.

The wind blows softly, the curtains swirl, and then he senses, rather than hears, her wander out to join him, an arm reaching lazily across his shoulder, then their hands clasped together as young lovers. Their thoughts unite, wandering back to the events of the past hours, months and years. As their gaze takes in the vista before them, their minds drift, wondering how this all came to pass, and how could they ever have let it…

1

Where Do You Go To?

The broadcast from the BBC washed over them in a tidal wave of evocation despite the fact that they were in very different places.

"…and now straight in at number one in our classic chart, the iconic "Where Do You Go To My Lovely" by Peter Sarstedt; a landmark for all you groovy flower children back then in heady 1969. Hey, love and peace, guys, right on." The voice of Tony Blackburn resonated, bringing their past to the present.

> *But where do you go to my lovely*
> *When you're alone in your bed?*
> *Tell me the thoughts that surround you*
> *I want to look inside your head, yes I do…*

They both heard the broadcast at the same time. Jenny had arrived at the Four Seasons Hotel on East 57th Street in New York City from Washington DC the night before to represent her very rich, well-heeled, well-connected, and very well-corrupted client in an

Internal Revenue case. Frankly, she despised the brief, the work and the pressure, although the fees were very attractive.

Peter was in the bustling, ultra-modern, glistening metropolis of Dubai, looking out over the Creek from the Hyatt Regency, where he was immersed in securing the urgent sale of property his Liverpool firm desperately needed to complete. Frankly, he hated his mission, and was singularly unimpressed by the ugly, impersonal nature of his so spectacular twenty-first-century location; once a dream, but now a nightmare.

It was 10.30pm Dubai time and he wanted out of where he was; at 2.30pm in New York City, she was preparing for a trial, and she wanted out of where she was. The music played and they were both stilled in a moment of intense reflection, disturbingly dreaming, drifting back over the years and reaching.

Tell me the thoughts that surround you
I want to look inside your head, yes I do…

As one, they stopped what they were doing. She sat on the bed and realised with surprise that she had tears in her eyes; he opened the sash door to his balcony and felt the warm blast of desert night air, then breathed a long sigh of solitude. It was a deep loneliness they were both experiencing.

The years of their lives, as they listened, had compressed, bringing the dreams of yesterday washing in a wave over their today. She suddenly felt a crazy impulse to make a call, though she rarely dared to embrace such urges. It had been one of those which had sealed their fate back in July 1969. She recalled her dash across the beach, drawn into the arms of a complete stranger, yet their seizing of the moment was so crazily *not* crazy in that time, nor in the weeks that followed or in the heaven of their sharing. That was then but, in her mind as she listened to the evocative music, their then was still their now.

The song played on and their awareness was heightened as the words reached out to them, sweeping their thoughts together until they were gathered into a unity of one. Each was irrepressibly drawn to the other, and the desire to take a step towards yesterday was almost impossible to resist.

I know where you go to, my lovely
When you're alone in your bed
I know the thoughts that surround you
'Cause I can look inside your head

The words and the notes danced as they looked inside their heads that day, and they both knew the thoughts that surrounded them.

Jenny lay wide-eyed in contemplation of reckless thoughts, mischievously embracing a moment she was tempted to seize again. For the first time in such a long time, she felt emboldened to once more make that dash across the beach as she had done a lifetime ago. Although she was highly successful, confident, and very poised, she wanted to do something out of character and reach for the person within herself she had locked away for far too long. She had never felt such total fulfilment than the experience that she had shared in the summer of '69. They had once made a Covenant to one another, and so why the hell not seize a crazy, crazy moment and invoke the promise? Back then she had felt so alive. *Oh my God, how I lived!* She had reminded herself many times before hiding from the truth that was, once again, now tempting her from the fetters of her reality. "I refuse to be mundane; I am not growing old until I am ready." She spoke the words out loud.

Why could she not forget that summer? After all, she was just a teenager then, she reasoned. Throughout her life, whenever she thought of Peter, he had assumed an almost iconic status as a figure to be admired like a statue dedicated to her youth. From her earliest

3

years she had struggled to conform, feeling like life did not fit her; only with Peter had she ever realised a complete sense of her true self, a sense which she had then lost or buried. On the outside, she was a successful, dynamic lawyer with an outstanding, lucrative career. Her position had given her incredible opportunities and an affluent lifestyle, mixing with some of the most influential people in the world. She had dedicated herself to her work with a ruthless determination, and striven to achieve. However, she had never felt comfortable in the existence she had created, feeling, sometimes, like an imposter, or that she was playing a part in a greater drama that she had not written. The words of the Covenant she had once made were an ever-present reminder of the person she had been, and who longed to return.

Then go and forget me forever
But I know you still bear the scar, deep inside…
I know where you go to, my lovely

Peter turned and looked through the swirling curtains at the lights of the glitzy buildings twinkling down the Creek, reflecting on the still water. His mind was not calm, but was recalling and revisiting. The music had liberated a memory which was flooding him, despite his futile attempt to hold it back. He had never really left her, nor she him. Visions from that summer with Jenny had often haunted him; after all, his had been the decision to turn away. Frequently he sought to neatly file away the wonderful memories of his beautiful experience with a mantra: *That was then, this is now.* Yet, the Covenant he had made then had never left him, offering a lifeline that he once believed could draw them back to the happiest place he had ever known. His hand covered his eyes as he tried to make sense of the thoughts swirling around him.

Returning to the room, he poured himself a generous glass of Scotch, which he downed too quickly, causing him to splutter. Then, lying on the oversized bed, he thought back over his life in which he had felt trapped by so many contradictions. It had all seemed so simple once, until reality had intervened; or had he actually run away from the reality of a dream? He closed his eyes.

She lay before him, her long dark hair framing a cute smile welcoming him back into her arms as the sound of the sea on the shore whispers to them only yards away.

He awoke, and knew that it was time to break free.

2

The Journey Begins

Friday 20th June 1969
Dover Harbour, England

Peter had driven from Liverpool to Dover in his battered 1961 Volkswagen Beetle, surprising himself with how easy it was to break from the bonds of his life. Now, with meagre savings, his dreams, a small tent, a few clothes, and no planned future, the adventure was really just beginning. As he queued for the ferry, he looked from the dock road across the surprisingly small expanse of harbour at the open English Channel beyond. His thoughts drifted across the ocean of life that lay in front of him, wondering whether he would ever be the same again. He felt he was running away, but hoped it was into the arms of a new destiny wherein he could escape the past. He knew that a future was calling to him which, if ignored, could force him back into an existence driven by custom to which he was expected to conform.

Peter's parents were customarily dismissive of his idea to go off on his travels. In their day, he would have, and should have, been working the boats on Liverpool Docks. His father, James Chainey (Jim), had entered the docks as an apprentice at the age of fifteen, working busy twelve-hour shifts loading and unloading ships, just as his father had done before him. Tragically, his dad had been killed in a wartime bombing raid on the docks in 1941.

After the funeral, Jim felt he had responsibility for his mam and the family. He hadn't time for any feelings, and never showed them. The loss of his dad had given him an unswerving loyalty to the dockyard community, the union and the workers. Then after marrying Rose, a sugar worker from Tate & Lyle whom he met at the weekly dockyard dance in 1948, their son Peter was born in 1949. At first, they lived in Jim's mother's home, taking over one of the three tiny bedrooms. After three years, helped by the docks scheme and a gift from his mam, Jim and Rose bought their first home in 1952, an end-of-terrace on Hope Street which provided the setting of Peter's first memories.

The terraced houses were a close-knit community but Peter grew to hate neighbours constantly dropping by with endless gossip. He was something of a loner, and longed for the privacy that would descend when he went to bed. From his earliest years, he had sought refuge finding places to wander within his imagination, and once he learned to read, he had become captivated by books. Here, he discovered a world outside his own which mesmerised him with a kaleidoscope of exciting people and places.

As they had no TV, Peter would often retreat early to bed, escaping in his reading to wide open spaces, or exotic locations he could only dream of. Each week he waited impatiently for the mobile library van to come to the corner of Hanover Street, ten minutes from his home, so he could excitedly select his next adventure. Books transported him to realms where brave knights jousted for a place at the Round Table, and on journeys across the oceans to exotic South Sea Islands, or in biplanes to fight wartime duels in the sky above the Flanders trenches.

From an early age, he yearned for adventure, feeling confined by his surroundings. In make-believe, Peter found freedom; a place where he could be himself. He was an only child and did not mix with other children easily, although his parents would make him go out and play. He learned to fend for himself in street games of football, cricket, or hide-and-seek amongst the derelict houses on the old bomb sites. At school he reluctantly joined in playground games, often feigning enthusiasm. He went to Beaufort Street Primary – 'the Bewey' – walking the mile there and back each day from the age of five.

Peter hated primary school, with its rigidity, unswerving discipline, and emphasis on conformity to a norm to which he felt alien. Yet, despite his reserve, he found that he enjoyed some lessons, particularly reading and writing. He developed a talent for expressing himself in written composition, encouraged by one teacher, Mr Stanley, who seemed to care rather than harshly punish as others did. He would ask pupils to write about their lives, or to make up imaginary stories which he then read out, inviting comment and criticism from others in the class. Mr Stanley encouraged and praised Peter, giving him a confidence he had not had before. Praise and recognition were not things he had been used to at home, where his mam and dad rarely showed emotion.

Increasingly, despite his achievements in writing, he became increasingly introverted, suffering from the fear some of his teachers inflicted where any perceived lack of respect or obedience was rewarded with harsh punishment including being beaten or slapped. The wooden ruler was applied across the back of the hand regularly, with a viciousness that haunted Peter for years. In time his fear became a sullen disengagement; so much so that, by the age of seven, he had already grown resentful of authority.

Peter's sense of individualism took seed at this time, as he would refuse to cry or react on receiving physical chastisement. This would have the effect of enraging some teachers even more, but inside he triumphed, despite the anguish and the physical pain. He would bite his lip hard, looking without blinking at the master who inflicted his punishment. Once he was slapped in the face by a red-faced teacher for his insolence, but still he stared at his tormentor, who then appeared unnerved and walked away, strengthening Peter's resolve.

He told his parents, who both agreed, "Well, you must have deserved it, so learn your lesson and it won't happen again." His detachment from both them and authority took root in the pain he felt, and reinforced the loneliness in the distance from the care he longed for. He felt a need to be recognised, and would never accept that he should ever be looked down on by the teachers whom his parents referred to as his 'betters' whom he should never, ever question.

His determination grew, and by the age of eleven he was performing well in school, sailing through the eleven-plus and ending up at the Liverpool Institute High School, otherwise known as 'the Inny'. This was one of the single most important factors, he acknowledged later, in giving him the foundations of self-belief that opened the door to success. The school, on Mount Street, was a centre of academic excellence, drawing some of the most talented and eccentric teachers of the day, who created a dynamic learning environment in which Peter excelled. Here he was motivated to read, write, and be creative; his self-confidence soared.

Teachers encouraged rather than disciplined, and the cultural mix from all social levels created a fertile ground for self-development. The academic and creative atmosphere was inspirational, and pupils' attention was drawn to the opportunities that existed outside the world they had grown up in. Peter felt emancipated, relishing the attention from staff who seemingly wanted to share in his life, listen to his thoughts, and motivate his thirst for the treasures of new knowledge. For the first time, he developed a confidence in just being himself, and his mentors gave him the courage not to accept, but to reach out. Teachers spoke openly about a revolution in music, thinking, expression and freedom. From this foundation, he was determined to prove himself. The school boasted former pupils such as Paul McCartney, George Harrison, Les Chadwick of Gerry and the Pacemakers, and Len Garry of the Quarrymen. They were all giants on the Mersey music scene in 1968 when Peter left school, and they inspired him to seek the new life he knew he could create for himself. Hence, with excellent 'A' level results, he applied to, and was accepted into Sheffield University in 1968.

The seeds of self-improvement and development were sown. He knew that he sought more than working on the docks as expected by his parents. Conformity was not an option. Peter began to openly challenge his father's ways, and the claustrophobic values that his trade unionist creed appeared to foster. Jim Chainey had tried to instil in his son the working man's values he had inherited, and for which he perceived his own father had lived and died. Peter, however, could see beyond the old life, and was drawn by the confidence bred at the Inny to a different destiny. He saw his father's attitudes as old-fashioned, belonging to a former era of working-class struggle. Despite his admiration for the workers, by his mid teens Peter felt there was a need to embrace a new age of tolerance, understanding, and even love.

Years later, he confided in Jenny that he had never seen his parents kiss or show any affection. The word 'love' was never spoken, except in derision when in the '60s they began to see posters extolling love and peace. His dad made it clear: "There'll be none of that gobshite in this house, or long hair like them Beatles with their shouting music."

Liverpool in the 1960s was changing, and finding a new cultural confidence in music, comedy and politics, but it was that confidence which divided as much as it united. Thought varied from unswerving loyalty to traditional left-wing radicalism to New Age idealism; from revolution to self-focused mystic meditation.

In this confusion, some sought refuge in the psychedelic relief of LSD. Peter sought his release from reality in reading and, in 1969, a decision to travel in order to expand his horizons and prepare him for life.

Tuesday 1st July 1969
John F. Kennedy Airport, New York, USA

Jenny and her friends chattered excitedly, the college minders watching over them like a brood. They were the lucky ones, escaping life in the USA to reach beyond and seek new experiences in Europe, and to revel in the art and culture they thirsted for – or so their teachers and parents thought. At nineteen, Jenny wanted to find a new way. Her dreams lay not in education but in breaking the ties that bound her to a life that was square and just so normal. "I will not be straight; I'm goin' to drop out," she repeated to herself each day, like a mantra. She was caught up in a desire to seek, to find answers, and to explore how she might make a difference. Her generation wanted change; she would never meekly comply with what was expected by her parents or anyone else. This was her time, her generation, and she was part of the revolution, of 'where it's happening'.

As she watched the BOAC VC10 aircraft crawl sluggishly towards the boarding steps, she marvelled that this silver bird would take her to another world, and a thrill of anticipation and the impending unknown made her shiver.

Jenny had always been very independently minded, determined from the earliest days of her childhood to do things how she wanted to. As a toddler, smiling acquiescence had not been her way, and she had found a means of expressing herself by refusing to cooperate, exasperating her mother with her wilful attitude. She had been christened Ginevra Maria by her Italian immigrant parents, but by the age of three would only answer to Jenny, dotingly used one day by some visiting American friends of her father when making a fuss of her. She delighted in her mischievousness, often smiling when she sensed her parents or others were backing down. Her mother would despair of her, though she could do no wrong in the eyes of her father. That was until, as a teenager, she began to openly rebel against his wishes.

Her life had been kind of easy, yet also complicated by her parents' passions for her future. Her father, Giuseppe Baronio, was a driven man who seized opportunity at every corner. He had emigrated from Genoa in Italy to New Jersey, and was determined to create position and status for himself in this New World. Her mother, Gina, was from Milan, and, despite the hopes of her family after commencing studies in Law, had never completed her degree, giving in to Giuseppe's incessant demands as a passionate suitor. Theirs had been a brief courtship which was more about the young man's impatience to make his mark; he had no time for long romances when he could sense opportunity. His motivation lay in a drive for the heights of success that beckoned him away from Italy to America; a land that encouraged enterprise.

Italy had held no hope after the corruption and confusion that followed the dictatorship of Mussolini and his fascist government. Giuseppe had initially admired *Il Duce*, who he believed represented power, strength and a nationalist pride. Then he felt betrayed, despising Mussolini for his self-promoting posturing, his ineptitude in foreign policy, and especially in his aligning himself with Hitler. After the end of the war in 1945, Giuseppe wanted to seek a new life in America, which was welcoming those escaping from the shattered remains of war-torn Europe.

His parents were originally travelling-show people who had opened a small food store in Genoa in 1936. Giuseppe had eagerly watched how money could be made, learning from his father when he expanded the business during the early years of the war. Food was in short supply and it was not long before he was operating a lucrative black-market business, bypassing the rationing regulations. Giuseppe was quick-minded and adept at recognising a chance to set up, or spot, a deal. His self-assured, confident nature had been expressed as a youngster in rebelling against authority; an independent characteristic that he would later proudly claim had been inherited by Jenny.

In 1947, the chance came to escape from a country in turmoil. At the labour exchange, when Giuseppe was offered a subsidised emigration ticket to the USA, he seized the opportunity. During the subsequent voyage to New York, there was much celebration on the ship, including dances, during one of which he met Gina.

She had begun studying Law at the University of Milan in 1945, and had only completed one year when she was forced to cease her studies because of her father's sympathies with the former regime, and his subsequent imprisonment. On his release, eighteen months later, the family sought a new life away from the darkness of the past. Gina was pleased to accept an offer to continue her studies from the American resettlement authorities. She had only completed one year of law school by the time Giuseppe persuaded her to marry him in 1949, abandoning her studies despite her parents' protestations. Giuseppe would never be deflected from his ambitions, whether in affairs of love, design or business. They settled in Atlantic City, New Jersey, where Gina soon became pregnant, and Ginevra was born in 1950.

Neither Giuseppe nor Gina shared love easily with their daughter because it was not something that had easily been shared with them. Their families had been exposed to the horrors of war. He had cowered in shelters during the bombing of Genoa and seen bodies of those he knew being brought out of ruined houses. She had witnessed her parents' vineyard turned into a battlefield, and the destruction of their family home. Gina had built up a horror of violent conflict during this period, which she instilled in her daughter throughout her childhood, saying that the world must never, ever return to war. This was a conviction that stayed with Jenny all her life. Gina despised fascism, passing on to her daughter a hatred of all things to do with power politics, ambition, and violence in any form. Love was rarely displayed other than in the ritual of being part of an Italian family unit, and that was important.

Giuseppe had inherited a long family tradition of the fairground and circus, or 'show business', as he called it. He had ambition, setting up a stall in Atlantic City, borrowing money to build his business, at exorbitant interest, from those cashing in on the opportunities in the post-war growth in leisure. When Jenny was born, her parents were devoted to one cause; namely that she would never suffer the deprivations or the violent destruction that they had lived with. Her father was strict but giving, calling her "*mia principessa*" ('my princess').

The family soon prospered, with Giuseppe running The Palace, a seafront amusement arcade he developed off the Boardwalk. Gina gave birth to a son, Matteo, in 1955, and Jenny loved to play with him and look after him. This was, at least, one area in which she found she could give and experience love.

Despite Giuseppe and Gina's efforts to create a disciplined family environment, their princess developed a highly individual streak. Gina would report to her husband that their daughter had caused problems at school, where she was called wilful by teachers, but he was fiercely protective of her, always excusing her despite the accounts of difficult behaviour and nonconformity. He would say, "Hey, what do they know about her? They should teach, not criticise. If they taught properly, she would be a good girl." He knew she was naturally bright, and her results were excellent at school. Her parents conceded from an early age that it was Jenny's way or no way but, as Giuseppe said, "*Lei nuoterà nell'oro.*" ('She will swim in gold', meaning 'She'll make good.')

Her mother would explain to other parents, "She refuses to behave, and just plays her own games; nobody can tell her anything until she has decided it for herself. She is worse than her father, and he *non sapere che pesci prendere.*" ('Doesn't know what fish to take', or 'has no idea what to do'.)

At the age of fourteen, she was accepted into Atlantic City High School (ACHS), located at Albany and Atlantic Avenues, a couple of hundred yards from The Palace, so her father would drive her there each day. In her studies she excelled, especially in English and History, the latter giving her an interest in Law as she learned about the formation of the American Constitution and government. Despite this, she found conforming to the code of behaviour tough, and began to learn the art of more serious rebelling. She would customarily argue with teachers for little reason other than a for a little devilment in refusing to accept a represented viewpoint. She found her studies easy and was frequently caught reading material not sanctioned by the school. She loved underground comics such as *Zap*, which explored new ideas and published images no one had dared print previously. She found revolutionary ideas irresistible but hated violence, embracing the early expression of love and peace. Ultimately, by the age of seventeen, she decided her future lay in 'dropping out', but dared not tell this to her parents.

Jenny often skipped school, wandering down to the Boardwalk where she would watch strolling visitors with fascination, enjoying the thrill of being where she should not be. When rock and roll was banned from the home by her father in 1965, she immediately ran out and bought her first record by the Beatles, 'We Can Work It Out'. The words resonated that life was short and that time was precious. She felt that no-one around her was seeing it all as she could. She wished her father could see it her way and then questioned what was her way. She felt lost and out of place, needing something or someone to hold on to or simply care about and share love with, despite her fierce independence. She often felt very alone, but no one would ever know because of her uncompromising drive and determination to succeed in whatever she sought to achieve. With those qualities of purpose, despite her desire to rebel, she applied to, and was accepted by, Harvard Law School in 1969.

America's involvement in the Vietnam War gave a focus to her teenage years, joining protests, marches and sit-ins against the wishes of her parents. She was incensed by her father's unswerving support of President Lyndon Johnson's commitment to the war, justified as a way of preventing the spread of communism. Jenny was affronted by the President's words – "Just like the Alamo, someone had to go to Vietnam's aid" – glorifying his sending troops to war. She could see no glory in any conflict, but only devastation and suffering. Well, heck, her generation was damn well going to change everything.

3

The Meeting

Friday 11th July 1969
Plage de Cabasson, Domaine de Cap Bénat, Côte d'Azur,
Southern France

On the beach with friends she first saw him; a slim man with a gorgeous, toned body, his fit, muscular frame drawing her gaze as, with difficulty, he pulled a colourful cart down the sands of Cabasson beach. He chanted loudly like a street vendor, "*Eskimo Glace et chocolat, demandez les*"; then, comically, "Get yer ice creams here, lads" in a curious British accent which she later learned was from Liverpool, like the Beatles. She was instantly drawn to his comic daring; a wicked, mischievous, challenging look; his long brown hair with soft beard just evident; and an easy, cheeky smile. Suddenly, on impulse, she threw caution to the four winds and ran towards him with a sense of complete abandon. She had no plan, but her young energy and vibrant sense of the now took her and she flew down the beach.

"Hey, man, you are so cool," she laughed as he looked at her with dancing brown eyes, taking in her brief bikini, her long, dusky dark hair, and her teasing pouty look.

"You want an ice cream or you just want to reach for a whole lotta love?" he quipped, and that was their beginning; a story that was never written when their lives reached to create it. Their eyes met and they fell headlong into an abyss that drew them helplessly into a fate they could not know or resist.

She quizzed him on how he had come to France, and they ended up cross-legged on the sand for hours. Very few ice creams got sold that day, but by the end of it, they had woven a thread that was to bind them both, tentatively at first, but then with a beautiful bond of awareness. They talked and talked and talked some more, she waving away her startled minders anxious to mother her back to the gîte they were hiring. "I'll give her a lift," he called, unreassuringly to those concerned to protect her from herself, and him.

Jenny did not return until late that night, calling her college party from a phone at the bar bordering La Favière beach in the little port of Bormes-les-Mimosas not far from where they had met. Here they had decided to sit and watch and share the world that evening. As they sat on the edge of a low quay, they splashed their feet in the water by the shoreline, chatting and seeking to know more of one another. The attraction was total, and just as her stomach jumped each time she looked at him, he was utterly captivated by her softness and her lovely smile with pouting lips; a deep, intimate connection surrounded them. Their first kiss was not hesitant, but flowed naturally from a knowing look, then the briefest touch before their lips softly moved together, seeking, sensing, tasting, awakening something more. Their joy in each other was incomprehensible to them both, but their senses reeled and understanding mattered not as their hands clasped and their eyes sparkled in the lights from the few bars on the cobbled walkway by the port. Jenny was in a dream she had once reached for, so many years ago, as a romantic fantasy; yet this was real and, wow, she knew already, as they said back then, that this was where it was all at.

On being dropped back at the gîte, her friends quizzed her excitedly, but she found she was reluctant to say too much as the evening had been so intimate. Peter had asked her to spend the following day with him, she informed her team leaders. She did not add that he had also asked her to stay with him for the entire summer. That night her excitement overflowed, and before dawn she decided that she would leave the gîte and not return. This was her moment and she was going to take it and seek the freedom she knew awaited her; a revelation that she could be herself and live in a world in which her ideals were embraced, not mocked or belittled. She was in love already, despite her girlish denial, but she could only lose that argument because Peter was definitely just the grooviest guy ever.

In the morning Jenny took down her case, packed her clothes, and wished her open-mouthed but envious friends a happy summer before brazenly announcing to her college minders that she was leaving them. They were shocked by her wilfulness, urging her to return to the US with them and threatening that this would affect her career ambitions, but their words were not heeded. "I guess I'm dropping out of all that. So you enjoy. This is my new world and I'm going to embrace and feel the love. I'll send you a postcard. Oh, and I'll tell my mom and dad, in the words of Martin Luther King, I'm free at last. Peace, man." With that, she flounced cheekily to the waiting VW and was gone.

It had taken less than twenty-four hours since arriving in France for Jenny to take the step she had often promised herself and drop out. She cared not for the establishment lifestyle, having long decided that her way was part of the new revolution. She was going to embrace this age of enlightenment and seek the changes that it would bring to her life, not least in being immersed in the spirit of love and peace. She was happily leaving behind the failures of being conventional, which she wanted no part of. She was leaving her parents and their tired generation that dwelt in convention, power, politics and conformity. That day, Jenny took a path that liberated her from the past.

She wanted to challenge everything, accepting nothing that people who were square would tell her. There had to be a way of preventing the staggering cruelty of napalm being dropped by her country on civilians in Vietnam, of massacres like the one in Mỹ Lai when US troops had opened fire on civilians. This was a time to be ashamed of being American. There was no condemnation of the teenage soldiers; she was one of the flower children despairing at the sad faces of conscripts torn from family and home. They were ordered to fight a faceless foe with whom they had no argument, but against whom they had to use 'modern warfare', devastating whole populations including women and children.

"What sort of war justifies what we do, and for what values?" she asked openly, especially within her family. In her eyes, the older generation were too respectful and accepting of authority. Whenever President Johnson gave a speech about Vietnam on TV, her father would applaud, often ending with him standing with his hand on his heart as 'The Star-Spangled Banner' played. Didn't they get it? "What is wrong with you?" she would exclaim angrily, to which he would respond that he loved his country and so should she. Well, this was 1969, and she was joining her generation in protest.

That first day together after Peter had picked her up, they walked through the pine forest bordering the beach nearby, stopping occasionally at a bar where they would take a beer, then sit, hands clasped, chatting endlessly about their lives. She found welcome solace with Peter, who did not simply accept all she said but debated with her, valuing her views and complementing them with his own. He was not adversarial but warming to be with, and she loved every second of it. As they talked, they both became aware of an intimacy between them that made his hands around hers seem so very natural. Their arms constantly reached for one another, warmly welcoming their connection.

Their day was timeless and ethereal, forging an instinctive togetherness. As the sun dipped, they sat by the shore, mesmerised.

They sensed a harmony of mutual realisation, each loving the other's voice, their thoughts enchanting, their touches exquisite. His deep brown eyes caressed her, drawn to her soft body scarcely covered by a bikini, gazing at her long legs, flat stomach, and her top clearly showing the outline of her breasts. She was so drawn to him, adrenaline flowing like falling off a cliff into a chasm, yet safe because she was pulled back to him. She took in his beautifully shaped frame, khaki shorts worn low at the waist with a line of hair trailing downwards from his navel. His tanned chest was almost smooth; her eyes soaked him up from his smiling face to his muscular legs, discarded sandals and bare feet. She was captivated by the intensity of his look, the gentle tone of his voice, and smiled at his accent as he pronounced words in a manner she had never heard before.

"Hey, baby, my tent is near here if you dare; I promise I'll be the perfect boy scout if you care to join me."

She laughed, saying that she never trusted anyone in uniform, especially if they were wearing a top with a 'commie' on, referring to the image of the Cuban revolutionary Che Guevara on his discarded T-shirt. She teased him, saying that Che was more handsome than he, which prompted being lifted bodily and then thrown screaming into the sea before he overbalanced and they ended up rolling over and over in the surf.

They walked arm in arm to the tent, hearing the waves echoing as they crashed on the beach, washing white-edged water up over their feet, yet sensing little but one another, as if in a dream. Once alone, they each drank in the other as they easily discarded their clothes, and then they were kneeling naked before each other, taking in the pangs of desire that drew them together, their skin so sensitive to their warmth. Their mouths met, kissing passionately as their bodies arched, needing and aware. Then he pulled her gently down to his bed, their eyes held by each other, savouring the exploration of their bodies, his fingertips seeking her soft curves, and hers around his hardness, gently caressing.

She lay back, rejoicing as she felt his pulsing desire against her, her hand reaching to guide him, and then he was deep inside her. She gave herself utterly to his embrace, surrendering to him, then wantonly pulling him to her, yearning him again and again, yet seeking more. Their gasps of joy celebrated the depths of their passion and their shared intimacy, so very natural to their moment. As they lay naked in their union of peacefulness she reached for him again, desiring him with a hunger she had never experienced before. She marvelled at his slim body, loving the feel of his taut skin. She whispered how gorgeous he was as he responded to her fingers stroking him in a primeval, instinctive rhythm that left him gasping. He drew her to him and she sought him once more, so close as he stroked her hair, looking deeply into her eyes, telling her how beautiful she was. His joy matched Jenny's, which was suffused with sheer heaven as she reached high after high, her cries only stifled as she eagerly sought his mouth, their tongues dancing. Then, as they embraced the calm, the music drifted sounds to them softly played from an unknown guitar outside in the stillness of the night's darkness.

Later, they lay together, talking long into the night, their subdued voices mixing with the almost reassuring rhythmic sound of crickets. Then sleep welcomed them warmly into a dreamlike serenity.

When dawn broke into their reverie, Jenny stirred, then, seeing Peter's half-open eyes, smiled at him, absorbing this moment, their moment. Leaning over him, she kissed him briefly before abruptly opening her bag and pulling on a bikini. "Come on, beach boy, time for our morning swim." She half-dragged him from the sleeping bag before throwing his shorts at him. "If I'm to stay with you, you have to promise to greet the start of each day by running with me into the sea."

As he began to protest, she placed a hand over his mouth, pointing determinedly in the direction of the ocean. Hauling himself up, he slapped her playfully on the bottom, then ran from the tent shouting, "Last one in makes breakfast."

Reaching the shore, Peter dashed into the small waves, gasping as the shock of the cold water caught his breath. As he half-turned, Jenny dived into an approaching wave, and he watched her almost balletic, yet powerful strokes with admiration. This was just all too far out, yet, even then, he felt he was running from a reality which belied the dream he felt he was living.

She beckoned him. "Hey, Mr Ice-Cream Man, you just too slow for me. I hope you can cook better than you can speak English!" A water fight followed as their arms flailed, creating huge splashes as they half-ran, half-swam to and from each other. Jenny was giggling, then screaming like a child, but as she emerged from the sea onto the warm sand she reflected that she had never felt such deep release and emotion in all her life. She placed her arm around Peter as he joined her and they walked slowly back to the tent, feeling the soft wind, heavy with the scent of pine, and utterly aware of each other. Few words were needed as it just felt so very right, so crazy, so groovy.

On entering the tent, he lay back, saying that she had exhausted him and he was too tired to make breakfast. After throwing a towel at him, she moved beside him, nuzzling into his neck. *This is all so natural*, she thought, loving the feel of his strong body next to hers. She kissed his brow, and trailed soft kisses to his neck. She hushed his weak protest with her finger before running her tongue across his chest, tasting him, and then down his flat stomach with its long line of downy, fair hairs. As she reached, he responded, and her lips encircled him and her tongue swirled around him.

Afterwards, she turned to him as he cradled her head into his shoulder. "What is your surname, sir – I don't think we've been properly introduced?" Following his answer, she responded, "Well, Mr Peter Chainey, I'm mighty pleased to meet you. I am Jenny Baronio and I think we are going to get along."

4

Haven's Reach

14th July 1969

Bormes-les-Mimosas, Côte d'Azur, Southern France

Two days after their first night together, Peter suggested they drive to St-Tropez. Everyone was saying it was an iconic place; like a beacon of free expression attracting the rich and famous from all over the world. "Sounds like a jet-set playground where it's really happening, baby – we have to see what we're up against," he said with a wicked grin. He also spoke enthusiastically of Port Grimaud, which was a few miles further up the coast. "Apparently, it's really something else, like a magical city rising up from the marshes; they say it's going to be a French Venice built on waterways, and it sounds far out."

It was as if they were already a couple, she mused, delighting in the feeling that thought gave her of a strange instinctive security. During the hours they had spent in each other's arms, they had continued opening up to one another, sharing their thoughts, dreams, hopes, and their joint ambition to make their world infinitely better than the one they had been born into.

That morning, just after the dawn broke, they swam, as Jenny had demanded they should, in the glassy, calm sea off Plage de la Favière, gasping as the cold water shocked their bodies. They cavorted and splashed, their laughter reflecting their happiness. Then they sat, hands clasped, on the soft white sand, warmed by the Mediterranean sun, she topless, and he in his brief denim shorts. There was such an intimacy between them, as their glances to one another were met with knowing smiles; then their fingers sought each other, and their eyes danced with the realisation of their closeness. They ran from the beach, buying croissants, jam, and café au lait from a small snack bar bordering a road leading to the pine trees beyond. It was Peter's day off and she readily agreed to the trip to St-Tropez, just a little over an hour's drive away.

The day was warm and scent wafted from the many blooming yellow mimosas, mixing with pine to create a heady summer perfume. They drove down the winding coastline, windows open, marvelling at the many beaches and coves as they rose over hills and then dropped down almost to the shimmering water's edge. His hand clasped hers for much of the journey, adjusting to the dramatic rise and fall of the undulating route through flashing sunlight in the trees to the sparkling Mediterranean dancing magically before them. Their happiness was in their togetherness, their joy still glowing from their mutual passion. They swapped stories, and he told her of one of his rare trips to the beach as a child, when his parents had decided on a picnic during the summer holidays. His dad drove them there in his grey Morris Minor. Peter was just six, and excited to be going to Southport sands with his two cousins. He recounted to Jenny how his parents had somehow herded the other children into the car and then driven off, leaving him behind. He still remembered the isolation, knowing that his family had gone but not being sure why. They had returned after discovering they were a child short, but dreams of that day had haunted him all through his childhood, and weirdly, sometimes still did.

Jenny responded with stories of her life by the sea in Atlantic City, in the little house in which she lived with her parents and her younger brother, Matteo. She hated sharing a bedroom but at least they had a proper bathroom. She told him she was from a long tradition of Italian circus folk who loved travelling, "So hey, Peter, you gotten yourself an all-Italian gypsy, *che cavolo!*" They both laughed as she explained that the words literally meant 'what cabbage', but were used as an expression like 'goddamn it'. Her parents, she told him, were proud first-generation Italian-Americans who could not forget their heritage, and from whom she had learned countless sayings without learning to speak Italian herself.

They arrived in St-Tropez suddenly, hardly realising they were nearing, having crossed country away from the coast on the approach before the road led back to the shoreline and the harbour, where they saw lines of fishing boats and yachts. Peter parked the Volkswagen by a wall overlooking the tiny port and they sauntered along the front. Arm in arm, they took in the quaint harbour, despite the cordoned-off areas where busy and noisy building work interrupted the wonderful panorama. Beyond the sea wall stretched a huge bay which curved to the left and then swept away to the right, behind which hills gave a dramatic backdrop to the view. Meandering as young lovers, they mixed with the people parading down the quay in a variety of dress, from fabulous chic clothes to those daringly wearing very little. Both extremes added to an exotic atmosphere that they found intoxicating. There were modern sports cars with vulgar, tuneful horns announcing their presence, whilst street vendors, musicians, hippies and the smartly dressed elite bustled the streets flanked by designer shops. The sights and sounds were exciting and vibrant, with music filtering around every corner, often complemented by someone with a guitar inviting others to join in with a musical mantra of peace and harmony. Many young people were wearing flowers in their hair or around their necks, and the scent of burning joss sticks added a touch of the bohemian. Smiles greeted them everywhere and a euphoric happiness hung in the warm air, within the heady freedom that they both felt.

"This is where it is really all happening, hippy chick," Peter said, using the term for the first time.

She countered with "And I'm with the beach bum I want to share it with", as they kissed.

They wandered, taking in this fresh new world, flinching at the impossibly priced clothing in shiny shop windows contrasting with stalls selling T-shirts carrying messages of love and hope for their new generation. Theirs was a time in which idealism was not about money but simply *being*, welcoming the thoughts of others. There were people sitting cross-legged, arm in arm, by the shore, covered in garlands of flowers; everywhere colour bloomed and blossomed like a new springtime. Way-out clothes and hair, and varied tastes, were welcoming in a kaleidoscope of youthful expression. The scent of marijuana floated everywhere, and people held hands, kissed, smiled, drank, smoked and listened, experiencing a universal bond.

Jenny and Peter explored, loving the heady cocktail of creative expression all around them, flavoured by artists showing their creations along cobbled streets, and amongst the cafes in the narrow alleyways leading away from the seafront. Soon, they joined a trail of people walking up the hill and away from the centre on a pathway that led them towards the beaches on the other side of the peninsula. As they neared Pampelonne beach, they became more aware of people celebrating the atmosphere of freedom and openness. Girls barely concealed their near-nakedness, with tops buttoned loosely and microscopic shorts stretched like a second skin, straining to offer any modesty. Men too strolled somewhat brazenly in brief swimming bottoms that accentuated their physiques, which, as Jenny commented, certainly drew the eye, resulting in Peter's playful slap on her backside.

On the beaches, they watched a group chant, "Hare Krishna"; some dressed in long white robes, walking into the sea, then returning to the shore in a rhythmic, swaying dance, their cymbals shaking, almost hypnotic in their undulating mantra of harmony.

Jenny led Peter by the hand. "We have to experience this, baby," she implored, pulling him towards these people who looked so beautifully in tune with themselves.

The swaying entourage drew in others who chanted with them, and they welcomed all. "Yeah, man, anyone can take part, and we want to celebrate our consciousness of peace with you. We seek freedom, tranquillity, serenity and harmony. Come, feel and experience our calm through our overcoming of our outward awareness."

Peter and Jenny joined hands, laughing with others who opened their arms to them. They both sensed the calm and release the chant gave them, and the group moved slowly down the beach, their cymbals drawing attention. Then they paused, raising their arms, beckoning others to join. No one pushed them or tried to persuade, but there was a celebration of understanding between all, uplifting their spirits. They walked on, hand in hand, then turned to each other, and their intimate closeness gripped them in a spontaneity of reaching. Their kiss was sensual, yet not passionate, uniting without need, bonding with no demands, and they both felt the beauty in their increasing awareness of each other.

As they meandered further along the sand, they noticed that virtually all the females were topless, whether lying, walking around or just standing. After a few minutes, Jenny stopped, slipped her simple blouse off, then shrugged out of her bra, revealing herself. Openly walking around half naked for the first time, having previously restricted herself to lying on the beach or early morning swims, she felt a sense of brazen liberation. Peter pretended he had hardly noticed but she was knew his surprise, which made her all the more daring. He looked at her, her body so gorgeous and shining with the sun oil she had applied earlier, then, laughing, he ripped his T-shirt off and they wandered further down the shoreline, both feeling rather naughty. As they ventured further up the beach to seek another way back, they became aware of couples lying together, totally naked. "My God, Jenny, they are wearing nothing; I think I'm embarrassed to be clothed for the first time in me life," he said in his adorable, sing-song Liverpool accent.

Jenny looked at him. "OK, big boy, you ready for me?" she giggled, then, sitting on her shirt, she wriggled out of her shorts and, as Peter watched in some shock, stripped totally. He knew she was beautiful, but in some ways never more so than in that moment as her body was so unexpectedly revealed.

"OK, sexy girl, be shocked by my depravity," he threw back at her, standing proud as he pulled one leg and then the other from his shorts.

Jenny giggled, not at his nakedness, but at his obvious nervousness despite the bravado of his actions. They experienced a feeling of utter freedom as they stood together, soon losing any shyness or self-consciousness. Jenny turned to Peter. "My God, how liberating, but if I told my papa about this, I would be out of the family."

Peter cast his mind back to Liverpool, the docks, the life he'd had, before comparing it with their now. "If me dad could see me now, he would cut my balls off," he said directly, his accent adding emphasis to his claim.

Despite their love for the liberation they were discovering, they felt in some ways out of place returning to the Port when looking in the shop windows that evidenced a rich 'establishment' embedding themselves on this enchanting coastline. As they explored, they mixed with those who strode around like peacocks in expensive outfits dripping with jewellery, belying the age of freedom they both espoused and embraced.

Despite the slight misgivings that money was encroaching on the area, St-Tropez captivated them. They were drawn by the excitement of life, music, and diverse cultures clashing yet living side by side; each reaching out to the other as though the old was seeking affirmation from the new, and the new reassurance from the old. They sat by the port, looking across the bay, discussing the contradictions of establishment versus New Age, of freedom versus reactionary commercial interests, of war versus peace. They agreed on so much, and shared their impatience at the older generation which showed diffidence to, or shunned, their beliefs.

Their days in St-Tropez would become many as the heady atmosphere drew them back again and again with its crazy mixture of those from, or embracing, the hippy culture with those who had made it financially; a modern clash between idealism and superficiality. Their 'Haven's Reach', as Jenny later christened it, was a port of contrasts witnessing a transformation in culture. The residents they spoke to were philosophical about the changes that were affecting their lives. The world was coming to them, and, with a shrug, the saying was *"Pourquoi pas?"* – 'Why not?' After all, they had never had such opportunities to prosper, and so they welcomed the invading visitors on their hedonistic search for understanding or pleasure.

Jenny and Peter returned to Bormes-les-Mimosas that evening, refreshed by their experience, delighting in the exuberance, and the dawn of their Summer of Love. On the way back, they diverted to the new 'Venice' being built at Port Grimaud. They passed an exotic archway entrance accessed by a bridge spanning a creek. After parking their car next to the beach beyond, they returned to the entrance and crossed over the waterway. There was a large square on the other side lined by new buildings, some of which were already occupied as shops and restaurants. Although they could see that much was under construction, they resolved to return to this enchanting location.

Their day was drawing to a close; time had captivated them and they were absorbed by their experience. Her last words before she drifted into her dreams that night were that they had found their Haven's Reach; not just referring to St-Tropez, but to the unlocking of their minds, freed to be together.

5

Foundations

Peter had found a job the day he arrived in Le Lavandou, a small town nestling on the western edge of the French Riviera coastline. Having wound his way through the hills and mountain passes since leaving Aix-en-Provence, he descended via Hyères, his first glimpse of the blue Mediterranean giving him a thrill of excitement. He knew he needed a seasonal job and a place on the coast to stay. He parked by a bar and took in a cool beer overlooking the sea, then asked the barman if he knew of any work going. He was told there was another Englishman – well, an American – working on the nearby harbour who might help him. This man normally called in for a drink around that time of day, so Peter waited.

He felt achievement having driven some 1,100 miles since leaving Boulogne, taking diversions along the way to meander through villages, avoiding the Autoroute toll charges, and enjoying the drive down the *route nationale*. He had been fascinated by the French towns and villages, their character so different to what he had known back home. Many of the roads were long and straight with trees uniformly planted either side, giving a mesmerising symmetry. Most of the houses had shutters at the windows, giving them an enchanting character. He relished his journey, staying in campsites at Amiens, Moulins, and then Chartres to view the magnificent cathedral. As he drove further south, he noticed the climate becoming warmer and more humid. He camped in Lyons, Orange, and then came his final stay in Montélimar as he planned to reach the coast the following day. He had been in no hurry but now, arriving in the bustling town of Le Lavandou, he wanted to find a home for the summer.

As he sipped his beer, he experienced a feeling of elation at breaking away from his roots. He was on his second beer, musing over his long journey, when he noticed a tall young guy entering the bar. He wore a straw cowboy hat, and had long, dark, wavy hair. Peter thought he was just so hippyish, with his square sunglasses and long moustache. Denim shorts, sandals, an old T-shirt, and beads around his neck completed the look. After speaking briefly to the barman, he came over and offered his hand.

"The name's Jonas. You come a long way, boy?" he offered with an engaging smile in a deep American accent. "I'm from Dallas, Texas, but don't let that bother you none."

They soon became immersed in conversation, exchanging and relating experiences from their very different lives. Jonas was the son of a rancher who had made a pretty good life for himself, and had been raised a "country boy" despite living only thirty minutes from the city. He confessed to Peter that he was "seeking the meaning of life". He didn't accept all the "bullshit" Americans were being fed by their government and institutions regarding history, politics, Vietnam and "most else besides". At twenty-four he was older than Peter, and admitted he was "sorta running away from it all". He had started a small DIY store in Balch Springs, a little town not far from Dallas centre, and had decided to leave it for the summer, and find some adventure and freedom.

Jonas worked for a couple delivering boats around the coast for the jet set, and he found the work easy; plus it kept him "in grass". He rolled a joint in front of Peter and told him to relax as "Everyone's doin' it here, man." Working there had earned him a lot of contacts, and he reckoned he could get Peter fixed up with a job from his friend Pierre, who ran a business hassling on the beaches, which meant selling gifts and drinks to tourists. They chatted some more and Jonas was fascinated to hear of Peter's Liverpool background – "Where all that British rock 'n' roll is coming from? That's so cool, man." They took in a couple more beers, finding that they had a great deal in common, not least music, both admiring diverse artists such as Bob Dylan, the Beatles, Jimi Hendrix, The Who, The Animals and the Rolling Stones. They spoke of politics and their despair at the war in Vietnam but, as they agreed, it was up to their generation to make changes.

They left the bar, and by sundown Peter had accepted a job 'working' four beaches, and secured a place on the campsite where Jonas was staying, just outside the port of Bormes-les-Mimosas. He was introduced to other young people who had come to the area to find out "where it's all at". By nightfall that first day he felt comfortable – well the worse for drink, but amongst a community of people he could relate to and relax with. The night was made more convivial when he played his guitar, opening a musical bridge to those from all over the world with familiar songs around a campfire until the early hours. After a day of relaxation he was on his first beach, testing his talents in selling ice cream and cold drinks. He was issued with a handcart he had to drag across the unyielding sand but, hey, it was work, and made him self-sufficient.

Jonas and Peter began to form a warm friendship as they spent long evenings together, telling of their backgrounds and discussing their beliefs. It was unusual for Peter to allow someone to get close to him but he found Jonas relaxed, easy-going and open; a sharp contrast to those around him at home. Late in the day, they often called in at Les Arbres, a corner roadside restaurant nestling in the pine trees just off the Domaine de la Ris Favière, for a late afternoon drink before the more serious guests arrived in the evening. The restaurant enjoyed a unique feature of olive trees whose spread branches formed a leafy canopy over the tables and chairs, creating a natural sheltering 'roof'. The atmosphere was relaxing and welcoming.

Although Les Arbres had started out as a beach bar, the owner, Monsieur Gaspard Devreux, had grown his establishment into a restaurant with a fine reputation. Capitalising on the wealthy clientele descending on the region from the USA and the UK, he offered a less strict French cuisine that pandered to their tastes. He presided over a highly unusual, old-fashioned and personalised waiter service, and it was not long before Les Arbres was noticed by the rich and famous. Jonas joked that when they returned home they could say they had been rubbing shoulders with people like Noël Coward, Cary Grant, Dirk Bogarde and even Brigitte Bardot, all of whom were not infrequent guests.

Monsieur Devreux, clad in a white apron and sporting a magnificent moustache, was fascinated by the younger generation who were driven by so much energy. They reminded him of his youth in the 1930s before so many of his ideals had been lost during the occupation of his country in the war. He had genuinely warmed to both Jonas and Peter, always greeting them with open arms and often giving them a small meal. "It is all I can do for the children of the liberators," he said.

It was natural, therefore, for Peter to introduce Jenny to Les Arbres' patron on the third day after they had met, and ask whether there might be a job for her. Monsieur Devreux bowed in a slightly overdramatised way, before kissing her on the hand and telling her she was one of the most beautiful women in all of France. She giggled and looked shyly away, unused to compliments delivered in such a gallant manner. Peter affected a jealous response, warning Monsieur Devreux off with a fist and a very impolite gesture.

"But, Peter, she is so gorgeous; my restaurant would be blessed if she agreed to work for me."

Jenny was delighted to accept as the restaurant was ten minutes' walk from the campsite. The patron kissed her on both cheeks, shook Peter by the hand and, with a broad smile, cautioned him, "I think you have fallen in love, *sois prudent, mon ami* ['be careful, my friend']; your life is in danger of being captured."

As they wandered slowly back to the tent that evening, they were euphoric. They had each other, the summer lay before them, Jenny had secured work, and they had a foundation for what was meant to be. Within three days their lives had changed and they somehow knew that nothing would ever be the same again; nor did they want it to be, as they instinctively knew that they were bound to each other.

Their lives drifted in a fantasy through the early days of their magical summer, in a rhythm they understood and with an intimacy they craved. It was a time in which they sought nothing but the joy they shared. Although they both worked during the day, this still left time for their hedonistic life to captivate their minds, bodies and souls. She often teased him, playfully calling him 'the ice-cream man'; she would imitate the first words she had heard him speak: "*Eskimo Glace et chocolat, demandez les*"; then, in an atrocious American attempt at a Merseyside accent, "Get yer ice creams here, lads." At this, Peter would jokingly admonish her for her disrespect of 'Scousers' with an appropriate playful punishment.

At 5pm on the 21st July 1969, they watched the news with Monsieur Devreux in the bar of Les Arbres; on a TV with grainy black-and-white pictures of Neil Armstrong gingerly stepping down from the Lunar Module onto the moon's surface with the words, "That's one small step for man; one giant leap for mankind."

The patron stood up, applauding and exclaiming, "This is *extraordinaire*, is it not?", before pouring them all a celebratory glass of Ricard and downing his own in one quick gulp. Peter and

Jenny felt they were part of living history at a unique time, with both their lives taking one small step.

As they left Les Arbres, Peter drew Jenny to him. "I will never forget these beautiful times; I sense you in every minute of every day." They held one another, saying nothing as they swayed, listening to the sound of the surf breaking on the shore.

Peter felt able to express himself to Jenny in a way he never had done before, opening up to emotion denied to him during his upbringing, when a tough outlook had been expected. As a child, he confided in her, he had craved more love than his parents could give. He'd wanted to be like other kids who talked about their mams kissing them goodnight, but had never had that. Jenny welcomed his deep honesty, praising his sensitivity and his courage in showing his feelings. As he spoke of his life with her, his stories brought both laughter and tears to her eyes. He told her of his refuge in books that brought his world to life, giving colour where there was none, and adventure to an existence which had little. He admitted to her that he had learned to display an outward confidence to others, yet few knew the insecurity he felt within. Here, with Jenny, Peter had blossomed in a new realm where feelings between them were openly celebrated as joyful.

One night, after a shower, she entered the tent, crouching before him as he sat cross-legged with his guitar. "Stop playing, my lovely," she commanded quietly, stroking his chestnut hair away from where it fell across his eyes. She sat opposite him, cupping his face in her hands, her fingertips gently caressing his temples. "No, you are not my lovely," she continued. "My beautiful man, you are my *love*, for in you I see all I desire, all I hold dear, all I need, all I ever want to have, not just for now but for always. My God, I am consumed by you, baby. Peter, I love you."

Peter was shocked to see tears rolling down her cheeks as she held his gaze, her blue eyes fixed on his, her fingers stroking his cheeks. Her words flooded him, warming his soul, and in those seconds he was complete as he had never been before. "Jenny, I love you too." He clasped her to him, each burying their head in the other's shoulder. They rocked backward and forward, together in the magic of this moment wherein they had just spoken all they had known to be, but had never before dared to share.

Jenny had been consumed by emotional turmoil all her life. She was strong, wilful, driven; an achiever yet she so desired softness. She accepted others yet often despaired of them, and was most intolerant of intolerance itself. She related to the actress Katharine Hepburn, who had said, "Life is hard. We are taught you must blame your father, your sisters, your brothers, the school, the teachers – but never blame yourself... If you obey all the rules you miss all the fun." Jenny had never been able to obey all the rules and, therefore, enjoyed a mischievous sense of fun. She had little respect for convention unless it contributed to a better life. Respect for others? She could give it, but if you wished to gain it, you had to earn it; if you had it to gain, you had to have the courage to claim it. With Peter, she felt a calm closeness wherein respect needed neither earning nor claiming because it was naturally theirs; she respected his giving persona, gaining her admiration.

6

The Gospel of Love

They lay together that Sunday morning in Peter's tent, lazily, warmly and intimately aware of the dawn. In the distance a bell chimed, summoning the local residents to Sunday morning worship.

Peter turned, gazing at Jenny, and she looked back at him as though drinking in his thoughts. "Do you believe in God?" he asked, as the church bell chimed through the morning stillness.

"I believe in love," she told him. Then, "That's what has struck me in recent times; like, Jesus was preaching love two thousand years ago. I guess he was a bit like an evangelist is today – you know, like that guy, Billy Graham. He sounds good but I feel like he is more for the establishment and those who are trying to keep our voices quiet."

Peter ran his fingers through her hair, musing, "I relate to Martin Luther King; like, he was so way out. You know, he led with his beliefs and inspired so many, yet he was still putting God at the centre; but I don't know where I am. It seems to me that

God is whatever people want to seize on for their purposes or their message. If God is love then maybe we should open to that, because of what we are discovering. We met three weeks ago and now have a testament to our creed of love." The bell continued a slow, rhythmic toll in the distance. "Let's go, then," Peter said suddenly. "Come on, we'll go to church and see what gives. What clothes have we got? We have to wear our Sunday best."

Giggling, they rummaged through what little clothing they had, abandoning their normal jeans or beachwear to dress as they imagined might be acceptable. Jenny found a long skirt, and borrowed a shirt from Peter which she tied at the waist but in a more demure fashion than her norm. Peter found a black pair of Levi's 606s which he claimed would look better than blue denim, and slipped into a maroon-striped cheesecloth shirt. She in sandals, he in hockey boots; she pulling on a floppy straw hat, he placing a beach trilby on his head; in minutes they were ready, anticipating and excited.

They walked hand in hand to the source of the echoing bell slowly ringing a welcome or summons. Within a short distance down a sandy track, they crossed a narrow road and came upon a chapel, a surprisingly small white building humbly announced by an unassuming sign: 'Chapelle Saint-François-de-Paule'. The priest was outside, mingling amongst his assembling flock, dressed in fine white-and-purple ceremonial robes. Hesitantly, Jenny and Peter moved toward the small number of people, who hardly noticed them, despite their unorthodox appearance. Neither of them had approached any church, except when forced to by circumstances, since they had been in school. Although Jenny's mother attended Mass every week without fail, when Jenny was fourteen she had given up trying to coerce her daughter to join her. Peter's parents had occasionally attended the local Sunday service and had registered him for Sunday school when he was five, but their attendance had dwindled and by the time he was eleven, church no longer played a significant role.

Jenny turned to Peter anxiously. "This is not for us," she said, gripping his arm, but he was sure of purpose and wanted to seize all that their new way of life was opening to them.

"I don't think Jesus throws hippies out," he retorted reassuringly, smiling with his wild, irresistible look.

As they approached, the priest looked up and walked towards them with hands held up as though in a religious pose. "*S'il vous plaît, vous êtes invités à entrer – ici inspire le calme et le repos.*" ('Please, do enter – here we embrace calm and rest.')

Tentatively, they entered the small chapel, and were struck by the cool simplicity of the interior plastered walls, contrasting with the two imposing gold statues of the Madonna and Christ in arched recesses to either side of the altar. There were small yet magnificent medieval devotional paintings around the walls, impressing upon them where they were, which, they agreed afterwards, had humbled them. Curved pillars supported sweeping buttresses blending into the roof. At the front of the chapel was a towering golden structure with an open-winged angelic herald either side, set in a huge arch in the centre of which was a painting of a medieval robed figure whom they presumed to be the saint after whom the chapel was named. All this was atop a white marble surround with steps leading to it, adding to the majesty and awe which emanated within the atmosphere of stillness. They were transfixed, and experienced a tranquil inspiration in the peaceful beauty that surrounded them. They clutched hands as they listened to the opening words of the Mass from the rear of the chapel where they had safely positioned themselves.

They watched, mesmerised by the ancient ceremony unfolding as the chanting priest processed slowly down the aisle towards the altar. After following a familiar hymn with unfamiliar words, they knelt in prayer, aware of the deep devotion of those around them. The words were irrelevant, but something held them in a moment of serenity. They joined in the Lord's Prayer, which they recognised despite it being in French, whispering the familiar words from their youth in English, pressing their hands together. As the priest turned and knelt at the altar, they looked at one another, nodded, and slipped quietly away without staying for the rest of the service.

Outside, they felt the need to share their moment and hugged; then, looking into each other's eyes, they both expressed how deeply they had been moved, sensing their own gospel of love. The seed of their Covenant was born that day, and, in their experience of the stillness, they sought more.

As they walked back along the dusty road, arms loosely around each other, Peter explored his experience of utter tranquility which prayer had evoked. "I'm not saying that I'm religious or turning to God and all that, but I do believe in love, like we should all have love for each other."

Jenny stopped him, kissing him lightly, and put her head against his. "I feel so close to you already, Peter; this is just so beautifully crazy, and if God is about love then maybe we have found him – or has he found us?"

They walked on in silence with an intense, unspoken awareness. As they emerged through the trees, looking out over the glistening sea, Peter broke their reverie. "Do you think that people should commit, like our parents, or should we be free from all that? Like, wanting to be with someone for all time, I dig that."

She kissed his hand, holding it tightly against her chest, whispering before she could stop herself, "I so want to give myself to you."

They carried on, without speaking, both sensing a lifelong bond already growing between them. Within these hours was sown a seed which grew and blossomed in the days that followed. They began to reflect upon a more spiritual unity – not requiring the blessing of custom or old-fashioned ritual, yet wanting to seek a way that would be eternally there, celebrating their love, and, just maybe, within that would be their God.

7

Ideals and Obligations

Jenny adored Peter's arms around her as they lay in the tent with the flap open, their transistor radio playing mainly British and American music with French commentary she did not care to translate. They were naked beneath their sleeping bags, which were zipped together, resting on a double foam mattress which folded to become a couch in the daytime. Their sense of one another was joyously consuming. "I feel wonderfully pure," she breathed as she caressed him intimately, "yet I am full of desire for you. It is sort of blowing my mind in the most fabulous way." There was no timetable to their intimacy, which was as natural at the close of day as it was in the dawn; theirs to seek in the middle of the night, or on impulse in the afternoon. Their awareness was constant, yet never pressing or demanding; just expressive of their need for one another.

On this day Jenny had awoken first and had lain for some time, trying not to think of a direction on their journey in case she faced an ending. As Peter stirred, she gently kissed him before rising and wrapping a towel around her. She undid the tent opening, gazing at the early dawn, welcoming in the freshness of the air, and rejoicing in the warmth of the sunlight peeping through the trees. She waved at others meandering around the camp and her thoughts returned to an air of complete calm; this was a time that was just theirs. She thought again of tomorrow and dismissed it, dwelling instead on the happiness of today, albeit with a guilty admission that she was living in an unreal bubble. Jenny was not ready to prick her happy bubble for a sad reality she refused to consider.

She turned, and saw Peter stir, then raise his head and smile at her, his deep brown eyes captivating her with their gentle warmth.

"Hey, bronzed boy, you going to welcome me back into that bed or freeze me out with your cool British reserve?" She affected an accent, imitating Vivien Leigh in the old movie *Gone with the Wind*: "*Oh, Rhett, where shall I go, what shall I do?*"

Peter threw the covers back, his nakedness so beautiful to her, poorly imitating the iconic reply, "*Frankly, my dear, I don't give a damn…* or, as they say where I come from, I don't give a shite."

She lay back cosily against him, reassured by his welcome embrace, running her hands through his long brown hair, then her reaching fingers caressing his obvious and awakening desire. Kissing him briefly, she pulled back. "I want us to talk. Let's go in a boat with sails and be carried by the wind."

He had not sailed since venturing onto Southport Marine Lake as a teenager, but reassured her that he had the skill and that there were boats for hire on nearby Cabasson beach.

After a breakfast of croissants from the camp shop, which they smothered in jam, and coffee heated over their single-burner stove, they drove the fifteen minutes to their favourite beach. Peter was dressed in his usual tight denim shorts, over which a faded short-sleeved shirt was draped, open to the waist, drawing Jenny's admiring glances to his toned, bronzed body. She had thrown on a crocheted white bikini, over which she wore a long, flowery sarong skirt, and a crop top which equally drew his gaze to her tanned, slim midriff. Her wide, floppy straw hat completed the look, he thought, of the perfect wild thing, which, in his eyes, she was.

Cabasson was fringed with trees, providing welcome shade for the cars which lined the approach road on both sides. Many had shades fixed over the windows to shield the seating areas from the searing heat which would build during the day. A number of short paths led through the trees to the vista beyond, where sparkling sunlight danced on the ripples of the ocean. As they entered the beach, the view they loved greeted them: the calm, welcoming sea, with gently sloping sands on a rounded bay, opposite which the Fort de Brégançon towered from a small island about half a mile offshore, adding a touch of magic. As so often upon their arrival, Jenny threw off her sarong and bikini top running like a sun nymph into the shimmering waters of the Mediterranean, shouting for Peter to join her. The sand was soft, the sun warm, the wind calm, and they were there, held within their rapture.

They soon hired a small sailing dinghy – without tuition, based upon Peter's false yet solemn assurance to a doubting attendant of years of experience in the Royal Navy. They had brought a small bag containing a baguette, ham, cheese, and a large bottle of wine. A light wind caught the sails, and to Jenny's delight they were shortly gliding effortlessly through the wavelets. The sound of the water sluicing by was enchanting, yet there was tranquil quietness too. As soon as they were a mile offshore, they both stripped naked and Peter let the sails down, and then they were drifting on a flat, calm sea. They sat on a platform at the back of their dinghy with their legs dipped into the Mediterranean. The bottle of wine was opened and both took generous swigs, absorbed in nothing but all they were sharing. They looked deeply at each other in silence, so very aware, the kiss that followed melting them in the moment. Then, lying back, they absorbed the tranquillity, and the gentle creaking movement of the rocking boat.

As they relaxed, Jenny felt a need to place the events of the past weeks into a context that she was struggling to understand. Suddenly, she turned to Peter, raising the subject that she forced from her mind almost on a daily basis. "Hey, beach boy, what are we going to do when this is all over?" The future was so uncertain, yet their present was so now.

Peter was prising open the baguette, placing a slice of ham on each piece, and breaking lumps of cheese as they had no knife. "I love you, hippy chick, but I don't know where the wind is blowing us. There will come a time when we ask whether we seek or need more. I want to explore forever with you, but there is a reality ahead which we will have to face. Maybe we have to ask ourselves whether we want to create opportunity, or wait and see where the wind takes us? Do we want to try and change the world, or just live the dream?" He knew, she knew, that the questions raised answers neither wanted to face.

"Baby, I want to know more about what jives in your head," she ventured. "Like, do you really worry about the world; I mean, does it matter to you? I have always wanted to change so much."

Peter held her hand in his and explained, "In my world, Jen, we are ruled by a class war where the inequality of our history dictates where we are today. Unlike yours, which was built on a set of values, our society was built on privilege, and exploitation of the working classes. It is in the distribution of wealth where our grievances lie and change is needed. Like, the rich get richer, many through inheritance, whilst the workers rarely get the chance. My father is a proud trade unionist chained to these working-class instincts. But I wanted to seek opportunity, break free from my background, and learn from this new age of love and peace. I believe that love can help us make changes; not just the love we have, but in opening our arms to humanity. Peace is not just some idealistic dream. I agree with John Lennon, who said that peace is possible and violence is not inevitable... the gift of love is like a precious plant that needs constant watering, looking after and nurturing. He comes from the same place as me, and I dig what he has to say. I hate money, but maybe we need it to change things. One thing is for sure: I know that love needs no wealth."

Jenny looked at him with admiration. "I love you," she said simply, before standing up and diving into the wavelets gently rocking the boat.

Peter watched her swim, transfixed by her and drawn by her alluring body. She returned to him, holding his legs, treading water as she reached up to kiss him deeply, her tongue lightly caressing his with a soft, almost imperceptible touch. In their intimacy he was surrendering his very soul to her. Then he looked directly at her. "Your turn, foxy lady – tell me the thoughts in your head. Like, what really rocks in your world?"

Jenny hauled herself up onto the back of the boat, shiny droplets running down her naked form. "My country is not all built on its originating values, Peter. We have Vietnam, the struggle for civil rights, open racism, political corruption, and mass exploitation. They call it equal opportunity; that opportunity is based on a system supporting the growing wealth of the haves rather than taking account of the have-nots. Our country is not so beautiful, but relies on a system which corrupts values for greed and opportunism. You think the Brits built power on the enslavement of workers – well, ours is being built on enslavement of nations. We even stole the land off our own indigenous population that existed before the New World. It wasn't new to them. Both our nations should be shamed by our history. What equality did we represent to the Africans who were torn from their countries, carried across the oceans and then forced to work for us in slavery? I have fought for change, Peter, and I will continue to fight for real values. I do not intend to conform, nor sit idly by, nor sell my soul to the Devil. We are ruled by square people who need to wake up to the real New World."

They were both conscious that they had answered the questions about the future they wanted to hide from.

This time, it was Peter who stood up, stretching before her, his chest thrust out and his stomach flat beneath it. He turned to her and smiled. "We are both naked as jay birds," he stated in a mock Southern American drawl. "We have no values or propriety; I am ashamed of you, tempting me to bare my all for your hungry gaze, craving the attention of my manhood."

That was too much, and his reward lay in being pushed from the boat followed by the shout, "Peter Chainey, you are disgusting and depraved."

"Guilty as charged, ma'am; you'd best come and arrest me. I think you need to take me in." His teasing words prompted them to end up wrapped around one another in the sea, their kisses drawing their bodies closer until she felt him enter her deeply, filling her as she pulled him to her, her hands grasping his firm bottom. They rocked slowly in the swell, delighting in their sensuous arousal, until their shortened breath and eventual collapsing gasps evidenced the height of their release.

As they headed back towards the shore, they both felt reassured by the honesty of their values. Yet they were also increasingly and uncomfortably aware that their desire to effect change would inevitably lead to a return to reality. They were victims of their ideals in an age in which they felt they could make a difference. She possessed a fierce determination of spirit which would draw her to pursue her aims, whilst he approached what lay ahead with a more resigned commitment not to be tied to the past, by creating a better future.

They began to realise they were close to shore, and still naked. "You think they will notice?" she said, breaking the silence, coquettishly raising a leg in the air, stretching languidly and arching her back. "Because I think some of those boys would love to see me right now, like this!" She was rewarded with a slap to her rear, and they laughed as they playfully donned their beachwear.

Both realised that day that time was being inevitably drawn into, and invading, their den of cosy unreality.

8

Echoes

Peter watched Jenny, captivated by her, as she followed him from the sea after their customary morning dip. She was so wild, her dark hair shimmering in the sun as she danced before him, the water dripping off her tanned body. He reached for her and she fell into his arms, giggling with delight. He had been dreading this moment, but knew there would never be a good opportunity.

"My love, we must talk," he said, reality shunning his hedonistic instincts.

"So hold me tight… don't let me go."

She turned to him and he put into words the truth that they both knew was a shadow over their summer.

"You know we must part one day and face what awaits us. We will need to consider when we are leaving here."

She looked deep into his eyes, almost pleading. "Peter, our love is for now, but it will endure and lead us back. I know we will part." Her tears cascaded down her cheeks, and although he

48

comforted her, he too succumbed to feelings of desperate sadness at their awareness of the inevitable.

Each day they had created a routine of togetherness, without the pressures of a world they cared much for but considered little. After their swim, Peter would shower in the campsite block before sauntering down to the beachside store, seeking croissants to welcome their morning and taking them back to Jenny like a hunter, briefly sharing the start of the day before he strode out to work his beaches. His emotions were more alive than ever, and he constantly dwelt upon the joys of their union as he laboriously dragged his trolley cart through the sand.

Jenny usually fell back to sleep after he left, loving the scent of him that remained as she stretched languidly inside the sleeping bag, enjoying her space. She felt free from the restrictions that life had placed upon her before meeting him. She would often wander the beach for an hour or so, dwelling on her newly discovered life.

By noon, she had to be ready for her job serving in Les Arbres, only half a mile from the campsite. Monsieur Devreux would customarily bow to her when she entered, as though it was his privilege that she deigned to work for him. The magic of the tree-fringed restaurant had gripped Jenny from the time she was introduced to it, and she had found new confidence there in meeting others from so many walks of life, backgrounds and cultures. The openness of the new age she was living in liberated her. Not for her the heavy, drug-laden nights exploring endless, hopeless, idealistic philosophies like some of those they mixed with. She was drawn to those with real vision, charisma, and vitality for life.

Serving in the restaurant one evening, she kept being drawn by one man; not attracted, but just held by his magnetism. First, there was the pronounced, crisp timbre of his very English voice, which was like Peter's but clearer and more clipped. He was dressed immaculately in a safari-style jacket over a light blue shirt, under which he wore a cravat; the outfit complemented by cream-coloured trousers which were impeccably pressed, and a pair of white shoes. He was somehow familiar but she knew not why. His smiling eyes and easy-going ways were charismatic, and she became distracted as he displayed dramatic gestures throughout his conversation, with an air of supreme self-confidence. She noticed he sported a slight pencil moustache which reminded her of 1930s movie stars, and something about that look stirred a memory.

Having served drinks to his table of four, for which he graciously thanked her, she returned to the bar area where the patron inquired as to whether she recognised her customer. He appeared amused by her response, and drew her with him to the table. "Monsieur, I am sure you may be delighted but this mademoiselle has no idea who you are. *Peut-être*, one of the very few, I think."

The imposing man rose immediately to his feet, bowing in an exaggerated manner like she imagined men would do in a royal court. "*Enchanté*," he said with an engaging smile, kissing her hand. "Mam'selle, I am delighted to make your acquaintance. I am David Niven; may I be honoured with your name?"

She was mortified as she immediately recognised him, and as his warm blue eyes met hers, she felt utterly disarmed. His charm was magnetic as he playfully remonstrated with her for her failure to swoon. He then invited her to join him and his acquaintances, with her boss's permission, for an after-dinner brandy, which, with the nodding approval of Monsieur Devreux, she nervously accepted.

After dinner, Niven strode over to Jenny, stating that he would be "most honoured" if she would join his party. She was introduced to an older couple and a woman in her late thirties, whose names she did not recognise but who, her host said, were involved in the production of a forthcoming French movie called *The Brain*, in which he was playing a bank robber. "Can you imagine anything so extraordinary? I am a former British Army officer but, I suppose, a scoundrel too!" She found him to be self-effacing and utterly genuine, if not somewhat sensitive. He asked her where she was from and about her family, listening with interest as she explained that she found it hard to conform or fit in, feeling that the modern world was changing too fast for the establishment. She felt utterly at ease expressing her views and her idealism, which he seemed to welcome with genuine interest and openness.

"Well, my young rebel, I can tell you, nothing changes, then, because I felt the same. From my 'failings' at school – I was expelled," he laughed, recalling his parents' horror, "to my desertion from the army; in peacetime, I hasten to add. Then I ran away to Hollywood and pursued my dreams. I was meant to go to Eton, but my waywardness put paid to that. Gosh, it didn't work out too badly for me, old girl. Your ideals are admirable, but never forget we all only get one shot at this show. I still can't quite conform and some call me a bit of a cad, but I did return to England when duty called and the Jerries decided to try it on in the war. My advice as a very old officer with, perhaps, a touch of a gentleman remaining, is to pursue your goals but never betray your ideals, and if you are tempted, never be too hard on yourself. I followed an adventurous path, and I have had an awful lot of fun." He smiled broadly at her, finished his brandy, leant over and kissed her hand. "Good luck, old girl; keep up the revolution. Who knows, one day you might be one of us, heaven forbid." He stood up, bowed and left.

His words stayed with Jenny, and in time she would often reminisce about how he, amongst so many others, had helped shape her destiny. She was learning fast, gaining understanding of a generation she often wrote off as 'squares', realising that they too had once had their visions, hopes and dreams. Pragmatism was taking root , although her principles remained fiercely intact.

One night she sat with Monsieur Devreux, after she had finished work at Les Arbres, watching Billy Graham on TV.

"I do not understand you Americans with all of this," he proffered, almost tentatively. "Why is this man so important to your country, yet you continue an unjust war in a place even we French abandoned?"

Jenny watched the evangelical radiance of the enthusiastic, energetic man on the black-and-white TV. They were in the lounge behind the bar area, just off the corridor through which food was being carried out to the well-heeled clientele. She found the 'gospel of love' being preached on the TV empty as it failed to address the important issues of the day, such as human rights and the realities of the war in Vietnam. Graham contradicted her own beliefs, and it was a gap she could not bridge. Here was a man sharing platforms with Presidents and Prime Ministers, gathering enormous admiration in a new wave of Christianity. Billy Graham, Bible clutched in his outstretched hand, appeared utterly convincing with his powerful words. He spoke about God and the Son of Man in a way that she had never before seen, yet she felt indifferent to his message. Despite her admiration for his ability to convey appealing sincerity, this did not feel like the love she instinctively knew, but a betrayal.

Monsieur Devreux pursued his point. "Your country is conducting war whilst embracing peace, *n'est-ce pas?* Is this not, how you say, a little cynical? I fought *les Allemandes* who occupied our country in the war, but I knew what I was fighting for. The violence, I hated it, yet I knew it was a necessity. Vietnam, and the way your country represses so many others, remind me of dictatorship."

She could do little but agree. "I accept all you say, *mon patron*, but I am not part of it, nor is the majority of my generation complicit in this. We are conscripted, bullied and cowed by the authority of unrestrained capitalism, whilst the alternative in Russia fails in an authoritarian communist corruption of individual rights. *Plus ça change, Monsieur Devreux, plus c'est la même chose.*" ('The more it changes, the more it stays the same.')

That evening Jenny felt ashamed of her country and the utter hypocrisy of the establishment with its corruption of history, freedom, religion and human rights in the name of democracy. She determined then that she would make it her life's work to fight against injustice in all its forms, and never to be bound by conventional restrictions, or discrimination against origin, creed or colour. In the comfort of their tent later, she expressed to Peter her utter dismay at the craziness of the world, and that it was up to them to do something before it was too late. He comforted her in the warmth of his embrace, telling her softly that this was their time to make a difference.

"Jenny, my love, it is in our music, our cool generation, our absolute passion spreading across the world. It is in the principles of peace, love and openness. It is in our realisation of equality with individualism; our freedom to express. These principles are what unites us. We are the future, we are where it's happening, we are part of it all and each other."

The crickets played out their unceasing rhythm, then quiet descended and little could be heard other than the waves breaking gently but repeatedly on the sand close to where they lay. The air was balmy and their tent open, revealing the unfathomable pattern of stars over which floated occasional wisps of silver cloud. As Jenny wrapped herself in Peter's arms, she felt safe and secure as her thoughts slowly rested, contentment surrounding the welcoming serenity of her sleep. Peter stayed awake, listening to her longer, slower breaths, holding her to him with a sense of primeval protection in which he too drifted.

In the future their words would stay with them both, haunting them like unwanted ghosts from the honesty of their past with a question. Is it not better to accept what is, with a commitment to change what can realistically be changed, than to lose the prospect of any change at all, sacrificed to unachievable utopian idealism?

9

The Commitment

They held one another in the dawn of every day as they built their own Summer of Love in a time when there was already excitement in the air from a life they could feel was changing. Everywhere they went, they were greeted with smiles, and even those much older than themselves, like Monsieur Devreux, were showing an interest this new, vibrant young age. In the evenings they spoke excitedly, sitting on the sand outside their tent, of their role in a society where nothing would ever be the same again, sharing with others from diverse cultures and countries.

In contrast to a time of peaceful revolution, in late August, they noticed the French students they mixed with becoming loudly enthusiastic about a "*révolution dans les rues*" (a revolution in the streets), proclaiming that they were on the verge of seizing power in Paris. Some enthused about storming government buildings when the time was right, and taking France by force. "If people get in our way, so be it. Some may get hurt but this will be the price for taking away the old and replacing it with the new." Violent student protests were breaking out across France, and television images depicted riots, water cannon, and violence, alarming Jenny, who had witnessed America's Civil Rights demonstrations a few years earlier.

"My God, Peter," she said one night as they lay together, "these guys are well crazy, man. I want change too, but not like that. They talk peace but want violence to achieve it, which is not my way, baby."

Peter embraced her, adding warm reassurance with the words, "We represent the new age of love with tolerance; they promote ideals enforced by intolerance. Love will win because there are millions like us that will make it so."

The students on the campsite were becoming increasingly militant, and they both felt uncomfortable, chatting with Jonas about finding somewhere different to camp. He was typically resigned about the situation. "These guys are full of bullshit, and if they gain power, I'm outta here like a squirrel in the headlamps, man. Last time they acted like this, they started choppin' heads off in Paris – no, man, no way. If you leave, guys, count me in, because, well, shit, I'm wrapped in some kind of love story with you two and it's groovy."

That night the students' revolutionary songs reverberated through the campsite, amongst cries of "All power to the revolution", followed by the more menacing, "Down with the state." For once, it did not seem like a place celebrating peace, but a military camp preparing for violent insurgency. Peter, Jenny and Jonas decided that they would leave together the following day and head for Port Grimaud.

The drive up the coast road in the morning brought welcome relief from the tensions which had surrounded them. Their spirits were lifted by the journey, with the sparkling Mediterranean Sea on their right, passing small coves and inlets, and reaching their destination after around an hour. They passed the grand entrance with its stone arch proudly announcing Port Grimaud, and admired the developing town which boasted houses with glistening white-painted walls, ridge-tiled roofs, smart frontages and gleaming window shutters.

A few hundred metres further on, they reached the main beach campsite. As they pulled in, Jenny shouted, "Stop the car!", before running into the sea fully clothed.

Peter stepped to the ground, waving, then slowly absorbed the beauty of their location. It was a curving crescent of a beach, about 750 metres long, with the rising Port Grimaud emerging to the right. In the distance, he could see the circling bay reaching around towards St-Tropez, which he could just make out through the shimmering haze, the Esterel Hills giving a dramatic backdrop to the view.

Jonas joined him. "Hey, man, this place is cool but, like, hot, you know what I mean?"

They finished taking in their surroundings, then Jonas gave a long Texan whoop and they both ran into the sea, joining Jenny in a frenzy of splashing. This was a welcome, euphoric celebration of their new home, for this was where they had decided to settle. For Jonas, it was easy; Port Grimaud was a harbour used by the boat-delivery business he worked for. Peter and Jenny had opted to travel to their respective places of work together, knowing that their hours could be adjusted to suit.

That night, as they climbed into their sleeping bag, Jenny turned to Peter and whispered, "You are my always I want us to be like forever." Their consciousness united with their subconscious in a harmony of shared joy.

His eyes met hers and he spoke without thinking. "My beautiful hippy chick, I am drawn to you from the dawn of day until the night draws in. I want you for always." Their joy was beyond their ability to comprehend but it captivated their souls, as Peter said, "Not just for this time, but for all time."

For a while, they lay in silence, listening to the rhythmic sound of the crickets, their fingers clasped. The oil lamp flickered and shadows danced around them, and the waves could be heard breaking gently on the shore. Peter opened the tent flap and tied it back, leaving a view of the stars, before relaxing back again. They spoke little but sensed so much in the semi-darkness as each of them searched within themselves to reach for and create something even deeper between them.

It was Jenny who spoke first. "Hey, baby, you recall that day we went to church? Like, we discovered something then; it was pretty way out, right? We spoke of commitment but I think we were, like, reaching out to each other."

Peter leaned over her, his brown eyes intently seeking her thoughts, drinking in the deep moment of intimacy.

"I want to make a commitment to you, my beautiful love," she whispered. "We should make a promise to give ourselves to each other, bound by our own words." She sat up, her eyes sparkling in the reflection of the moonlight. "We should make our own vows to each other, like a Covenant of Love with words we create from the heart."

He responded with enthusiasm. "That is so far out; a Covenant just for us, and maybe we could have our own ceremony of unity."

As their idea took hold, their whispers became more excited, and through the night they spoke of a plan that would give them the symbol of union they desired. They both instinctively felt the need to dedicate their destinies in a way which would bind their minds and souls for all time. Their spirits soared as the idea of a personal ceremony, which they would make especially their own, took root, broken by gentle kisses and words of love.

At 4am, they woke a protesting Jonas in the next tent, with whom they shared their excited thoughts. He took a deep draw on a freshly rolled joint before saying, "This is so cool – crazy, man, but it's just way out of sight. So am I playing the role of the goddamn priest?"

They all laughed, lying back and watching the stars fade as the still dawn broke. And so Jenny and Peter decided that they did not want marriage, nor anything restricted by religion, politics or creed other than their own, but they wanted their Covenant of Love. Theirs would be a marriage without marriage, bound by secret words that each would keep from the other until delivered.

That night they conceived their Covenant and by morning had fixed a date; a commitment they vowed they would hold sacred for life.

10

A Beautiful Friend

Already, it had become almost routine for them to be together, yet their time remained unique, with a wonderful freshness. Their days were spent apart, working, and they both enjoyed the experience of meeting and mixing with so many people before joyfully returning to their beach haven. Some evenings they strolled lazily across the small bay into Port Grimaud, which had become their retreat from the world, and sampled the new waterside cafes. They adored exploring the surrounding towns and villages, driving in the hills bordering the coast, swimming at sheltered, secluded beaches, and soaking up the atmosphere of the Riviera. Their dream 'Venetian' village, despite being popular with tourists, held a charm and a unique flavour. They wandered around the waterways which criss-crossed the quaint streets, with occasional bridges overlooking walkways alongside which restaurants and shops nestled. It was here that they discovered La Cave de Grimaud, 'their bar', where they were always welcomed by the patron, the ebullient and cheerful Monsieur Albert Le Fèvre, who became their smiling confidant, their listener, and even their mentor.

A portly middle-aged man, Albert had slicked-back dark hair, a small pencil moustache, and typically dressed in a colourful waistcoat with a neckerchief tied under an open-necked shirt. He wore a beret, which, he proudly announced to them, ensured that French custom was maintained. He would always greet them with a theatrical bow, showing them to a table like a head waiter in a luxury hotel; a position – or vocation, as he viewed it – he had held for many years in Cannes. His wife was also on the larger side, and would bustle around the bar helping to prepare food, occasionally stopping to ensure that Albert was attending to the tasks she allocated to him. She would rarely chat to the clientele, leaving that to him, but she took a liking to the young lovebirds frequenting their bar.

La Cave de Grimaud lay at the end of a group of buildings facing the sea on one side and the waterways on the other; an enviable location, although far enough from the centre for it not to be overcrowded. Peter and Jenny loved strolling the twenty minutes from their campsite to sample the hospitality of Monsieur and Madame Le Fèvre, often accompanied by Jonas. He took a particular liking to their croque-monsieur, and announced to Albert that he was so inspired, he was tempted to open some restaurants back home in Texas and call them Croque-Albert. "Git 'r done [slang for 'It's achievable'], hot damn, man," he blurted one night. "I reckon I could make your face famous, like 'Colonel Sanders'. We gonna be bigger than Kentucky Fried Chicken." That was typical of Jonas; seeing another business proposition in every situation.

Their friendship with Jonas had become very special, and he became a close companion, joining them on many of their trips, although he was always careful to give them time to themselves. He injected humour and a pragmatic, laconic realism into the era of free thought in which they were living. They both loved his easy-going ways and relaxed, self-assured manner, and his habit of elongating his Texan drawl, stamping his identity on his words. As Jenny joked, "Your accent is harder to understand than Peter's, and I'm American."

Jonas was wise and intuitive, with an ability to cut through bullshit in very few words. His dress typified the hippy image – flared jeans and a T-shirt, topped by a bandana or occasionally a flamboyant Texan Stetson. They teased him, calling him a cowboy, but in fact Jonas had studied at Harvard Business School and graduated in 1968, exceeding all expectations, not that he needed any qualifications. He was already expanding his small hardware business with a third store, based upon his unshaken belief in the new generation of homeowners seeking to better their lives. He had entered university older than most at twenty-two, and now, at twenty-six, he was using his late father's inheritance to build his new enterprise which he pursued with relaxed enthusiasm. In June of that year, he had felt a need to understand the world a little more, and so had decided to explore the dropping-out thing by travelling to Europe for a while. Jonas was a little puzzled by the new generation, but hell, if love and peace could add a little something to the world, then more understanding might benefit his business too.

His father had died the year before after a brief struggle with cancer. Jonas had spent hours with his 'daddy' in those months of 1968, debating and sharing so much with him. Randall Barnier had created his life opportunity from hard work, growing from a small investment in cheap land in the early '30s to the development of a thriving ranch, helped by the energies of his family and a very supportive community. He had tried, with little success, to infuse his son with the energy that he felt for his ranch.

In his final months, he had desired to give Jonas guidance. "My life has been hijacked by war, son, and your generation is right on one thing: this war in 'Nam ain't got no justification. We gotta stop any more wars unless they can be justified with truth. Back in

'44, we knew what we were fighting for and I'm goddamn proud of what we achieved." During his illness, Randall would drift, talking of the Normandy beachhead and the incredible challenges the Allies had faced against impossible odds in June 1944. He had been around the same age as his son on D-Day, when he leapt from a landing craft into the water at Omaha Beach, under heavy fire.

He instilled in his son the hopelessness of war, stressing the futility of pitting man against man. He stressed the importance of "always standing by your comrades, and remaining loyal in all things". In his final days he told Jonas that he had no faith in those in authority. "Don't believe a word of their bullshit, son. They are responsible for killing off the finest President we had, and Lee Harvey Oswald, he was a patsy, used for their cover-up. Kennedy was killed because he was committed to uncomfortable change." By the time his beloved father died in August 1968, Jonas was determined he would not be just another cog in a machine. No war was going to take him, least of all Vietnam.

He had so far escaped the draft into the army because he had been looking after his ailing father, but now he expected further papers to be served. He told Peter and Jenny that he would have faced prison rather than go to war. Jonas was instilled with a belief in America, yet loved to rebel against anything unjust, especially the politics of big business. Often during that summer, they had spoken of their lives and sentiments around the campfire and found that they were united in so much, inspired by love, peace, and rock and roll. Their idealism drove them, joining sentiment and emotion in a bond where thought could be freely expressed and opinions debated openly. Jonas was totally against what he saw as an inwardly corrupt system feeding on its own capitalistic greed. If he was aware of the irony in his simultaneously nurturing a growing enterprise, he was never challenged on it. As he said, "You know what, guys, in the words of Timothy Leary, we all need to 'Turn on, tune in, drop out.'" He would often excuse himself to roll large joints, from which he puffed deeply whilst giving of his wisdom.

Jenny had always been drawn to dropping out but turned away from the drugs scene, although many of her friends took LSD, speaking poetically about their highs. Peter had tried smoking joints at home but preferred a good few pints of bitter in the pub; a habit he was not anxious to break despite his desire to abandon convention. They loved listening to the words of wisdom Jonas was keen to offer, as he drew inspiration from copious puffs of marijuana which he would freely share with anyone joining them.

"Maybe this is the end of war," he had declared, as they watched the huge crowds of people in Washington on a TV in La Cave de Grimaud, demonstrating against and deriding the American offensive in Vietnam. They had conducted an animated discussion on whether their generation was behind President Nixon's pledge, given in a sombre yet almost triumphant tone the previous year, that "we shall have an honourable end to the war in Vietnam".

One evening, after they had sat around the fire for hours, talking and drinking wine, Jenny turned to Jonas and said simply, "You know what, Jonas, you are one pain in the ass, but you are a beautiful friend to Peter and I. I really think we will always know you, because none of us will ever want to say goodbye. Can we be your forever friend?"

As the date they had fixed for their Covenant approached on the last day of September, they had entrusted Jonas with the role of supervising their exchange of words, despite his protestations that he had not been trained as a priest. Inwardly, however, he was proud to be part of their celebration of love, although he wondered how their pledge would fare in the inevitable return to reality.

11

The Covenant

Jenny stood in the centre of the beach, her long, rich raven hair reaching to her waist, tied loosely at her back with a single blue silk ribbon. Her Grecian-style dress was of fine white cheesecloth, a light golden plaited belt drawing it in at the waist, then draped beneath to the ground, a diaphanous covering over her body. Her awareness of her near-nakedness added a sensuality to the poetry she felt inside her, the verses drifting around her consciousness awakening so much within. The light framed her soft figure, her breasts clearly outlined beneath the fine muslin, whilst the shadow of her long legs added to her sensuous silhouette. She was wearing flowers in her hair, and holding the stunning blooms of fragrant cistus and lavender given to her by Jonas which, she thought with a giggle, had most certainly not been a purchase.

Jonas had been waiting on the beach to welcome her, in his floor-length white kaftan worn over sandals, his long dark hair and thick moustache drooping around his smiling mouth, carving an

64

iconic image, Jenny thought, but not of a priest. She felt that this day had an almost religious mystery of its own, in a ceremony of their making, celebrating the love and deep understanding that she shared with Peter.

She held the flowers tightly to her as Peter entered the beach from Port Grimaud, walking slowly towards her, his shirt open almost to the waist, and singularly beautiful. She was so very aware, yet nervous, but her life was his and his was hers, and this moment was the most wonderful she had ever known. She blissfully absorbed the soft sound of the waves caressing the beach only yards away, and she positively ached with joy.

Peter had spent the morning in St-Tropez, walking past the newly opened smart boutiques and chic polished-glass shopfronts announcing piously that he did not belong. He had been searching, but felt derided by the displays parading their fancy labels, above which mannequins stared soullessly at him through dark glasses. He walked down the front, past the small harbour bustling with people in chic outfits, feeling pretty smug in his mission. Finally, walking around the bay, he came to the beach and the sporadic hut shops, outside which was an array of floaty white clothing billowing like sails in the wind.

Approaching a double-fronted store, drawn by a track he liked and knew well, 'Wild Thing', he entered, breathing in the scent of joss sticks. He stood behind a makeshift rack, peeled off his old and faded yet faithful jeans, and tried on a pair of white denims, pulling them tight over his muscular thighs toned by his summer of dragging carts of ice cream across the beaches. They fitted like a second skin, and below the knees, the flares spread over his sandals. Stripping to the waist, he selected a button-fronted, tailored white shirt with a light frill down the front. He chose a thick belt with an exaggerated silver buckle, then stood in front of the broken mirror. This was their time, he thought, and this was their forever day. Shirt open to the middle of his chest, he found a wire-framed pair of sunglasses to complete his outfit. A quick smile, and he paid the store owner.

Swiftly retracing his steps to the harbour, Monsieur Le Fèvre, their loyal patron, awaited him, having filled his old boat with fresh fruit from St-Tropez market. He looked at Peter quizzically, his customary Gauloises cigarette dangling from his mouth, whistled and said laconically, "*Toujours l'amour*, ah, to be young – you look like Steve McQueen, *mon ami*." Then, ramming the old diesel engine into gear, with a crunch and a large puff of smoke from the laboured motor, they cruised the half-hour across the bay to Plage de Grimaud. Peter watched the shore getting ever nearer, and wondered whether anyone could really want him this much, but he knew that, so unbelievably to him, Jenny did. When he stepped ashore, his thoughts were reaching for her, his heart pounding, and he felt breathless with anticipation.

As he approached the far side of the beach, he saw her and was spellbound by her sheer loveliness as she stood framed against the sea; an exquisite vision. She smiled almost shyly as he came closer, looking down, but his eyes drew her gaze back with a look so deep, so longing and so complete, born of a feeling the like of which he had never known before, nor ever would again. His senses were reeling, her beauty was mesmerising, teasingly revealed, captivating, the light suffusing her dress with her body hazily outlined. She was motionless by the shoreline, although the warm breeze washed over her, giving gentle swirls to her flimsy clothing. He drifted the last steps to her, drawn not by conscious thought, but instinctively, despite shaking with nerves.

As Peter walked towards her, he seemed to Jenny to embody a spirit of all they understood, and all they did not. As they stretched out their hands to one another, she felt their entwined fingers were binding the very essence of their beings. When their eyes met, smilingly, she knew with certainty where this was taking them, although she remained so very blissfully ignorant of all that could follow.

Jonas spoke surprisingly softly in his Texan drawl. "I want you to kneel, my beautiful people, and face one another – oh, and, Peter, man, take off the shades."

They turned to each other, the sand warm upon their skin, and Peter's eyes met Jenny's, a smiling recognition of primeval love, so natural to this, their time. They had memorised their words, each secretly from the other, in a professed desire to express their love and their joy in one another.

Jonas continued. "My wonderful friends, I want you guys to say whatever words you have written, looking into each other's eyes; this is your testament for all time, and, Peter, I guess it's you that goes first if we doin' this by the book. I'm not sure if I'm allowed to say this, but God bless you both." He laid his hands upon their heads for a second before standing back from the kneeling couple.

They both reached into their souls. Peter took Jenny's hands in his, and as his eyes met hers she drank him in, her long dark hair blowing wistfully in the wind, her lips parted in a reassuring smile. He spoke with a softness, and yet a strength that projected his love, conviction and his desire to share and unite his being with hers. As she listened, she felt him within her, and her spirit rose to a place beyond where they stood.

"My love, for that is what you are, I yearn to hold you not just for this moment, but for all time; not for any one reason, but for all reasons; not for myself, but for ourselves; not just for this life, but for our forever; not to seek you, but to find you; not to understand, but to wonder.

"My Jenny, my love, my all time, my every reason, for ourselves, for our forever, to hold, and to wonder, I Covenant that my life will remain open to yours for all eternity, and that I shall never deny you or all we have and all that we have discovered within us. I pledge that I will always love you, and that is my bond I give to you."

His words were uttered from his very soul, and she was scarcely aware of anything but the joy flooding through her. She listened intently to his caring, soft voice, knowing that she wanted nothing more, not ever, than this beautiful person who could lend reason where there was none, captivating her thoughts, her dreams, her aspirations like she had known him for a thousand years. In her mind, he was part of her for all time and she was part of him; she craved to be closer to him than with anyone she had ever met, and this day gave him to her as she gave herself to him.

Jenny swayed as she gazed adoringly upon him, her deep blue eyes so drawn to his, warm tears trickling down her cheeks, her hands gripping his, trembling yet so joyful. The sound of the waves seemed to increase, cascading over the sands again and again and again; their awareness of the stillness of their emotions was conducted by nature's symphony gracing their union, as their hearts beat together, sensing one another. Peter's Covenant had enveloped Jenny warmly, serenely and sensually. She was held in the still calm that descended upon them and over them.

Jonas looked at her, giving her reassurance and strength as he guided the occasion. "Right on, man. This is your moment, Jenny; I want you to rock the world with the love that is inside you, a love I have witnessed as, just there, so pure, you know what I'm saying; like, it's really happening." He placed his hand over theirs then nodded warm encouragement to Jenny as he stood back.

She turned to look at Peter, her eyes meeting his and melting their minds into one, her voice so gentle and yet reassuringly strong in its commitment. "Peter, you are my rock of life, for you, my joy, are my revered foundation; you are my river upon which reason flows; you are my mountain of strength; you are my calm sea; you are the sky that I reach beyond; you are the wind in my hair, the soft breeze that breathes upon me; you are the heaven we reach; you are the wild, tempestuous storm of passion within me, yet you are the stillness within my quietest places.

"I Covenant to you that I will hold you in every season of my life: my wonder at the spring, my sun shining in the summer, my forever in the fall, and my warmth in winter. I shall never leave what we have together, and wherever I am, I shall always return upon your call. I love you."

Peter's heart pounded, overcome by the beauty of her words and the intensity of emotion they carried. *I shall always return upon your call. I love you.* Those words embedded themselves in his mind.

There was a long pause before Jonas finally whistled through his teeth. "Right on, man," he breathed. Then, with an irreverence that still held the occasion, "Shit, that was so darned far out; outta sight – wow, like, *way* outta sight! Hey, man, I guess you better kiss each other."

Afterwards, they all walked to La Cave, Peter and Jenny hand in hand whilst Jonas took a toke on a well-earned joint. Music to welcome them was already playing as they left the beach, wafting towards them from the welcoming familiarity of their bar at the edge of Port Grimaud.

Just a month before, they had known that they wanted to make a commitment, not bound by convention, but freed from outside reality into the dream of what they knew was real. The Covenants they made that day were made more poignant by the haunting awareness of time eating away at their nirvana of playful joy.

12

Nirvana

That evening, their love was intoxicating, overflowing as they rejoiced in all they thought and all they shared. There were never-ending toasts but, for once, Peter and Jenny merely sipped at their drinks. Their laughter joined with others', filling the warm evening, which was suffused with music. Monsieur Le Fèvre insisted on playing his accordion, and entertained them all more than once with a somewhat strange rendition of 'That's Amore' in his deep French accent. They danced and sang, but yearned to seek the refuge which would allow them to celebrate their passion for each other and the sweet serenity of their union.

Finally, they departed amid applause, despite their attempt to leave quietly, waving shyly before mounting the stairs beyond the bar area as Jonas gave a Texan whoop. As they entered the room prepared for them on the first floor of La Cave, they delighted in the white flowers that were draped from the beams, the garland over the simple wooden table on which an oil lamp flickered, and more strewn across the old farmhouse-style bedhead. The windows and shutters were flung open, revealing the sea beyond sparkling with the lights reflected from around the bay, the moon bathing the Esterel Hills behind in a silver cloak, and the Gulf of St-Tropez stretching before them. As the slatted door closed behind them, she reached for him, and he held her. For long minutes they savoured their moment, suspended in time, facing the beautiful vista beyond. They kissed, then swayed to the music drifting from below: 'The Wind Cries Mary', the seductive riff of the guitar chords echoing off the narrow cobbled street and mixing with the sound of the waves beyond.

After blowing out the dancing flame of the oil lamp, the only light came from the wall lantern opposite the windows across the street, and the room was bathed in a magical soft golden glow. He was captivated as she stood there, her body clearly silhouetted against the light, like a Greek goddess. She was his Helen of Troy, the face that launched a thousand ships, as he drank in her young body, her nipples teasingly outlined against the whiteness of her robe. She undid her belt and lifted her dress over her head, shaking her long dark hair back over her shoulders. Her naked, tanned body was revealed openly to him, whitened enticingly where her bikini bottoms had protected her from the warm summer sun. For a few seconds, she stood as though teasing him silently, coquettishly showing her body, angling herself before him. Her pert bottom and breasts, so full and firm, drew his admiring gaze; her legs so exquisite, the skin accentuated by the sheen of the cream she had applied. His eyes travelled down to her waist, captivated by her perfect shape, then to her darkened triangle of soft, downy hair that graced the apex of her long thighs. He was breathless in the face of her beauty.

His hardening arousal pulsed, pushing provocatively against the front of his jeans, over which her fingers playfully trailed as she kissed him, tasting him, sensing his desire mingling with hers. She shuddered as she felt his straining for her, so urgent, yet gentle, he arching towards her and she to him, almost balletic in a dance of primeval passion. She kissed his chest, then followed with light feather kisses downwards, then undid the thick buckled belt at his waist. She relished his desire throbbing against her as she began, button by button, to free him, sliding her hand inside, her cool fingers wrapping around his erection, marvelling at the spasms of his excitement. She could feel his slippery silkiness; her finger explored his tip as she sensed her own wetness melting her thighs wantonly, opening, yearning to just take him. God, she wanted him so much, it made her gasp with need.

His hands were pulling her against him, his hardness against her naked skin as his jeans were stripped from his muscular thighs and, at last, he was revealed to her. Jenny pushed him from her; she wanted to rejoice in this moment, to hold all within her, savouring the intensity. She was in awe as he stood in front of her at arm's length, absorbing him with his gorgeous, smiling, longing face, his gentle beard so sweetly framing his cute features, his little-boy nose, and his pouty lips, as she called them. His long chestnut hair fell carelessly to his shoulders, above which his bandana, tied carelessly, gave him the carefree, happy-go-lucky look she so loved. His shirt was now open to his waist, revealing a chest scarcely covered with wisps of fair hair, above a flat, muscular stomach with rippling lines and a valley defining his athletic physique. He was slim, yet so magnificent in his maleness, with a strength and an irresistible sensitive side that she adored. A trail of hair on his lower abdomen drew her eyes down, down his oh-so-soft yet taut skin, to his obvious excitement as he was upright, pulsing, and utterly desirable. His body seemed poised; restrained, yet beautifully straining. A drop of his arousal caught the light as she knelt and drew him to her.

His lower body and thighs were against her as she pulled him closer, her lips encircling him, feeling his spasm as she swirled her tongue eagerly around him, tasting his salty maleness. She yearned to take him, to satisfy, to please, to surrender herself, spellbound by their mutual desire. Her mouth took him hungrily, sucking his swollen manhood deeply, greedily even; her hands around his shaft, she began to rhythmically move his skin as she slid her lips over him. He was groaning and she revelled in his excitement as he neared his peak… but then he pulled back, gasping, then guided her pushing her gently back onto the bed.

He kissed her, tasting himself, which added to his arousal, before his mouth began trailing down her neck, nibbling, licking, kissing; down over her breasts, tickling their tips, teasing gasps of delight from her. His tongue ran a course down the middle of her stomach, making her whimper, wanting, whispering, her back arching upwards, opening herself, until his mouth was buried between her thighs, and she cried out as he licked intensely then softly, teasing her most delicious centre before making gentle, tantalising circular movements, his fingers reaching inside her as she climaxed, unable to prevent her passionate release, yet still demanding more. Her lower body began to move as though guided by an unknown force, in a rhythm of love, craving and needing, as their desires soared to become heavenly waves washing and cascading over them, before retreating and then returning once more.

He moved his body slowly upwards, his hardness brushing in a languid manner against her as she reached to caress his wonderful erection. His hands cupped her naked breasts, seeking her swollen nipples, so responsive to his touch, hardening as he lightly ran his palms then the tips of his fingers over them, as she responded jumping at his touch, crying out. She lifted herself and began stroking him more urgently as she sought to heighten his desire; sensing her need, he gently pushed her backwards over the cool sheets, and their mouths met with melting, yielding passion. Her tongue danced upon his as they became as one, their bodies pressing together, her thighs parting feeling him enter her, thrusting deeply and totally. She yearned for him, guiding his hardness so naturally, like a shaft of pleasure between her eager thighs.

They moved together, their mouths joined, then parting, their gasps of desire as each craved the other more; she needing him to fill her, and he desiring to give completely. Their words of love were absorbed into the welcoming night air, and inside themselves, carrying them to a distant place of union, wrapped in their joy of one another. He moved with gentle strength; her fingers reached between them, caressing them both, enthralled at his arousal and responding wantonly to her own; she welcomed his urgency, which grew as he moved more intently within her. Her hands sought to pull him more urgently, grasping his body and demanding him. Her need was to give herself utterly, yet embrace what was hers to take, and share in a way that unified them.

Their sounds of love were a symphony of intimate music as they reached their crescendo as one, her waves of utter heaven joined with his deep spasms of release. Shuddering with joy, they moved and moved some more, savouring their joining, and never wanting to part. They were only slightly aware of the soft music which blended with their passion in the warm evening air: 'Nights in White Satin'. Their night would never reach the end because with their eyes they spoke the truth of their love that would never reach its end. The letters they would never send held the words they spoke to one another, echoing the music. "I love you" – and yes, that was their truth.

Before they went to sleep in each other's arms, Jenny turned to Peter and whispered, "I shall never leave what we have together, and wherever I am, I shall always return upon your call. I love you."

Peter ran his fingers gently through her hair, his eyes dancing yet profound in the dim light, his voice gentle and strong, yet reassuring. "I Covenant that my life will remain open to yours for all eternity, and that I shall never deny you or all we have and all that we have discovered within us. I pledge that I will always love you, and that is my bond I give to you."

Neither left the passionate highs nor the following stillness of their revelation of love that night, but they each held and rejoiced in the purity of their ethereal discovery. As explorers, they had awoken to an undiscovered place wherein lay their infinite. Their forever was their now, but their evermore was yet to come…

13

Île du Levant

Time was creeping up on them like a shadow falling across the life they had created, and their sanctuary felt increasingly exposed. Their 'Island of Paradise', as Jenny called it, had been blissfully isolated from reality, but as the summer drew to a close, their awareness of the end grew. In those latter days, as work finished with the season, their escape was found in travel beyond Port Grimaud. They would follow the winding coastal road, its numerous hidden bays and coves with beaches teasing them through the trees, as they weaved in and out of the slow-moving traffic crossing the Côte d'Azur through Saint-Raphaël, Sainte-Maxime, Cannes, Juan-les-Pins, Nice and Monaco.

In Nice, they wandered the streets, giggling at their blending in with the rich and famous, as though they shared their wealth. No one knew who the elite were; lines had become blurred as the jet set took on the habit of wearing jeans and T-shirts, whilst women's high fashion was being cheaply mass-produced, enabling anyone to achieve 'the look'. They drifted, hands clasped, soaking up the atmosphere, then stopped for a drink, sitting outside one of the many cafe bars, from which they watched life unfold around them. Their joy lay in the simplest times, yet they increasingly recognised that their lives were suspended without a plan or direction.

In their ideal days, there was no future, no past, and they wanted nothing to distract them from their hedonistic union. Every new experience was written upon their consciousness and welcomed by their souls. They kissed, they held, they reached and were joined in purity, yet lost in sensual release as they soared to heavenly places. Their love and their peace were inside one another, needing no drugs, and the music they danced to, they danced to together in the symphony of life.

By October, they sensed the lengthening shadows of summer's end and an acceptance of the future. On a whim one day, they decided to take a trip to Île du Levant, an island not far offshore where, they had been told, an atmosphere of total freedom prevailed; where intimacy was celebrated, nonconformity welcomed, and open artistic expression encouraged. This attracted them as they were openly expressive and sought to embrace new ways of thinking. From holding hands as they walked, to deep looks in each other's eyes, from arms that linked in careless walks down the beach, to fingers drifting to their faces as they sat chatting with others, theirs was a love that did not hide.

Île du Levant lay approximately twenty kilometres offshore, reachable by a boat service operating from Le Lavandou near the campsite they had left weeks before. They joined a small number of mainly young people for a calm crossing to the isle in radiant sunshine. The boat helmsman turned to them on the way over, asking if they knew about their destination and informing them that it was a place that celebrated freedom of spirit. *"Ici nous célébrons la liberté et la santé."* This openness included nudity being virtually mandatory. Neither Peter nor Jenny had any inhibitions about being naked together, either privately or publicly. A freedom they often enjoyed was being au naturel on many of the beaches along the Côte d'Azur, where nudity had become synonymous with the openness of the new generation.

They had seen images in magazines and newspapers of that summer's music festival at Woodstock, where people had been photographed dancing naked. When Jenny had seen these in *Paris Match* magazine, she had grabbed Peter's arm excitedly. "That is so far out, man; like, beautiful and free."

During that warm summer, she had become used to wearing little; like many others of her age, she rarely rarely wore a bra even under the skimpiest of tops. Jonas would often remark, with his customary directness, "Shit, I'm a hot-blooded Texan. You girls have quite an effect on a man, you know. I need some restraint in the southern regions, you dig, but hell, I ain't complaining."

On the island, they headed down a track which led away from the boat jetties, seeking La Plage des Grottes, which, they had heard, was a pretty beach location in a secluded setting. On the way they met other people, mostly wearing little or nothing. They felt liberated and stripped naked, walking arm in arm, relishing the daring openness they felt in no longer confining their nudity to beaches. As Peter pointed out, "Look, if I find you attractive clothed, then it would be crazy if I didn't when you're in the buff. Am I meant to pretend I don't find it sexy? Well, I'm sorry, because right now I do."

"Peter, you are a bad, bad boy," she giggled. "And you know what, thank God almighty, because I'm horny." They hugged, and she knew he was telling the truth because it was obvious, and hey, she liked feeling him against her, and they walked on, very aware of one another.

Reaching their beach, they were struck by its stunning location, surrounded by a rocky peninsula sheltering a small, white sandy stretch with waves lapping gently at the shoreline, beyond which lay a calm lagoon. The beach was not more than seventy-five metres in width, and enjoyed a sheltered, quiet setting. Pine trees overhung from right and left, framing the vista that stretched before them. In the distance to the left, they could see the shores of the island beyond, but low, rocky cliffs to either side of them gave an enclosed, comfortable security. There were few people there, and all were wearing nothing. A woman who, Jenny remarked, must have been well over forty walked past with just a gold chain draped around her midriff, from which coins hung provocatively like an exotic belly dancer. Jenny turned to Peter. "That looks so beautiful. You know what, she is sexier, I guess, than if she had nothing on."

To Peter and Jenny, the openness of nudity was not only freedom of expression, but also a sensual, erotic art form. Many they had spoken to vehemently disagreed, saying that this purity was above any form of sexuality. In private, the couple had their own thoughts on the subject, rejoicing in their lack of conformity. In fact, they had coined a phrase: "Are we conforming?" If the answer was no, they loved the feeling of individuality this lent them. As Peter said, "If we follow convention, we can never be ourselves and express our individuality, or lead our own way." Nonconformity was a creed they had come to live by. They celebrated their openness, enjoying the exploration without it ever being perceived as a threat to their relationship.

They lay back in the sun, allowing the balmy air to play over their bodies, opening a bottle of wine and toasting one another. "Hey, Mr Ice-Cream Man, you are groovy," she teased.

"Hey, Miss Hippy Chick," he responded. "Never forget me smooth chat-up line: 'Get yer ice creams here, lads.' So, pretty lass, was it me Scouse voice that drew you to me because I sound like John Lennon? I used to look for birds like you on the Dock Road in Liverpool; someone a bit tacky, like, that I could have me way with."

The wine was about to be slowly poured from her glass over his head, before he reminded her that they only had one bottle. As they lay back, he admired her body: her long dark hair spread over delicate shoulders above her proud breasts; the gentle valley of her stomach; her lovely soft, tanned skin; her long legs shiny with oil – his eyes drank her in, right down to her carefully painted toenails. *She is just exquisite*, he thought, his interest prompting him to roll over onto his stomach.

Jenny's head rested on his back between his shoulders. "I love you, Peter. You are breathing life into me with every breath you take."

He felt liberated in their closeness, enhanced by the affirmation of their caresses. Their Covenant was a tribute to their love, and their intimacy a signpost to their souls. They knew instinctively that they would never find this again, and in their recognition was a fatalistic resignation to the duty of life overriding the nature of being.

Jenny broke into Peter's thoughts as she tugged him by the hand, begging him to join her in the ocean. They ran to the edge of the breaking surf, hesitating before plunging in, splashing one another. They swam away from the shore, then, clasping each other closely, giggled as waves of desire coursed over them and through them. She reached for him, savouring the hardness of his passion, and loving his straining need. She pushed against him, wrapping her warm body around him, her nipples grazing his taut chest and her urgent desires matching his own. When they joined, she gasped with shaking, convulsing release, her breathless moans igniting him as he followed in seconds, their mutual ecstasy expressed in cries of delight.

"You are so disgraceful, Mr Chainey," she teased, as she swam backwards from him.

"And you, Miss Baronio, are a tart," he replied, resulting in swirling armfuls of water being directed at him.

They swam ashore together, hardly noticing the half-smiles of some on the beach who had observed, suspecting. As they sat drying in the late afternoon sun, Peter broke into their dream, revisiting the reality that they both knew was to come. As he spoke, Jenny felt like she wanted to put her hands over her ears, to hide under the towels or run from anything that burst their bubble of freedom.

"Jenny, my love, we are going to have to think of our future, baby, and face where we are." He saw the deep sadness in her eyes, and hated himself for acknowledging the truth of their situation. "I'm due back at university for my course, and you are overdue for Harvard. Jenny, you have become more to me than I could ever have imagined. I love you and my Covenant is real, and yours lives within me and always will, but life is summoning us."

She burst into tears and he held her, giving comfort yet feeling strangely isolated himself. He knew the spell was being broken, and their enchanted kingdom was about to change forever.

As they left the beach on the Island of Paradise, they clasped their hands together, stopping every so often, their eyes meeting, seeking; hugging and needing each other. Their need grew and would never diminish, not ever.

14

Idealism

They were awakened by a violent shaking of the tent. "Hands off cocks and on with socks, hippies; it's time to get them wagons rollin'. Yee-haaaa!" Jonas was never one to announce himself quietly but they knew why he was calling them; the fateful bell was tolling the end of time on their island of bliss.

"Will you piss off back to Texas and leave us to our peace, man? Like, haven't they called you up yet? If the Viet Cong hear your voice, they'll retreat all the way to Ho Chi Minh City. Hey! Then the war is over."

Peter emerged from the tent, followed by Jenny, and they stood together in silence, facing the sea. The calm waters hardly rippled, the waves kissing the beach with a soft swish, as if holding the moment in a calm embrace. Jonas rolled a joint, deftly completing the move they had seen him carry out so often, with a delicate flick of his tongue down the Rizla paper before completing a tidy-looking smoke. His were never untidy, like some they saw with wide, unfinished ends; nor did he have a pipe as many did around them. He looked just like he was smoking a cigarette, although he would draw deeply, and often took pleasure in exhaling slowly, creating either a few large smoke rings or a multitude of smaller ones which made Jenny giggle.

"Hey, I'm serious, Jonas," Peter continued. "If you go back, you could be drafted any time. Maybe we should all stay here and just drop out. They would never find you. You could grow a neat moustache for a change, and we could call you Pierre or Roget."

They knew Jonas was leaving as they had discussed their 'return to reality' over the preceding days. They all agreed that they needed to be a part of the life they had escaped from. Jenny wanted to make her mark and drive change in the world. Peter was passionate about finding a career in which he could make a difference in the city where he had grown up. Jonas was more relaxed, but said that his aim was to live a little, give a lot, love a little more, and create opportunity for others along the way. "I got a pragmatic streak that just gave me the idea of gettin' a business, then, shoot, next thing I knew, folks were queuing up. So I opened another store, then another, but I gotta return 'cause that business ain't goin' nowhere without some help from me. Guess we all need it; just a little pragmatism." Jenny retorted that idealism was a critical part of pragmatism, arguing that the latter without the former was directionless and, therefore, pointless. "Phooey," Jonas responded. "You are going to make one shit-hot lawyer, ma'am."

They sat on the groundsheet outside the tent. The dawn was warm despite the lateness of the season, and the sun's rays speckled through the trees to the left of them, throwing patterns across the sand as they faced the ocean. There were few people around, although some were also sitting outside their tents, enjoying the tranquillity of the emerging day.

"Well, I hear they movin' the draft system to some new shit selection by lottery, and hell, I always been lucky so here's hopin'." Jonas lit his freshly made joint and the scent of marijuana filled the air. "Anyways, Nixon has gotten in on a ticket to finish conscription so maybe this whole goddamn thing will end."

Peter drew out a bottle of white wine and poured drinks to welcome the day. Their togetherness was bound by friendship, woven by the heady atmosphere and held by the threads of all they had shared together.

Jonas would be flying to Paris and from there to Dallas. He was being driven to Nice Airport by the couple for whom he had worked all summer. Sailing and navigating boats around the Côte d'Azur had enabled him to enjoy the somewhat hedonistic freedom which he had sought. He was not sure what had driven him to France that summer, but knew that there was a life he would never find unless he reached for it. He had felt stifled by the United States and its self-assured arrogance on a world stage that no one seemed to understand had changed. He had watched in horror and with increasing frustration as young students were attacked for their peaceful pursuit of civil rights. The whole concept of democracy seemed to be unravelling as the establishment came under closer media scrutiny. There appeared to him to be a breakdown of the order that had previously given America stability and the appearance of universal democratic unity. Society was being rocked by events.

The assassination of President John F. Kennedy had heralded a series of catastrophic events that destroyed the foundations of natural justice, signalling, many felt, corruption at the heart of power. After the assassination there had been the Warren Commission Report which sought to investigate and rationalise what had occurred. This was met with derision across the country, and especially in Texas, forging a division in the community between those who refused to accept conspiracy and those who, like Jonas and his 'daddy', felt that there were unanswered questions. Vital witnesses had disappeared or died in unexplained circumstances, and those who attempted to raise legitimate questions over testimonies not being considered were publicly ridiculed, their integrity called into question. Then, four years later, Bobby Kennedy too was shot during his run for President, levying a further tragic cost upon that family. Had they asked too many questions? Jonas felt the distrust of an entire generation.

Two months before Bobby Kennedy, Martin Luther King was shot; he had been viewed by Jonas and many of his compatriots as a blazing light amid the dark shadows of discrimination. King's commitment to non-violent protest had achieved so much that force never could have, breaking down the battlements of entrenched resistance to change. In 1963 Jonas had listened with hope to Dr King's powerful words of having a dream "sitting at the table of brotherhood." He recalled King's reference to "meeting physical force with soul force", which resonated with the empathy that Jonas felt with the growing peace movement. Yet, even with the capture of King's killer, James Earl Ray, there was a further story gaining credence that he too had been part of a wider state-sponsored conspiracy. Jonas had become disillusioned and cynical.

His disenchantment with all things establishment grew with the riots across the US, culminating in open gun battles in the streets between police and Civil Rights activists. His disaffection was compounded by the deep mistrust his father had held for anything to do with the exercise of power. In the final three months of his father's life the previous year, Jonas had had some of the most profound and meaningful conversations he had ever had with him. During the summer of 1968, he had spent hours talking to the man he admired as the strength of his family. As Randall Barnier's health deteriorated, he still relished debate and discussion with anyone who would join him, especially his son. It was as if he wanted to give Jonas as much wisdom as he could in those final months.

"Son, you are gonna take over this family, so you be sure to watch over your mama. Maybe you can find her a job in that goddamn junk store of yours." Randall had never understood why his son had not joined him on the ranch, but his derision of his son's business was always in good humour. Jonas had developed a close bond with his daddy, enjoying his counsel despite often ignoring it, instead drawing on the experience and resourcefulness that Randall had used in building his cattle business both before and after the end of the war.

"You know what, boy, I got no illusions; you need to look after number one because corruption is everywhere." Randall instilled in Jonas that he could not trust authority. "Look what happened to JFK. He didn't move quickly enough in some areas, and moved too quickly in others, trod on too many toes, so they got rid. This country has lofty ideals it will never live up to. Hell, Europe is no better, and that's where a lot of my buddies lie because we fought for freedom. You should go see France, the country we liberated. We had beliefs back then, son; I hope you find peace with yours." That was one of the last conversations Jonas had with his father, who sank into a coma a few days later.

By the end of 1968, Jonas was frustrated and disenchanted with his country, and this, combined with the loss of his father, left him with a need to find meaning behind it all. He had developed a wry sense of humour and a ready smile, but a deep scepticism about life. By early 1969, he had determined he was going to follow his daddy's advice and seek life experience in Europe, leaving his mama to oversee administration in his business. All that summer, he had been in no doubt that he would return to Texas, and by October, he knew the time was right to face his destiny.

Peter too had always known that he would return home. Even after meeting Jenny, his going back was never in doubt, although he wasn't sure how it would all fit with her. His struggle was in balancing a changing world against the traditions in which he had grown up. He had never felt he fitted in, and had determined many years before that he would take a different direction. A new life beckoned to him, in which opportunity offered hope.

There was a lot of crazy stuff going on too that he did not subscribe to. On TV he watched his fellow Merseysider John Lennon creating a movement called 'Bagism' with his partner, Yoko Ono. Peter had been brought up to deal with practical issues in a practical way. He just could not appreciate such an abstract concept as believing that you could get rid of prejudice or stereotyping by living in a bag. As for 'bed-ins', they seemed to him an excuse for two people to draw attention to themselves in a self-publicising stunt, designed to shock, rather than make a statement. He did share Lennon's aims and beliefs in one area, feeling that the world needed to find peace, but crawling into a bag or a bed was not the optimum route to achieving this.

In 1968, he had left the Liverpool Institute for Boys with glowing academic achievement. He bowed proudly to the sincere applause given to him by his teachers and fellow pupils when returning to the school to retrieve his A Level results, in which he achieved three 'A's. These grades were more than sufficient for him to accept the offer from Sheffield University to take a degree course in Economics and Business Studies. His parents were wary of the direction their son was taking, although secretly prouder than they showed. Peter was delighted to pursue a new life in Sheffield, immersing himself in his studies and relishing the freedom to live in a different environment.

In June 1968, he began planning a trip across Europe the following year, for which he knew he needed money. His father secured him a temporary holiday job in admin, following an interview which appeared to concentrate more on his political beliefs than his aptitude. Peter's work in the Dock Administration Office was tedious. The days dragged by and he watched the clock constantly until the siren announced the end of the shift at 5pm. At home he watched the violent breakdown in society on the nine o'clock news on his parents' black-and-white television. He was alarmed by the growing unrest, with street protests in London, and even more violent outbreaks in Paris, the United States and

Germany. He sympathised with the need for a fairer distribution of wealth and protection of civil liberties, but did not condone violence from whichever quarter. He despaired at the use of water cannon and tear gas on the streets, at seeing students hurling projectiles at the police or setting fire to cars; but there was hope, too, in the growing movement of peace and love breaking out across the world. By the summer of 1969, he was more than ready to seek time away from the restrictions that bound him.

Jenny had suppressed any thought of parting since her first night with Peter, when something told her that this was where she belonged. For years, she had felt isolated, torn between two cultures, wanting to be accepted into the American way, but suffering her father's obsession with their Italian roots. Giuseppe Baronio was fiercely proud of the country of his birth, despite pledging his patriotic belief in America, a contradiction totally lost on him. He would proclaim his daughter was a true Italian, adding richness to the culture of the United States to which he proudly dedicated his allegiance. Jenny had come to loathe his view of her heritage, although she suspected that her Latin background had led to some of her directness and passionate nature. She had no time for nostalgia, but recognised and respected the needs of her community to follow *la via Italiana*; the Italian way. This was not her way; her mother's surrender to all that Giuseppe desired was definitely not going to be Jenny's swansong. She felt frustrated by her parents' refusal to embrace the changes she hungered for.

Conforming had never been an option; she knew she was different, always seeking adventure, or something more outside the family home. Jenny related to the protest movements of the early '60s, developing a desire to rebel, but by 1969 she was a pacifist revolutionary. She despised her father's nationalistic views, and the traditional past her mother reminded her of. Gina's security in her role as the wife of the master of the house was just too straight, too hitched to a past that denied the excitement and opportunity of the present. Jenny did, however, respect her mother; more so than her father, whom she tolerated with little admiration and a more distant relationship.

Jenny's later education had taken place at the Atlantic City High School, to which she walked daily, its clock tower always imposing, but rarely telling the right time. Here she developed an even fiercer of independence, seeing a passport to a life to which she might truly belong. Her life had an urgency of purpose inspired by the social injustice that surrounded her. She had a conviction that this was her time, and that fate, or providence, was playing a role in which she was determined to do 'her bit'. Her frustration with her family and her growing recognition of inequalities had caused her to cry, when younger, but now this had been replaced by steely determination. Her life would be dedicated to the new revolution in thinking. War was an unthinkable sin, waged by the establishment for their own aims and, she believed, their economic or corrupt betterment.

After leaving high school in May 1969 with outstanding grades, Giuseppe was reluctantly persuaded that she should pursue her own wilful ambition to study Law instead of working for him. He secured her a place at Harvard, or at least pledged to fund her higher education, shrugging it off with, "Hey, I need insurance – who is a goin' to look after me? She will make the money and take care of her mother and me, huh?"

She wanted to see a little of the world before university, so readily enrolled on a foreign trip being advertised for alumni of her old High School. A former teacher had recommended it, as the trip fees would be cut if she was acting as a minder for some of the younger students. She had a burning desire to travel and escape from the claustrophobic society she was determined to change. Freedom called, and she craved it.

The three friends sat on the sand that October morning in 1969, realising the highway of life awaiting them for an unknown journey. They were all aware that this ending was the beginning of a fresh chapter, but for Peter and Jenny, the idea of parting was a private agony. They intertwined their fingers as Jonas told them of his plans to return home and develop his business, but also diversify to give a fresh interest to his life. "You know what, my wonderful amigos, you have become true friends this vacation, and I find you both crazy and beautiful."

They, in turn, expressed the warmth of their own feelings for their bond with him. "After all, you were the presiding priest at our Covenant, which makes you so special to us," Jenny observed. Peter smilingly affirmed. "And very godlike you were too, rolling a joint before we'd left the altar."

They reminisced as the sparkling waves slowly made their way across the bay to break with a slight hushing sound into small, white, foaming fingers that reached up the sand before retreating again. The tree-covered hills overlooked them, and they could already see the workmen meandering over the upper floors of the new city a few hundred yards to their right. Time was stilled by their peace, but they all knew that this was the end of their dream.

Jonas was unusually philosophical, offering his reflections on his future in which he saw a need to build a life for himself whilst still caring for those around him. He saw a sad futility in the idealism being expressed by the new generation when these wonderful beliefs were set against the immovable force of government. He had arrived in France, he said, utterly confused about where life would take him, and had since concluded that the control he himself took would decide his direction. He admitted an element of selfishness in his conclusions, but said that any change he could contribute for a better world would resolve from his own strength of purpose.

Jenny stated that she wanted to help what she saw as an ongoing revolution, but that she had concluded that she could achieve more from within than from without. "Demonstrations, sit-ins, violent protests and riots are not the right way. I once placed flowers in the barrels of guns drawn against us at a demonstration, and truly, I was proud of myself then, but little has changed as a result. I despair at the crazy way we seek a more peaceful world by becoming more violent. Martin Luther King was right, and that will be my way: soul force. What has changed in me this summer is that I learned to love. That has made me stronger, and I will hold that gift inside me always." She hugged Peter, and the realisation of the finality of these days ached in both of them.

Peter's mind was set on following a career path which would ultimately decide the direction his life would take. He stressed his determination to find a way of improving the city he loved for the people he related to and the community he felt part of. He had a deep drive to succeed, exploring opportunity without being tied to the expectations of the past. Money, he said, was of little importance; making a difference from which others might benefit was his true goal. "My gorgeous hippy chick has helped me put it all in perspective through the gift of love we have shared."

A car horn sounded, and Jonas stood, turning to them and placing his hands on their heads. "I am not a believer, but I want God to bless you because I have met two of the finest people ever these past months. You are just far out, and you have blown my mind. I hope, my friends, that we will reach out to one another again – who knows? But I'm outta here and need to find myself again; a journey you two have already helped me on. You know what, we got a better world out there waiting for us, and between the three of us, we gonna kick some ass."

He kissed Jenny on both cheeks, hugging her, and threw his arms around Peter. Their bond had been forged and they realised their karma as Jonas walked away. Jenny cried, Peter tried not to, and they held hands as Jonas waved from the car window. They knew they had come to the inevitable crossing that they had avoided so many months ago, and from which they had attempted to escape, knowing that there would be an end, and the challenge of a new beginning.

15

The Parting

They gave themselves just one week after Jonas left, determined to live to the full in their last days together with no work. The holiday season was over and now they would ignore their future which played little part in their final days as it was too much for either to contemplate, but it would emerge at night. "When we part, we will still have our Covenants to bind us," Peter whispered to Jenny as she lay in his arms one night in that final week. "I think we should agree a period of time when we part without speaking to one another so that we can commit to the lives we seek."

Jenny clutched him to her. "My God, Peter, I will be inconsolably unhappy without you. Why is life so cruel? Why?" She then reached within herself for the inner strength she had always possessed when her security was threatened and, surprising herself, added, "We must agree not to speak for at least one year. That will give us both time to adjust."

Peter kissed her forehead but had already acquiesced, knowing she was right, as they drifted into troubled sleep.

Each day of that week they were determined to make special. One was spent on the beach at Cabasson, now curiously deserted. Peter playfully suggested that they make love in full view of the Presidential Palace at the Fort de Brégançon across the water. Although they abstained it was still warm enough to picnic and enjoy sparkling white wine as they sat taking in the late summer sun, reminiscing over the dreams they had shared. A return to St-Tropez, where, once again, they wandered down the harbour front, taking in the atmosphere, which was still vibrant, although more peaceful. A trip to Le Lavandou where Peter had first landed, meandering round the shops, then calling into Bormes-les-Mimosas and the campsite where they were first together, followed by a swim at Plage de la Favière, where they had first swum together. On one unusually warm day, they sunbathed au naturel together one last time on the beach at Cavaliere, with much wine, laughter and love. On an impulse, they took the short drive to Sainte-Maxime, where they walked, hands clasped, around the harbour, the old town and the shops, buying gifts for family. Their conversation was as if there would be no end to their happiness. They enjoyed lazy drinks in waterfront bars flanked by the charming old-world buildings mixed with modern villas that dotted back from the harbour up the hillside.

Early one morning, Peter drove them down the long, winding coast road overlooking the Mediterranean to Cannes. There they walked down the smart boulevards and admired ornate buildings, sensing the wealth that permeated. They parked their battered VW Beetle, which they had named Herbie after a movie about a similar car, just off the Promenade des Anglais, oblivious to the Porsches, Maseratis and Lamborghinis in adjacent spaces. They walked, arms around each other, carefree yet inwardly conscious of the sands of time running out. They laughed, as carefree lovers, exploring the opulence that they could only dream might be theirs.

In the evenings, they lay together, absorbed in their union, held by one another and the dream they had created and lived. Often in those final nights, they would awaken, asking in a low whisper if the other was asleep, before a reassuring response heralded more exploration of their thoughts, hopes and lives.

"Why did we meet, my love? Do you believe in fate or divine intervention?" Jenny asked in the early hours of one morning.

Peter was wide awake. "I have no beliefs or disbeliefs, Jen, but I sense that this was meant to be and will one day lead us somewhere. We were given to one another, a gift we should cherish always, and even in our darkest places our lives will be lit up by the beacon of love that has drawn us together. I will always seek you, as you will me, but whether we will be drawn back is an unknown. Parting from you tears me apart, but in many ways our lives haven't even begun."

The practicality of his reply stunned her, yet she knew his wise words were right. She had a path to follow, yet somehow in the magic of those months, their direction had blurred their focus now yielding to a clarity they shared. This was their defining decision: to seize the life that awaited them, rather than abandon themselves to a hedonistic, delusional existence. Though idealistic, Jenny was fiercely practical and felt she had no less of a destiny than Peter, who, whilst he hated the prospect of leaving, knew that opportunity was beckoning. It was in these moments that they transformed thoughts into a vision that they could embrace.

On the last day, their practical heads drove them to awaken early, and – strangely, Jenny thought afterwards – they did not make love. They had a timetable, and she had to be at Nice Airport for 2pm.

They had started their goodbyes the previous night in La Cave de Grimaud, having a few glasses of wine with Monsieur Le Fèvre, who offered words of advice. "Never leave love, *jamais, jamais*, because love will seek you out, *mes amis*, and haunt you. Love needs to be embraced, savoured, tasted and treasured for always.

C'est pour toujours, mais vous cherchez la vie ['It is for always but you seek life']. That is the modern way, find your way in life, but remember what I tell you. Love will seek you out."

They parted after extended embraces, followed by Monsieur Le Fèvre seizing his accordion and singing to them, for the last time, the song 'La Mer' in both French and English; a song they would never forget. As the words echoed off the narrow cobbled streets, they found his voice singing, *"Au revoir... bye-bye"* so poignant, and yet their instinct was that this was not the end. Their lives would be sailing somewhere, as the song said, awaiting their return from beyond this shore, embracing as before.

As they left the restaurant that night, they were immersed in sadness, though trying in vain to balance their sorrow with anticipation for what was to come. Later they lay back, looking up at the stars, listening to their thoughts, and tearfully sharing the joy of all they had experienced. They had found the keys to release them from their nirvana, yet neither wanted to escape. They wrapped their arms around each other, whispering words that were not needed, and seeking thoughts that needed no expression. Then they fell silent, holding one another, so very aware in the calm they created within; they sought nothing more, as they knew what mattered in that silence.

In the morning, they packed quickly and easily, for they had not collected much in their long summer. At the top of their sleeping bag lay a folder, inside which were the words of their Covenants, written down by Jenny so they both had copies. On the front was written, in Jenny's neat hand, 'The Covenant.' They took the folder down to the water's edge and faced one another. Tears began rolling down her cheeks, and he choked as he said just some of the words, although as he looked at her, he knew he did not need to read them as they were imprinted upon his consciousness: "My love, for that is what you are, I yearn to hold you not just for this moment, but for all time; not for any one reason, but for all reasons; not for myself, but for ourselves; not just for this life, but for our forever; not to seek you, but to find you; not to understand, but to wonder…" He broke off, his brown eyes full of emotion, stifling the grief he felt, then, "I shall always remember with wonder, and I will be willingly bound to the memory we have created until we reach our forever."

She set the folder down, clasping both his hands, her voice wavering as she sought to escape thoughts of their parting. The wind blew softly, barely rippling the wavelets by their feet, and there was an embracing calm inside despite the aching grip of adrenaline that held them both. She looked deeply into his eyes. "I Covenant to you that I will hold you in every season of my life: my wonder at the spring, my sun shining in the summer, my forever in the fall, and my warmth in winter. I shall never leave what we have together, and wherever I am, I shall always return upon your call." She could hold her feelings back no more, and sobbed against his chest.

For both of them their thoughts were sacredly and profoundly felt. They held each other, and swayed as the experience of just being cascaded over them like a wave, carrying their thoughts and memories in a kaleidoscopic spume of awareness. Then they walked across the warm sand to the edge of the beach and, turning one last time, paused. After gathering themselves, they stifled all thought beyond that of where they now needed to be, and walked away.

Peter drove Herbie back towards Le Lavandou, frequently glancing to seek a look of warm reassurance from Jenny. Despite his determination to reach for the life that awaited him, he felt vulnerable with a feeling of disorientated panic. Jenny sought solace in the memories that flooded her mind; from the joy they had shared, to beaches, villages, scenery, music, love, laughter and togetherness. She rejoiced that they had experienced it all in a new era of hopes, visions and dreams.

They pulled in at Les Arbres to be welcomed by the ebullient Monsieur Devreux. "Ah, the most beautiful American girl in all of France. You notice, I dare not insult my countrywomen," he joked, then added intently, "but I am extremely saddened by what is happening. We seek love always, like a quest that never ends for many, and never begins for others, but you, you have found that which so often eludes, yet you are running away. I despair of the English, but you Americans are more – how can I say? – adept, and know how to seize love. First you find this gift, then you abandon it. You have, so to speak, panned for gold, then, on discovering it, you give it away. This is a cause for a drink, no?"

They sat sipping Ricard with iced water. Peter explained that they were not running away, but facing their future; not hiding, but seeking; and if they allowed their journey to cease before it had started then they would be denying themselves what life held for them.

The Patron questioned them further about their intentions in a world that had gone crazy, and in which there needed to be another way. "You young people have the answers, not us; the new world needs to be driven by the youth, powered by ideals like this 'love and peace', *et pourquoi pas?* It is only twenty-four years since we had the horrors of world war, and now we have more wars, and more threats against us."

Jenny gripped his hand. "Gaspard, it is because of the need for change that we are both inspired to do something; not by violence or disorder, but through the influence we can have. I want to contribute to the future, and Peter has given me a renewed of a life and love that has strengthened me."

"You know what, it's like a new beginning I'm seeing," Peter interjected. "There was the Civil Rights movement in America, which was met with violence; there was violence against students in Paris, against peace protestors in London, against those protesting against poverty, and against those opposing apartheid in Rhodesia and South Africa. I've seen the workers in Britain demand and demand, and no wonder, because they have been used by the privileged classes throughout history. You had your revolution, and maybe we need ours, but peacefully, man. That's what our generation is about; across this planet we are awakening, united by the realisation of what love and peace can achieve. Listen to our music reflecting the need to change and I want to do my bit. There's a whole generation out there, you know, feeling disenfranchised, disillusioned and shocked by the breakdown in democratic freedom, or the illusion that we ever had it in the first place."

Jenny admired Peter's ability to express himself in such logical, direct ways, yet complemented with the poetic. She shared his views as though he spoke from her heart. They were in unison, like rivers flowing together, adding to the force of their conviction. "You speak of the war, Gaspard – my Father was a fascist before he was aware of the violence they inflicted. Despite his beliefs, he did not wish harm on anyone. In order to prevent abuses of power, we need to understand them. I want to help change things. In Vietnam, my country is acting like a fascist regime, taking people my age and forcing them to go to war, imposing their will with overwhelming superiority against a population with few resources. We can excuse the draft in World War I, or World War II on the grounds of principle, but not in Vietnam. But you know what the Viet Cong have? They have belief. This is a war fought on political differences, backed by greed and the need to maintain a cosy global political status quo which has nothing to do with the needs of the Vietnamese. I'm ashamed of my country, and so we return from this summer as idealists, yes, but with a purpose that is committed to change."

Gaspard Devreux was moved by their passion, and he rose from his chair, clapping his hands slowly – not mocking, but in awe of their fervour and commitment that far exceeded his own at their age. He hugged each of them in turn, his grey eyes filled with sadness. "You modern people, you think you know it all, and in many ways I think you do, because you voice an awareness we either never had or never dared to express. God bless your lives; I hope you can both remain true to your principles." Those words were to echo through both their lives in the years that followed, as though Gaspard sensed the pressures that they would face. They all embraced, with tears in their eyes, then waved as Jenny and Peter drove away until they could see Gaspard Devreux no more.

Their last stop was the campsite where they had spent their first night together. Here they held one another in the spot where their tent had been pitched, laughing as they recalled their impetuousness. They kissed deeply before setting out on the drive to Nice down the coast road, together for the last time.

As they approached the airport terminal, a false normality descended over them as they could not bring themselves to talk or think of what was to follow. Their emotions were held in check as Peter took Jenny's baggage from the front bonnet of the car, but then they both stopped, as though frozen for a second, and looked deep into each other's eyes.

Jenny sobbed, dropping her head to Peter's chest. "Please never forget me, us, or our precious times – this has been our heaven on earth, Peter."

They held each other, both so very aware of the sacred nature of all they had reached for and realised. The moment filled them with the chasm of the unknown into which they were throwing themselves. Surely, this could not be the end, she thought, as Peter's warm embrace and words helped to steel her for what lay ahead.

"We will always have our Covenants, my dearest love, and they will bind us for all time. We are not gone from one another, but remain part of each other, and will always. These words will remain with you: My Jenny, my love, my all time, my every reason, for ourselves, for our forever, to hold, and to wonder, I Covenant that my life will remain open to yours for all eternity."

Her tears welled up in the grief of their parting and her voice wavered as she responded, "I Covenant to you that I will hold you in every season of my life... I shall never leave what we have together, and wherever I am, I shall always return upon your call. I love you."

Peter helped her towards the terminal. One last hug, then they pulled away. Fingers slipping apart, hands dropping slowly, they tore their eyes from one another, and began to walk towards their unknown. Then, turning again, they saw each other for the last time. They both smiled despite their agony, waved, and walked away without looking back.

16

Autumn and Winter 1969

The parting hurt Peter beyond anything he had expected. Pulling into a lay-by close to Nice Airport, he sobbed in a manner that shook him to the core. He was stronger than this, wasn't he? Yet now he felt more vulnerable than at any point since he was a child, and equally exposed. He looked across to where she had been sitting only minutes before, as if hoping to see her smiling face, but there was nothing. Nothing except the rain which lashed down in a metallic rhythm, drumming in his isolation and wreaking heaven's revenge upon the direction in which they had allowed their lives to take them. Suddenly he was alone, and far from the life-seeking person he had explained to her they both needed to be.

The drive home seemed even longer than the three days it took; a journey without comfort which became a blur of places that meant little, as he faced a life he was no longer sure he wanted. After sharing each night with the highs of their love, he was in the loneliest place he could ever remember. The basic functions of eating and sleeping were mechanical, and he no longer felt the joy in each day. As he drove into Normandy, he began to look forwards to the normality of his parents and a home where he could at least hide himself. He called from a public phone in Calais to alert his father that he was returning. The familiar voice was warm and gave Peter a much-needed sense of belonging, but this was the advent of a new life rather than the haven in which he had sought refuge throughout the summer.

Arriving back at his parents' home, he was welcomed by his relieved mother and father, but they were a world away from his experience and he did not want to share it with them. He skated over his meeting with Jenny and the feelings she had awoken in him although his Mother somehow knew there was more. Amongst the post that awaited him was a letter from the faculty administration informing him that he needed to reapply to continue his studies, and that his place was not guaranteed. He felt the judgement was harsh, not least because his own senior tutor had encouraged him to open his mind and travel, challenge accepted norms and embrace new ideas.

He had discussed travelling during a tutorial review in 1968, in which Peter had confided that he felt confined by his upbringing and restricted in his experience of life. His tutor, Professor John Quiney, was in his early fifties, wearing a sports jacket with leather elbow patches, looking somewhat dishevelled with a receding ginger hairline, yet retaining a youthful full moustache. Thick, round brown-rimmed glasses could not hide the piercing blue eyes that gave him a commanding air of authority. He lit his pipe slowly, the flame dancing as he began drawing and puffing clouds of aromatic smoke into the air. "You should go travelling, Peter, and seek to expand your horizons. When I was your age, most of us had to break off our studies or careers and join the war effort. I ended up as a tank major in Monte Cassino, where we took a hit from a German aircraft, hence my stick and hobble. You, young man, have the freedom to travel, and you should take it before your career prevents you from having another opportunity. Remember, this is your generation; I only wish I'd had the chance."

Professor Quiney's wistful words stayed with Peter, as did those of so many who had mentored him during his life. He relished the guidance and counsel of others, and genuinely valued experience upon which he might draw, but by which he was not always swayed. From his earliest years, he had been fascinated by stories, and, as he grew older, those stories spurred his imagination and drive to seek. He had a natural inquisitiveness which would lead him to ask questions of others; as a youngster occasionally earning him reprimands for impertinence. However, his inquiring nature rewarded him later with a wide range of views and a tolerance learned from a wealth of knowledge and opinions. His urge was to travel and, as the adventure books he read would say, 'seek his fortune'; a phrase which still had an exciting ring to it.

Peter called Professor Quiney in late October 1969, asking if he could visit, and travelled to Sheffield two days later by train. For some days since his return from France, his beloved VW, Herbie, had declined to start in the mornings, thumping and emitting clouds of white smoke in protest. However, as he proudly announced, Herbie had been purchased for £225, and had carried him across France – a distance of around 1,300 miles each way – without so much as a murmur.

Leaving Sheffield Station, he took a cab up towards the university, passing the old bomb site that was still there some twenty-five years after the last bomb had fallen on the city, reminding him of the many similar sites in Liverpool. Then up The Moor, across to Brunswick Street, and the approach to the university. This was where he had spent his first year of study, in a student house on Endcliffe Rise Road, thirty minutes' walk from the university, sharing with three other students: a mechanical engineer, an electrical engineer and a physicist. He had revelled in their competitive banter, in which he was labelled the capitalist, whilst they claimed to be socialist revolutionaries driving research to assist the workers. Their logic was, he countered, quite farcical, as his background was rooted in working-class Liverpool whilst they were from the privileged middle class. He stressed that his revolutionary credentials were impeccable, like those of Marx, Lenin, Trotsky and Stalin, none of whom had ever studied engineering or science. His studies in economic theory, Peter claimed, albeit without conviction, were laying the foundation for the New Age philosophy which would bring triumph to the workers.

That first year had been a mixture of serious study and many raucous nights in which exposure to alcohol without the constraints of parents led to enjoyable excesses. Though Peter enjoyed the conviviality, he preferred quieter nights when he could escape into his adored books. At university, he began to explore the library, discovering the literary joys of Shakespeare, Keats, Byron, Coleridge and Shelley. He relished the talents of Tolkien, Rider Haggard, Jane Austen, D. H. Lawrence, Virginia Woolf and others who pushed the barriers of the day or the accepted conventions of their time.

Peter was introduced to his tutor, Professor John Quiney, at his university interview in November 1967. He was a strange mixture of talents, having studied English Literature at Oxford before taking up another degree in Economics, finishing with a PhD in Business Studies. As he drily observed to Peter, "I felt it necessary to learn the art of writing from the masters before attempting to persuade others of the merits of my business philosophy. Although these days, the future of economics lies in rock and roll. Clearly, that is where the money is to be made; not in studying economic trends, the FTSE 100 or fiscal policy." During the long interview they had discussed literature, art, music and politics, the professor eagerly entering into discourse with the much younger man, drawn to Peter's enthusiasm. He made him an offer of a place there and then, although, he stressed with a twinkle, he would deny it if challenged, as officially speaking such matters had to go through the proper channels.

Throughout his first year, Peter found Professor Quiney's guidance in both academic learning and life edifying, giving him confidence in his ability to succeed in the future. His professor's passion for life mixed with a healthy distrust of society's boundaries, and that, in the changing climate of the late '60s, was an attitude with which Peter felt very comfortable. "If only we had been granted the freedoms you enjoy today," Professor Quiney said ruefully. "You should seek out, and embrace ideas with the young of other nations. If there had been more of that in my day, maybe we could have avoided war. Pursue your dreams, my boy, pursue your dreams."

Peter had fully intended to return to his studies in September 1969, but unforeseen events had intervened. He had written a postcard to Professor Quiney in August of that year; a view of the beach by Bormes-les-Mimosas, with a simple message:

Sir,
I pursued my dream and I regret I will not be returning for now. Please forgive the rashness and ideals of youth.

The professor had smiled upon receiving the card, delighting in Peter's youthful impulsiveness, with a pang of envy for what he himself had been denied. He was equally delighted to grant his student an interview upon his return. "Come in, Peter; tell me about your journey into hedonism. Did you seduce the French maidens, or vice versa? Do you now feel that the draw of John Maynard Keynes has the edge over profligacy?"

Peter was quick to dispel that indulgent fantasy. "No way, man, but," he replied with some earnest, "I did fall victim to Cupid's arrow, and that appears to have been my downfall. I left a haven with her to reach for a future, and in so doing, Professor, I also left behind a person who transcended all, beyond any perception I may have held about love or romance." He paused, looking into the distance, then gave a deep sigh before continuing. "My words are out of touch with my generation. We embrace love, but all the commitment that goes with it is seen as kind of weird today.

I know the beauty of it if you open your mind. We opened our minds, but still decided to run away from it, or at least I did. I knew I could succumb to the crazy reality of what I felt, despite it being impractical, abstract, with no relevance to career and self-improvement."

Professor Quiney shook his head, giving Peter a disparaging look over his rounded glasses. "Then, Peter, you may have walked away from the reality of what is important – not that which you perceive, or about which you can be taught, but that which is within us, waiting, if ever we are lucky enough to release it. Once upon a life I met a young Italian girl called Marina. She helped nurse me following my injuries at Monte Cassino. She was so beautiful, with big dark eyes and long wavy hair, and very coquettish. We saw each other secretly at first, because in 1944 it was not good for Italian girls to be seen with those who had, for a time, been the enemy. We had meetings outside the hospital, and fell utterly in love. We were inseparable, passionate lovers, but also developed a deep bond. We discussed everything, and even wrote poetry to each other. It was paradise for me to go from the violence I had experienced and the utter futility of warfare into the open arms of someone I knew was my true love.

"I wrote home, telling my family that I might settle in Italy. I was twenty-seven, and my parents would have none of it. I remember my father writing back to me and saying it was time to finish the job, get home and return to a real career. He said he would fund my studies at university to become a teacher, but only if I returned alone. I took his advice, or accepted his demand as 'the right thing to do'. That was a popular expression then, and it meant a lot."

He looked Peter directly in the eyes, removing his glasses, and Peter could see the emotion he barely held back.

"Despite my happy life with my wife, I have never forgiven myself for abandoning true love and seeking 'the right thing'. It wasn't; I left Marina and carried that regret with me always, never forgiving myself. Time and again, I have nearly reached out to her, but life and duty intervened. The philosophical point we have to consider is: should we follow the most attractive instincts, or pursue our own sense of duty? Or is that misplaced, meaning a duty to others?"

They sat and talked more, Peter opening up with all his pent-up feeling from the two weeks which had passed since his parting from Jenny. He told the professor that he thought of her every day and often dreamed of her at night, awakening believing that he was in her arms. He was committed to the decision he had taken, but racked with loss, and the two were irreconcilable foes.

Professor Quiney stood and walked over putting his hand on Peter's shoulders. "Then, my boy, I will put myself out for you; you will have your place restored here. I have influence, but I want you to do something for me." He looked earnestly at Peter, patting his shoulder, then moved to the large window overlooking a playing field where he stared into the distance. "She too will be feeling what you are feeling, but perhaps more so, because despite modern thought, females are innately more sensitive than we are, and have both the strength and the weakness that their emotion gives them." He returned to sit behind his shabby desk. He lit his pipe, puffing clouds of smoke from the side of his mouth. "Write to her, tell her how you feel, and 'do the right thing', old boy. I didn't, and it has haunted me for the rest of my life. Do it for me, do it for Jenny, do it for my Marina, but also, you must do it for yourself." He puffed even more on his pipe, and a flame leapt above the glowing tobacco core, adding to the haze in the room.

Peter felt absolved by the exchange, having shared for the first time his experience, his uncertainties, and the thoughts which haunted him. He was now committed, he told his teacher, to a course he had to follow, but not without looking back.

"Then, Peter, you must not close the door behind you, nor shut off from your feelings, because that will take away a part of you which shields and protects your ideals. Too many of those my age have become devoid of the drive or vigour to uphold the beliefs they once held. Some of us were idealistic once, but the war destroyed much of that; emotion and love were no longer relevant or real. You know, Peter, it is important to have feelings because they drive us, but losing them because we run away from truth leaves a scar which may not heal. My advice is to stay true to yourself, and whilst your opinions may change, you should value the gift that your emotional experiences give you."

They shook hands, and then enjoyed a beer in the local pub before Peter caught the bus back to the station, both relieved and challenged by the advice he had been given. Although his mind was made up that he had to move forwards, he looked back with a wistful longing and Jenny remained in his heart. Their journey was never-ending, and in his dreams, they returned to it.

When Jenny left Peter, tears streamed down her cheeks as she walked towards the airport terminal. Turning one last time, she saw his face, often so mischievous and incorrigible, but now so serious, so lost and so vulnerable that she wanted to run back to him, to reassure him. Yet it was he who had written this chapter, although she had not resisted as she now so wanted to do. She could not comprehend how they had reached where they were, nor why he would not be there to snuggle into her that evening.

Inwardly she had screamed for Peter to announce that they should abandon their plans to return to their normal lives. But he had reassured her that they needed to find their way in life, strong in their commitment to the ideals they shared. "We have to be aware of reality and return to it, because this is the only way we can develop and bring about real change," he had told her as they lay in their tent. They were by the edge of the beach, listening to the waves breaking on the shore. Why should they part from the simple peace within which they had found so much joy? Jenny wanted to make a difference, but hated the conflict in herself. Her hopes focused on a world in which peace would replace war, poverty would be met with generosity, and race, creed and religion would merge in a pool of human understanding. She ively knew that Peter was right, but yearned to remain in their cocoon, shielded from life.

She sat in the airport lounge, numb with shock after Peter's departure. Everything seemed to have happened so quickly. One moment they had been sitting hand in hand, discussing life with Monsieur Devreux in Les Arbres, and inside two hours, they were parted from one another, and none of it made any sense. She was tortured by her thoughts. Should she call Peter on her return to Atlantic City, or accept the path they had chosen and walk away? The question stayed with her.

She endured the journey home – via Paris, and then the long flight to JFK Airport in New York – with an ache in her stomach, a feeling of emptiness, loss and despondency. She barely acknowledged the meals offered on the aircraft as she had no appetite for food; nor for meeting her parents, who she knew would be waiting for her. She had run away from something that every instinct drew her back to, and her denials were no match for her convictions. She had lost her security, her rock, and the best friend she had ever known.

Descending the steps from the Boeing 737 on her arrival, Jenny felt displaced, missing the reassurance that she had always had with Peter. Nothing seemed to make sense. Approaching the terminal, she entered the long, sweeping building, with its impersonal columns and circular framework, with disinterest, and a foreboding about her future. She had been driven all her life by a fierce independence, yet despite this, she felt that she could only be herself when with Peter. Even when they had disagreed, their debate united them, each seeking to understand the other.

She marched beyond Immigration towards the doors to a new life that she neither wanted nor welcomed. For the first time, she felt directionless and without motivation, such that, when she finally saw her parents, she ran into her mother's arms and sobbed into her shoulder, unable to contain her feelings. "Mama, I met someone so incredible and now he is gone"

"*La mia bellissima figlia, non essere triste. Una ciliegia tira l'altra.*" ('My beautiful daughter, do not be sad. One cherry throws up another.') On the way home, she told her Mother about her Summer and how she felt meeting Peter had changed her life. Gina felt for her, recalling her own hopes for love that she had once cherished.

Giuseppe was less understanding. "You need family; you need to be here, not wasting your time with English hippies. *Sei stato uccel di bosco.*" ('You have been a bird in the woods.')

In the days that followed, Jenny was a recluse in her room, before deciding to seek help from the only man in her former life she felt any real connection with: Father Michael O'Leary from the church she had hated in years past. He had been so kind to her when her parents had despaired of her in her teenage years. He had visited her school and taken time to talk to her, discussing her views and principles. She had found in him someone whom she could genuinely trust, despite her refusal to embrace the Roman Catholic Church as her parents demanded. She wandered the fifteen minutes from her parents' home on Winchester Avenue up to St James Church on Atlantic Avenue, a block away from the Boardwalk she had come to hate because of her father's business.

The one element of the church she liked was the historic look of the building, and, as she approached, her mind wandered back to the day she and Peter had entered the Chapelle Saint-François-de-Paule – so long ago, it seemed – in Bormes-les-Mimosas. That had been a time without end, just endless beginnings and the urge to seek. Once she entered through the unimposing wooden doors, her memory was jogged as she stared around at the stained-glass windows and the Norman style arches surrounding the nave with its vaulted ceiling. A place she had endured as a child now seemed to hold a calmer atmosphere, the quiet contrasting with the bedlam of the developing Atlantic City beyond. Here there was an air of tranquillity, and she sank onto a pew, surrendering to her reflections, yet holding back the urge to cry.

"Jenny, isn't it?" The warmth of his Irish burr was unmistakable. "Forgive me, but I have a good memory, which is needed in case I see someone who has not visited here for some time." His gentle chiding was delivered with a smile, which she attempted to return with as much sincerity as she could. "What ails you, Jenny? Your sorrow is written on your face. You look lost, child. Would you like to join me in my room for a wee chat?"

She acquiesced with a nod, and welcomed his outstretched hand helping her up with reassurance.

Father Michael was from Letterkenny, Donegal, Ireland, and had been a priest at the church for fifteen years. He was well respected as an active and enthusiastic man who reached out to his local community with evangelical zeal. In his mid forties, he considered himself an ambassador of Christ with a duty to bring the Gospel to the people. He possessed a quick wit, and a lively, sociable demeanour that made him a welcome dinner guest in the area. He was tall, played tennis with enthusiasm and some skill, and was not averse to a few tots of Jameson's, his favourite whisky. His hair was unruly and, unusually, he wore it in a bit of a quiff, which had not gone unnoticed in his early days in Atlantic City when, despite protestations, he was compared with Elvis.

He welcomed Jenny into his office behind the nave and bid her sit in an armchair beside his own, separated by a table on which sat a pile of books. She looked around uneasily, having never entered this part of the church before. The theme for the room was endless books, with shelves surrounding the walls, then a break for an arch in which hung a framed picture of the Madonna. On one side was a pedestal desk covered with faded green leather, in front of which was a padded captain's chair. A picture of Pope Paul VI looked benignly upon them, his right hand extended as he sat upon a grand chair or throne. The long window looked out over a grassy area fringed with trees. She found she was shaking as she sat wondering how to speak to him, or even what she should say. She had no plan, just a need to share with someone who might listen and understand.

"Father, I have no idea why I should come here," she almost blurted out.

"Then, my child, you are in very good company, as many have no idea either, despite attending Mass regularly. Perhaps we should start at the beginning?" His tone was disarming and comforting.

Jenny then told him of her Summer of Love, respectfully not referring to the fact that she had slept in the same tent as Peter, but unburdening herself of the torment she felt at leaving him. "I am not here because I am weak, Father, but because I need to find my strength. I have always had purpose in my life, but I lost it when I left Peter. I know I must face my future, but without him it seems impossible."

Cups of tea were brought in by an elderly lady who quizzed Father Michael on how long he would be, reminding him of a later appointment.

"She tries to bully me, so she does, but she'll never win because the good Lord made me very obstinate."

Jenny smiled, this time with ease as she felt relaxed with him. "Father, I need to reach out for a new way but I am finding it impossible to choose a direction in which to go. I think I am lost." Her emotions surfaced again, and she could not hold back her sobs.

"I think…" he said slowly. "I think your words have just given you the direction you need without any help from me. If you make a plan, Jenny, that is the place to start. You know what, you will never reach your destination without a plan or a route, so it is not whether you take the journey, but whether you have planned it. That plan will give you the direction you should take; create your map, and then you will arrive."

She turned to him, and before she could stop herself asked, "Father, do you believe in love?"

She had caught him off guard with her customary outspoken nature. A look of sadness came into his eyes for a moment, then he gave a sigh and a pause as he looked far into the distance.

"I was in love once with a lovely girl and it broke my heart to walk away. In many ways, I never recovered; like you, I turned from it to seek my direction. Do I look back? Of course I do, for that is the temptation that I had to resist. In my life, Jenny, I have had to make many sacrifices for my faith, but for me the greatest love lies in my vocation. I do believe in love, but I dare not dwell on the love from which you suffer at this time. If we had love for one another, then the world would be much better. So yes, I believe in love and I pray for peace, and, you know, that was the message Our Lord preached. The Lord Jesus promoted the Gospel of love despite the many ways it has been corrupted and twisted by mankind throughout history to justify inhumanity. You feel love for Peter; that too is sacred but only, at this point, to yourselves – unless, of course, one day you are fortunate enough to unite in marriage and have a family."

Marriage had not featured anywhere in Jenny's thoughts about her beautiful summer, but she recalled the Covenant she and Peter had made; a bond which was sacred to her.

"The truth is, Jenny, you have become blinded by your love and cannot see the life that awaits you, and, from your words, it appears you are aware of that. You do not need a priest's reassurance, but perhaps a little guidance to find your route map. My thoughts are that you should write to Peter, tell him it is right that you both find your paths, and put his mind to rest too, as the poor lad is probably feeling as bad as you, if not worse." Father O'Leary stood up, walked to the shelves and selected a hard-backed blue book, which he handed to her. "God bless you, my child; read this, it may help. You have the answers but just need the strength to start your journey. Now take your time, tread carefully, but be resolute and you will carry yourself to what awaits you. I can feel it; there is so much waiting. My final words of the day to you are: make that plan and be resolute in following it." He shook her hand and clasped both of his around it before guiding her to the door.

As she walked back down the aisle, she looked down at the book, *Little Women* by Louisa M. Alcott, which she determined to read with a new-found purpose. It was a very different Jenny who returned home that day; a transformation which she would remember for the rest of her life. Their journey was never-ending, and in her dreams, they returned to it.

17

Letters

It was on Sunday 14th December 1969 that Jenny took two steps forward on her journey. The first was agreeing with her father, for once, that she should reapply for entrance to Harvard, and pursue her interest in Law. In the weeks following her meeting with Father O'Leary, she had formulated a plan and committed herself to it. She had been inspired by Charles 'Chuck' Morgan Jr, a young lawyer who had won a landmark cases for the Civil Rights movement that had altered the course of history. She had watched in awe as the attorney from Birmingham, Alabama, had stood up to the blatantly abusive, corrupt and racist voting system in state legislature, taking his case to the Supreme Court and winning the right of 'one man, one vote'. That was one of a series of high-profile cases Morgan took, another was defending Muhammad Ali against draft evasion charges for his refusal to fight in Vietnam.

Jenny felt her destiny was to fight intolerance, abuse of power, and inequality; but she recognised that to be successful in her objectives, she needed the authority and influence to succeed. She called her father at his office and stated simply, "Papa, are you sitting down? I'm taking your advice and I'm going to re-apply to Harvard Law School."

There was a shocked exclamation from her father before he excitedly replied, "Harvard and *mia principessa* is *come il cacio sui maccheroni.*" ('Like cheese on macaroni' – a perfect combination.)

The second step she took the same day, after witnessing some particularly annoying music on *The Ed Sullivan Show*. *This is music with no meaning*, she thought as she watched a new group, The Jackson Five, being introduced for the first time. Jenny dismissed the repetitive rhythm as music driven by commercial interest without inspiration or ideals. Dwelling on her own idealism and how she had committed to move forwards, she decided to take the priest's advice and write to Peter.

My beautiful Peter,

I have thought about our time together so very often, and craved your arms around me daily since our parting. I seek you in the dawn of day and in the stillness of night. I yearn for your whispered words in my ear and the soft sound of your voice, the joy of waking to your touch and my boundless desire for you. I crashed from the heights of our heaven into a pit of despair when we parted. Even writing this I am trembling as I miss you, my hippy love, and part of me has been left for all time in the places we visited and the dreams we shared. I never wanted to wake from those dreams, nor ever see or feel the inevitable, relentless curse of reality ending what had been an endless beginning.

Peter, you were my beginning, and when I left, I felt you were my end too, but I know I have to seek life, not succumb to it. You were right and I suppose we met at the wrong time for both of us, but inside I knew it was the right time too. In the weeks since we left France I have weighed up these contradictions, and now I recognise that I must map out my future; one inspired by our time together, our shared thoughts and our experiences.

Each day we were together, there was no other world but ours. How could I imagine anything other than a life with you in which there was just the joy of sharing? Isn't it so sad that the sacred dreams of two young people untarnished by life are the most unrealistic when we compare the ideal with the real? I recoil from the real, yet know I must face it, and I admire your strength in guiding us to the conclusion we had to reach; though every part of me wanted to cry out for freedom. Was it so wrong to dream? We are young, embarking on life, and I wonder at how lucky we were to find each other and experience our joys together.

Yet, my Prince of Dreams, I now know your strength of purpose was what we both needed to give impetus and context to our lives. Yours was the wisdom and mine was the fairy tale, but sometimes, just sometimes, isn't it wonderful to believe in a myth? Many would call that delusion, but I know it to be true because I have the strength to imagine, and in imagination, we can escape. Our sin was to live the dream and never want to wake up.

So where do we go now? What is in your head? Are we prepared to break the bonds, and do we have the right to do that to ourselves or each other? I don't know the answers, and have so many questions to which there can be no answers. The cruelty of life has overridden my fantasy, but I shall never deny my Covenant; that remains as true today as the day I watched you walk across the sand towards me. You were, remain, and always will be a joy that I hold within me, never to let go but never to hold back, and it is in that impossible contradiction that our dream rests. My secret hope is that, as in the fairy tale, one day my Prince of Dreams will rescue his waiting princess, who may have slept for a hundred years before being awoken again.

My joy, my life, my hope, my dream, I will always hold you within my deepest places and treasure you for as long as I live and beyond. You are my calm sea; you are the sky that I reach beyond; you are the wind in my hair, the soft breeze that breathes upon me; you are the heaven we reach.

Thank you for being my dream.

Always yours,
Jenny xx

Monday 22nd December 1969

Rose Chainey picked up the striped airmail envelope and examined it suspiciously. On seeing the United States postmark she was tempted to tear it up, thinking of how her son had been led astray by an American siren that summer. *She's like that Wallis Simpson, leading our Peter on like that woman did with the King. That's what they're like, these Americans, just like me dad said. It was the same in the war, he told me; they had a saying then: 'Only three problems with the Yanks: they're overpaid, oversexed and over here!' Well, Mrs bloody Simpson isn't having my son.*

Despite her views, she took the envelope to Peter's room. "A letter from Wallis," she shouted, and threw it round the door before returning to the kitchen to blame an unsuspecting Jim for everything before he left for work.

Peter had found solace in talking to his tutor with his reassuring words and experience. The advice to send a letter to Jenny he had been a little more reluctant to heed. Peter knew life dictated that they could not be bound by an idealistic union that had no direction. But he wrestled with his thoughts, knowing the truth that screamed at him to turn back from his chosen path.

He had intuitively known during that summer that he had to escape his past yet sacrifice his present in order to find a way forwards. He did not want to live on the streets by the docks, but needed to expand his horizons as he could see other young people around him doing.

Despite his resolve, he was shaken when he looked at the envelope, instantly recognising Jenny's writing, and ran his fingers over the paper, caressing where hers had been only days before. He could sense her. His heartbeat quickened as he kissed the handwriting, then slowly prised apart the tissue-thin envelope and unfolded the contents. He read, then read again, trying to restrain his tears. A deep sigh announced the realisation that he could not turn away and fail to reply. He rose and approached his homework table, set up for him years before by his parents, and began to write.

Hey, my unforgettable hippy chick,

It's yer beach-bummin' ice-cream man here, kind of trying to be cool, but after reading your words, that just isn't easy. Remember that first day we met and you couldn't tear your eyes off me, bowled over by me Merseyside accent and irresistible charm? I look back with disbelief at our amazing experience and, my God, we were close to dropping out, and I blame myself for not doing that. I will probably spend my life regretting the decision to return, but despite the joy of us, I sort of knew we had to.

I think about what kind of life we would have given one another, and what we would have denied each other. I could have turned back to you as I walked away at the airport, and, as I sat there, parked up close by, every part of me wanted to. The truth is, you are the most beautiful person I ever met, and I not only loved you, but admired you. Your wonderful ideals and principles and your hopes for the future were expressed not in terms of yourself, but for mankind. I think that is so amazing. If we had dropped out, so much of you would have been wasted, because I sense such a future for you.

Am I making excuses? Probably – every day I question myself – but I have a drive to escape to a better place. Everywhere there is opportunity as so much is changing, much of it driven by us young people. This, I feel, is our time, Jenny, to seize life and all it has to offer us. I sense I'm at the start of a long road, and a destiny awaits if I reach for it. I curse myself for these thoughts when our Summer of Love had everything I – we – needed. I was lost in that. I was tripping on love and I still feel it, you and us every day. But I had to come down from that trip, even though it was so far out. I feel like stark reality is all I have ever faced, and even as a child, I knew I had to get away. I hid in my books and escaped to magical places far away from where I lived.

What a bummer, eh? We meet, fall in love, and then realise that our paths have to split; but maybe one day we will thank each other for allowing ourselves that freedom. Many love stories are built upon impossible foundations; books, plays and poetry are testament to that. Love needs truth too, and if I had given up my life for us I would have betrayed myself, and I suppose that is the greatest betrayal of all. I need to make a life, to seek a life, to build a life, and you do too. We are at the start of an amazing journey with an ending we can create. I think that's just – wow – incredible to think about.

So where did we go wrong? We met too early and loved too deeply, too quickly, but so beautifully. I think of you on those beaches. God, you were so foxy, baby, and we were so heavy. Some days I think I am running away from the light and into darkness. I cannot imagine ever finding anybody else like you, and the truth is, I don't want to because I want to hold the vision of you, who filled my life and opened my eyes to a world I never imagined.

Jenny, our lives demand that we turn away and embrace what awaits us. I hate this, hate myself, but do not hate the joy that was us and remains with us, tempting us back. I know I have to resist the love which still holds us. I made you a Covenant and meant it, and that will bind our memories and nurture us in our futures.

How crazy is this? I feel my heart is broken, a phrase I never understood but the tears in my eyes now witness my sadness and the devastating fact that I may never see you again, hear your voice, breathe your scent or hold you close. Bless you, my gorgeous love, for that is what you are, and what you will always be. In my deepest places I shall seek you, and in my dreams I shall find you. Forgive me and find the life path you deserve; at a different time, we would have walked it together, hand in hand to our forever.

My love, I yearn to hold you not just for this moment, but for all time; not for any one reason, but for all reasons; not for myself, but for ourselves; not just for this life, but for our forever; not to seek you, but to find you; not to understand, but to wonder.

Forever in my thoughts,
Peter xx

The distance between them now grew, despite the need they felt to turn back. Although each of them, in their separate lives, occasionally and secretly reminisced about their time together, they seldom revisited the Covenants made in that summer of 1969. It was as though they sensed that reaching into that time might open up a part of themselves they were hiding from. Perhaps they were avoiding acceptance of the ending before they had found or understood their beginning. The truth that they had to face was to carry them, as Jonas had sardonically put it, "back to reality".

18

Jenny

Jenny was now resolute in her commitment to contributing to change. However, instead of freeing herself of all the material elements of her life, which had once been her goal, she had accepted that she would accomplish more by being part of the mainstream. She was accepted into Harvard Law School with the blessing of her delighted father, who could see his gifted daughter achieving success that would only reflect well on his growing status. By now he had expanded his Boardwalk empire and taken on new ventures including an ice-cream parlour, a bar, an arcade and a restaurant.

Jenny took to life at Harvard, burying her head into her studies with a determination that she would emerge to make a difference. She looked back at her time with Peter as a wonderful memory, but had grown to accept that a pragmatic approach was needed to succeed in her strategy. Learning about law and the priciples that had driven the legislation and the democratic structures of the United States made her more focused than ever on securing a role in which she could help achieve or promote justice. There was no more contact with Peter, but she never lost a secret desire to invoke their Covenant to reunite upon a call.

Jenny met Braden Trelawney at a Harvard summer ball in August 1973. She had not even wanted to go, but her law professor had invited her to join his table, where he wanted to show her off as his prize student. She had been a star all her third year, excelling at every stage; her grades were way above what had been expected when he had taken her under his wing as a protégée. She had a rebellious side then, yet he recognised that that was what led to her forthright style and her unwillingness to accept any statement, evidence or thesis until she had dissected the arguments.

It was during her first-year dissertation in mid 1971 that she first saw Professor Wostenholme, who appeared just to the right of the stage upon which she was speaking. Her speech was on civil rights, with the title, *The Power of Peaceful Protest in Achieving Change*. She was passionate in her delivery, drawing much applause at the end, when she noticed the dark-haired, slightly dishevelled yet smartly dressed bespectacled man nodding enthusiastically, gesturing approval with his fists in the air. He wore a pinstriped suit which contrasted greatly with the more flamboyant attire of the other academics, who sported cravats, roll-necked sweaters or open shirts. Removing his glasses, he walked over with a broad smile and she immediately sensed the bearing of a powerful person. Introducing himself, he indicated that his role was to assist students who showed great promise and help them secure successful careers.

Professor Leopold Wostenholme had a keen mind, and held a highly respected position as a consultant and adviser to many leading organisations including the US government. As a young lawyer, he had served at the Nuremberg war-crime trials in 1946, during which he had made a name for himself cross-examining Nazis on camera in what even he recognised were show trials, although important for global humanity. This was an opportunity for him to represent the United States on the world stage and, in turn, show off his skilful advocacy in contrast to the crude and rather lacklustre performance from Soviet lawyers.

He had met the former Deputy Chancellor of Nazi Germany, Reichsmarschall Hermann Göring, in his prison cell, with whom he held a number of eloquent exchanges on the politics of post-war Europe. It was terrifying, he reflected, that such an engaging, genial, keenly intelligent man could have aligned himself with such an evil mindset and been complicit in the persecution of Jews and others. He recalled Göring's words, which he had often repeated: "Never trust a leadership that seeks to hide its authority or its actions behind institutions. Power should be entrusted to those who have the courage to be honest." However, Göring had also been chillingly cynical, claiming, "Democracy can only have a future if those with power can take decisions without concerning themselves about the opinions of the people who placed them there." Wostenholme knew about power, because he helped maintain it.

He had been selected by his mentor, Lawrence R. Houston, who worked directly for the Attorney General's office, with links to the CIA, which he helped create in 1947 and for which he acted as legal counsel. His job was to tell the agency what it could do under American law and, more covertly, to give guidance when laws had been transgressed. Wostenholme had learned much in the very short time he worked for Houston of the somewhat Machiavellian skills required in interpreting law in the exercise of power. His rise had been nothing short of meteoric, working for various government agencies and with initial involvement in the defence of President Richard Nixon during the Watergate scandal. However, he had been removed by Houston from the presidential team because his mentor knew Nixon would not prevail. He was given a position at Harvard Law School, but with special responsibility to the CIA. In this role, he retained links with the White House elite, with whom he frequently consulted and for whom he acted, under the direction of Houston.

At Harvard, he performed a critical role in assessing those who might warrant special attention, and who might be groomed to be of use to the government and intelligence services. Jenny had excelled in her studies, with alacrity of thought combining with imagination and foresight. After taking an initial interest, Wostenholme had followed her progress, holding regular reviews with both Jenny and her tutors. He soon recognised she was destined for greater things, and, having waited for years to nurture a student of such ability, he was going to ensure that she reached a position worthy of her.

As Jenny stood by the dance floor at the summer ball, Braden approached her, asking if she was a student, then inviting her to join him for a dance. She accepted his approach as a distraction rather than out of any particular interest, but he was sort of nice in a goofy sort of way. They danced together, and at least, she admitted to herself, she liked his smart dress. He looked a little like her father, she thought, although much slimmer, with a crop of dark hair that refused to lie down. He had a neat parting with an Elvis-style quiff more akin to the 1950s than to current trends. He wore a suit with a velvet collar and a thin tie which might have been fashionable a few years before. His hair was shortish and he wore round glasses that reminded her of the new British rock sensation Elton John, which maybe did interested her.

The music was loud, and as they could hardly be heard, she allowed him to accompany her back to her table, where an affable Professor Wostenholme invited him to join them. "You are welcome for just one more aperitif; then this gifted lawyer must return home, like Cinderella, before she loses her glass slipper."

"Oh, Leo, you are so square," she laughed, but accepted the situation, in reality quite glad of his presence as her chaperone. She was in the middle of a treatise on legal rights in relation to state property and land ownership. Her studies tied neatly in with research into Native American Indian land rights and the legal injustices that had followed the so-called 'settlement' policy a century earlier.

Professor Wostenholme asked Braden about his background.

"Oh, I'm from Wisconsin, sir, and I work for Western Union Insurance. I moved to Boston when I gained a role in our regional office to head up the new Life Division."

Leopold explored further. "OK, young man, you are embarked on a career and therefore your future is tied up with our country's stability. So how do you feel about the whole Watergate thing and the effect it has had on the authority of the presidency?"

Braden replied that he felt that the issue had probably been exaggerated by the press, and that this was not a matter that should threaten the integrity of the President of the United States. He said he believed in the nation's system of government, which he felt was being undermined by those who wanted to cause instability.

Jenny felt uncomfortable with Braden's words but decided this was not the time for debate. She did accept his request that they swap phone numbers, more as a gesture than out of a desire to meet again.

The evening ended on a pleasant note after Professor Wostenholme asked Jenny to walk him back to his carriage. In the ensuing days, she was surprised that he took almost a paternal interest in her meeting with Braden. He spoke of him in glowing terms, saying that he possessed a refreshing presence, and urged her to "Give this young man a chance."

Two days later, Braden called and invited her to dinner, which she found rather cute. Her parents and their friends did that kind of thing, but she was more used to being invited to gigs, or for a drink either on campus or in downtown Boston. She asked him directly over the phone, as it had been bothering her, "Do you really believe that scumball Nixon is innocent, because hey, man, that is crazy?"

Braden replied that he never liked to get too deep into stuff he did not fully understand, and that he was prepared to listen to any argument. So they agreed to meet at Jack & Marion's on Harvard

Street, Brookline, which served as the local standard-bearer of a quality New York-style delicatessen.

Jenny had not dated seriously since returning to the US in 1969, but had endured a series of suitors whom she had seen as a diversion from her studies and her ambitions. Whilst she enjoyed mixing with friends from Harvard, she had no time for the introductions made by her hopeful parents to one "great guy" after another in Atlantic City during her vacations. They wanted her to join the developing business, but as Giuseppe purchased more property, installing a long line of so-called 'amusement machines', she became further disillusioned with all he represented. He would return home, often late at night, with groups of Italian men, and their laughter and raucous ways haunted her. Giuseppe would often call her and parade her in front of his acquaintances as his "beautiful *principessa*", which she despised. Her mother would serve beers and Jenny would hear the careless chatter about making "*molto scharole*" (much money), and feeding the "*spaccone* scum", as they described the officials enjoying their financial gifts. They spoke openly of their 'persuasion' of those in office to ease restrictions on the legal casinos gradually being permitted, and to ignore the many illegal establishments they operated. She never knew whether her father was involved with the Mafia, but knew that his business associates were dubious.

Sometimes, Giuseppe would stagger upstairs to the bedroom her parents shared and she would hear his slurred voice becoming excited and breaking into loud Italian as he berated her mother, calling her "*stupida*" and "*pazza*", or crazy. Then came the retaliation, usually starting with a string of expletives about how useless he was. It was as if he sought out the worst things he could say to hurt Gina and then decry her responses as hysterical. Their arguments were commonplace, but Jenny knew they took a toll on her mother.

One night, when she was just fourteen, she had heard her father shouting that he could find better whores walking the streets than the one in his bedroom, and prettier ones too. Jenny had run to their bedroom, screaming that she was ashamed of him and that he was not worthy of being her father. He threw open the door and her anger became more intense, passion driving her words. "You are nothing but a low life, Papa, because you don't know respect, and if I walked the streets, I would find a better father than you." He slammed the door in her face, but she knew she had hurt him. She remembered him shouting to Gina that her daughter was out of control, and that it was her fault.

Later that night, her mother crept up to Jenny and put her arms around her. "*Grazie*, my daughter; he does not deserve you, but I am proud of you. You have strength and you will go far. Never allow a man to be this way with you."

Her father apologised to her the following day, begging her forgiveness, but she never gave it. Instead, his ways instilled in her a fierce self-preservation.

Jenny tried to build bridges with her mother, offering support as Giuseppe became increasingly drawn into his business, with less time for his family. Gina had long despaired of her husband's ways, but defended their marriage, telling Jenny, "He is my husband and he protects me – I must be here for him." Whilst Gina would berate Giuseppe loudly for his misdemeanours, it was done as was often customary in Italian families *di Milano* (like normal), and almost a source of pride for him. One night, Jenny's mother said to her, in between sobs after suffering another attack from Giuseppe, "My wonderful girl, no man must ever treat you like this because we are worth better, and you, *mio bambino*, are going to *be* better because of your studies, which he denied me. Your father is sometimes a lost soul but I will love him and support him. Promise me you will find a proper man, eh?" She hugged her daughter, and from that point, Jenny knew that no man would ever dominate her.

For a while, she had hated men, until her joyful summer of 1969. No man had touched her since Peter; nor had she ever wished for such intimacy, as it was sacred to their time, their place, and their union to which she knew, despite the passing of time, that nothing else would ever compare. Other hopeful suitors she laughed off, although she revelled in the fun times she enjoyed with friends at Harvard.

The night approached for her dinner date with Braden, presenting the challenge of what to wear. She chose a long aquamarine-coloured skirt, a headscarf over her long dark hair, and a white blouse with a neck ruffle and puffed sleeves. She completed her outfit with a tan suede full-length jacket and boots. She wanted to lift her image from that of a student, but not to dress in the formal style she had been taught for court appearances.

She caught a bus from her apartment just off campus for the ten-minute ride to Brookline. She had never eaten at Jack & Marion's, although she had passed it many a time, her attention drawn by the slightly psychedelic sign. As she waited outside, the brief sound of a car horn caught her attention and Braden drove past, waving from a red Ford Pinto. He parked across the street and strolled towards her in a fawn corduroy suit, a long-collared, patterned white shirt, and a floral tie smartly worn with a large knot; a striking look finished with tan ankle boots. He was certainly different to the guys she mixed with at law school, who, in the main, wore jeans, T-shirts and waist jackets in various colours and styles, creating the student 'look'. *Wow – a far cry from my hippy roots*, she thought, but quite enjoyed her arm being confidently linked as they approached the entrance.

After discussing the evening of their meeting, they relaxed as their conversation drifted to their different upbringings. At her request, he related to her his life growing up in Wisconsin; the adventurous days spent exploring the vast tracts of countryside, lakes and mountains. He told of his time in Green Bay on the banks of Lake Michigan, and how he had developed in the quite inward-looking community. His educational achievements at the local high school had been low- to middle-grade, and university was not an option. He had started his career working in a meat-packing factory, but was eager to escape the area, jumping at the opportunity advertised in the Green Bay News Chronicle to become a life insurance sales executive in 1971 at the age of 21.

She, in turn, spoke to him of her life in Atlantic City, her restrictive upbringing and how she had longed to escape. She sensed his disapproval of anything anti-establishment, and so skirted around her time joining protests and her sympathy with the Civil Rights movement in the mid 1960s. Her sabbatical in France in 1969 she described with no reference to Peter, Jonas, or the life she still cherished within. However, she quizzed Braden on his views of Martin Luther King. "Man, wasn't he cool back in 1963 when he just captured the spirit of the age with that speech, 'I have a dream'? The words really spellbound me; held me, you know, like a realisation of the truth of it all."

Braden's disappointing response was that he had found King's speech just "OK, but change was pretty inevitable, and I worry about civil disruption." The reply contained nothing to share or warm to, but it was, she supposed, kind of safe. Maybe it was time that she pursued a safer path. Braden stated that there were changes in society that they all had to adjust to, but that it was important that there was respect for the American way. He added that he was not convinced that civil rights were being pursued in the peaceful manner their advocates claimed, and that there were times when federal authority had to be respected.

Jenny asked him whether he had been enlightened or inspired by President Kennedy, but gained little from him other than that he had been too young to appreciate the man. As for the much-discredited Warren Report into his assassination, Braden said that they had arrested the culprit and, as there was no evidence of a cover-up, it was time to move on and cease asking questions.

The disappointment she felt that evening was to re-emerge time and again, but Jenny did feel reassured by Braden's conventional ways. They contrasted with the constant turmoil of revolution in which she had felt embroiled for so long. Braden was grounded, treating her as more than a student. He seemed to represent a security and an order that had been lacking in her life. Strangely, she felt drawn to him, despite him not being her type.

19

Peter

Peter had returned home in October 1969 with a heavy heart, convinced that his life would never again embrace the freedom he had experienced that summer. He and Jenny had agreed not to contact each other for at least a year, and that hung over him like a shadow, as if he was living in a vacuum without meaning or direction. He felt lost – having found a reason for everything, he now had none, but in a way that drove a new resolve to seize every opportunity he could find. By late 1969, he had been accepted back at Sheffield University. The desire to progress through study drew him back with a yearning he had not known since his inspirational education at the Inny.

Reaching for a career was his motivation as he rejoined his course in Economics and Business Studies. His parents never understood him, but proudly boasted to their neighbours of their son's achievement. "Our Peter's a student," Rose would announce over the fence as she shared the daily ritual of pegging out clothes to dry on the line. Housewives would chatter from the strips of garden that those in the growing estates of semi-detached properties were lucky enough to possess; a lifetime away from the terraced houses most of them had grown up in. Rose had never understood Peter's needs, having been brought up in a family in which men acted like men even when they were boys. To her, bringing up her son was part of her duty, making sure he learned to do what was right rather than all this hugging and kissing she had seen some mothers do.

There had been little time for feelings or sentiment during the war when she was growing up. You just had to get on with it, or 'Keep Calm and Carry On', as the government slogan urged people. Her teen years were spent praying that the German bombs would miss them as she crouched, trembling in fear, with her family in an Anderson shelter, which felt and looked so inadequate. The sound of deafening explosions shaking the ground would cause many to cry out in sheer terror; terror that would never leave her. The war seemed to engender a toughness in spirit in those around her, in which sentiment played no part. She locked herself away in a secret life, finding some escape in books; a trait Peter inherited. She did away with emotion altogether shortly after being told, at the age of fifteen in July 1944, that her father had lost his life in Normandy after D-Day. Only six weeks before, he had given her a smiling hug at Liverpool's Lime Street Station, saying that she should be strong whilst he was gone. When Peter was born, she had a fiercely protective instinct for him that was devoid of softness, because that was the only way of showing love that she felt was safe.

Peter's father hoped he would become more aware of his working-class roots and use his university education to develop a career that would help the workers and stand up to capitalism. He reminded Peter that trade unions were the new place to be, citing the fact that the Labour Party and related organisations were attracting and needing those who were more educated. He was proud to be a registered dock worker in Liverpool, and fiercely defended his hard-earned right to pass on his job, with all its enhanced privileges, to his son. From his perspective, if the upper classes could pass on their privileges then so could he; his enhanced pay had been fought for through industrial action, and that was modern Britain.

Despite these views, by 1970 he confided in his son, after the Conservatives won the election, that there was a betrayal within the working class by those who 'factionalised' their claims over their 'brothers'. Trade unions were competing for power by flexing their muscles, challenging authority without consideration of consequences. The Labour Party under Harold Wilson was increasingly pursuing policies which no longer seemed to have anything to do with protecting the working man. Peter and his father became increasingly concerned when the unions contributed to the fall of the government in 1974 after a miners' strike. As Jim ruefully surmised, "this was no victory, but a surrender."

He conceded to his son, "We have become like those we were fighting against; a new generation of union leaders has emerged, motivated by greed and power." By 1972, he began to encourage his son to seek a better life; a life he had never known, nor aspired to. As the country was held to ransom once again by industrial action in the late 1970s, he conceded that democracy was being sacrificed to civil unrest and anarchy. As a lifelong believer in socialism, he felt betrayed and, a few years later in 1979, he joined with many from the working class in seeking a new way by voting Conservative, under the banner of unified opportunity being offered by Margaret Thatcher.

Peter formed the closest relationship he had ever had with his father during his time at university. They often visited The Frayne (an Old English term meaning 'The Stranger'); an evocative pub, formerly known as The Trawler, on The Strand, where socialising commonly coincided with the dockers' shift changes. Here they joined others in debating issues of the day, enjoying the community spirit. Many of the locals knew Peter, and often spoke to him about seeking a better life. "Get out of this shite, lad, and seek somethin' berrer – and good luck to you."

His father felt proud of what his son was seeking, and began to speak openly to others about his achievement in gaining a place at university. "Just as long as you don't take any notice of them Yorkshire gobshites," his compatriots would warn, before Peter travelled back to Sheffield after a break staying with his parents.

One day in September 1970, after being driven to Lime Street Station, he was completely taken by surprise when his dad walked around the car and uncharacteristically threw his arms around him. "Peter, your mam and I are not only proud of you, son, but we admire you; you are very special to us. Now bugger off and learn to earn enough money to keep us in our old age." Peter would always remember that moment, treasuring the warmth between them that he had rarely felt before.

From his earliest days he had had questions about emotion and love, and now, he wondered over the his feelings for Jenny. They called to him, reached out to him, refusing to be forgotten. He had learned to shelve such thoughts like files that could be neatly stacked for some time in the future but they remained within his consciousness.

Peter excelled in his studies and, on receiving his degree, recognised that at last he could realise his aspirations to lift himself beyond the dismal, claustrophobic life he had been expected to follow on the docks. As a graduate in October 1971 he was snapped up by the Merseyside property business, Granvilles. They specialised in developing plots on the old bomb sites and where slums were being cleared. Here he met Rubin Granville, the founder and inspiration behind the business. Peter could not help but be impressed by the single-minded determination of this refugee from Germany who had fled persecution by the Nazis arriving with nothing in 1938, yet had striven to create a thriving business. His success had been earned as a result of incredible sacrifices in the early days in terms of income and living accommodation.

Before joining the company, Peter had undergone an interview with Mr Rubin Granville which had been singularly unconventional. The offices were situated in a three-storey Georgian building just outside Liverpool city centre, on Rodney Street near the Anglican cathedral. There were no big signs, but on the double varnished doors a polished brass plaque announced, simply, 'Granvilles' in black lettering. Once inside, Peter approached a smoked-glass window, and pressed a bell for attention. As he waited, he looked around the mahogany-panelled walls, on which hung framed black-and-white pictures of various buildings, each with a label underneath detailing the area and the type of property. He was shown to an office on the second floor with a varnished oak-framed door by a smartly but severely dressed bespectacled lady with swept-back grey hair who, he later learned, was Rubin's cousin. She knocked, and dutifully awaited the unexpectedly loud but soon-to-become accustomed "Come" in a German accent which made the invitation more of a command.

Peter was met by a smart silver-haired man in a dark suit and grey waistcoat, from which a watch chain hung. He wore a bow tie, pince-nez glasses and, very unusually, a monocle hanging down his chest. He was short of build and yet, as Peter often thought later, he assumed the stature of a much taller man.

"Come, come, young man; I am Rubin Granville, but I want to hear all about you." His voice was genial, yet commanding. His smiling face was quizzical, and he had sharp, piercing blue eyes.

Peter had forwarded a CV which he had rather clumsily put together in line with Sheffield University guidelines, and which, he felt, totally failed to project who he was as a person.

"So, your résumé is convincing, your education is good, your degree impeccable; but your achievements are yet to be proven, so we have to find out who you are. Please tell me who you are and how you came to be in my office today?"

This was Peter's first interview and he was very nervous, yet he felt an immediate affinity with the man sat in front of him behind a large, imposing leather-topped cherrywood desk. His captain-style chair wrapped around him like a wooden palisade, protecting him with worn leather-topped arms. The room had photographs of old Liverpool, black-and-white or sepia, placed evenly around the walls, which were covered in striped paper. The carpet was thick, yet worn, suggesting busy success. There was a slight odour of pipe tobacco, further emphasised by a rack of pipes to one side of Granville's desktop.

"Sir, I'm really not sure what you wish me to tell you; are you seeking to know more about my course at Sheffield, or my potential skills?"

"No, Peter," the older man responded; "I want to know all about you, your life, and how you came to be here – take as long as you want."

Peter hesitated before asking what period he should cover, and was told to start from the beginning. As Rubin Granville explained, he wanted to hear about his life – and, he said, "In return, I may one day tell you a little of mine."

Peter recounted his life, starting with his earliest memories in the street-fronted terraced house they had occupied, his escape into books, the determination that had driven him in school, and then, hesitantly, he recounted his desire to seek adventure in the summer of '69. Before he could stop himself, mention was made of his connection with a beautiful person who he said had given him inspiration for life. Rubin took an interest, questioning him on his motives and how he could let such a bond pass and walk away. In truth, Peter found that an impossible question to answer as he had never quite understood what he was reaching for – he'd given up the most meaningful period of his life, and for what? He had not worked out convincing answers, and explained to Rubin that he had pursued his ambitions. The older man took an interest in his life, recognising his honesty, combined with spirit and determination. He had made up his mind in the first hour that he would invite Peter to join his business, yet they spoke for considerably longer, both feeling a relaxed warmth between them.

On his first day at Granvilles, Rubin escorted Peter to his office, where he explained his philosophy. This was to strive for the best deal for his clients, maximising a return on their investment which would, in turn, more than justify the commission he charged or the fee he negotiated. "I want my faith in you to reflect the ethos I have created here, but equally I want you to exercise your own judgement, provided the final decisions are always agreed with me."

Peter's role was that of a scout; to seek out derelict or run-down property and decide whether it was suited for demolition and redevelopment, or repair and renovation. He was proud of his new job and determined to develop his career, fuelled by an ambition shared with so many of his generation to 'better' himself. He smartened up, exchanging his dishevelled Afghan coat for a suit and thin tie, although cut slim in the modern style and worn, as per the fashion, with slip-on ankle boots.

After only eighteen months, he had cut something of a reputation for a sharp mind and a natural affinity for a good deal. Rubin, nearing retirement and recognising Peter's quick yet steady mind, promoted him, and Peter became a property development manager. This gave him more responsibility to find, place offers and secure purchases on building plots and properties throughout Merseyside. He applied himself enthusiastically with a passion born of a desire to succeed and a wish to contribute to his city. Despite not following the Liverpool family tradition, he, like so many Merseysiders, had a strong loyalty to the city and the community he belonged to. He had a keen eye, spotting sites that had potential to develop into more desirable neighbourhoods, or those streets that could be resurrected and reformed, yet retain their character. He eschewed the tall, faceless, impersonal blocks of flats others had built in the '60s, and some were still racing to build, destroying neighbourhoods in the process. He soon gained a reputation for his ability to develop with taste and generate a generous return on investment.

Rubin saw in Peter so much of the energy he had possessed when he was young, and wanted to reward him with a financial incentive for his achievement. He gave him a cut of the return they received on each development, which soon became a lucrative income. "It is an ill wind, Peter, but we must always take advantage of the circumstances we find ourselves in, and create better from a business that cares, eh?" he said in his sage, faintly Germanic Western European accent. This was a time for learning and teaching, the growing relationship between them fuelling their mutual success.

Rubin was giving but exacting, telling his protégé that he would only succeed if he trusted no one but his family, and even then, never to trust completely. His principle was to offer the lowest cost as if it was the highest he could possibly afford, and equally if he was made an offer at no matter what level, he must then convince, with utter sincerity, others of the sacrifice it would cost him to accept that offer. If he was making a final offer, then others must believe it was thus, and the lowest cost, Rubin stressed, must never, ever be the lowest he would consider paying or receiving. It was a creed by which he lived, and one that his family had taken for their own since as far back as he could remember. "We are in a drama, and if we learn to play our part convincingly, then we live better, and from that, others will benefit from the wealth we create and the money we spend." It was a simple case of economics wherein the survival of the fittest benefited those less well off who gained through employment opportunity or support – Rubin cited his generous gifts to charity as an example.

Peter began to enthusiastically embrace Rubin's creed, thriving in creating and making property and land deals, his ready talents in negotiation resulting in very lucrative returns. Sometimes he was drawn to reflect, haunted by thoughts that he might be betraying the aspirations and beliefs he had once shared so meaningfully with Jenny. But heck, 'That was then, this is now'... wasn't it? Sometimes, this mantra he used to cover his feelings when he moved on in life was not always convincing.

20

Seeking Life

After their first tentative meetings, Jenny and Braden dated very conventionally, and she felt comfortable in a relationship that took her from her chaos of uncertainty into order. They met twice a week, usually once for a restaurant meal, and on other days for walks, drives, or exploring local attractions. They both had an interest in historic buildings, but shared little in the way of motives or beliefs that inspired them. She spoke with Braden about civil rights, Vietnam, Watergate, women's liberation, music, and the new age of enlightenment, trying to elicit common areas of belief between them. Frustratingly, he was very dismissive, saying that the future lay outside these issues, and beyond what they had the power to influence. His view was that this was their world now and they had their future careers to think of. "Jenny, those matters may have appeared important to you but they are student-days issues." The only words he uttered that she identified with were, "It is our world now", but she realised that for him they came from a very different viewpoint.

Jenny frequently returned to the summer of '69, despite all her efforts to ignore or run away from her previous life. In her sleep, she was aware of the crickets, the balmy scent of the lush French vegetation, the sound of waves upon the shore, and Peter's reassuring arms reaching for her. She knew she had not escaped, but she was drawn to opportunity and doors were opening to her, although not closing on her past. She could not reconcile the feelings she still held, deeply and secretly, for Peter with her admiration for Braden's solidity. She was experiencing a security she had not felt before, yet Peter remained so real and vibrant to her, like a chivalrous knight who in her dreams would ride off into the unknown with her in his arms. However, her daytime reality refused her a refuge in which to hide.

On the 14th September 1973, on the CBS evening news broadcast, the veteran anchorman, Walter Cronkite, announced that President Richard Nixon might face impeachment proceedings through demands being made by Congress over Watergate, and Braden kissed Jenny for the first time. They were walking near their favourite restaurant, Jack & Marion's in Brookline, where they had just eaten and heard the news. They were making their way down to Riverway to take in the remaining sun over the waterside walk. Jenny was excited by the dramatic events, which might herald the removal from office of a President for whom she had no time or respect. She talked animatedly about her hopes for change before Braden stopped her, drawing her head towards him. Their lips met tentatively, and then with a natural surrender. She felt a passion in him which, although she did not return, she enjoyed as a sign of his attraction to her. He held her to his shoulder for a moment, then, stepping back, said that change was less important than planning ahead. The government's difficulties would fade away, but their career challenges were their future, and that was real. Though his reply was disappointing, she was at least reassured by his interest in her, which felt, well, almost loving. After all, she told herself afterwards, she would learn to love him in time, despite her emotional detachment and his refusal to be drawn into debate on any issue that was important to her.

By the end of 1973, she was immersed in her studies, and Braden was a social attachment, although she convinced herself that there was more to their relationship. He was considerate and took her out regularly, joining in conversations although he never led them. Despite the fact that his dismissiveness of her values filled her with disquiet, she coveted a security wherein she could fulfil a meaningful role and develop a career. She was seduced by the opportunities that were opening up to her; not only via her success at Harvard, but through the security afforded by a stable partner. Braden was handsome in his own way, although a little dreary. He shared her interest in history, but from a very different perspective. She was motivated by the pursuit of justice, freedom, humanity and social development, whilst he was fascinated by architectural achievements and the growth of commerce. She persuaded herself that these differences were unimportant, surrendering to the desire to build a future, perhaps even one with children.

Two months after Jenny and Braden's first meeting at the ball, Professor Wostenholme summoned her to his study. "Well, as you have passed your exams with grades higher than I myself achieved, I shall start calling you 'Your Honour', because I have no doubt that you will rise to the top of your profession. Now, I hear you and your young man are cutting quite a dash in Boston. I would like to invite you both to the Law & Commerce Lunch I am holding with colleagues from Washington at the end of the month. I think, with your mind and his experience as a young business executive, you could both contribute and, I might add, perhaps oil the wheels of your career journey which, young lady, I think is unstoppable."

Three weeks later, Braden and Jenny boarded an Eastern Air Lines flight, travelling on a voucher curiously issued by the federal government via her professor. Jenny felt like they were pretty special, like they had real respectability and status. On landing in Washington, they were met by a driver who issued them with security passes before taking them to the Washington Hilton. There, they were asked to show their passes before being ushered to the Lincoln Room, where they were met by Professor Wostenholme, who greeted them with smiles, a brisk handshake for Braden, and a hug for Jenny. His thick, round glasses were hanging by a chain over a surprisingly smart black pinstriped suit. His hair was ruffled and he wore a spotted bow tie which was slightly askew as a result of which, despite his suit, he still presented a little untidily. Jenny had elected to wear a long skirt with a close-cut maroon jacket over a plain white blouse. Her hair was tied up, an affectation she felt gave her an air of authority and professionalism. Braden, as always, looked immaculate in a dark grey three-piece suit and a silk blue-and-red-striped tie.

"You may recognise some of my colleagues," Professor Wostenholme announced as he led them to a cocktail bar, next to which champagne glasses were being handed out by waitstaff. Within seconds, they had met Congressman Gerald Ford who, they were told, worked with the White House; he was most genial and polite in his greeting. He seemed genuinely interested not only in Jenny's progress at Harvard, but also in taking time to quiz Braden on his career. Then they shook hands with various dignitaries in dizzying succession, including the newly appointed Director of the FBI, Clarence M. Kelley; Vernon Walters, the Deputy Head of Central Intelligence; and James R. Schlesinger, the Secretary of Defense. They were toasted as a young couple and offered good wishes for their future, before joining a large group of other young people from varying backgrounds across the USA. There were graduates and undergraduates, business executives, and junior officials from government departments, plus interns working for prominent Democrats and Republicans alike. Although from a host of disciplines, they were all eminently talented and bright, representing the cream of the area in which they specialised. Following an hour of socialising and discussion, a flamboyant lunch was served, with the young attendees dispersed around the tables and joined by the dignitaries.

Afterwards, speeches concentrated on the need to integrate regulatory control of industry and commerce more directly under federal jurisdiction. With polished oratory, the policy was championed by Senator Edward Kennedy of Massachusetts. Then they joined various brief workshops examining future US commerce policy, with debates on direction. Jenny was in her element, vocalising her opinions with customary directness, attracting attention and admiration alike. She shone in the debate with an enthusiastic contribution offering her progressive ideas on increasing business confidence through more focused regulation, whilst deregulating to allow greater entrepreneurial flair.

After lunch, she was invited to briefly meet with Deputy Director Louis Tordella, the Chief Operating Officer of the National Security Agency, on her own, whilst Braden remained in an open discussion group. She was shown into an anteroom adjoining the suite in which the conference was taking place, where a smart man with an engaging smile rose to meet her. After she was introduced by an aide, he greeted her warmly with, "Hi, I'm Louis, and I'm delighted to make your acquaintance. Let's sit down." Then, after briefly touching on her studies, he asked, "Would you mind if I asked you a couple questions? We are planning the future of state security, and with that in mind, we want to recruit the best and most outstanding talent of our time. Jenny, I am delighted to tell you that that's why you are here, but don't tell anyone, huh?"

It was a light moment and she smiled with him, but did not interrupt, sensing his command of their discussion.

"Jenny, we are seeking to create positions for an elite on whom we can rely to help protect our great nation. You are bright, your academic achievements are outstanding, and your future could potentially be more successful and rewarding than you might believe. I have two questions. First, do you believe in your country? And second, would you like to benefit from the opportunities which I can promise will flow from being part of the elite being created now? I can tell you it matters not what your politics are, Republican or Democrat, although if you're a commie it could be a problem."

They both laughed.

"We merely seek to establish your potential interest in helping us create an America in which generations to come may live in confidence and prosperity."

Jenny thought briefly and could not see anything negative in what he was asking of her; quite the reverse, and she even allowed herself a feeling of pride in being selected. But she wanted to be honest too. "Mr Deputy Director, I am deeply honoured, but in answer to your first question, although I love my country, I am not content with it; there is much I would change, not least in creating more equality, improving civil rights and spreading global peace. In terms of benefiting from opportunity, of course that is appealing, but always subject to strict principles."

Tordella rose, smiled again and shook her hand firmly. "Miss Baronio, welcome to the future. I look forward to you playing a full part in creating a new America. I hope you will treat all this with the strictest confidence. Thank you for your time." The meeting was over, and secretly, Jenny was excited.

After she and Braden returned to Boston, they both received a letter signed by Gerald Ford, thanking them for their contribution, on headed paper from the White House. Jenny had hers framed and it remained proudly displayed in her offices throughout her career, which, from that moment, was monitored very closely indeed, with reports being sent every six months to the Director and Deputy Director of the NSA. She could not have known then that two months later, Gerald Ford would become the thirty-eighth President of the United States.

Jenny's parents took to Braden, with his display of deference and respect always prevalent. That autumn the couple were invited for a weekend at the Baronios' home, and Giuseppe delighted in sharing with his prospective son-in-law, as he already viewed him, his business achievements and the opportunities he had seized in Atlantic City. "Hey, don't let anyone stand in your way, but seek out your fortune and protect your family always. Gina, don't I always protect you?" he shouted across the drawing room in the general direction of the kitchen.

"Giuseppe, you are a low down stealer of young, innocent girls from Milan, and you know what, Braden, he does nothing all day and still makes me cook; he is a no-good pain in the backside, *che palle!*" ('What a pain!') The banter was part of the better times in the Baronio household which, for once, Jenny welcomed, joining in the laughter.

Her parents had tried to ignore the 'unfortunate' summer she had spent in France, which, as a result of their disapproval, she refused to discuss further with them. She had abandoned her duties then, and caused embarrassment to the family for which her father said he would never forgive her. Jenny dismissed his outbursts, as she did her mother's moments of excitable disdain, exhibited with less anger but in typical Italian style. She shrugged off her heritage – she accepted her Italian roots, but she was American. Giuseppe blamed her waywardness on her mother. "She is like you, and has no respect; what kind of daughter you give me? *Che malanova mi hai* ['I can't believe it']. You know what she will do? *Spazza il pavimento* ['Sweep the floor']."

To which her mother replied, "At least she will not be a *faccia brutta* ['an ugly face'] like you, with all your drinking."

Still, a sort of peace and stability descended on Jenny's relationship with her parents in 1973 that she had never before experienced. Harvard served a purpose in opening the door for her to thrive, whilst adding to Giuseppe's status. She was fulfilling the dream her mother had missed out on, which drew them closer together. Braden's entry to the family seemed to lay the ideal foundations for all that was to follow.

21

Perspectives

Since their parting, Peter had heard little of Jenny, other than through Jonas Barnier, with whom they had both kept in touch. By 1974, Jonas had developed his DIY business, expanding to fifteen stores, and diversified by investing in property whilst still leading a somewhat unconventional lifestyle. He remained within a former time that denied all he had achieved, rocking to music from the '60s, living in flared Levi's and T-shirts, and just was not for conforming. He sought freedom on his Harley-Davidson motorcycle, roaring down the freeways away from civilisation. He often hooked up with fellow bikers, who had no idea of his considerable wealth and commercial success, and with them he was most comfortable, feeling no need for status or recognition. If he could just be himself, then that was 'right-on'.

Married in 1973 to a sweet girl he had recruited as a sales executive, they started out well but drifted inexorably apart as they wanted such different paths, splitting up two years later. There was no enmity between them, just a mutual recognition that they were not meant to be. She desired to grow in a secure family, and he wanted to seek meaning in life through music, deeper thought, and ideals he retained from another age. He had no desire for children, although he loved entertaining them with his lively humour and a wildness they adored whilst he felt more at ease with youngsters where he was neither threatened nor judged.

Jonas had built up a genuine respect for Peter's sincerity and rare open, sensitive nature when they had first become friends in 1969. They had communicated by letter from time to time, learning of each other's developing lives and growing success. In July 1974, having been told about Peter's career in property, Jonas contacted him by phone, quizzing him about the UK market and finding his incisive knowledge highly impressive. "So, boy, can you help an old Texan freewheeler get rich? I want to invest in the UK, because from where I'm sittin', there appears to be a whole heap of building goin' on there."

To Peter's amazement, Jonas then suggested that he fly over to discuss options, and a week later, Peter found himself waiting at Lime Street Station for his old friend to arrive from London. He was strangely nervous about the meeting, but Jonas had insisted that it was a great idea, and he was a hard man to dissuade. It had all been so easy back in 1969, but this was the real world and Peter felt unsure of himself, despite his early success in the business.

When dealing with others, he was self-assured, confident, and appeared every inch the successful business executive. He possessed a natural charm, backed by an aura of professionalism and a lively wit, which engendered trust, putting others at ease. Investment in Merseyside was not an easy prospect to sell, but he was proud of his native city, and very good at selling it to others. He would dwell on the culture, the maritime history, the hard times experienced during the war, and the indomitable spirit of the local inhabitants. Music and comedy, for which Liverpool was now famous worldwide, were symbols of the creativity, resourcefulness and inventiveness of the Scouser. He would talk animatedly about the historic buildings, and the achievements of industry and commerce. He cited the iconic factories which underpinned the stability of the city, such as Tate & Lyle, Meccano, Dunlop and Kellogg's, together with the car manufacturers Vauxhall, Ford and Triumph. He spoke eloquently and with genuine pride about shipbuilding, the docks, his local roots, and above all, the city's growing business opportunities. His energy was unceasing, and he had a passionate belief in his mission to deliver opportunity for Liverpool through redevelopment.

Despite his outer confidence, however, encouraging foreign investment felt out of his league, as he confessed to Rubin. However, his boss would hear none of it: "My boy, you are what this city needs; you are young, ambitious and very bright. Frankly, you remind me of myself many years ago, but I was an impatient man, whilst you have a wise wariness. So my advice is go for it, and cease being too wise. Be careful, but never hide from your instincts." As always, his employer's words acted as a catalyst and filled him with a renewed drive, but despite this, the prospect of selling investments to his old friend was daunting.

On arrival at Lime Street, Jonas was unmistakable still, with his thick moustache. His hair was mercifully tidier, and he sported a cowboy hat, jeans, and boots with silver toecaps. He wore a denim jacket with the words 'Love and Peace' emblazoned on one lapel, and on the other, a circular ban-the-bomb symbol. Peter was dressed in the business suit and tie expected by those he dealt with. Jonas strode over to him and threw his arms around him before slapping his friend on the back. "Shit, man, you look like a goddamn news reader on CNN. I swear you are the spit of Walter Cronkite. Where's my hippy? Hell, boy, you became one of them!" Peter laughed, amazed at how, in a bizarre way, nothing had changed between them, except that this was Liverpool, England, and there was no Jenny.

Over dinner, the conversation flowed as though they had never parted, as they discussed their lives and the directions that had opened to them, or those they had taken themselves. They agreed that they had similar objectives, investing in what they perceived would bring a return; in Peter's case, a fee or a share, and in Jonas's, an upturn on the value of whatever he placed his money into. Jonas used property as security in expanding his portfolio. By now, he confided, it was a little academic, as his market had taken off in the US so this was just a little insurance. He listened intently as his old friend related the story of the growth in Merseyside property values and the investment return on developing former derelict sites.

As they sat in the bar of the Adelphi Hotel, drinking brandy after a long dinner, Peter tentatively raised the subject of Jenny, asking how much Jonas knew of her. His heart pounded, as if he were almost frightened to reopen something he had tried in vain to suppress.

His companion waved for two more drinks, and sat forward in his chair. "I been chattin' with her and, wow, she's doin' real good, man; like, she is goin' to be one damned hot lawyer." Jonas reached inside his jacket, pulling out a cigarette from a silver case, lighting it with a neat flick and click of a Zippo lighter, and taking a deep draw. "Man, you guys were really where it was at back then, but hey, she is movin' on OK. She's with some insurance guy from up north but, hell, do I think she is happy? No way, baby; that girl is motivated by all the wrong stuff. Like, she is all establishment now, doin' all the shit we hated. I don't think she's settled. Back then, we believed in something, and you know what happened? Life, man, life just got in the way." For a moment, Jonas paused, looking a little wistful before sighing. "Hey, look at you, boy, look at me; so what is it all about? Maybe we all grew up a little. I tell you truly, she will always hold a candle for you, Peter, but it will only return to you guys if you both have the courage to reach for it. The question is, was that just some fairy tale, or was it real? I guess that's a question only you guys can answer."

They stayed over at the Adelphi, reflecting long into the night over brandy upon where their dreams lay, and what their experience of the '60s was all about. Reconvening the following day, they toured some property sites, examined costings, and agreed a strategy. Jonas was to give Peter a costed budget but, incredibly, also gave him his trust to make the key decisions as he had total confidence in the skills of his enthusiastic friend. That night, their business concluded, they had another dinner together at the revolving Tower Restaurant atop St John's Beacon. Peter wanted to show off his cosmopolitan city, but Jonas countered that the US already had a turning tower restaurant in Seattle, called the Eye of the Needle. Nevertheless, he was still mightily impressed. "I guess there may be more to this city than boys with guitars," he joked. They reminisced about their earlier lives together, and what they sensed might never be the same again. "You got strikes and your coal miners hold your government to ransom, and in my country our President is getting kicked out of office for lying and being part of a cover-up. Not sure which of us is worse off, but there has to be better times ahead, my friend."

The following day, Jonas was gone, and Peter buried himself in his work once more, but something had awoken in him, presenting a dilemma; perhaps he should reach out? But then, his life was secure and he was developing his career. He knew he was convincing himself, and so he buried his thoughts, knowing that hiding would avoid the danger of them overtaking his rationale. Going backwards was not an option.

Braden Trelawney had followed his career and his company's expectations like a sheep. From door-to-door life-policy sales in Wisconsin, through to regional insurance sales, he had moved with his job to Boston. Seeking to join the more rewarding business sales sector in 1972, he had applied for and been given a position as a commercial insurance salesman, calling on businesses across the state of Massachusetts. In 1974, he became the area manager, controlling a small team of four sales executives from an office set up for him in central Boston. His position gave him a company car, a Chevrolet Monte Carlo, of which he was enormously proud, often polishing it at weekends, which to Jenny represented a pointless diversion when they could be doing more exciting things.

A driven man, albeit within the confines of a defined structure, Braden was systematic and methodical, liking routines, in which he sought security. He had watched his parents struggle financially when he was growing up, and he wanted to do better. He was the youngest of three children, and his two elder sisters never let him forget that he was the odd one out, teasing him incessantly. Although he had little ambition, he wanted to break away and carve out a life he could call his own. His father was a hard-working blue-collar worker for an agricultural machinery manufacturer. His mother, a proud housewife, came from an immigrant family who had arrived from Norway at the end of the nineteenth century.

Both his parents were determined to raise their family in a secure environment, and their dedication to their home was reinforced by their close bond. His father had been in the Army Corps of Engineers, serving in Europe in the last eighteen months of World War II, helping to both destroy and build bridges; an irony never lost on him. His wartime service at nineteen years of age had given him a determination that his family would never suffer the insecurities of his youth. His warm, infectious nature characterised his family roots in Cornwall, England, before his parents had seized the opportunity to escape the declining tin mines for the opportunities in 1920s America.

Braden had inherited the hard-working ethic of his father, and a strong order and routine instinct from his mother's Scandinavian background. However, he also suffered from feelings of inadequacy, covering these up with a personality that revealed little of himself but much determination. He was not going to suffer life as a worker; he would not be a cog in a factory, but wanted a career in which he could earn sufficiently to be comfortable. He sought stability, nominal status and security with a relaxed lifestyle, avoiding conflict, or involvement in division and protest like others of his generation. His American dream lay in respecting the rules, abiding by the law, and being a responsible member of the community.

Jenny found his lack of concern over pressing current issues such as the war in Vietnam and political earthquakes like Watergate, and his apparent disdain for human rights issues, utterly incomprehensible. Braden seemed to have a built-in refusal to acknowledge anything which went against the status quo. "We don't need to get involved in all that stuff, Jenny; we have real lives to lead" was his typical response when she raised these issues. They spent much time together in the late months of 1973, exploring their surroundings rather than who they were to each other. To Jenny, Braden represented security and stability, and brought a calmness to her life that she had not had when growing up. She wanted to create a foundation and settle, despite her dedication to her idealism. Perhaps, she mused, it was time for other people to take the mantle whilst she helped others when she became a lawyer. Her beliefs were as strong as ever, but she felt that through her career she could make a difference, despite the nagging reservation which served as an internal advocate arguing against her.

In October 1973, Braden purchased tickets for a Broadway show, *A Streetcar Named Desire*, at the St James Theatre, New York. Jenny was electrified by the performances, especially that of Lois Nettleton in the role of Blanche, whom she referred to as her heroine after the show. Braden was singularly unimpressed, neither fully understanding nor appreciating the drama or the story. To him, it represented domesticity in a state of cataclysmic collapse, but to Jenny, the resilience that she saw in Blanche was liberating. Her dramatic character personified strength, challenging the status quo, and then, having been corrupted through no fault of her own, she had been removed from society, losing contact with reality as she embraced realisation. This had a resonating connection for Jenny, who wanted to challenge, yet still felt a need to conform somehow in a swirling contradiction that she struggled to reconcile.

She still wandered back to the place where she had been four years before, especially as she drifted into sleep. Often at night, in silent moments, Peter's thoughts were with her and hers with him; as they lay in the stillness they connected, even without the awareness of the other reaching or seeking.

22

Reawakening

9th August 1974

The phone rang in Peter's parents' three-bed, proudly semi-detached house in Huyton, Liverpool. His mother called to him, "Peter, there's some girl called Jenny on the phone; she sounds like one of them Yanks and says she knows you from years back." Then, in a derisory tone, recalling the love affair she thought had seduced him away from reality, "Is she that Wallis Simpson woman that led you astray?"

Incredulous, his heart pounding and his stomach in a knot, Peter ran downstairs to the hall and grasped the receiver to his ear with apprehension. "Please tell me this is who I think it is?" he started tentatively, even nervously.

"Hey, Peter, baby." Her distant, yet still so familiar voice washed away the years that had passed since they had last spoken. "This is just the craziest thing, but I wanted to tell you – like, right now – that I think of us so often; you are still with me, Ice-Cream Man."

A pause… he did not know how to respond.

She carried on, and incredibly, it seemed normal, as if five years had never passed. "Guess what, Peter – President Nixon resigned today; and, even more amazing, we did get out of Vietnam. Isn't that something else? Do you still recall our dreams? Those were our times, but a coming of age for the world too." She spoke quickly, the words tumbling out as she reached for the courage to tell him her news, struggling to know why she needed to.

"Jenny," he gasped, his thoughts reeling, trying to put words to his uncompromising emotions which challenged his present by invoking the past. "Jenny, my far-out hippy chick… but why now? My God, I have thought of you too, very often."

"Peter," her voice caressed his thoughts, "I really wanted to reach out to you so many times and… and then I ran away; I was like a frightened child because it was all too much."

There was a pause before he replied, "But why now, why? You know, like, that was then, this is now, man… I do still love you in my dreams. You know what, that was the purest love and I will forever treasure our time together. I still keep our Covenant close, I do hold it in my heart…" He could not justify, nor did he want to justify, the sentiment he expressed. His deepest thoughts often directed his aspirations without a compass, towards a destination he knew not where. "Jenny, we were such a beautiful part of that time, and I think our lives were enriched by all we shared. We had wonderful ideals back then, and, yeah, it's cool to still have them." Peter felt his words were ridiculously inadequate.

"Hey, you know what, Peter, the flower girl just became a lawyer – I am joining the establishment. Have I betrayed all we believed in then? God, I wish we could be back there, because every time I look back, all I see is just so fabulous. There was music, there was love, there was hope, and there was us."

Both held the receivers to their ears as though clinging to one another; wary, yet so very needing. They spoke openly, yet avoiding any reawakening of what had never slept, as though dancing around what they desired, swapping summaries of where they were in life. It was all far away from the heady days of 1969. Yet, despite that distance and the chasm of time, they were drawn to one another as they discussed the hypocrisies of their era, from the lies of Watergate in a corrupt White House, to the abandoning of principle in the Vietnam War. Peter painted an equally gloomy picture of government in the UK under Ted Heath failing to stand up to anarchic trade union power and betraying democratic sovereignty by enrolling the UK in the EEC.

They talked animatedly about their aspirations. Jenny wanted to build a life as a lawyer fighting injustice, whilst Peter was committed to creating new urban communities in Liverpool. She was energised and driven by her success at university which had opened up a career path with a leading law firm. He was equally motivated by his achievements in property investment and the increasingly lucrative returns he was generating. They felt excitement at their development, which, they tried to justify, upheld the principles they had held so dear back then.

Jenny knew she had to tell him, even though she was embarking on a journey she was no longer sure she wished to make. "Peter, I need to tell you something." The seriousness in her voice arrested the conversation. "I am going to be married next month."

There was a long pause. His heart was thumping, and he felt utterly unable to respond coherently. Then, in a trance, he heard himself say, "Hey, that's wonderful, Jenny, and my congratulations", though inside he felt a dreadful, pounding emptiness. He could neither justify nor vocalise how he felt. There was no logic to feeling this much emotion after so long, yet he did.

"But, Peter, my Covenant remains for you always..." Her voice trembled, almost pleading, yet it was insistent, as though conveying that their time was theirs for all time.

He recovered enough to wish her a wonderful future, and meant it.

The end of their call was too sudden for both of them, yet despite her yearning, it was Jenny who brought it to a close. "Hey,

Peter, we were a groovy couple but I guess it's time for us to say to each other, 'Have a nice life.' But, God, I wanted more. I still do. Honey, never forget me…" Her voice broke with a half-sob, then, before he could respond, "Goodbye, Peter. Take care, baby." And she was gone.

After the call terminated, he was left with a dreadful loneliness. The memories he held were his karma to himself, to her, to their special places that only they knew. He sought to justify that his life was so very different now, yet nothing could convince him to turn away from or against what lay within him.

That night he sought refuge in escaping reality, in dreams, as he so often had in his life. The years disappeared and he was back with her, walking hand in hand. They were barefoot on the warm sand of the beach at Cavaliere, by the calm Mediterranean sea which caressed the shores of their heaven. Their discovery had stayed with him throughout the years since, remaining vibrant. He remembered so much, recalling with a vividity that often surprised him but which drew him back to a place he longed for.

This was where they had swum, shared so much; where they had giggled frivolous hours away, or talked from dusk until dawn, and made love in the sea off a quiet beach, rejoicing in their intimate secret. Her voice had evoked so much, like poetry he had forgotten, though so many years had passed. She had beckoned to him with her words, drawing their Summer of Love back into his mind, his focus drifting to places he thought he had forgotten, yet never really had. He could see her as she lay beside him inside the tent, her long dark hair spread across her brief white top, tied at the waist over her bronzed stomach and low-waisted denim shorts. Her soft, sensual figure; her long, slim, tanned legs drew his gaze, and his heartbeat quickened, drinking in her loveliness, her arousing beauty captivating his mind and body.

Jenny had awoken that night in 1974, not sure why she wanted to call Peter, other than to share the stunning news that President

Nixon, or 'Tricky Dicky', as she and her fellow students called him, was gone. The news evoked feelings from her past which cascaded through the present. She also knew that she had to tell him about her forthcoming wedding, although she dreaded it. She never had called before, although God knows she had wanted to, but had resisted the desire, telling herself that life was different now… but it really never had been. After the call, she reflected deeply on where she was.

Jenny had always been strong, absorbing all around her, developing beliefs about the social justice issues of her age from her earliest years growing up in Atlantic City. Aged just nine, she had asked at the family dinner table, "Papa, why can't white folk go on Chicken Bone Beach, and why don't coloured folk go to the same places as us? Do you not like Negroes?"

Challenging views, which she knew she was doing, was a brave move where the wrath of the somewhat fiery Giuseppe Baronio could be raised, and regularly was. He berated the Beatles when she applauded them for refusing to perform at a concert where there was segregation. "Those goddamn long-haired Limeys should get the hell out if they don't like our country, *Dio mio!*"

Jenny had walked out that day, calling her father "a right-wing racialist". She was fired with enthusiasm, listening avidly to the words of Martin Luther King in 1963, firmly positioning herself behind the Civil Rights movement and championing the cause of the oppressed at every opportunity. She embraced his dream that the nation would rise up and live the true creed supported by the words from the Constitution; 'We hold these truths to be self-evident, that all men are created equal.'

By 1963, her father's business had expanded, bringing more comforts and a move from their tiny two-bedroom homestead on the edge of the Inlet to a modern five-bedroom home in the fashionable new development on Winchester Avenue, with a smart stairway ascending above street level. Their new home came complete with air conditioning, a fridge, a clothes washer, and every modern luxury including a colour TV. Jenny was drawn to watching the news, which excited her as it depicted authority being openly challenged by the young flexing their muscles in a new generation, often backed by the music she adored.

In 1964, Giuseppe Baronio had been a proud supporter of Lyndon Johnson's campaign for nomination as the Democratic candidate for President. The convention was held in Atlantic City, and Jenny despised Johnson and his patronising, warmongering speeches. Her father's unswerving support for the brash Texan gave even more impetus to her belief that the American dream was a gross deception favouring the elite. Her future was ordained in these times of growing civil unrest and the thirst for new answers and new freedoms.

As her teenage years passed, she became increasingly incensed by Giuseppe's admiration for Johnson, and his outright support for the war in Vietnam. She was determined to make a stand. On the 21st October 1967, Jenny enthusiastically joined the march of war protestors to the Pentagon, facing down the National Guard for the cause of peace in Vietnam. This was the time to stand up to political corruption; the people versus the establishment. She smilingly recalled the banners proclaiming, 'Make Love, Not War'. She was just seventeen when, with a floral bandana round her head, dressed in a crazy blouse and a pink miniskirt, she marched proudly, facing the weapons of authority. She looked into the face of a young guardsman, who flinched visibly as she put the stem of a white flower into the barrel of his rifle with the words, "We just want to love you, man; be free." The peaceful gesture really hit him, she thought, the irony of flower power not lost on her. And she was right, because weeks later, he refused an order to confront a further protest and was court-martialled.

That day Jenny was arrested, along with hundreds of others who protested, which felt a little like an honour. Initially she was treated roughly by the 'pigs', but she remained uncompromisingly defiant. She found that looking each of them straight in the eyes disarmed them; after all, they were only men. Her father had to travel from Atlantic City to the court in Washington DC to have her released on bail, followed by a $500 fine. She often laughed at the fact that she was accused of 'disturbing the peace' when all she wanted, and was fighting for, was peace.

She despaired even more when the Democrats lost the election in November 1968, Nixon defeating Vice President Hubert Humphrey; but hell, no wonder, she thought, he was such a nonent. She was working a vacation job as a waitress at Ed Zaberer's Restaurant in North Wildwood. Ed inspired them all with his tales of starting at the bottom. He told them he had begun as a lowly washer of dishes, and now look at him. He was an imposing, flamboyant man, who exuded show business with his dramatic gestures and relished entertaining his guests. One day, he announced that Richard Nixon was coming to town and would be dining there. When the President-Elect arrived in December 1968, Jenny was underwhelmed by his alleged charisma, although she recalled his dark eyes. His brows were furrowed and his expression overly grave as those around him scurried to offer sycophantic pandering. He grunted thanks to her as she served him without hardly realising she was there. Later, she often laughed that she could have poisoned the thirty-seventh President of the United States and "saved all that Watergate shit".

23

The Wedding

Despite her reservations, Jenny had willingly accepted Braden's proposal of marriage when it came in April 1974, shortly after he had received an unexpected promotion to area manager, and she achieved a position as junior attorney with the very well-respected firm Latham Ellis Piper with offices in Boston, New York, Washington and LA. They had carved out something of a reputation as highly effective defence lawyers during the Watergate hearings, and were closely associated with Professor Wostenholme. He had introduced Jenny to the firm, and had accompanied her for her initial interview two years earlier. Ostensibly, he had taken no part in it; yet he appeared at lunchtime to join her and her interviewer, together with other senior partners. She thought nothing of the influence being exerted, other than reasoning that her abilities were being more fully represented. She had excelled in all her exams, fully justifying Wostenholme's faith in her. He called her "a future Supreme Court Justice", which she laughed off, but then he turned to her with a surprisingly steely look. "We never misjudge those we choose, Jenny; you are destined for greater things, and in time, you will earn the privileges which surely await you." His words thrilled her at this point in her burgeoning career.

On one of the regular visits Professor Wostenholme made to her comfortable office on Union Street after her appointment, he went further. "You know, Jenny, there are people taking notice of your progress, and I mean important people," he told her earnestly. "I have taken great interest in your career, as you know, and I can tell you that there are enormous opportunities for you out there. You have ideals and we embrace those, but, Your Honour, it may be time for you to build a little security for yourself." He told her that the sooner she embarked on her family life, the more opportunities would flow from that. Citing a new generation of women assuming more powerful positions in both the Senate and the House of Representatives, he stressed that their families enjoyed more stability because of their early commitment to marriage. "So it may be, Jenny, that this is the best time for your career to consider where you are going with the young man in your life." He stressed that it was little business of his, but that he only wanted the best for her.

She confided in him that Braden had proposed just a few days before, to which the professor responded with appreciative applause. The wedding was planned for September 1974, and Wostenholme stated that he would use his influence to assist by securing a donation for the event, in gratitude for her and Braden's contributions to the conference they had attended in Washington. Gesticulating with a wide sweep of his arm, he told her to select any venue and it would be paid for. "You impressed many people during that conference, Jenny, and this is our chance for the government to thank you with a gift, but," he placed his finger on his lips, "don't tell anyone apart from Braden."

Afterwards, an excited Jenny confided in Braden about the gift, which delighted him, not least because he knew, if he asked them, his parents would struggle to assist financially. Soon, they selected a location they both loved in Boston, and nervously put it to Professor Wostenholme. The Omni Parker House was a historic hotel on School Street. Its mid-nineteenth-century opulence had not faded with time but, on the contrary, had been enhanced by the glitterati who frequented it. Movie stars from Joan Crawford to James Dean, and Presidents from Ulysses S. Grant to John F. Kennedy and more, had stayed there. The interior was lit by graceful crystal chandeliers; the floors, from marble to deep carpet, welcomed guests with a service second to none; whilst in open lounge areas, larger-than-life circular seating invited visitors to sit and converse in discreet alcoves, not unlike a private club. Professor Wostenholme responded to Jenny's telex tentatively proposing the venue on the day he received it with five simple words: 'I will propose the toast.' On receiving this message, Jenny's heart leapt, adding to the euphoria she felt at so much falling into place, both in her career and in her home life.

She made a decision at this time that she did not wish her identity, including her name, to be changed by marriage, which caused something of an argument with Braden. She announced to him that, following the ceremony, she would be known as Ms Baronio. Braden normally acceded to Jenny's choices in life, although he never expressed any enthusiasm for her ideals, which he dismissed as the whims of a student of the era in which they lived. For her not to adopt his surname, however, was a slight against his standing in the community, which, he suggested, demeaned his status. Her response was brief, if not characteristically concise: "Bullshit!" He remonstrated with her, pointing out that it was customary and that he wanted to blend into society without being compromised by modern fads. Jenny was never one to be trifled with, and she damned well knew it and was not going to change her mind, pointing out forcefully to Braden that his "square ideas" had no place in a modern world, and certainly no place in hers. "So, Mr Trelawney, you can stick your Cornish name up your ass, because I have been a Baronio for twenty-three years, and that is not going to be changed – not by you, and not by anyone. On that, my decision is final." Never one to create more waves than he was capable of calming, Braden accepted defeat, but harboured a resentment which stayed with him.

Braden's life began to undergo something of a transformation as his prospects developed. Despite the average sales results achieved by the team he managed, his career was on an upward path. He was summoned to an interview, at short notice, in September 1974, just one week before his wedding to Jenny. He approached the door on the top floor of the building with trepidation, wondering if he had committed some misdemeanour.

"Come in, Mr Trelawney." Bernard 'Bernie' Walters puffed on a large cigar.

Braden was facing a room with a large desk at one end, from which extended a meeting table with chairs either side. There were three seats behind the desk, in the centre of which sat Bernie, his manager at Western Union Insurance, flanked by two others he did not recognise, both dressed in dark suits.

"These gentlemen are from our Upper Division."

They barely acknowledged Braden, other than with a nod; nor did they offer to shake his hand.

"We been thinking that you should be rewarded for all the hard work you put in here. What do you think, kid?"

The meeting had been called unexpectedly and he had been summoned shortly before he was due to leave for a business appointment with General Electric; a meeting he had fought for months to secure. However, he had been told to postpone and rearrange it due to unforeseen circumstances, and that was decidedly unusual, breaching normal Western Union ethics.

"I'm kind of wondering what to say," Braden responded, then regretted his words. He had never been good at self-presentation. "I mean, sure I want to progress in the company, but I am not sure what is being suggested."

Bernie took a long draw on his cigar, exhaling slowly. "We want to give you an opportunity to show what you can do, OK? You are getting married, right? She is a bright girl and, I understand, well thought of, so you deserve to be up there with her." His New York accent added an edge to his words, like this was not an offer but a decision. Bernie leant across the desk, taking his glasses off, adding a touch of emphasis. "You will take over the position of regional manager of commercial sales, overseeing our entire Central Eastern operations here. You will be covering from Maine, right down the Eastern Seaboard states to Virginia, including New York and Vermont."

Braden was almost too shocked to speak, stumbling over his response. "I guess I'm surprised, grateful and honoured all in one," he managed.

"Well, kid, you clearly are favoured by someone, somewhere, but remember – you will be watched, and not just by me, so don't let them down. One other drawback: you will be reporting directly to me, so be careful, huh?"

Braden's salary was to be almost doubled; a decision which had already been made. He and Jenny felt like they were riding the crest of a wave with their respective careers taking off together. They set the date of the wedding for the 14th September 1974; just five weeks after the resignation of President Nixon, which Jenny felt was a positive portent and an opportunity for a fresh start.

On the day of the wedding, Jenny was driven to the gates of the historic Church of the Covenant on Newbury Street, Boston, in a large white Rolls-Royce in which she sat with Giuseppe, who waved from the windows like royalty. "See, Jenny, *mia principessa*, how impressed they are now? We Italians can show these Americans a thing or two, eh?"

Even at that moment, she felt distant from her father. She was American, and determined that her identity lay nowhere else. Strangely, she even felt slightly distanced from the entire proceedings, as she entered the church recalling, with a shudder, a simple yet more beautiful time in a quiet French chapel in Bormes-les-Mimosas in 1969. Shaken, she pushed the memory away on this, the happiest day of her life.

Her dress had been chosen by her mother, despite some resistance from Jenny, but she wanted to please her and, for once, empower her. For Jenny, the idea of something simple appealed; remembering, with a secret inner smile, the diaphanous, sensual outfit she had worn to mesmerise and almost seduce Peter in their beach ceremony five years before. The contrast could not have been greater, as Gina was determined that she should make a statement deserving of the Baronio family. A traditional long white dress was chosen, flared wide from the waist, edged in lace on chiffon fabric with silk sleeves, and tailored so that the bodice showed Jenny's figure, albeit softened by the lacy outer layer. A subtle low cut to the front added a further hint of femininity, over which her bridal veil was draped before the ceremony, falling from a collection of white satin flowers bunched at the back of her head. Pearl earrings, and pointed white silk shoes with a ruffle heel, added just a touch of *amore a prima vista*, or 'love at first sight' to everyone who saw her.

Jenny could not help feeling a sense of occasion as she arrived at the church to find crowds of people awaiting her appearance. She and Braden had selected the Church of the Covenant as she refused to comply with her parents' request for a good Catholic wedding. Gina and Giuseppe were, at first, united in their shock at their daughter's almost blasphemous decision to deny her roots. Giuseppe had stormed off, saying that he had no daughter and that God would never forgive her. But eventually they compromised when the Church of the Covenant was described to them by Braden as a Nonconformist church, enabling Giuseppe to climb down without losing face. The significance of the iconic building whose name contained the word 'Covenant' was not lost on Jenny, whose mind was in turmoil throughout the process of planning her dream event, thanks to her past.

Led from the car by her father as the door was held open by the chauffeur, they approached the church steps. She looked upwards, taking in the lofty tower to the right and the shorter but no less impressive Norman-style tower to the left, and hesitated. Filled with an awareness of 'no going back', it was as though to go forwards held a finality that challenged her. The three arched doorways in front of her reminded her of an ornamental weather-forecast house from her childhood, from which figures had magically emerged to predict rain or fair conditions, yet today she was to enter the central door without knowing what was to follow. Her father coaxed her up the steps, telling her that "Our Lady is watching over you"; words which offered her no comfort.

Processing between the Norman arches lining the nave on either side, she could still feel the occasion, or perhaps it was just the majesty of the building, but she also felt a tinge of trepidation and emptiness. There was a finality as her father slowly removed his arm from hers, kissed her hand, and left her to walk the final steps to where Braden stood, somewhat stiffly, in a black three-piece suit and a frill-fronted white shirt complete with a grey silk cravat. He turned slightly as she joined him with a brief half-smile, but then looked straight ahead as the priest raised his arms to welcome the assembled. His words were lost on Jenny as a mist of misgiving took hold of her, almost sending her into a panic. She wondered whether the 'happiest days' of other people's lives were like this. Did other brides suffer the same uncertainties, and why now, at this moment in their union?

The service seemed to proceed without her, yet she uttered the words "I do" with rehearsed confidence, despite her misgivings. She had made a Covenant once before, and felt the waves of emotion from that time crashing over her now. The intimacy displayed with such honesty then far outweighed anything she almost wished she could experience now, in this ceremony she was sharing with so many others. As she and Braden were invited to seal their union with a kiss, she silently begged forgiveness as she could see the face of another framed against the Mediterranean shoreline; her body silhouetted in the sunlight against the translucent material of her gown, drawing the gaze of her beloved.

She truly sensed her God, offering a secret confession to him, in the blessing. "The Lord bless thee, and keep thee: the Lord make his face shine upon thee, and be gracious unto thee: the Lord lift up his countenance upon thee, and give thee peace." She felt a connection, though whether it was more with her own soul or the Almighty she knew not and cared not, but attempted to find the peace within that the benediction should have bestowed upon her. Yet, somehow she already knew that that peace was a Holy Grail which eluded her then, and which destiny would continue to keep from her.

After their exit into bright sunshine, it was not long before she began to resent the photographer forcing them into poses she was not comfortable with, and which represented no spontaneity. Braden seemed relaxed, smiling as he grasped her arm, and she dutifully went through all the motions; it was just all incredibly unreal. She thanked those she spoke to for coming, and laughed obligingly at well-worn, clichéd quips: "She's made an honest man of you, Braden", or "Keep him on his toes, Jenny; a tight hold on the purse strings, eh?", or, even worse, "What date are you planning the christening?", at which she smiled with a level of detachment matching her mood. Perhaps, she thought in the Rolls-Royce taking them to the Omni Parker House, it was the weight of the church occasion that was overbearing, and all would be better at the wedding breakfast.

They alighted, and were met by a procession of guests offering greetings, through which they walked, shaking hands and accepting congratulatory hugs, before being seated. They were placed at the centre of a long table covered with the *Tricolore* of the Italian flag on one side meeting the Stars and Stripes draped across the other. Jenny immediately knew who was the author of that idea; a conviction which was soon confirmed by Giuseppe.

"Hey, we Italians bring some beauty to America, eh? Our wine the best, our cooking the best, and our women – *Dio mio*, remember, *chi non ha moglie non ha padrone.*" ('A man without a wife is a man with no master.') He laughed at his own comedy, as always, encouraging others to join him. Oh God, she felt so detached, as if she was watching herself.

After the dessert was served there was a short break, during which the master of ceremonies invited those who wished to smoke to do so before the formalities to follow. At this point, Professor Wostenholme appeared at the top table, beaming, offering a hand to Braden before gallantly kissing Jenny's. "For both of you, this is the beginning of a new chapter – one, Jenny, that will bring a world of opportunity to you and, dare I say it, your family." He laughed at Jenny's shy look of disdain, but concluded, with a smiling gesture to the room, "Just look at all this, and think: it is given with the gratitude of the federal government because of your achievements. Here's to your futures, and to the destinies that await you." He bowed, lifted his glass of Bollinger champagne, and clinked the crystal with each of them.

Braden turned to Jenny. "We are lucky to know people like him. Our future awaits, Mrs Trelawney."

She winced.

When the surprise came, she was unprepared for it, having never expected it, but her focus on the words she heard was total.

Braden's best friend from his days in the office in Green Bay, Wisconsin, had given a dreary speech, complete with gaps as he fought to find his place in the notes he had written. His words drew polite laughter and much heckling, and then gave way to telegrams. He read two from distant relatives of Braden from Cornwall, England; then one from a fellow student of Jenny's at Harvard who was now working in the American Embassy in Moscow. She had known him as another of Professor Wostenholme's protégés. The words brought her a genuine smile, adding to the surreal nature of her feelings.

Zdravstvuj ['Greetings'],

Mr Brezhnev, Mr Kosygin and I would like to send warm greetings — well, maybe cold ones — from Moscow. We are all embracing detente on this joyous occasion. We hope that your relationship will be warmer than Soviet Russia this night. Dasvidaniya. ('Until we meet.')

"Then, ladies and gentlemen, we have one which carries the address of no less than — wait for it — Number 1,600 Pennsylvania Avenue — the White House."

There were gasps before the room fell silent.

"This reads…"

I am honoured to have made your acquaintance on your visit to Washington DC, where you gave valuable input to a conference on the future of business and government. My wife Betty, and my staff and colleagues, join with me in sending you both our best wishes from the White House. God bless your union.

Congratulations from President Gerald R. Ford, the Oval Office, September 14th 1974.

A ripple of applause filled the room, and one by one the guests arose, giving spontaneous cheers and then louder applause. Braden stood, gallantly clapping Jenny as if to bestow the honour entirely upon her. The room hushed again, and a greater surprise followed.

"And finally, ladies and gentlemen, there is one from Liverpool, England."

Jenny's attention was shocked into focus.

Greetings from a Scouse ice-cream vendor. Eskimo Glace et chocolat; get yer ice creams here, as you did in 1969. Not for any one reason, but for all reasons, I send you memories. Remember, the answer will always be blowin' in the wind.

The latter part drew a flutter of laughter, and a quizzical sidelong look from Braden whilst her heart leapt. This moment meant far more to Jenny than the day itself, yet she could not, dare not share it with anyone. Peter's words magnified her awareness, evoked so much inside her, leaving her senses reeling. She suppressed the exhilaration which flooded through her, smiling to herself and feeling a warm fulfilment not from her wedding day, but from so much more. A candle remained flickering, bringing light to what was surely impossible, but nonetheless beautiful to contemplate.

That night, on retiring to their magnificent bedroom in the bridal suite which Professor Wostenholme had announced was part of their wedding gift, she knew she had to face another hurdle, but *Why the hell not?*, she thought. Braden and Jenny had not yet made love. They had had clumsy fumbles but it had never seemed right, and in any event, he had made it clear that there should be no sex before marriage. On one occasion, after some prolonged kissing, she had attempted to give him oral sex, but he had recoiled, telling her he was not ready, or even sure he could do "that!"

After several glasses of champagne, she felt giggly and just a little wicked. It was time to bring him into a more sensual, open world. She changed into a thigh-length, delicate cream silk-and-lace nightie, but left on the stockings she had worn for the wedding. She pirouetted in front of him coquettishly, but Braden was embarrassed, awkward even, as if unsure of what was expected of him. He felt uncomfortable and wished he were able to be more spontaneous. He put to Jenny, in a very balanced tone, that they both needed to get used to this new aspect of their relationship in a sensible way, which would take time. She did not wish to be sensible, and felt betrayed by his lack of excitement or reaction. She climbed abruptly into the oak four-poster bed and, a minute later, he joined her, comically dressed in blue-striped pyjamas. Suddenly, it was she who wanted to be sensible; she would rather have gone to sleep.

When he entered her, it was after a series of clumsy kisses, grasping her to him and thrusting; but the moment had passed for her. The sweeping, overpowering orgasms for which, in another life, she had never had to wait did not flow through her. Braden's passion was expressed in half-stifled grunts that gave her little except, unknown to them both, the beginning of a new life. Her mind drifted as she welcomed blessed sleep, escaping to a far-off beach in France where she knew Peter would be waiting. There, she most certainly would not have been sensible, she thought with a wicked, mischievous smile.

24

Opportunity Knocks

Peter's relationship with Rubin flourished as he earned his teacher's trust and helped develop Granvilles into a leading property investment and development business. They spent hours together, debating and discussing their opinions. Rubin gently berated Peter for his romanticised view of life; and yet, he said, in many ways he coveted it.

His early life had been a fierce struggle to protect himself and those around him from the real threat of persecution. He had come to England in 1937, fleeing the wave of anti-Semitism sweeping Europe in the wake of the Nazis. His family had arrived with very little other than the possessions they could carry, reliant on the goodwill of others in their community who helped them start their lives afresh. They often discussed the summer of '69, the events of which fascinated Rubin in that Peter had not followed his instincts, but had been drawn by the lure of a career rather than the joy of love. Rubin felt that the world was lacking enough love. He was fascinated by the philosophy of love and peace embraced by the young which, despite the impossible utopianism it represented, he confessed would have been a wonderful antidote to the horrors of 1930s Europe, the subsequent war, and the Holocaust.

"You are like a son to me," he confided to Peter one day in 1979, "and I am proud of you. My boy, you have shown that you are wise and have excellent judgement, although maybe not in matters of the heart, I seem to remember, eh?" He rose from behind his desk, walked slowly over and hugged Peter, patting him on the back.

It was the parental type of affection Peter had once craved, but could rarely recall receiving. He thanked Rubin for all he had done for him, and pledged his loyalty.

"No, Peter, you have no loyalty to me, but only to your own – and for that, you need to take a wife."

It was then that Peter told him of the Covenant he had made in 1969, and so much more about the girl he let go. Rubin sat, swallowing with emotion, listening to the younger man's story which he so understood. His thoughts drifted back over the years to another time and to his treasured Rebecca, from whom he had been parted at the age of twenty-seven in Hamburg, never to see her again. Theirs had been a secret and passionate relationship of the heart, in which they pledged their love for each other. They had built a castle of dreams in which they both wanted to dwell forever. Rubin's family had fled when Germany was taken over by the Nazis promoting violent anti-Semitism. He had assured Rebecca that he would return when it was possible, and she had accepted his promise, looking searchingly into his eyes for reassurance. He had never forgotten the day they parted, nor the tears streaming down her face, their fingers touching until the last second. He'd watched from the cart as they drove away down the cobbled streets until he could barely make her out in the distance, and then she was gone. He had been left with an ache in his stomach that he could still feel whenever he thought of her; a lonely place from which he had never recovered, but upon which he never dwelled.

"My boy, you turned away from a life opportunity, which is unforgivable if you really loved her; that was the choice forced upon me when I was your age. Maybe, I think, a part of her will always wait for you."

A sad look occupied the older man's face as he recounted a little of his turbulent past, even allowing himself to speak of Rebecca. His family had been amongst the lucky ones, leaving Germany when the dark clouds of Nazism began to descend. Over the ensuing years, they settled in England, assisted by the generosity of others in their community, who helped Rubin establish a fledgling business in Liverpool. Loans were agreed and interest rates accepted, giving a return to his sponsors and an invaluable start to Rubin. He had quickly transformed his first property into flats, generating security of income before investing in another, this time bringing in developers and selling on to make a profit. He changed his name from Rosenberg to Granville, to give his image a touch more class; thus, Granvilles began to flourish under Rubin's determined control. He met his wife, Esther, in 1942 at a bar mitzvah party, entering into conversation on finding out that she was from Munich, and that she too had escaped from Germany in early 1939, just before the mass round-ups.

They were married in 1946, living a contented life with a singular determination that they would share the enjoyment denied to so many of their family and friends who had perished in the Nazi death camps. Esther had been assaulted during the Kristallnacht pogrom in November 1938. A group of brown-uniformed young men, some of whom she recognised as childhood playmates, had smashed their way into her parents' business and announced that they were no longer welcome in Germany. Her father had been arrested and she had stood in front of her grandfather, protecting him from their intimidation, and been rewarded with rifle-butt blows to her head and body until she fell unconscious to the floor, her assailants laughing mockingly. Her injuries were life-threatening due to internal bleeding, but fortunately their neighbour was a doctor. Although he had been banned by the Nazis from practising, as had virtually all Jews, Esther was secretly nursed by him and his wife. When she was well enough to depart Germany, her family emigrated to Britain. However, as Rubin told Peter with some undisguised feeling, her injuries were such that they could not have children; one of his greatest regrets.

By 1952, Rubin's debts were paid off, and he had begun to expand his business with a ruthless determination to distance himself from the past and create a new life. "You, Peter, have still not turned away from that Covenant you made. I see it in your eyes, and as the years pass, you will return to it again and again. It will haunt you, as my failure to seek out or return to Rebecca haunts me to this day. You should seek what the good God has given you."

Peter felt the depth of sincerity in the wise man's words, and the ring of truth in what he had correctly surmised. No, he had never forgotten those magical days, but he had moved on, hadn't he? But the answer to that question he found impossible to face.

His relationship with Rubin had stretched beyond the boundaries of business, and Peter savoured the closeness of their bond. Rubin's encouragement was genuine and warm; yet, as he reminded Peter, "You see, I'm not as stupid as I may appear, because you have not only enriched my life with the pleasure of your company but," he added with a flamboyant gesture, "you have enriched me financially." They would often laugh together at Rubin's philosophies of life and the conclusions he would draw, like a sage imparting invaluable lessons to his pupil.

In November 1980, Rubin agreed to sell the business to Peter as he was suffering the first warning symptoms of heart issues which, at seventy-one years of age, he thought were the signs to quit. Peter could not afford the price but agreed to jointly guarantee the transaction with Thomas 'Tommy' Wilson, a trainee sales negotiator in the company. Tommy had worked closely with Peter, both joining Granvilles at the same time, although he was in a much more junior role. He had none of Peter's flair for seeking out or sensing the potential of land or property. He had watched, with some envy, Peter's star rise in the firm with a grudging respect for the skill he exercised. Hence, when Peter confided in him that he was struggling to find the money to buy the business, Tommy saw an opportunity for advancement. To buy the business required an immediate payment of £250,000 which, Tommy assured Peter, his family would cover. He said he wanted nothing more than an equal share of the business, and a future job as a partner once he had built up the experience. They had to guarantee to follow the initial deposit with annual payments of £200,000 for the next ten years.

It was a generous offer from Rubin, who called Peter in on his last day. "My dearest boy, it pains me to leave you, especially as this deal you have struck is not as good for you as it might have been in my mind. Remember, this was the lowest offer I could possibly accept, and yet, just maybe you could have argued a little more on the price; perhaps a little less." His smile was broad, and their laughter followed. As Rubin walked away, he paused and turned back, placing his hands on Peter's shoulders. "I told you to trust only family, but then you are family to me. Be careful; I do not trust that Mr Wilson. I am so sorry to be leaving you, my dearest boy, but I am always here." He clasped Peter's hand with both of his.

After that parting, Peter felt very alone; excited by what was to come, yet with a deep sadness. Later that evening, he went to a drawer in his bedroom and opened a small container, from which he extracted some paper tied with red ribbon. He carefully undid the bow, reading Jenny's Covenant to him, and reached for her within his dreams.

25

Power to the People

The Covenant they had made stayed with Jenny in every part of her life, although she never shared it with anyone because it was priceless in its purity. She had memorised it, repeating the words to herself in her darkest moments. No longer just a Covenant, it was a tribute to and a connection with a part of herself that she still longed for. The words unlocked a place of comfort wherein she sought solace, evoking the beautiful love she so missed. Sometimes she found herself writing about her feelings, analysing herself, but then she would dismiss her thoughts as too intrusive and self-absorbed. Still, later she would return to what she had written, reflecting upon her motives in all she had achieved, for achievement had come easily to Jenny.

She had majored in contract, commercial and finance law at Harvard, turning away from the temptingly lucrative matrimonial and civil compensation fields which were taking over an increasingly litigious culture. She wanted to practise in a serious area of law which would tax her naturally investigative and intuitive talents. Very soon, she was building a reputation as a ferocious defence lawyer, and, with a sense of theatre, she began to exercise a gift for performing in front of judges and juries. She loved the drama of holding centre stage, pursuing truth as she perceived it, or represented it. She would not be concerned about where the truth really lay in her ruthless goal of winning her case. Sure, she may have defended those with a touch of guilt, but surely a minor indiscretion could be forgiven, or even perhaps ignored, for a greater purpose? Jenny had learned to mix her idealism with pragmatism, flavoured with a forgiving mind that justified her intervention which allowed others an opportunity to change their ways.

Her professor often visited her, taking her for lunch and hearing about her progress. He had introduced "sensitive political cases" to her, briefing her on the implications which, he said, he felt she was uniquely able to appreciate. Ongoing investigations were still flowing from the Watergate crisis and, as he pointed out, impeding effective government. He was always so reasonable; infuriatingly so, as he seemed to address all her concerns before she raised them, then deal with them effortlessly, prior to reaching the conclusion that inevitably suited his purpose. Sometimes she felt that their meetings had been choreographed, so well were his arguments rehearsed, It was as though they both knew the charade he was enacting, and conspired together invisibly.

Braden took to the post of regional manager of the Boston office with a resignation that it was good for his career and status. He was not ambitious, and was content to remain in his post, overseeing the office and ensuring that regional targets were met.

In June 1975 Jenny gave birth to a girl they named Maria Gina Baronio Trelawney, reluctantly acceding to her husband's insistence that the child should bear his name. Braden was delighted, although unprepared for the changes that would ensue, having expected Jenny to assume a more Motherly role. His hopes were soon dashed when she returned to work within five days, leaving Maria with her mother initially, before employing a nanny. She firmly informed Braden that she was wrapped up in critical legal matters and that she was needed by important people. Whilst he voiced his disapproval, using the diplomacy he had learned, to his cost, was necessary, he acquiesced when she assured him that she would give Maria her unreserved attention at weekends. This was an assurance he welcomed initially, but subsequently felt cost him in terms of the companionship they had previously.

Despite initially finding that she lacked the prenatal maternal instinct and enthusiasm shown by other mothers, Jenny was surprised in subsequent months to be captivated by Maria. Her daughter's thick dark hair already covered her head, and she had adorable wide blue eyes like her own. Even in her first few days, she appeared to be absorbing all around her, heralding the inquisitive character that was to become her way. She was assertive, her crying demanding attention or bewailing the fact that she was not receiving enough, and Jenny relished playing the role of mother, loving the developing bond between them. She devoted herself to Maria at weekends, normally dismissing their nanny, Carlotta, at around 7pm on a Friday and immersing herself in motherhood until 7.30am on Monday, when she returned to work.

Their life was comfortable, and in 1975 Jenny and Braden's combined income was sufficient for them to move from the apartment they had rented initially in the centre of Boston to a four-bedroom house on Goodwin Avenue, Malden; under thirty minutes' drive away from the areas where they worked. Their new home had been built in the early 1960s, with a white timber frontage, a modest plot with a front lawn bordered by trees, and off-road parking for their two cars. Initially, Jenny felt content as she got into the routine of working hard during weekdays and then playing the role of devoted mother at weekends. What the marriage lacked in passion, it gave in the balance to her life and the secure home for Maria she desired.

March 1977
Boston

She had been expecting him but, as customary, he was a little late. There was always something pressing with Professor Wostenholme, usually dismissed as "affairs of state" or urgent matters of academia rather than admitting to his inability to be punctual. Jenny's secretary announced him around twenty minutes after the appointed time. After a knock, he entered, wearing his signature trench coat and his glasses on the end of his nose, with untidy, wispy greying hair half-covering his ears under a grey trilby hat. She helped him out of his coat and hat, beneath which he wore a tweed jacket, a matching waistcoat, and fawn-coloured pants which, she noted, had probably once been pressed.

"Your Honour," he started in his usual manner, after an embrace during which he kissed her on both cheeks, "it is always so good to see you. How is the baby? Running around now and into everything, I would imagine?"

He was correct; Maria was walking, and into everything they had not placed out of reach. She already possessed an inquiring, restless nature, and Jenny's parents, doting on the baby, blamed Jenny for her wayward spirit. "*Madre Mia*, what have you given to us?" Giuseppe moaned. "She is like your mother, impossible; and like you, *avere un chiodo fisso in testa*." ('She is fixated on what she wants, like a nail in the head.')

Gina responded, with equal but good-natured gusto, "*Il Diavolo fa le pentole ma non i coperchi – e tu sei il Diavolo.*" ('The Devil makes the pots but not the lids – and you are the Devil', or 'What goes around comes around – and that's your doing.')

Jenny smilingly related her parents' words to Professor Wostenholme, but admitted that she was not being the best of mothers by too often giving in to her daughter's demands. She adored Maria, yet still found taking any time off for family reasons a frustrating interruption to her work. Jenny had reached the stage where she could see that she was capable of making a difference. Whilst still holding on to her profound beliefs, expedience was confirming to her that she could improve the system from within.

It was at this meeting, following the exchange of pleasantries, that Professor Wostenholme produced two dossiers from the briefcase that rarely left his side. He stressed to Jenny the utter confidentiality to which they must now commit themselves. Each file had a name neatly typed at the top in capital letters, beneath which was stamped one word – 'Authorised' – in red. Wostenholme stood up and walked to the window. "Those buildings over there have to be some of the ugliest I have ever seen." He gestured towards the Boston City Hall complex. "They should never have been constructed, and had there been a proper consultation, they wouldn't have been. That is what motivates me in my work: giving power to democracy where it is needed, while democracy must respect the power of those who direct it."

He continued that the entire US political system had been corrupted over time, which was what had led the country into Watergate. "Jenny, there are two names in front of you of individual American patriots who have served their country very well. They were involved in the cover-up; plus they took part in the security operation during the break-in, but it was not of their own volition. Their duty was performed, however misguidedly, out of loyalty to our country and in the interest of protecting the office of President of the United States. That office is greater than the individual; it is a historic institution, and one of the greatest bastions of freedom in the world. Respect for that freedom must be protected at all costs, and it is in this noble endeavour that you can play a meaningful part. These men had no alibi but played no significant role in the Watergate cover-up; they have both served their country with honour, defending Korea in the military, and operating in our intelligence services to safeguard America. It is our duty to protect this type of integrity, Jenny, and that is where you come in.

"Inside the dossiers, there are the names of four White House interns. They are all distinguished in their service to the United States and are men of the utmost honesty; but that honesty also lies within their pledge to ensure the future of our revered democracy. We would like you to undertake the defence of the two accused, and present to the judge that the statements of the four witnesses in the dossiers, which give alibis to our people, have been obtained late because of national security issues, not least that they work for the CIA."

He paused, then, "If I may paraphrase Churchill, he said that it is fine to be honest but also very important to be right." He paced the floor, explaining to Jenny the burdens of great office which he had helped protect after the dark days of World War II. "I have often wrestled with my conscience," he admitted, "but always my actions have been for the greater good of my country. The men I hope you will assist are two of the finest, and of value to the new administration. I can tell you that the request for help has been sanctioned directly by the President, but we needed a lawyer without a major reputation to prevent unwanted press attention. The President is anxious to move past Watergate and direct our national energies into creating a more balanced society in which human rights and equality are the standard-bearers of change. It would be an real honour for you to accept this mission, but any authority given by this administration to do so will be denied if ever questions are asked – and, Jenny, that denial will include myself"

After breaking off, he sat down, almost as though exhausted by his address. As he had started to speak, she had sensed unease, but then felt that she was being entrusted with an opportunity to play an important role in the new political climate. By March 1975 her head had been completely turned by someone who seemed to encapsulate so many of her ideals. She had heard him first on a newscast, the words spoken in a folksy, endearing Georgia accent: "My name is Jimmy Carter, and I'm running for President."

Jenny had immediately warmed to the easy-going nature of this charismatic man who appeared to be inspiring the nation toward a new style of politics whereby things were going to change for real. Right up to the election in November 1976, Carter introduced himself with those words as if he was still unknown, drawing laughing approval from his audiences. Jenny had been inspired by the decisiveness and commitment of his stated aims when he issued an amnesty to Vietnam draft dodgers in January 1977. If the President wanted change, she would lend any assistance to the process.

She looked from the dossiers to her old mentor, friend and guide. "Professor, I'm on your side and I will accept the case. I will play my part in making this country a better place, and to that I am totally committed."

Wostenholme stood up, solemnly clasping her hand. Then, after embracing her, he declared, "This conversation never took place, but it gives me enormous pleasure to congratulate you on the promotion you are about to be given. You are to be awarded the status of junior partner with Latham Ellis Piper, with effect from January 1978. Be assured, Jenny, I have every confidence that your reputation as an attorney can only grow based on the matters that those I associate with want to entrust to you."

Jenny felt a wave of euphoria sweep through her, and excitement that her life had just taken a major leap forwards, and so fast; yet she felt deserving of it. It was she who had driven her career, backed by her beliefs.

"You will be moving to New York City," Wostenholme continued, "but heck, they have terrific offices there. A little further away for me to keep my eyes on you, but I will always look after the interests of my star student."

He began to digress, as she saw it, moving on to ask Jenny about her intentions in terms of growing her family. She knew he was, as usual, circumventing the direct question he needed to ask, which was whether there were likely to be any further interruptions to her career. Having established that the reason for the meeting had been addressed, she did not wish to be manipulated further.

"Professor, get the hell out of my office, before I inform the White House that you are committing a felony: that of being a pain in the ass."

After he left, she reflected on the burden of the task she had been given, appreciating the trust placed in her and the justification based on the greater needs of the country. She felt pride in her task, in her career development, and in the part she was playing in creating a new beginning for a better America.

If only she could feel the same purpose and belonging in her home life. The truth was that, despite the joy of giving birth to Maria, there was something missing.

That night, as she drifted, she could see Peter walking down the beach towards her...

26

Guardian Angels

In late 1977, following final confirmation of Jenny's appointment as junior partner, she and Braden moved to a newly built property in South Spring Valley on the outskirts of New York City. Braden had put in an application to relocate to the New York office of Western Union Insurance and had almost been expecting the summons from his boss, Bernie Walters, confirming yet another promotion after a charade of an interview. He was in and out of Bernie's office within fifteen minutes after being told he was lucky to have good connections "There are some born to succeed, some learn how to, and some just have good connections" were his boss's parting words which riled him.

Whilst outwardly stable and secure in their marriage, Jenny felt a growing frustration with her life outside of work. She had been uplifted by the election of President Jimmy Carter, believing he really was breaking down old barriers. She would turn excitedly to Braden as they watched the television news, seeing the President greet guests in jeans with his easy-going, hillbilly style, and say, "My God, this man is gonna kick ass – isn't he just crazy and beautiful?" It was as if Carter belonged to her generation, and she felt her hopes rise with those of the nation.

Braden would typically respond, "This is not strong leadership, Jenny, and it's not what our country needs. We need strength, not hippies in the White House."

On many occasions, she would walk out of their living room and bang her fists on the wall in frustration. Braden was so not on her ticket, and was going in another direction.

On one occasion in 1978, she cheered out loud as the Camp David Accords were announced, bringing about a peace agreement between Egypt and Israel. "So is this so-called hippy a statesman or what, honey?" she announced with triumph and a barely hidden note of sarcasm.

Braden's retort was that she was an idealist, ten years out of date, and that stronger leadership would have secured more. He was adamant that the Democrat style of politics was not suited to the modern world under the threat of nuclear Armageddon.

Jenny began to appreciate that their political differences were symbolic of the wider gulf between them. Braden openly and regularly derided virtually everything she believed. She questioned whether she loved him, and indeed whether she ever had; then knew in her heart that she had loved only once. Each time her doubts surrounded her, her mind cast itself back. She would try, in vain, to erase the thoughts of Peter that still flooded her soul. She would see him in the ocean off Cabasson, mocking her for not joining him before diving away, leaving her utterly unable to resist the urge to follow him. Had she ever felt like that with Braden? Of course she knew the answer to that question.

In June 1978, Jenny was invited by Professor Wostenholme to Washington to join a conference which was to consider the law, the Constitution, and the energy crisis. This time she travelled alone and was met by a black limousine upon landing, which whisked her directly to Professor Wostenholme's Washington office at the State Department on Virginia Avenue Northwest. Upon her arrival, a marine snapped to attention, before opening her limo door and escorting her to the reception area.

After only a couple of minutes, she heard the voice she knew so well. "Jenny, Jenny, Your Honour, thank you for coming to see your old friend." Wostenholme shuffled across to her, his worn tweed jacket as crumpled as ever, complemented by equally worn trousers over lace-up shoes which, perhaps, had once seen polish. As customary, his glasses were balanced precariously on the end of his nose. "We must go to my office, I have someone I want you to meet, but how is Maria?"

She felt his genuine warmth, and had come to really enjoy their meetings which always seemed to herald important events or decisions in her life. They walked down a marble-floored corridor, flanked by pillars, stopping before a rather plain door on which was a nameplate – curiously simple, Jenny thought – bearing the typed name 'Professor L. Wostenholme'. He ushered her in and she sat in front of his somewhat understated modern desk; not at all what she expected in Washington, especially when compared with the lofty atmosphere of the building. There were piles of papers which did not appear neatly ordered, although she knew, from her previous dealings with him, he was meticulous regarding detail and order.

The professor pushed his glasses down his nose and looked at her directly. "Jenny, forget the conference today; I have something far more important to discuss. You will know that the President has embarked on the most ambitious platform of reform in our history. He is committed to the causes of human rights, emancipation from discrimination, and a liberal foreign policy. He is, I think, closely aligned with many of your ideals, but his programme could stall. There are some who seek to derail his policy by any means they can, and that includes character assassination. Watergate opened the floodgates to intrusive press investigation wherein any of us can and may be targeted. Woodward and Bernstein were just the beginning, inspiring a generation of young reporters who will do just about anything to make a story. I think you can help, and in return, there is a great career opportunity for you."

He looked at his watch and told Jenny he had someone he wanted her to meet, then picked up his phone, announcing that they were ready. Moments later, after a rapid knock on the door, a smartly dressed dark-suited woman entered, announcing, "The Secretary of State."

Cyrus R. Vance was an imposing man and, in contrast to Professor Wostenholme, impeccably dressed, carrying himself with a military bearing. He had a warm, engaging smile, with which he greeted Jenny. "Ms Baronio, I am impressed with all I hear of you, and a fellow lawyer, too. Your husband is in insurance, as was my father, so we have much in common."

Jenny was shocked by his entrance, stuttering her response, and shaking the Secretary of State's outstretched hand.

"I believe you are a bit of a firebrand in court, Ms Baronio, and have a reputation as a fierce opponent. I also understand that you are an idealist, and that is why I am here. I am not one to, as they say, beat around the bush, so I shall come straight to the point. The President and this administration are embarked on a crusade of change, and you might understand this is ruffling quite a few feathers. We now find ourselves the victims of an over-interested press who are hungry for a story. As Richard Nixon once said, the press are 'wallowing in Watergate'; I guess, for once, I understand how he felt. This administration is being hounded by journalists seeking a reputation. Last year, we lost a very capable member of the White House staff, Bert Lance, who worked closely with the President and was forced to resign. The guy was squeaky clean, Ms Baronio, for Christ's sake; he knelt praying with the President every goddamn morning in the Oval Office."

They were interrupted by the smartly dressed lady entering once again, this time informing them that she had "a call for Mr Vance from the President", which he took, to Jenny's astonishment, right there in front of her.

"Good morning, Mr President. You will recall, sir, our conversation regarding the resignation of Bert Lance, and the pressure being brought on others? I am speaking with a young lawyer right now by the name of Jenny Baronio, sir, who comes highly recommended by Leo Wostenholme. She has already carried out sensitive administration cases and I am briefing her on the press difficulties. On the issue of Israel and Egypt, sir, and the Anwar Sadat matter, I intend to make a call right after this to square things with Menachem Begin and calm troubled waters." Once the call terminated, he turned to Jenny and said simply, "The President sends you his best wishes, and hopes you can assist us at this difficult time."

Cyrus Vance highlighted to Jenny the critical need to safeguard the reputation of the administration against forces that were determined to resist change. The difficulty was that they were being targeted by those who were uncomfortable with the major reforms they wished to enact. "Our greatest achievements are yet to be realised, but realise them we will, if we can escape from the wolves who seek to hunt us down. We need someone who will assist in defending those affected by press attention, and someone who has the capability to delay progress in cases being brought against those supporting us. This person cannot be anyone prominent; nor do we wish to be seen to be in any way involved in this process. Your name was put forwards by Leo here, and, after studying your credentials, I am delighted that you have been selected for this very important task. After today, Ms Baronio, this meeting will not have taken place. It has been a pleasure to meet you, and Leo will fill in the details. I hope your undoubted skills will assist us in gaining momentum in our reform programme." He turned, waving a hand in the air towards Professor Wostenholme, and was gone.

The meeting had lasted all of forty-five minutes, but it left Jenny feeling a little disorientated. Wostenholme bid her sit on the couch along a wall of his office, in front of which was a low coffee table. He explained that there were a number of regrettable cases being pursued by investigating committees upon which court hearings might follow, and the critical need was to find and present irrefutable evidence to back up any defence. The imperative was that they took all steps necessary to protect the integrity of the White House, especially as it was embarking on a crusade to transform the way the United States was being governed. Jenny's role, if she accepted, was to fully brief Wostenholme on what evidence was required to ensure either that such cases did not reach court, or that if they did, there was a viable defence. "Whatever is required, we will source it. We have at our disposal a number of bodies who can assist us, covertly if necessary."

There followed two briefings: the first given by an impeccable military officer in uniform on dealing with secret communications from the State Department or the White House; the second by a smartly dressed man from the Press Liaison Division of the CIA regarding a number of key cases in which they required scrutiny and direction.

Jenny flew back to New York that evening carrying case files she had been given feeling both pride and unease in her mission. She was torn between her passion for all the good that she saw in the changes being made by the administration, and concern over the support she could call on to assist those who were helping her country. Could the end justify the means?

That night, she went to her daughter's bedroom, and watched Maria sleep in the subdued comfort light that stayed on until morning. *Such innocence in my child*, she reflected, *and so free from the choices that I have to make.*

All her life, she had stood up for the virtues she believed in: love, truth, integrity, justice, and human rights. Should she compromise so much for the greater good, or was she merely assisting in ensuring an outcome which should be reached in any event? The self-justification haunted her, and she silently prayed that Maria would never be exposed to this side of life. A wave of emotion swept over her, bringing tears to her eyes which began to trickle down her face as she wondered how life had taken from her the dreams she had once had.

27

Connections

In Liverpool, both the commercial and domestic property sectors were providing Peter with opportunity. Vast areas of the city had been left without any coordinated policy of regeneration apart from the programme in the 1960s to demolish terraced houses and build blocks of flats. This short-sighted scheme to transform whole streets into vertical towers had destroyed the communities which were the strength of Merseyside. An understandable bitterness grew as political decisions were made without recourse to the social consequences. The result: a militant left-wing backlash which combined with those who felt an ethnic isolation or victimisation.

Initially, Peter had little thought or concern that those with whom he was conducting business at Granvilles were the 'haves' of society, believing that his work would assist in reversing the decline in the social fabric of the city he loved. His involvement in property speculation would, in his view, raise standards through investment, and by transforming derelict areas into either smart property or pristine office developments, the city would benefit. Those he did business with were the city's elite, with a substantial concentration in the Jewish community, flowing from contacts with his former boss, Rubin Granville. However, as the 1980s approached, he began to have gnawing doubts about the changes they were making.

Peter had felt sufficient concern to prompt him to say to Rubin in 1979 that his clients were taking historic property and creating soulless replacements. He argued that they were removing what could be turned into affordable housing for the poorest and replacing it with commercial property or building developments – for a handsome return, but at a social cost.

Rubin reassured him that the money generated would filter down into the community. "We see an opportunity, Peter, and seize it, making the city better and thereby attracting investment. From this, more money floods into the local economy, resulting in more rates and more income for local government. That should feed into housing, but politicians need to be pushed to pay for the development of affordable property. If we can assist with the process, we should not deny what I call 'the natural way': those who have will create opportunity for those who have not. This is where socialism cannot work, because it gives money without direction to where it may not be deserved or needed. Opportunity is always far better created where those reaching for it feel they have contributed to it. We need to help those who have not by empowering them."

Peter was reluctant to accept Rubin's 'natural way', yet could not deny that opportunity had lifted him into a successful, rewarding career and a move to a smart house in Long Lane, Wavertree. His parents were full of admiration for his achievement and his new centrally heated home, looking in awe at its modern kitchen complete with electric oven, Formica units, and cushion floor that looked like real tiles. There were fitted wardrobes in the main bedroom, with sliding louvred doors and brass handles. The latest shadow-pile carpets covered the floors, whilst his bedroom boasted a cream carpet which his parents had never seen the like of before. He had invested in a VCR unit, miraculously allowing him to record one TV programme whilst watching another. His mother Rose would spend hours at his home, catching up on *Coronation Street*, *Emmerdale Farm* or *Crossroads*.

Peter was not oblivious to his community and knew there were frustrations in the city regarding housing, jobs, and failures in inward investment. In 1981, a single event was to transform his fortunes, springing from a day and night of civil disobedience in Liverpool so severe that it rang alarms in central government.

The Toxteth Riots began in Liverpool on Friday 3rd July 1981, sparked by a single arrest which was handled a little heavily by Merseyside Police. Tensions were already high due to the frustration of the black community, the appalling state of the city infrastructure, lack of investment in regeneration, unemployment, and poor housing. This all combined with left-wing political distrust in the way in which the police were controlled. The tinderbox sparked, prompting nine days of often violent rioting, resulting in CS gas being deployed for the first time on mainland Britain outside of Northern Ireland.

Prime Minister Margaret Thatcher was only too sensitive to the 'power of the people', having witnessed the miners' strike of the early 1970s which had brought down a government of which she was a member. 'The Iron Lady', as the Russians had nicknamed her, was not to be trifled with. Despite her bullishness and an innate refusal to countenance compromise, she had foresight and knew she needed to show a rapid government response. Alarmed by the prospect of spreading civil unrest, she appointed Michael Heseltine, a well-known 'big hitter', to tackle the issue and create a symbol of resolute government action.

Like many others in Merseyside, Peter was not surprised by the riots, although their ferocity shocked him; he understood without condoning them. He could appreciate the frustration of communities who felt abandoned by a system that appeared to favour the privileged. Liverpool was not naturally a city in which communities took to the streets in civil unrest. It was a home for many who had been displaced from all over the world, giving it a richness of cultural diversity cemented by a fierce pride. Merseyside had a strength of spirit which had radiated and rippled out from the city centre in the 1960s. Merseybeat music, comic talent, growing new businesses, trade unionism, and Liverpudlian humour had contributed to a proud, renewed identity – a great deal of which, by the summer of 1981, had been lost.

On Tuesday 7th July 1981, the phone rang in Peter's office, and his secretary announced that the call was from the Environment Minister's office in Whitehall. Peter accepted it with some surprise, and then heard a faintly familiar voice saying, "Mr Chainey, this is Michael Heseltine. I am informed that you are well versed in local real-estate issues. I would like to invite you to assist me in exploring ideas for redeveloping Merseyside. I want to involve you in a consultation meeting I am having tomorrow with local people on the ground. Our task will be to formulate a plan for the regeneration of Liverpool."

Peter readily agreed to the meeting, but felt he was being summoned, such was the minister's natural authority and charisma.

The following day, Peter attended the Town Hall on High Street, which, uncharacteristically, had police outside, standing either side of the entrance. He was asked to wait in the vestibule, and calls were made before he was ushered up the ornate red-carpeted staircase, above which impressive plaster ceiling cornices added to the grandeur of the first-floor access. He was challenged near the top by the statue of George Canning, a 19th century Liverpool MP who became Tory Prime Minister, above which hung a portrait of the Queen – just to put him in his place, Peter thought. He recognised the figure of Chief Constable Kenneth Oxford standing outside a door with some other people, some of whom he thought he faintly recognised.

They were ushered into a room which, Peter later learned, was known as the Dining Room. Sitting at the head of a series of tables positioned in a rectangle was a surprisingly youthful figure in a fashionable double-breasted striped suit, sifting through papers. He gestured to all to sit. His wavy light brown hair with its customary centre parting was iconic, but the command of the room Michael Heseltine showed was total. "Gentlemen, we have got something very wrong in this city. My job is to find out what, and to put in place the mechanism to put it right. I will not execute what is required, but those of you with foresight and strength of purpose will. I am here to facilitate, but you… you are here to deliver. I want a single sentence from each of you summarising why the dreadful scenes we have witnessed have taken place."

There would be no argument or dissension in the room; merely answers to questions Heseltine would ask. No wonder, Peter reflected, that the press had nicknamed this powerful man 'Tarzan'. No one present was in any doubt as to who was in charge that day. He fixed each speaker with an icy but genuinely interested steely gaze, his benign appearance and smile belying his alertness to the task. Peter listened to the answers to the minister's question, given in turn, including "A failure to invest in the city", "An isolation of the working class from the privileged elite", "A decline in inner-city culture", "Poor policing with institutional racism", and "Unemployment and no prospects for the young", all of which seemed to him to be lacking in positivity.

When his turn came, he stood up and said simply, "This city deserves to retake its strength from our unique character and identity as witnessed by our music, culture, history and architecture. All we need is investment to enable the city to develop and modernise. We just need to be given the opportunity."

He was hardly aware of the "Hear, hear" uttered quietly by the minister.

The meeting was over in ninety minutes, surprising all, but Heseltine called it to a close, announcing that he would be touring key areas of the city that day. He stated that it was time for a change not just in attitude, but in the real way actions were taken by those in power locally. Stressing that he wanted to listen, he was determined to put in place measures which would transform Liverpool from the dock front to the suburbs. Afterwards, he detained Peter briefly and asked for his view regarding investment to regenerate the docklands, which were in serious decline. He was keenly interested in Peter's success in transforming derelict sites, slums and buildings into attractive investment returns. He asked Peter to give him a written briefing on target areas for improvement, but instructed him to keep his submission concise and precise in its conclusions, "And preferably, the initial brief should be no more than two A4 sheets."

Within a week of doing so, having completed his task in a couple of days, Peter was invited to join the task force advising and spearheading an investment programme for urban regeneration. From that moment, his business became linked with the new investment strategy in Liverpool, acting as consultant advisers to the government, and reporting directly to Michael Heseltine. The minister wanted local involvement in leading every step towards regeneration in an investment strategy he would organise. Areas were targeted, and Peter was not discouraged from using the knowledge he gained through confidential discussion to benefit his business. The minister was interested in action led local leadership involvement requiring minimal briefing other than to be shown there was priority being given to achieving the objective. Peter was in the extraordinary position of seeing where the investment might be directed, and hence, had the opportunity to direct his attention to land and property in these areas. His contribution not only benefited the city but allowed his business to grow far more rapidly than he could ever have envisaged.

He jumped at the chance to help redefine investment in Liverpool, seeing it as his duty to make a lasting contribution; he led teams of business visitors around the city, highlighting areas targeted for redevelopment. The initiative soon gathered momentum, attracting more inward investment and transforming the inner-city areas, As his former boss Rubin pointed out to him, "Remember, Peter, what I told you: this is the natural way, where the haves create opportunity for the have-nots. You are part of the process and your success is well deserved, my boy." Whilst Peter could not deny the euphoria he felt at the growth in the business and the impact of his new role, it was not without some unease.

Since their reunion in 1975, Peter had spoken regularly with Jonas, advising him on progress with the investment plan until, in February 1977, they concluded the final transaction. Jonas wanted to hold on to the properties and land he had secured without injecting further capital. The communication between them then dwindled to an exchange of Christmas cards, and the odd fax from Peter advising Jonas of his portfolio valuation, which would occasionally prompt a light-hearted response such as 'Hey, Walter, keep up the good work.' All were realising higher valuations than projected, increasing Jonas's respect for and trust in Peter.

Five years were to pass before Peter spoke to him again. In March 1982, his receptionist called through to his office announcing that there was "a fella called Jonas on the phone with an accent like J. R. Ewing", referring to a major character in the TV series *Dallas*, then dominating prime-time viewing.

"Tell him you are putting him through to Cliff Barnes," Peter replied sardonically, joining in the themed banter.

The voice was as familiar as ever. "Hey, is that Walter Cronkite? it's your buddy from the Deep South, and I got a proposition for you."

Peter smiled at the nickname Jonas had used regularly in communications since their last meeting eight years before.

This time, it was a different and daunting proposition, but not without excitement. Jonas sought risk capital for a property investment in the United Arab Emirates to match his own. "Hey, man, since they screwed us in with increases in oil prices in the Seventies, those Arabs now have more money than they know what to do with. So, here's the deal: we build, and they buy or rent. I think it's pretty simple even for a cowboy like me. They ain't got the skills, but hell, we have. We can double our money almost as soon as we make the land purchase. Goddamn it, Peter, it's just too good to miss, and you did fine good with me in Liverpool so I wanna include you, and I'm gonna make you an offer you can't refuse."

He invited Peter to inject capital into his venture, and guaranteed that if the return was not positive within a year, all monies would be repaid. He needed an input of $3.75 million US, equating to £2.5 million at the time, to match his investment. Peter was excited by the prospect, relishing the thought of expanding into overseas investment. He knew he could raise the capital from property security that Granvilles owned, but he had a business partner and the deal would leave the organisation exposed financially. He promised to give it some serious thought, hesitating as his old need for security battled with the thrill of developing a new venture.

"You got six months, Peter, then I'm gonna haul your ass out of that little island you inhabit and show you the wider world."

Jonas then departed from his proposition and asked his old friend, directly but gently, "You heard from Jenny? Hey, she has a daughter now, but every time I hear from her she still talks of you. I had a letter from her just a couple weeks ago, and in it she said, 'Tell Peter, when you speak again, that I will never forget him or our Covenant.' She enclosed an envelope for you, askin' me to send it on as she ain't got your address. I been meaning to contact you to check it was OK. I guess she's been thinking some. I got her letter here. Should I open it and fax it, buddy?"

Peter wanted to say no and walk away, because as he often told himself, that was then and this was now. Anything more would compromise his peace of mind, and yet he knew he could not walk away. He asked Jonas to fax him the letter, surprised by the adrenaline he felt. His heart began to pound as he sought to rationalise his thoughts. For a moment he stared out of his office window, across towards the docks and the River Mersey beyond, wondering what it was that seemed to drag him back to Jenny again and again. Those days were no longer relevant in his present life, yet his thoughts were drawn back there so often.

He heard the ringtone of his fax machine behind his desk, and could almost hear the thumping rhythm of his circulation as the paper tightened and began a slow creaking and whirring as the copy began to emerge. He could not bear to watch until he heard the end-of-message beep. Turning slowly, he warily pulled the paper to his chest and sat back in the large leather chair behind his mahogany desk. *God, if she could see me now*, he thought, *she would wonder what's happened to me and everything we believed in.* Sighing deeply with apprehension, he leant forwards and read.

> *My handsome ice-cream boy,*
>
> *Forgive me, because I swore to myself I would never try to contact you again, and maybe this is the coward's way as I will not have to face you as I did on that beach all those years ago and speak these words directly. I guess that is the lawyer in me finding a means to justify the way; thank the Lord for Harvard, which taught me how to justify almost anything.*
>
> *In my work, the truth is often hidden in the words I use, but right now I cannot hide from what I so want or need to say to you. I have never forgotten you; you're still within me, and our words come back to me as I write this. My God, Peter, I have a wonderful daughter now, a lovely home and a good career, and I guess I should be happy but I still look back wistfully to our time together. Do you? I hope so – they were beautiful days and we were beautiful too.*
>
> *Remember this: "I Covenant to you that I will hold you in every season of my life: my wonder at the spring, my sun shining in the summer, my forever in the fall, and my warmth in winter." I still hold those words dear and I regret nothing.*

Yet, I do regret… or perhaps I do not. I cannot turn my back on my words or the memories that still light up the shadows of my life.

Peter, I want to remember you now, as then, and hold that intensity within me always. I ask why, but I have no answer to the question, and I know my dreams may be impossible but, despite reality, I am still Wendy cherishing and seeking my Peter Pan.

God bless you always.

Your hippy chick – forgive me, forever,
Jenny

Her words washed away the years; the waves of intensity flowed over him and he fought back the tears that filled his eyes.

For days, then weeks, he dwelt on how to reply, failing to find the right words. It was not that he did not want to, but he knew that it would require him to venture out from the sanctuary of security into a dream.

28

Corruption

In March 1980, Jenny was again invited by Professor Wostenholme to join him in Washington, but this time it was a very personal invitation and one which he said she must keep strictly confidential. "My colleagues in Washington are very interested in your progress, Your Honour," he stated in an earnest tone, "and this visit may be the most valuable to you in securing the best contacts with the most influential people."

Shortly afterwards, she was visited by a young man who announced that he was from the State Department Bureau in Washington. She was asked to sign a pledge of secrecy regarding her visit, reminded of the seriousness of any breaches, and informed that this was a matter of national security before he gave her a business-class ticket. On the day of her trip, the same man picked her up, drove her to the airport and escorted her directly to the departure gate, having informed her that she could bypass normal check-in.

On landing at Washington National Airport, she was redirected by smart, dark-suited men away from the other disembarking passengers to a gateway through which she was ushered and then met by a smiling Professor Wostenholme. He guided her to where a large black limousine awaited. They exchanged light conversation but he spoke little of the purpose of the trip, other than stating that it was of grave importance to her future.

They were whisked down Pennsylvania Avenue, and Jenny's heart beat with excitement as she recognised the White House railings so close. Noting her interest, the driver pointed out, "That's where everything is decided, ma'am", before they swept right onto 19th Street, and back up Virginia Avenue to the front of the Harry S. Truman Building housing the State Department.

They were clearly expected, as the second the car halted, a member of the military opened her door, and snapped to attention as they alighted. She was experiencing both anticipation and an almost childlike excitement, though she attempted to appear cool and dignified. They walked to the doors of the building, which were held open for them to pass, Professor Wostenholme absently nodding thanks to the immaculate marines who stood at attention as they entered. They were ushered through a long marble hallway, past ornate columns and wall friezes that reminded Jenny of a vast Roman palace. At one end of the expansive corridor, a classical painting depicting angels leading a scholar of antiquity projected colour and a sense of majesty. Then they were taken through more ornate doors to an area which alternated between lofty windows and marble walls flanked with long velvet-covered seats on either side. Statues lined the imperious walkway, adding more grandeur and a projection of power.

They sat for a short while, during which Professor Wostenholme turned to her. "The next minutes may decide your destiny, Jenny. I am profoundly delighted to share this time with you, and I will support you all the way."

Another man in uniform approached, his chest covered in medal ribbons. "Hey, Professor, good to see you again, sir, and this will be the M/s Baronio we have been hearing of." He extended his hand and was introduced to her as Major General Herbert Marshall, US Marine Corps. "May I call you Jenny, ma'am?"

He continued without waiting for a response. "I just need to deal with a little protocol here. You are about to meet a very important man, but he likes to be treated directly and without ceremony, although respect is paramount. Although he is not officially in office, we still treat him with a courtesy that no other enjoys and, therefore, you are advised to refer to him as 'Mr Secretary'. Please speak frankly and answer any questions he has with honesty, no matter whether you think he would like to hear it or not. He does not suffer fools gladly, and if he perceives that you are misleading him, the meeting will be terminated immediately. Oh, and good luck."

He then led them to double doors upon which he knocked; a rather archaic action, Jenny thought, in such opulent yet officious surroundings, clearly at the heart of power. The anticipation was becoming almost unbearable as she still had no idea whom she was meeting or why. Wostenholme had insisted it was imperative she both accept the invitation, respecting the national security reasons for the secrecy, and travel without question to the Capitol based upon his assurances.

The doors were opened, and two attendants allowed entry before exiting themselves. A long floral carpet led past book-lined shelves to the most enormous polished desk she had ever seen, upon which was an equally imposing gold eagle. An elaborate crystal chandelier added to the palatial majesty, but it was the waiting figure beyond who captured her attention. Henry Alfred Kissinger was standing, hand outstretched, with a broad, engaging smile. She had seen him on TV many times, and recognised him immediately. Nervously, she stepped forwards, ushered by Leo Wostenholme's reassuring arm.

Kissinger's handshake was strong and somehow resolute; longer than normal, yet reassuring. He was shorter than she had imagined but she could sense his utter authority and command, combined with an uncompromising aura of power. "My dear Leo, this is the protégée you spoke of; so young, yet full of wisdom, I believe. Ms Baronio, please sit."

Drinks were brought in on a silver tray, with a choice of tea, coffee or sparkling water, a glass of which was poured for their host.

The former US Secretary of State was dressed in a dark grey three-piece suit and sombre maroon tie. His wiry, whitening hair with its traces of deep chestnut appeared somewhat unwilling to lie down, suggesting something of his formidable reputation for an implacable yet unconventional nature. He looked at Jenny very directly, his thick glasses accentuating the intensity of his blue eyes. "We have watched your progress with profound if not admiring interest, Ms Baronio." His German accent somehow warmed his opening, and the words were spoken deliberately and with pronounced eloquence. "I believe you have ideals and concerns about our country, which is good. Please enlighten me with these, and how you would change the United States?"

His directness was not a challenge to her, but an invitation, she felt, and her response was honest but delivered with respect. She momentarily recalled her meeting three years before with the Deputy Director of the NSA and decided, as then, that complete sincerity mattered and was needed to do justice to her deeply held beliefs.

"Sir, our country is divided by inequality, riven by injustice, and stifles both civil and human rights. We attempt to change the world but forget to look at ourselves and our own injustices. We fight wars without judging consequence, and forget to promote or prepare for peace in our hurry to impose our way on others. Are we not like the British, pursuing imperialism instead of upholding our Constitution? I believe those in power need to understand that the people require to see change not only inside the United States, but outwardly in the promotion of peace and understanding."

She paused as Kissinger leaned forwards, and wondered for a moment whether she would be ushered out by guards. Yet his words were non-condemning and welcoming.

"Then you and I, Ms Baronio, are united, despite what you may have read or surmised. It was I who pushed for peace in

Vietnam, and, although I detest self-promotion, it was I who attempted to return my Nobel Peace Prize after the failure of those peace talks. I have promoted detente to rid the world of nuclear weapons, a policy which I still advocate, and as for China, I opened the dialogue for others to continue. Our legal system is already under reform to ensure racial equality. Progress is being made, but it takes time to carry opinion, which we need to do because – unfortunately, some might say – we are in a democracy."

He paused, taking a sip from a glass of water before sitting forwards and placing his hands on his knees; relaxed yet imposing. "We need strength and conviction in the exercise of power; then, with patience, preparation and pragmatism, we can make decisions the people may never have agreed to or voted for. The question must surely be how we reach those decisions and who we select to make them. We need an elite who can guide with principle which ensures that power is not abused. Your ideals are laudable, Ms Baronio, but achieving your aims requires an element of what might be termed… practicality. Leaders come and go, but direction is, I think, critical irrespective of whoever is in power." His slow delivery gave impetus to the strong, sturdy voice that she had often heard, albeit dismissively, when he had appeared defending the policies of the Nixon administration.

Her own conviction emboldened her response. "Mr Secretary, I hear your words but what can we see to encourage support for a system that in my view has failed its founding principles? 'All men are created equal', and yet the US government is guilty of repression of the individual, interference in foreign countries' affairs, a refusal to recognise certain basic civil rights, and bellicose words to inflame the might of the Soviet Union. I am no communist, but we are embroiled in so many parts of the world, propping up regimes that hardly warrant our support and that fail to meet basic standards of human rights. Look at Nicaragua, Angola, El Salvador, Haiti, Afghanistan, Chile and South Africa…" She faltered as she realised her words had ended more like an outburst.

"Your passionate exuberance is a credit to you, Ms Baronio, and is much like my own after I left Germany in 1938. Do you think we supported Adolf Hitler or even dared to criticise him openly after his attacks on Jews? Expediency allowed my family to escape because we waited until the moment without making ourselves heard. That same expediency I have applied throughout my life to achieve what otherwise may have seemed impossible. We must embrace realpolitik as a weapon to defend us from too much idealism, which ironically can stand in the way of change. I have learned patience, which may be anathema to you as a young idealist. Occasionally, I have even been known to compromise. For you, change needs or is part of revolution; for me, I learned how to achieve change through study, speaking and writing; then I realised change needed power for it to be achievable. My own power followed, but only after making waves inside what you would call the establishment."

He paused to take another drink of water, then leaned forwards, looking at her with an authority and directness she knew would brook little argument. "Achieving change is not about insurgency, but persuading others to reach the conclusion you have already committed to, and by whatever means – within reason – for the greater good. Ms Baronio, you were brilliant academically and now you are in a position where you might reflect upon this question. Should you seize opportunity with the goal of change, but make idealistic sacrifices in the pursuit, or retreat in the face of realism, refusing to make the compromises that those of us in power have to make?"

There was a knock, and staff appeared with more trays of tea and – curiously, considering the gravity of their discussion, she thought – a variety of cookies.

Professor Wostenholme interjected. "Jenny, we respect your views and we are all on the same side here, recognising that we need change; but to succeed we also need the energy of young crusaders like you. You will recall the cases that I have briefed you on. This was in the interests of protecting the integrity of our nation, with the aim of a better future which I know you support. Change is slow but it is coming, Jenny, but we want you and others like you with our movement."

Henry Kissinger arose slowly from his seat and beckoned her to the windows. "You see, all of this – these majestic buildings, this Capitol, this great nation – can only survive if the elite amongst us band together to help others reach the inevitable conclusions that democracy will then support. It is power exercised by the people for the people, but forged through greatness of purpose and a realisation of destiny." He took her hand in his, and she sensed his sincerity in the gesture and a zeal matched by the sincere look with which he again fixed her. "I am out of government now, but play a key part in our world and its future, helping others to reach those inevitable conclusions. We want you to be part of a new order which crusades for a better future in which your ideals may take root, but with a chance of flourishing; not withering in the darkness of corrupt power, as happened in the country of my birth under the Nazis. The benefit to you will be immediate and the success of your future career will be assured. All we ask for is your commitment to a cause which favours the brightest amongst us to make the decisions. You can help us seek a more noble destiny where we can disagree, but from mutually assured respect for each other's intellect and integrity."

He placed a hand on her shoulders. "Ms Baronio, we are already established and have in our midst the most capable, influential people of this time from all over the world, including former and current Prime Ministers, Presidents, business leaders, academics, writers, and even Civil Rights leaders. We are the makers of the future, but our strength lies in those who will govern our tomorrow. If you want to be part of this, then you can make a difference. If you do not, I invite you to leave the room now, without any rancour from me, and no more will be said of this meeting." He returned to his desk, and began sipping a cup of tea like a benign, paternal grandfather.

She looked out of the tall windows over the vast array of grand buildings which signified the exercise of democracy in the United States. She felt privileged, proud, overawed and humbled. She realised that seizing this opportunity could help deliver her vision of a future fuelled by the idealism which had inspired her past. She turned, walked towards the two men and, with a awareness of destiny, shook the hand of first Dr Kissinger and then Professor Wostenholme, who hugged her.

As they left the building, Wostenholme said, "This day will stay with you, Jenny, and will herald what is to come." The words were prophetic. Up to that point, as a lawyer, she had learned to accept expedience in the pursuit of truth and justice. After all, she represented a system of adversarial law in which all had the right to a defence even where guilty. She often reminded herself of the Constitution and the Declaration of Independence, the lofty words of which she felt she was upholding:

We hold these truths to be self-evident, that all men are created equal, that they are endowed by their Creator with certain unalienable Rights, that among these are Life, Liberty, and the pursuit of Happiness.

Her role in justice lay in upholding the rights of the individual against the oppressor. Her ideals were still there; they were the principles she had stood up for all those years ago when she had marched on the Pentagon. Then, she was a rebel, but now she could make real changes from within.

In August 1982, Peter was summoned to the Liverpool Council offices to address a meeting on the progress of the investment strategy. He approached the event somewhat warily, as he knew that there were deep divisions in the Tory/Liberal coalition running the city. He was also conscious that into this mix of volatile politics had entered a growing left-wing group known as

Militant Tendency. His father had warned him, "They are a real shifty lot with dodgy intent. They are after helping no one but themselves, hijacking the working man to support their half-arsed militant aims." Peter respected Jim's deeply held convictions as a lifelong socialist, and was dismayed that an organisation whose main aim was to seize power via an internal 'revolution' had taken root in the Labour Party.

As he approached the Municipal Buildings on Dale Street, he looked upwards to the proud Victorian clock tower capping the majestic and imposing structure, its spire and Doric columns announcing its imperial importance to visitors from all over the world. This had been the centre of the city's administration. From the base of the tower, he noticed a banner hanging crookedly from the windows with the slogan 'Better to break the law than break the poor.' With some trepidation, he approached the entrance, anxious to say nothing to affect the uneasy peace which Michael Heseltine had brokered with local politicians.

He was ushered into a long room with whitewashed walls, on which were tall wooden frames displaying the fading names, dates and positions of previous leading members of the council. At the head of the room hung a portrait of a distinguished-looking man in Victorian robes edged with crimson, identified by Peter's young guide as William Henry Watts, who had served as Mayor of Liverpool in the late nineteenth century. He was asked to wait by a long table before being joined by a number of other delegates, officials and councillors. He recognised Derek Hatton and Tony Mulhearn from Militant Tendency, who were quite well known from their many appearances on TV. Peter noted sardonically that their smart suits were hardly representative of the working man they purportedly represented. The local Chief Constable, Sir Kenneth Oxford, was there; together with local Labour MPs Eric Heffer and Robert Kilroy-Silk, and Shirley Williams for the SDP.

Peter kept his talk brief, avoiding areas of political controversy, highlighting his aims of establishing effective targets for regeneration and the allocation of inward investment. A hostile line of questioning from Derek Hatton followed, during which Peter was asked if he was a government lackey and if he was aware of the current mismanagement of funds by the ruling coalition. Both questions were slapped down by the chairman, but Peter did stress to the assembled that he was his own man and that he had been selected to assist as the owner of a Liverpool business with knowledge of local issues. There were more considered questions regarding the involvement of a locally represented voice in the decisions being taken. Peter reassured them that there was constant consultation with local government, but felt uncomfortable knowing that much of the decision-making took place behind closed doors.

After he had completed his presentation, he was thanked and left the room. As he walked down the corridor, he was approached by a tall, thin, grey-haired man smartly dressed in a dark suit, striped tie, and white silk pocket hanky. "Mr Chainey, can I ask you to join me, please?" It was more a command than an invitation, uttered in a strong, authoritative voice.

He led Peter into a small office, where he bid him sit before settling behind a simple modern desk. He opened a file, on the front of which Peter was intrigued to catch a glimpse of the lion-and-unicorn crest and the words in red, 'HM Government – Confidential.'

"Mr Chainey, my name is Major Richard Ashford, and I work directly for the Home Office." He offered his outstretched arm, to which Peter extended his own for a brusque handshake. "Amongst other duties, my department is responsible for matters of national security, and that is the reason for this meeting. I work for government at the highest level, and my department assists with strategic planning to avoid any threat to our nation – or, if you prefer, to protect our freedom and democracy."

His voice was clipped and unwavering. Peter noticed he had an unblinking stare, which he found somewhat disconcerting.

"Mr Chainey, I will not beat around the bush: this city is facing a threat from political militant infiltration which directly affects the security of the United Kingdom. If I have spoken out of turn, or you are uncomfortable with the statement I have made, then please leave now and we will terminate this meeting. I can assure you there will be no repercussions, nor any record of this conversation." He paused, raising his eyebrows as if to give Peter the opportunity.

Major Ashford took papers from the file before continuing. "You are assisting government with the inner-city regeneration project; a job in which you have excelled, which has not gone unnoticed in the highest quarters. Please understand, Mr Chainey, we take no sides in political matters; nor do we take orders directly from government. We only become involved where issues may affect national security."

There was a knock on the door and a man entered, also dressed in a suit, somewhat bizarrely placing a pot of tea and cups on the table before leaving. Peter watched with some amusement as the major poured the tea with all the grace of an English butler.

"Our concern is to ensure that the development of this area is targeted in the right way, which requires careful selection. You recommend to government areas for development – building projects, dockland improvements and the like. We have compiled a confidential list of approved investors – in which, I hasten to add, your company is included. Your job, if you accept, is to ensure investment is carried out in the interests of the area, assisting those listed in making successful bids on developments that you will select. The militants are intent on seizing the initiative for political gain; many of them with mischievous and destabilising intent. State ownership of property is a dangerous aim, and the militants, if not checked, could cause catastrophic consequences for this area and for democracy."

The major stood up and walked to the large window, staring at the familiar skyline of the Roman Catholic cathedral and the

River Mersey beyond. "I fought for this country in the war, Peter," he used his guest's Christian name for the first time, as if to add sincerity to his words, "in Belgium, France, and later Italy, before ending up stationed in Germany at the end of hostilities. I am old enough to have seen what extremism does, whether on the right or the left. It takes hold of people, conquering reason, leading to fanatical support of an ideal no matter how perverse. Obsessive dedication to a cause justifies the worst actions, and I witnessed the human cost of that. My job is to apply pressure by whatever means on those making decisions to ensure the investment strategy is not compromised. Your job is to put the right people forward for selection. With your help and influence, we can more easily control the direction of development. Again, I give you the opportunity of leaving, which will in no way affect your position or the work you do."

On his return home, Peter studied the list of approved investors, among which were a number of names he recognised both locally and nationally. There was no heading to the document, no purpose identified, nor indeed any identification as to the source.

29

An Arabian Dream

Monday 23rd August 1982

Peter had driven to the office early listening to the comforting broadcasting voice of Brian Redhead on Radio 4's Today program yet the news gave reports of a deteriorating situation in the Persian Gulf which certainly put into question the joint investment endeavour with Jonas Barnier. The region was becoming destabilised by Saddam Hussein's Western supported Iraqi forces drawn up against against those of Iran under the regime of Ayatollah Khomeini. He began to reflect on the reason why there was any need to expand and what it would do for him. Despite all he had achieved he wondered at the definition of happiness or contentment as he felt he had not reached either. He recalled a former time and the books in which he had sought solace and escape. He had wanted more from life then, and, despite all that was happening around him, he wanted more now.

To all on the outside Peter was successful, one of Margaret Thatcher's finest. He found it hard to associate himself with the fashionable terms of the day as a "yuppie" (young urban professional), or a "Yumpie" (young upwardly mobile professional) yet that was exactly what he was. He had taken himself from the humblest beginnings to become the head of a growing, highly successful business, for which he was recognised and respected by his peers. Yet he questioned himself about his good fortune and how much resulted from entrepreneurial skill, how much from luck, and how much from his connections.

As he sat at his desk, Peter mused over the previous year. He had never been so busy, even working through the day of the wedding of Prince Charles and Lady Diana Spencer in July 1981. The whole country had been mesmerised by the event, yet there had been further violence on the streets of Liverpool the night before. It had been a dramatic period. Months before, he had gone down to the docks to watch the departure of ships scheduled to join the task force sailing to the Falklands War. He had been summoned to help government, given unprecedented influence over inner-city development, the freedom to invest and benefit from his position, and yet, despite his meteoric success, he felt uneasy. This did not feel like the purpose that had once motivated him when, a lifetime before, he was studying for his degree.

Peter knew he was becoming increasingly cynical in his outlook, despite still craving the idealism of youth. He argued with himself that he could justify virtually any of his actions because they were performed for the greater good of his city. Part of him felt guilty, yet he was achieving real success for Liverpool: a proposed regeneration of the dockland areas, more rebuilding – and, he had to acknowledge, a growing income. Dealing with approved investors could be justified by increasing the prosperity of the area through stable sources rather than bringing in the social ownership proposed by the more militant inside the local Labour Party, which, in any event, seemed to be at war with itself.

Just up the road in Crosby, a new political party had made its mark, with Shirley Williams enjoying a landslide victory in the

November 1981 by-election. Peter had watched in admiration as the Social Democratic Party, or SDP, voiced opinions which embraced reasonableness and practicality. Their opposition to Margaret Thatcher's unswerving yet admirable dogmatism seemed far more attractive than Labour, which had suffered catastrophic demise under the leadership of Michael Foot, who encouraged the more militant in his party at the expense of electability.

When the call came through from Jonas, Peter's secretary was, as usual, chirpy in her introduction. "I have J. R. Ewing from Dallas, Texas, sir; shall I put him through?"

It was a welcome relief to get the call allowing escape from his work which had become increasingly stressful. There was also a worrying issue within Granvilles. In recent months Tommy Wilson had begun flexing his muscles, asking for formal management meetings with minutes recorded, and a more active role in management. Peter had placated him with the role of liaising with new clients to establish appropriate investment packages – at least it had the benefit of easing his own increasingly busy schedule. In between government meetings, he was keeping his eyes on the many opportunities which were falling into his lap from 'confidential internal briefings' deciding whether Granvilles or another selected party should be involved.

The slow drawl of Jonas's friendly voice was welcome, liberating him from his thoughts. "Hey, how's that cool property billionaire? You own that damned city yet? Better save some for me, boy, because I hear tell there is big opportunities there now since they appointed you a supremo. Hey, Peter, I still got an opportunity knocking and I want to share some ideas with you. The Emirates, man, they are one cool investment in one real hot place. The United Arab Emirates is full of unspent money and those guys are breakin' outta tents and into high-rise. There's plans in place to make it an ultra-modern metropolis and a vacation destination like no other, and specifically I'm talking Dubai, man; a gold mine being created out of the desert. I want you in on this and you will just thrive, my old friend; but hey, if making a fortune don't appeal, I'll get off your back and just get back to my ranch."

Jonas asked Peter to fly out and meet him in Dubai the following week, stay for just three days, look at the prospects and return. It was, Jonas assured him, "An investment with no risk and staggering potential."

Five days later, Peter was walking across the parched tarmac at Dubai Airport, catching sight of Jonas waving from the balcony of the modest, unimpressive castellated terminal building. As he flew in, he noticed that the airport was surrounded by sand and long straight roads stretched away to buildings rising from the desert in an almost haphazard manner with tracks in the sand leaving the roads heading in all directions. The overriding impression was uninspiring but, as the aircraft prepared to land, he had seen a metropolis sprawling across the wide open desert peppered with buildings, some high-rise, and a landscape dotted with evidence of development.

Clearing security with a brief showing of his passport to a smart-uniformed Arab in a startlingly clean white *shemagh* (traditional Arab headdress), he was rapidly through and shaking hands with a broadly grinning Jonas, who sported a generous Stetson over a safari-style jacket and light pants.

"Hey, man, let's get somewhere civilised and down a bourbon."

Peter expressed surprise at the mention of alcohol, and was rapidly cured of his ignorance as Jonas explained.

"Man, they are unlocking this place for us corrupt Westerners to create a playground for the future. It's what they want, and they are permitting alcohol to be sold all over. You don't buy it in the streets, but in bars and hotels. Even some of the Arabs have a snort, sitting behind tables with a shelf: coffee on top, snifter beneath. This place is rockin' and rollin', Mr Cronkite. Come on, I'll take you to a pub."

They drove out of the airport onto an unimpressive highway, and Peter's first impression was the lack of vegetation. No green, just a vast expanse of sand, and more sand. "That way is Sharjah," Jonas pointed towards a long, straight road intersecting theirs, "but we don't want that; they got the same desire to expand, but nowhere near the same money."

Peter was astonished at the contrasting variety of vehicles on the highway; some without doors, or with wings missing, exposing the wheels, whilst smart Mercedes would occasionally speed past. They reached a crossroads, and to Peter's surprise, Jonas turned off the highway and headed across the desert sand towards another road a short distance away. Then, as they swung back onto the carriageway, he was informed that this was common practice. There were no barriers, and so shortcuts across 'country' were the norm.

They came to a few buildings close together, with a shop, a small hotel, and a further building on the end which looked like it had been added as an afterthought. They climbed out of the air-conditioned Datsun into the searing desert heat, which hit them like an oven door opening. "Welcome to England," Jonas said surprisingly as he opened a door on the end building, ushering Peter in.

The blast of cold air was the first thing he noticed as he entered, and then he stood open-mouthed in surprise. They were standing in a traditional English pub, exactly like those he frequented back home, with a bar, beer pumps, bottles on optics, and Watney's Red Barrel beer mats competing with Worthington E spread across the dark, round tables. There was even Guinness on tap under an iconic poster saying, 'Guinness is good for you.' The contrast between desert heat and homely pub could not have been greater but, as Jonas explained, it had become a haven for expats. Two whiskeys accompanied by beers began to relax them and ease their thirst.

Their conversation flowed easily as they caught up on the changes in their lives since their last meeting, with the fortunes of both on an upward curve. It wasn't long before the inevitable subject arose. "Hey, Peter, do you ever think about Jenny? I hear tell she is not in a happy place personally, but hey, that girl moves in high places."

Peter replied that he now thought of it all as a long time ago, and that, after thirteen years, it was time to close the door. "You know, Jonas, I often think about those days with a 'that was then' view, as so much has changed, including me. I'm told I'm a yuppie, and I just see my future rising further and further, escaping from my roots. My Filofax is my boss now, and, in answer to your next question, I am in a relationship but nothing too serious, not yet; well, maybe not at all."

Peter had not developed any kind of romantic relationship since 1969. His energies had been concentrated on his studies, and then his career. He had no time for discos, or nightclubs as they were increasingly being called. He tried them but his experience was that they encouraged no social interaction other than the physical. There was no talk because of the deafening music; only girls dancing in a circle around their handbags who laughed at those who tried to break in. It was, as he often said, a self-perpetuating club of women who could take comfort from the company of their peers in the mocking rejection of male attention. Peter had no inclination to seek rejection or humiliation, although he recalled being grabbed for the customary last-dance snog, when men were picked like trophies by those who had avoided them all night. Men and women dressed to the nines sought to look cool by pretending they did not wish to be noticed.

A few meaningless flings had been his '70s experience, which he was happy to forget. He felt he could do better, but had no time to develop meaningful relationships. He preferred to spend weekends, if time was available then, in his new interest of playing golf, which also helped develop a network of business contacts. In the week, he had little space to fit in any dating; working long hours, attending meetings, and setting up investment plans. He tried not to look back, although he still sensed Jenny like a siren seeking to turn his head, and secretly dreamed of running back to her… but that was then, this was now.

Earlier in the year, he had met a girl at a business dinner dance. They began going out, but although he enjoyed being with her, the magic was missing that he had felt in his experience with Jenny. Barbara was twenty-one and slim, with long, straight dark hair, wide green eyes and dusky looks to match. She applied her eye make-up generously, accentuating her iconic early 1980s appearance, which Peter thought could easily have fronted *Vogue* magazine. With a love of fashion, she always struck a vibrant note, changing her look from day to day, teasingly relishing the attention she drew from male admirers. She possessed a flirty good humour and a typical fast Liverpool wit which Peter found challengingly irresistible. She worked for Woolworths, or 'Woolies', on Church Street L1 in administration but, when required, would also take her turn on the tills. She loved Peter's ambitious spirit, which she found exciting and so different from others'.

Despite Barbara's wish for more, Peter was not prepared to commit because his primary focus was on driving Granvilles forward. Thus, he told Jonas that he could no longer look back; nor be sure where his relationship with Barbara might go.

They finished their drinks and headed out into the blast of heat which took Peter's breath away, and then they were back in the car, heading for the Dubai seafront. As they approached the centre there were more and more buildings, many with long stretches of sand in between. They turned onto a wider boulevard with a dual carriageway, and the first unusual feature Peter noticed was a strip of grass down the middle, constantly sprayed with water. Jonas chatted excitedly about the development that was taking place. "Goddamn, Peter, these guys want to turn this place into a rich man's playground; the doors are wide open for business but they kind of prefer the Brits to us, and that's where you come in."

They drove down the seafront, where busy cranes witnessed building development, then veered right towards the Creek, in which Peter could see antiquated Arab boats, or dhows, along a ramshackle series of moorings. "One day, this will be a prime marina for the super-rich," his enthusiastic companion announced.

They turned into the smart car park of the Sheraton Dubai Creek. Jonas tossed the car keys to a smartly dressed concierge who reminded Peter of those he had once seen at the Dorchester in London when he stayed there with Rubin on a business trip. It did appear, however, somewhat incongruous to see a man in uniform with a top hat in central Dubai.

They walked into the smart, cool marble lobby, complete with fountains, and passed a number of British expats, judging from their voices, en route to a far corner where an Arab was standing, waiting to greet them. He was dressed in a long robe (*kandora*) with neat embroidery down the upper part. His *shemagh* was neatly folded close to his head, and he sported an immaculately cut beard. He extended his hand with a broad, welcoming smile as Jonas introduced them.

"Peter, may I introduce Mr Amer Hasan bin Sunil Al Maktoum? Almost a prince, I believe, and beware, because he is related to the royal family here. On this one occasion, he will permit you to call him Amer."

This prompted a laugh from them all, which immediately broke the ice.

Amer turned to Peter, looking at him directly. "*As-salāmu alaykum* ['Peace be with you'], Mr Chainey; it is an honour to meet one held in such high esteem, especially by this man, whose credentials are a matter of some conjecture from time to time."

Jonas responded, to Peter's surprise, in Arabic: "*Wa alaikum assalam.*" ('Peace be with you,' expressed as a response.)

Amer spoke in very clipped English with an almost imperceptible accent. "I believe you are from Liverpool; a place I visited many times during my education. I was at public school in Lancashire for five years before studying Economics at Oxford.

Sad to say, I am not a prince, but my family is directly related to the ruling Maktoums."

They sat in a corner of an enormous, carpeted lounge-bar area, above which towered a wall down which water flowed from many floors above. An enormous portrait of the ruling Sheik of Dubai hung on the panelled wall close by, whilst that of the Sheikh of Sharjah was hung a little lower, as though reflecting the hierarchy.

"We can talk of families and much besides, but I am, perhaps, unlike my countrymen in that I like to get down to business. I am very well connected, Mr Chainey, as are you according to my inquiries. No, please." He waved away Peter's affected polite protest at the accolade. "Er, Peter, if I may address you so, your reputation in Liverpool precedes you. You are achieving much, but a little bird tells me that you are, shall we say, well informed from the right sources. Here in the UAE, we do things in a very similar way, for it is who you know, always, that matters to us, plus respect, which must be shown; but only where it is due."

A waiter appeared and drinks were ordered, including a coffee for Amer. Three bourbons were delivered with it, one being placed by the waiter on the shelf below the surface in front of their Arab host.

"First, you will need introductions, which I can arrange; then you will need to look at the investment options available. I have prepared a list which we can peruse. All of these should deliver a return in ten years, of a minimum of four times your initial capital input, but we expect considerably more. Then, of course, we need to consider the small matter of my fees. As you will understand, my connections are impeccable, not least because of my family. If you decide and I endorse the introduction, the decision will be made and confirmed by a handshake."

The afternoon wore on into the evening, by which time it was clear that Peter needed $3.9 million US to join a venture into which Jonas would invest an equal amount. Amer would take a 25% share but without the capital injection; his input was influence.

The idea was simple: to buy up land on which they would erect both offices and apartments on what was to become a fashionable district on Sheikh Zayed Road. They would also develop a further centre in Kuwait to capitalise on the staggering growth potential from released oil reserves, financing a massive and ambitious city-development programme. Amer also had strong ties in Kuwait for whom he could vouch.

By 10pm, their overall strategy had been agreed. It was time for outline agreement. As Amer said, "We only need a handshake to seal this; in this country, that is all that is required. We are men of honour."

Peter knew he could raise the finance but that he might have a job to convince Tommy Wilson when he returned home. However, when Jonas looked at him with a raised eyebrow and a wry grin, he simply nodded.

Late into that night, Peter and Jonas sat drinking on the balcony of Peter's room at the Hyatt Regency overlooking the Creek. The temperature was still in the eighties but, unusually, there was a wind blowing, which made the evening bearable. They sat near the sliding door to gain additional benefit from the overworked air conditioning, which emitted cool air into the unrelenting heat of the night. As the Bollinger champagne flowed, they reminisced about the summer of 1969; only thirteen years before, yet seemingly a lifetime ago. Both laughed at their relatively short haircuts now, which they would never have entertained back then. Peter still wore his halfway over his ears with a slight curl at the back as his hair ran over his collar, whilst Jonas had opted for short sides and a squared-off cut. He had long ago shaved off his long sideburns, whilst Peter's beard was consigned to memory except when he was reminded of it by the odd photo.

True to form, however, Jonas lit up a joint, taking one of the deep, hissing inhalations that Peter remembered so well. "Holy shit, Peter, we are in our thirties and I don't feel grown up yet.

Seems like I was lucky – in the right place at the right time, man – but I still love the idea of taking a whole summer out. I guess I'm not sure I got the courage no more."

Peter's memories of that year were always overshadowed by what he had walked away from, and the person who, even now, remained within him. "I try not to dwell on those times too much. I have an expression: 'That was then, and this is now.' I'm in a different place, and I'm a very different person, but, just sometimes, I miss the person I was. I've worked my backside off, Jonas, and my business brings me stress, but better things in life have resulted from it; like, things my parents couldn't have dreamed of."

Jonas thought better of mentioning Jenny, other to than to say, quietly, "You know, I still keep a connection, if you ever want to seek out someone."

They laughed about the music, the TV shows, and their clothes back then, recalling flared trousers, flowery shirts, neckerchiefs, and tie-dye T-shirts. "Jonas, when are you going to grow up and stop wearing a bloody cowboy hat?" teased Peter in his dry Merseyside accent. "You look a right twat!" His friend looked at him solemnly as he slowly emptied the contents of his glass over Peter's head.

Two days later, back at Granvilles, Peter summoned Tommy to his office. As he walked through the door, Peter again recalled Rubin's words of warning. He realised that he needed to be careful in the way he communicated with him. Tommy was dressed in a pinstriped suit with wide lapels, looking slightly flamboyant for the office. Peter knew his 'partner' was enjoying the fruits of their increasingly successful venture, to which Tommy contributed little. His tie was untidily knotted and, noticeably, despite his suit, he wore odd socks under shoes that could have benefited from a good polish. He had steel-rimmed glasses, wore his hair unfashionably short, and projected little expression from his face.

Tommy Wilson was not a naturally warm person, but nurtured a suspicious, self-protective nature resulting from the disapproval he had constantly received from his parents throughout his life. He was never good enough, and never would be. Having failed his eleven-plus, he'd gone to comprehensive school, which infuriated his parents. They had made their money from building a number of grocery shops across Merseyside, starting with a little help from their own parents. They had sold out in 1976 to Asda, a new, expanding retail business buying out shops to create supermarkets. Their reward was enough money to retire and live a life they had never dreamed would be possible. Tommy had been brought up in a strict Catholic family in which discipline did not give respect, but demanded it. He resented those who 'had', and yet had no time for the have-nots either. He felt somehow cheated out of his inheritance and a career path by his parents, who had sold all before he could be given a chance to showcase his abilities. However, in 1981 they had supported his investment in Granvilles, recognising and compensating for their son's frustration.

Peter motioned him to sit down. "Tommy, as you know, I have tried to steer a careful course in the investment profile of this firm. We have taken decisions prudently, but I decided that it is in the best interests of the business to widen our portfolio and look for global opportunities. You will be aware that I have just returned from Dubai, but it was not just for pleasure. I saw incredible openings for fabulous development opportunities. This is desert – sandy, open spaces where there are no planning issues and no regulation other than keeping the elite informed; spaces which are soaking up the resources of those with an eye for this. The country is awash with money, and businesses there are flourishing, attracting global attention."

As he expanded on his investment strategy, the figures, and the massive return projections, he was little prepared for the reaction. "Peter, who the fuck do you think you are? I have allowed you to run this place, make the big decisions and take all the credit. You have committed *our* assets to the tune of nearly 4 million dollars and you didn't think to involve me. Is that because you thought I was a quiet irrelevancy, a nonent? Well, wake up, because this is the last time, mate. I want this organisation changing into a limited company where my rights and those of the business are protected. You thought you could run this place and get me to rubber-stamp it all; well, in your dreams. I own 50% of Granvilles, and from this point, you will respect that and respect my position as an equal shareholder."

Peter was utterly unprepared for the outburst, but equally a touch relieved that Tommy had not attempted to reverse his decision to pledge the business's assets. After their meeting, as his partner left, somewhat testily, he recognised that he was no longer in charge of the way forwards, but constrained by the input of another. He thought that there would unavoidably come a time when there would be conflict.

Although changes were forced upon Peter, effectively compromising his control of the business, he began to enjoy some of the fruits of his career. His lifestyle was changing to reflect his achievements. Despite his reservations, Barbara moved in with him in 1983, and they took up residence in a smart four-bedroom detached and gated property in Woolton Park. The house had a gravelled drive, satisfying one of Peter's childhood aspirations from reading of such houses. In the areas where his family lived, driveways did not exist. Those he had seen in other parts of Liverpool belonged to the chosen few; a choice his family could never exercise. Barbara and Peter's relationship suited them both, providing them with a relaxed life. She liked to play the domestic 'housewife' role, and his absence for long hours gave her the independence which she also enjoyed. They talked little of a future because they were content with their present, clearly augmented by his fast-growing income. They had spoken of marriage but it was not a priority for them and, in any event, so many of their friends were now living together. For Peter, life felt comfortable, with a secure home in a pleasant environment. He had a foundation on which he could build his future, cocooned from memories and the past he tried not to remember.

30

The End of a Beginning

April 1982

Although his former boss was officially retired, he took an ongoing interest in the business and Peter was grateful for his continuing calm advice in the massively changing if not turbulent times which followed the riots of July 1981. They met on the first Friday of each month at the Adelphi Hotel for a two-hour lunch complete with large brandies.

"I need to meet you the day before the Sabbath, dear boy, so that I can pray for you the day after," Rubin had said jokingly. He was enthusiastic about Peter's new role, becoming animated as he likened it to the rebuilding of Hamburg, to which he had directed both funds and investment after the war. It was at these times that they engaged in reminiscence, which Rubin loved, drawing on his experiences to direct his vision of the future. "You need a woman, my boy, to warm you, care for you and manage you. You should look back, maybe, to the person you once made a Covenant with. Never let time destroy what lies within your heart, but maybe let your heart seek what it truly yearns for. A

Covenant is, after all, a promise, is it not? And yet… I sense you still run from yours."

In 1983 Rubin suffered a severe, debilitating stroke, but he retained a fierce sharpness of mind, often analysing Peter's investment strategies and offering invaluable, incisive advice. Although in the months following his stroke his mobility was compromised, he always remained upbeat. He would enjoy making points with some drama using a silver-tipped cane, upon which he was increasingly reliant. "I am like an English aristocrat, no? I think I will soon be knighted, perhaps." Peter watched his mentor suffer from increasing health challenges whilst retaining a positive resilience. "I have lived a good life, although many might challenge that, but, on the whole, I have enjoyed every minute," he said with a smile at one of their lunches in 1986.

Rubin repeatedly returned to the past, urging Peter to make contact with Jenny, even just as a friend. He told him that, if they had truly loved, he should not hide from the experience, insisting that Peter should, at least, remain true to the principles he had once had. "You know, Peter, when I was young in Hamburg, we saw dreams fading, but held on to a light that was our guide in the darkest times. Most of my family were lost in the concentration camps, but I refused to lose my identity or the beliefs we had shared. Sometimes, my boy, the ideals of the young are more honest than the pragmatism of the old."

After Peter assumed control of Granvilles, he had become closer to the man who had asked him, ten years earlier, to tell him about his life. No longer his boss, but one of Peter's most valued friends, Rubin remained his mentor, giving advice that Peter would recall throughout his life. Still, despite their commitment to their monthly meetings, these became less frequent in the latter half of 1986. Rubin would send last-minute apologies, saying that something had interfered with his plans, and when they did meet, Peter would, with silent pain, notice changes in the man he so respected and loved.

Rubin did talk, however, with excitement about his seventy-eighth birthday, to which he was to invite all those business colleagues and friends "still remaining" who were important to him. He invited Peter to be his VIP guest. Peter received the invitation by post in December 1986, inscribed in Rubin's handwriting, 'To my apprentice, my confidant, and the one who is like the son I never had.' He attended the celebration in formal dress in February 1987, at the iconic Adelphi Hotel. The dining room was full of men in evening suits and bow ties, many wearing the kippah cap reflecting their faith. Laughter was everywhere, and Peter recognised and was greeted by many he knew from his property ventures. "Mr Chainey, you thief, you have robbed me of so much – but to good result, eh?" drew laughter from one group, as he was ushered to where Rubin sat at the head of a long table.

"Aha, *ben sheh-lee* ['my son']," he welcomed him. "Come, come, my guest of honour, and honoured I am to welcome you as an important man now in this city. Soon, maybe, I'll be calling you Sir Peter."

The dinner was attended by many dignitaries Peter recognised, including, he noted curiously, some of those who were on the far left of the political divide running Liverpool City Council. Despite their militant 'working-class' credentials, they were most definitely dressed as upper-class gentlemen, he thought ironically.

Peter was sat by Rubin, on his right side, and introduced enthusiastically as his successor to the other guests. Rubin gave a speech in which he related many experiences, finishing with, "And now, an important addendum to my long life. I met a young man ten years ago who has become like a son to me, and yet now he has embarrassed me. He has taken my business to a place where I regret selling it to him, and he dares to show up here when he is becoming more successful than I. For those who do not know him, this is Peter Chainey. It is he, my friends, who is helping to rebuild our wonderful city with the help of Mr Heseltine. So treat him well, and he will advise you where to invest, eh?" He raised his glass in a toast – "*L'chaim*" ('To life') – echoed by all in the room, giving Peter an ovation which he acknowledged, nodding in humble appreciation.

Afterwards, they met privately in the Titanic Lounge, where Rubin heaved himself up from his wheelchair. He bowed, then flung his arms around his protégé and, with tears in his eyes, addressed him. "My treasured friend, my son, the world is changing for me, for both of us. I have two things I must say. Peter, I will again counsel you to reach for the love I once denied myself; remember your promise, your Covenant." He confessed that he had never forgiven himself for not contacting Rebecca again after his family had fled Hamburg. When the war was over, he could not bring himself to inquire because, he admitted, he was like "a coward frightened of what I would find. You, my dearest boy, have a chance to grasp what I did not. I left Hamburg in 1937, and was lucky to be given a home here and find a new life with Esther, though we could have no family. But, God forgive me, I wonder if I should have stayed with Rebecca or whether we would even have survived, and that disturbs me."

He collapsed in his chair and grasped Peter's hands, his words tumbling as though he could not say enough in the time they had. "The second matter which worries me. Please do not trust that Thomas Wilson, I beg you; he is not a good man."

They shared two drinks and smiled as their thoughts embraced, reminiscing some more before Rubin heaved himself from his chair once again. "*Shalom Chaverim* ['Go now in peace']," he said simply.

In the days and weeks following, Peter was contacted by person after person announcing that they were friends of Rubin, and that they were interested in talking business. A procession of appointments followed and he was in a position to both invest and attract investment in areas of the city he knew were ripe for development. All this whilst receiving reward from government for his consultancy work assisting with the regeneration of the city.

He spent less time with Rubin after the night of the birthday dinner. Peter knew the obvious – that his dear friend was becoming weaker – yet they had long chats over the phone, during which Rubin would question him, and prompt thought through his endless stories and experiences before giving advice. "You must develop an adversarial mind, Peter, but hide it behind geniality which, even if genuine, is a wonderful cloak as you size up your business adversary. Victory is assured if you hold your nerve, and as I always taught you, your lowest never is, nor your highest the most."

Their last meeting was in April 1987 when Rubin invited Peter to his home; a place he had never been before, despite their close relationship. Driving down Sandown Road in Wavertree, he turned in, through tall iron gates with impressive gold-tipped railings either side, to a large white-fronted Georgian property. He announced his presence by means of a brass lion knocker on the polished black arched doors, and was welcomed in by a man introducing himself as Mr Granville's assistant before being shown into a reception room.

Shortly thereafter, he was greeted by a tall, yet slightly stooped lady, with thick, wavy silver hair worn proudly in a confident set style suggesting regular visits to a hairdresser. She was strong in her bearing, yet clearly not in the best of health. "Well, you must be young Mr Peter Chainey." She smiled. "I am Esther, and I have heard much of you from my Rubin. I am sorry not to have met you sooner, but I always stayed away from Rubin's business. You have brought him so much happiness, and yet now he is very unwell." She grasped Peter's hand. "He has had another stroke and is very weak, but he is so looking forward to seeing you; he says to me that you are his missing family. He lost so much of himself when many of those closest to him stayed behind in Hamburg. They were never seen again after they were transported to the camps. He still lives with guilt, despite me telling him we could do nothing more."

Peter felt her emotion, and sensed her pain. There was such power in the deeply expressed anguish about the past that he had come to recognise in so many Jewish families he had become involved with, yet a strength of pride too.

Esther slowly led him upstairs to a panelled door on which she knocked, entering to reveal Rubin propped up in a large bed. Dressed in a padded maroon dressing gown, he was studying a copy of the *Liverpool Echo*. His monocle was, rather comically, wedged in his eye; whilst his pince-nez glasses hung around his neck.

"Ah, welcome, dear *mensch*; I am sorry I never got up." He extended his hand to Peter. "You remember we had good times, did we not? I treasure what we have shared together. Peter, my boy, there are greater times awaiting you, but please, oh please be careful because where there is money, there is jealousy; where there is success, there is envy. And, my son, you have sadness within you, and I know why." The old man's hand gripped his. "You still have that Covenant and it is not revoked. Peter, do not run as I did all those years ago. *Mein Gott*, it has haunted me all my life, leaving someone with whom there may have been much, much more."

They talked of old times and new, with Rubin castigating those in power for no longer having conviction. He warned Peter away from politics, reminding him of those he had seen at his birthday dinner. "Do not believe I did not see your look of disdain, which, incidentally, I share, but those men hold the keys to our future. We must seek out opportunity to create a better tomorrow, but our insatiable need to secure our lives must not lead us to turn a blind eye to injustice. I saw them, Peter, with their designer suits and watches. They are not Marxists but greedy men hijacking a philosophy for self-gratification in the spotlight of status. They are like men admiring a Ferrari; they covet the image of something they have always wanted and could not have, and therefore, they despise it, but embrace the symbol of it."

Their discussion dragged long into the late hours until Rubin began to close his eyes as he spoke. Both men felt a connection and a deep unity. As the night drew to an end, Rubin held Peter's hand in his. "*Shalom Chaverim*, my protégé; you are, without doubt, one of my greatest friends but, more than this, you are the son I would have wished for. Remember pragmatism, but use it wisely lest it corrupts you. It is so very good to talk." He sighed, and Peter shook his hand in both of his as Rubin slipped into rest.

He descended the stairs, on either side of which classical statues adorned alcoves in the walls like a Roman palace; a testament to Rubin's success and his love of art. Accompanied by Rubin's assistant to the open hallway, he was led back to the reception room where he was met by Esther. "I am losing him," she stuttered, "but he will always remain within me, and within you, I think. He has enjoyed your fellowship so much. You have represented the family he lost, and you are his hope for the future."

Four weeks later Peter attended Rubin's funeral, fighting to hold back the tears at losing someone as close to him as anyone had been throughout his entire life. Never before or again would he meet another he could trust so much. During the funeral, he was astonished at the array of people from all walks of the community gathering to pay their last respects, including the Chief Rabbi in traditional Jewish dress; Eric Heffer, the local firebrand Labour MP; the Chief Constable; some of those from the city council Rubin had warned Peter about; and very many with whom he was already doing business. He felt he had lost a father and life guide but, despite his overriding grief, he also felt a deep gratitude to the man from whom he had learned so much.

Afterwards, Peter threw himself into his work with a renewed, ruthless commitment, thinking less of his mentor's words about the Covenant, and more about pragmatism.

31

Thanksgiving 1986

Jenny had kept Jonas informed about her life in letters, updating him on her marriage, her home, her career, and the birth of Maria. Jonas had also kept the communication going but they had not met up since he had left her and Peter on the shore of Port Grimaud beach in 1969. Peter knew that they stayed in touch and that the connection remained between them. He felt a strange comfort in that lifeline remaining, as he initially thought of it, though his own contact with Jenny had faded.

Jenny was not sure quite what drove her but, on a whim, she rang Jonas in the November of 1986. She was feeling euphoric and enlightened by global events; yet she also knew, hell yes, she was goddamn lonely. Sure, she had her daughter whom she loved so much, and yeah, she had Braden, but he really just wasn't what she had dreamed of. Life was good, but a little empty. In her heart, she knew, yet tried to deny, that she wanted to make a connection with something which would evoke awareness of what she had lost, and that something was Peter.

She felt an impending sense of history flowing from world events around them, which were generated by idealism and change she had not seen since the 1960s. Prime Minister Margaret Thatcher and President Ronald Reagan were talking in the media about doing business with Mikhail Gorbachev, the leader and General Secretary of Soviet Russia. A summit between the President and the General Secretary was fixed for late 1986. This was all the more remarkable because, only three years before, Reagan had publicly referred to the Soviet Union as "the evil empire". Gorbachev was already being seen by many, including Jenny, as a visionary peacemaker. The times were momentous, inflamed by a reborn optimism for freedom. The TV showed scenes that she had never imagined, heralding a new era of world peace which struck such a chord with her youthful aspirations. Human rights were being openly and meaningfully discussed between the leaders of East and West, with reports in the media of commitments being made by Russia. The nightly news bulletins seemed to become ever more dramatic as the momentum of global understanding and change gripped the public imagination. No one in the Reagan administration expected or was prepared for, nor were the public then party to, Gorbachev's incredible, if not staggering, proposal to eliminate not some, but all nuclear weapons within a decade. Perhaps equally unbelievable was the fact that Reagan embraced the idea.

Professor Wostenholme had called Jenny at her office, in a most unusually animated state, on October 1st 1986. "Jenny, this call has never taken place, but my God, I had to call you; you of all the people I know. The news here is way out of sight, as you might say. This is what you struggled for coming to reality; it is what justifies my faith in the importance of the office of President as an institution… my God."

Jenny tried to steady him. "Leo, what in God's name is going on? Have you been taking something? Tell me calmly what is happening?"

Wostenholme excitedly informed her that, just over one week before, Mikhail Gorbachev had called the President, stating that he wanted to propose the total elimination of all nuclear weapons to herald a new era of understanding and peace. "This guy means business, Jenny, and I wanted you to know that all you hoped for years ago may come to pass. People like you have helped strengthen our resolve, based on a foundation of strong government and leadership. That is the power of your work and mine. God bless you, and God bless America."

Even Jenny's daughter Maria was caught up in the atmosphere of historic change with the thaw in relations between the two superpowers. At eleven years old, she was already quizzing her mother about current news events, and had asked what getting rid of the nuclear threat meant for the world. Jenny was pleased with her daughter's interest, which reminded her of her own in the early 1960s. She recalled her idealism back then as she had embraced the dawning era of love and peace. Jenny and her daughter were close, enjoying a deep bond. She delighted in watching Maria's development, and in the sharing of ready smiles and easy laughter that flowed between them. Maria had a mischievous nature and a spontaneous, open humour. She changed the words of well-known songs to deliver a naughtier meaning, going into fits of giggles at the reaction, or cleverly mimicked others' voices or expressions. She was outspoken, but Jenny recognised in her daughter her own strength of purpose, and encouraged her self-confidence. She delighted in Maria's emerging awareness of natural justice and global affairs, which contributed to their bond. Their relationship sheltered Jenny from the growing isolation she felt in the family home.

It was seventeen years after her Summer of Love, and suppressed thoughts were breaking through. The TV news images of Reagan, Gorbachev and Thatcher renewed and inspired Jenny's dormant sense of purpose. It was as if a light had shone on her life, re-exposing her consciousness, contrasting her career with the honesty of her earlier beliefs. In that October, she lost the argument with the logical side of her being, which had told her to turn away from what she now chose to do.

She was at her walnut desk in her smart New York office on Eighth Avenue, surrounded by the symbols of her success. These included citations from the rich and famous, a Victorian silver inkstand on her desk presented to her by the then Governor of California Ronald Reagan, and signed photographs from other leading figures. All were dominated by a painting on the wall of the Founding Fathers, given to her by Professor Wostenholme on her election as a partner in the firm. George Washington and Thomas Jefferson held the Declaration of Independence outstretched, whilst John Adams, Benjamin Franklin and Roger Sherman stood behind. Washington was reading the Declaration to some assembled soldiers, adding strength to his stature and historic conviction. On the opposite wall were personally signed photographs of Gerald Ford, Jimmy Carter, and the present incumbent, Ronald Reagan, each obtained for her by the ubiquitous Professor Wostenholme. On the left side of her desk was another photograph in an ornate silver frame, in which a thoughtful Henry Kissinger appeared to be looking at her in a slightly whimsical manner. His arms folded, dressed in a grey suit, he looked straight at her; was it a challenging look or a warm smile? Across the bottom, he had written, 'Always, we must consider expedience for the greater good. *Yishar koach.*' ('More power to you.')

She thought about conviction and her career, and all that had gone before in 1969 and afterwards. Where were her ideals? What was intact from those heady days? How far had she travelled, and at what cost? Then, glancing up, she stared at the infectiously engaging look of Ronald Reagan smiling down at her, thinking that he was partially to blame for how she felt now. World events were bringing back focus on the ideals that had been her foundation in her teens and early twenties. The words Mikhail Gorbachev had used, 'glasnost' ('openness') and 'perestroika' ('restructuring' or reform) had become bywords for change; for tearing down the old and rebuilding a new future based on peace and understanding. 'Love and Peace', she recalled with a smile, had been written on walls once, and worn on T-shirts as a symbol of power to a new generation.

It was at that moment that she picked up her bag and left the office, returning a short while later with a card upon which she began to write, attempting to suppress a naughty giggle. Minutes later, she found herself holding back tears before picking up the phone and dialling a Texas number. "Hey, Jonas, it's a blast from the past," she said, after intriguing the receptionist by saying, "Tell him it's a hippy he knew in the summer of '69."

The long, drawling voice she heard next was unmistakable despite the years. "Hey there, hippy girl, reveal yourself – is it Joan Baez?"

Their greeting was warm, stirring in them both so much from their meeting seventeen years before.

"Wow, my God, darlin', you some kind of hotshot lawyer mixing with all those high-headed folks we regarded as straights back then. Shit, I'm just a poor guy trying to scrape a living outta DIY."

Her good-humoured response was, as ever, typical of one not used to being outgunned: "Mr Barnier, you are one goddamn rich son of a bitch with, the last I heard, fifty stores and owning a sizeable chunk of England."

They shared much, talking over old times and the directions in which their lives were going. Jonas sympathised with Jenny as she explained her growing frustration and loneliness in her marriage, although Maria was her wonderful respite.

"Hey, you should see me take out my life on the poor bastards I cross-examine in court. I've changed, Jonas, and I wish I hadn't, and I guess it hurts me to admit it."

He listened, then gently countered that maybe they were all changing with time, and perhaps that was not all bad. He told her how Peter had changed from the happy-go-lucky guy she had known into a serious property speculator and developer. He wore expensive suits, drove a nice Jaguar, and had a high-living lifestyle. "He's become a real business executive type, Jenny; somethin' I could never quite get the hang of. I open my stores and folk come in and buy hardware, and then others do the hard part. Peter, wow, he is a serious player with his property empire and he works for the government too; I done a few deals with him and he impresses me, but he is a long way off from the beach of Port Grimaud, playin' guitars on starlit nights. We reminisce and laugh about the past, but he gets a little sad when we speak of 1969 so I guess we seldom do no more."

"Jonas, I need a favour." She finally took the plunge. "I want to contact Peter, you know, just to remind him of who I was. Can you give me his address? Because right now, life is sort of like it was back then. We got real meaningful things going on out there with East meeting West and all this Reykjavik Summit stuff; it's like the ideals for which we fought are taking root. You know what really happened between Gorbachev and Reagan? I mean, heck, Jonas, it's just incredible. I'm trusting you on this, because my friends in Washington would stick me in Bedford Hills Prison if they heard what I'm telling you."

There was a whistle of anticipation from Jonas. "Hey, girl, tell me what's goin' on, because we all thought Reykjavik ended with some acrimony." He had seen the TV pictures of President Reagan giving a fairly brusque, formal handshake in parting from his Russian counterpart, in stark contrast to the optimism as they had met. The world's press had sensed that there was potentially something monumental happening, and that tectonic plates were moving to end the Cold War.

"You are not going to believe this, Jonas, but our President agreed to a proposal from Gorbachev for the total elimination of all nuclear weapons. I'm talking no more nukes, like, these guys were going to do what we wanted."

Jonas whistled with surprise. "So what the hell happened, if we were that close? My God, that would have been beyond awesome."

"We *were* that close, Jonas, but the Star Wars stuff wrecked it. Gorby wouldn't accept the US developing a space anti-missile system if both sides were giving up nukes." Jenny carried on to say that the affair had reignited passions inside her that had lain dormant for too long, and that she just wanted to reforge a link with Peter at a historic, evocative time. "We never said goodbye properly, we never broke our Covenants; we just faded away for all the right goddamn reasons, but for all the wrong outcomes."

By the time they finished speaking, almost two hours had slipped by, but that had only focused Jenny's mind more, turning a whim into a resolve. She never paused in the words she wrote, sitting in her office, but then she was hearing the surf on the shore close by, and feeling the soft, scented warm air blowing down off the Esterel Hills.

On the fourth Thursday of November 1986, Peter was about to set off for the office from his smart home in Woolton Park, his silver Jaguar XJ6 glistening in the morning sun. Barbara had left for work over an hour before to earn some overtime. The postman crunched up the gravel drive, whitened with the morning frost and glistening in the watery sunlight, and handed Peter an envelope with the iconic head of George Washington on the stamp. Puzzled, he ripped it open to find a card wishing him a happy Thanksgiving. He opened it slowly and felt the shock waves within as he read the words carefully crafted with flourishing loops in neat, straight lines.

Hey, Peter,

My Covenant is with you still, my tears right now belie the truth of my happiness in all we shared, and I savour the breath of life you breathed into me. For I still hold you within my secret places and will never deny this haven to you or to myself. I Covenant to you that I will hold you in every season of my life: my wonder at the spring, my sun shining in the summer, my forever in the fall, and my warmth in winter.

Remember your rockin' hippy chick forever, as I still yearn for your arms to encircle me once again, and seek you in my dreams.

Love and peace,

Jenny

He was riveted to the spot for a few seconds, feeling an aching chasm of loss, a denial he had hidden from; then he turned back to his door, wandering into his lounge, and sank into an armchair. A wave of deep sadness washed over him.

Suddenly, he was back in September 1969, reaching again for her hand. As he sat there, he began to reflect on what had taken his life from a place he thought he wanted to leave to a place he had not wanted to arrive at. He recalled their dread at the inevitability of their parting, from a time they lived their dream.

The thoughts that now haunted him were seldom visited as they caused him sadness, recalling his betrayal of love. He looked through his French doors onto the long lawn beyond, lifting his eyes to the trees, above which the grey clouds moved intermittently, blocking and releasing shards of sunlight that made his eyes flicker. His day ahead became less important as he sensed the dream he had once left for the rewards of the life he had fought for and created. Suddenly, he wanted to divest himself of responsibility, to run and not look back, to relinquish the discipline of his obsession with his diary. His beloved Filofax, clutched in his hand, with every section religiously entered binding him to his routines or meetings, now felt heavy, and he let it drop to the floor.

He began drifting, reflecting, and allowing his mind to wander back on a journey. He was in another place, his thoughts whisking him away from the cosseted comfort of his home to their time.

Now they were on the warm sand, her dark hair streaming as she ran teasingly away from his outstretched arms, tossing aside her clothes and diving naked into the waves. He was shouting at her to stop as they were too near open areas, but then he too followed suit, swimming strongly to her until she lay back in his arms. She was daring him to take her, her fingers encircling him there, feeling his response before diving away from him again. Their playfulness, so carefree, with little sense of anything but each other, had taken him to a place he had never again experienced.

Peter left his reverie and was back looking at his prize collection of original oil paintings; the winning horses from Aintree which stared deridingly, almost decadently at him from the wall. Why did he question himself so often about where he was when he was so successful? He was enjoying the fruits of his hard work with a successful business, and so much good fortune had become his since he had taken over Granvilles four years before. Yet, despite all that surrounded him in his smart four-bedroom home, he sometimes felt an unease he could not reconcile that he had neither reached his dream, nor lived it.

He looked again at the words in the card. Jenny's beauty, within and without, shone like a beacon, drawing him back to a time of happiness and freedom. *I was so young then*, he thought, *but I was also so aware of what life could give us.* He pondered whether he should respond, but then realised that she had given him no address and no phone number. The only way of contacting her would be via Jonas, but why would he? Why should he? He had never been good at instigating contact with people with whom he had lost touch. With a sigh, he decided that he would put the card with the papers he still held from so long ago, in a box tied round with ribbon but now in a trunk in his garage.

Suddenly, he could see her at the airport, as their arms let go of each other, and she turned, as did he, before they walked away, breaking free from the bonds of love to be bound by all that was so much more important... wasn't it? The question haunted him, searing his soul.

Where do you go to, my lovely...

He placed the card in the box and closed it, retying the red ribbon because, he told himself, he had to.

32

Marriage and Career

By the late 1980s Jenny's marriage no longer held any meaningful relevance in her life. She knew she had outgrown her relationship with Braden. He was condescending to her, never giving her convictions any credence other than to deride them, chiding her for her innocence. *Christ*, she often thought, *who the hell does this prick think he is, talking to me this way? I am protecting some of the most prominent people in the USA, and he has the nerve to question my mind!* Occasionally, this overflowed into a row when she hit back with a torrent of derisory words about his views, his short-sightedness and his shallowness. Then she would stop herself as she knew she sounded just like both her parents rolled together.

"There has to be more than this," she once confided in her mother. "Mamma, what makes you and Papa keep together? I wanted to love someone forever once, like in a fairy tale, but it never happened. Do you ever think you should have sought more?"

Gina put both her hands on her daughter's shoulders. "More – what more? *Dio mio*, how can you ask for more if you don't make it more? You must never expect more from a man, but only from yourself. Never rely on them, because they will disappoint and you will know you deserve better. Do not be asking me if there is more, but go seek it for yourself. If you do not, you become weak like me, eh?"

The slight rebuke was, Jenny reflected later, wise counsel, teaching her that it was in her own strength where 'more' lay, and not within the solace she thought she should get from a man.

Her mother pointed out that, whilst there might be some wonderful men in the world, Jenny should never surrender herself without keeping her strength and self-respect. "Allow the man to treat you well – *perché no? (why not?)* I have no time for the modern liberation ways of denying our sex. But being a traditional woman does not mean bending to his will as I have sometimes done. So, do not weaken, demand to be treated well and never tolerate anything less. If you do that then, like me, you may not allow yourself to wish for more." The contradictions in Gina's words were not lost on Jenny but, she thought, reflective of the different and changing generations from which their two separate perspectives had developed.

Jenny was strong and knew she had the confidence to rise above the shortcomings of her marriage. She and Braden rarely slept together any more, literally or in a sexual sense. He was uncomfortable sharing sexuality or expressing desire. The act, when they both permitted it, was perfunctory and dutiful rather than evidencing or reinforcing any emotional bond. Orgasm for her lay in the memories of Peter she held sacred and into which she would only occasionally allow herself to venture, amazed by the sensuality they evoked after such a length of time. How did he look now? What clothes did he wear? Was he in a relationship? Oh God, was she better than Jenny? Then she would stop herself, angry that she, a successful lawyer shrouded in the practicalities of mature legal argument, could allow such childish, tormenting fantasies to take over her mind.

Braden had felt increasingly uncomfortable from the time he recognised that their lives always seemed to have to fit

Jenny's agenda. He could not support her idealism either, which, although suppressed because of her position, still often surfaced, condemning the American way that he respected. Yet he saw a contradiction in her career in that she had become part of the edifice she had once wanted to bring down.

After the birth of Maria, they had drifted further apart when she did not play the traditional role of mother in the home as he had expected. They had disagreed over Jenny's surname, her career commitment, her principles, and the upbringing of their daughter. Communication became more strained, where there was any at all. Braden drifted into a heritage group which held weekend walks or visits to places of historical interest. This often took him away at the end of the working week, which Jenny loved. It was then that she could truly be herself, and share special times with Maria. Jenny and Braden's absence from one another gave a stability to their marriage that neither of them had the motivation to alter. The status quo was the easy option, plus Jenny was happy that this gave some security to Maria.

By 1990 Jenny felt Braden had become almost insignificant, and certainly, she felt none of the insecurities she had felt when she'd first met him. She had married for very practical considerations of stability, and, she thought back ashamedly, because it was easy, if not convenient. Still, at least his presence had enabled her to develop in her very demanding position at Latham Ellis Piper. Plus, he was not violent or demanding; merely a tad inconvenient to have around from time to time.

She immersed herself more and more in the very rewarding work which continued to flow from Washington, and which, in turn, transformed her income and her position. At forty years of age, she felt she was on top of the world, and very comfortable within it, apart from her marriage. She reached so many highs in her work and in her comforting bond with her daughter that her relationship with Braden no longer seemed to be an issue. However, she often still journeyed back to a distant place inside herself where honesty, openness and dreams played a much more prominent part.

The few close friends she confided in would tell her to get the hell out, but for what and for whom?

Her daughter had already developed a very independent streak, asking very awkward questions. Was it right that Maria should be asking her mother about her attitude toward the gay community? Heck, Jenny could not recall even knowing about that side of life at that age, but she recognised so much of herself in Maria's interest in modern social justice issues. Maybe, she reflected, she had just been naive.

By 1990, Maria was a fierce supporter of the Democrats, becoming an ardent admirer of Bill Clinton, who was already attracting much attention as a potential presidential candidate. Jenny was a touch concerned that her fifteen-year-old daughter had pictures of Clinton on her wall alongside Madonna, MC Hammer, Michael Jackson and Jon Bon Jovi. She could not see the relevance of the Governor of Arkansas assuming pop-star status; nor could she see relevance in the music of that era compared to the '60s, when it had all seemed to mean something. *Oh my God*, Jenny thought ruefully, *I'm turning into my parents.*

She was delighted to witness her daughter develop values, yet there did not appear to be the same purpose now in the young, nor the idealistic revolutionary fervour. The establishment that Jenny had once hated were back in total control. Ironically, that was her justification for continuing to do what she could to protect the government in a drive to bring about change. However, she missed the rebellion, the adrenaline and the hope that had once directed her life.

When she discussed Maria with Braden, as usual, he just did not get it. Braden was a Republican and, therefore, "a staunch supporter of America". He did not seem to appreciate that his statements often disenfranchised or excluded virtually 50% of the population. He did not analyse politics other than from a populist viewpoint, and had no time for those who sought radical change. Although Jenny had no political allegiance other than to an innate awareness of what she believed was right, she felt utterly removed from her husband. Her early mild annoyance at his failure to grasp any element of the beliefs or causes she espoused gradually, over the years, eroded into a dislike of him, and then contempt. She watched with sadness and anger as Braden argued across the dinner table with his daughter without allowing debate. He patronised Maria, leading to her running from the room in disbelief at his "racist, authoritarian, uncaring attitude".

Jenny was proud of her and intervened little, allowing her daughter to flex her political muscles and learn how to debate her beliefs. "Remember, honey, you need to understand the views of those that oppose you in order to win your argument. Get inside their heads and appreciate the reasons they disagree, and there you will find their weaknesses. I do it all the time in court."

One day, Maria turned to her and asked, "Mama, do you not think you betray what you fought for and believed in by doing what you do?"

That really made Jenny think.

33

Jenny's Questions

Maria announced proudly at the dinner table, in January 1992, that she was supporting the candidature of Governor William Jefferson Clinton for President. She knew her father would treat her decision with disdain, and guessed correctly that her mother would applaud her. "Hey, guys, I am nearly seventeen, so guess what – I'm volunteering to help bring this beautiful guy to the White House."

Jenny looked at her daughter with pride, recalling, with some irony, her own early idealism which had wanted to bring down the establishment.

"That guy is an opportunist," Braden retorted. "We got a strong President in George Bush; he proved himself under Reagan, and he has gained respect across the world as a patriot, businessman, politician and Vice President. As President he has paved the road to peace and nuclear disarmament, and kicked the Iraqis where it hurts. What has Clinton got to offer? He's weak, and watch the news, girl; there's someone called Gennifer Flowers showing what your man is: a cheap womaniser. He's just a backwoods Governor of Arkansas. Heck, he's only forty-five years old and has no experience. I think you need to get real, honey."

The ritual broadside was interrupted by Jenny. "I think I have more experience in these areas than you, Mr Trelawney, because I work with the White House. I have signed photographs from no less than four US Presidents, three Secretaries of State and, for good measure, Mikhail Gorbachev. You need to learn that democracy is not all about your view, but also about respecting those that disagree and celebrating the fact that they have the right to. You know what, I like our President too, but listening to Bill Clinton, well, it sounds like he's one breath of fresh air."

Braden stood up, dumped his napkin and walked out. Mother and daughter hugged one another.

"I am so proud of you, Maria," Jenny exclaimed. "You remind me of the person I once was; and you know what, hang on to all you believe and never surrender to pragmatism."

Jenny had been involved in resolving legal policy positions, working with the current President since he had been Director of Central Intelligence. She was intently creative in preparing legal arguments the administration or the President could use, dealing with the fallout from issues that could damage the institution or the individual. Two of those for which she was responsible had led her to question her own integrity. The first arose from a political mess labelled the Iran–Contra affair, and the second covered the US turning a blind eye to uprisings in Iraq appealing for help in the face of a brutal put-down.

The Iran–Contra affair was the first real issue that caused her to agonise about her work. She had briefed the Secretary of Defense, Caspar Weinberger, on a strategy for supplying arms to Iran in 1981 which might otherwise have been judged political suicide. The Iranians had only recently released American hostages taken from the American Embassy in 1979, and this had infuriated public opinion. A method of bypassing scrutiny was required, to which Jenny had contributed. The process was wickedly simple and, she proffered, entirely legal. The US should, through their connections with Mossad, the Israeli secret service, arrange for

Israel to supply arms to Iran, and then simply sell the weapons to Israel. All legal and above board, which was fine until Lieutenant Colonel Oliver North of the National Security Council used some of the covert monies resulting from the transactions to fund the Contra revolutionaries in Nicaragua. A leak from Iran resulted in the illegal funding coming to light in the press and an investigation by Congress. In 1986, Jenny was requested to begin preparing defence positions for senior members of the administration including, potentially, President Reagan. Damage limitation resulted in the Secretary of Defense being indicted, together with thirteen other administration officials – but not the President. The irony of being both one of the architects of the policy and the one tasked with resolving the issue was not lost on Jenny, but it was a realisation that brought no smile; simply weight upon her conscience.

Sometime afterwards, a courier arrived at Jenny's office announcing that he was from the CIA. He personally handed Jenny two packages. In the first was an antique silver inkstand with an imposing marble American eagle in the centre. On the front, engraved on the silver base, were the words, 'Liberty, Freedom, and Independence.' In the other was a large framed photograph of a smiling Reagan sitting at his desk in the Oval Office. Scrawled across the bottom were the handwritten words, 'To Jenny, with my sincere gratitude to a true American patriot. Best wishes, Ronald Reagan.'

In 1989, under the new administration of President H. W. Bush, she had worked to delay proceedings against those involved in the Iran–Contra affair until it was judged that sufficient time had elapsed since the scandal. Subsequently, in 1992, the President issued pardons, effectively ending an episode which could have resulted in fatal damage to the office of President of the United States.

The Iraqi insurgency issue in 1991 was one which really tested her conscience in that she implicitly felt that it was wrong for the

US to turn its back on people fighting against oppression in Iraq. The Gulf War, which had been fought to liberate Kuwait from an Iraqi invasion, was ending. General Norman Schwarzkopf, the five-star general leading coalition forces, had stated in a meeting with the President, which Jenny attended, "We can chase this bastard Saddam Hussein all the way to Baghdad, and get rid of the evil son of a bitch."

The President warned that chaos might result, and that oil supplies would be further affected.

The general had replied, "I fight and win a goddamn war and get defeated by politics and commercial greed. I hope you don't live to regret that decision, Mr President. Christ, imagine if we had left Adolf Hitler in power." He abruptly left the Oval Office, waving his arms in the air dramatically.

President Bush shrugged his shoulders, saying calmly, "He is one hell of a guy and a great American."

Over the ensuing months, the Kurds of Northern Iraq were brutally massacred by Hussein's military in a campaign which included mass execution to stamp out any disaffection with the regime. He also ordered massacres of Shia Muslims in the south of the country. Jenny had found the argument she prepared to justify America's refusal to become involved unjustifiable but, once again, it protected the presidency. Nevertheless, the statement was used that interference would violate the United Nations Charter by attacking the sovereignty of a member state. The old word 'expedience' had returned again to haunt her. She shied away from ever labelling her contribution as corrupt, but it had crossed her mind.

Half-truths and lies always resulted in a mess she had to clean up, and although she saw it as working for a greater good, a growing cynicism began to affect her. She questioned whether her role was really supporting the aims of the United States in its goal of world peace. She was often haunted by the words of Henry Kissinger, many years before, talking of the need to "embrace realpolitik".

She knew that democracy was a fragile driver of change unless the will to achieve it was exerted from a position of strength. However, the suppression of her ideals was a sacrifice that she often reflected on, feeling that she had lost the person she once was.

Throughout the '90s, she felt progressively disillusioned regarding her role, which increasingly included covering up not only many decisions made, but also clandestine meetings between powerful men and women from across the globe in both business and politics. The meetings or conferences were held in secret, and the organisation was known as the Bilderberg Group. Those involved included current and former holders of high office from many countries. Jenny came to understand that these were power-broking meetings during which global policy decisions were taken without involving the 'inconvenience' of democracy or debate. She was aware of the power they were exerting but was always told by Professor Wostenholme that they helped democracy find its feet and direction. Despite her misgivings, she allowed herself to be convinced that this was for the future benefit of mankind. Wostenholme was clear on this: "We need strong direction, Jenny. Nationalism has resulted in two world wars in living memory, killing millions, and this new order is helping to stabilise the world. Some of our greatest thinkers, politicians and strategists are involved. Past Presidents, Prime Ministers, business leaders and even royalty, all coming together for the global good. Men and women who have the experience of power are creating the politics of the future."

Jenny attended these conferences at un publicised locations and, sworn to secrecy, was amazed to see people involved she recognised from not only the United States, but across the world, including the Soviet Union. One figure stood out by her absence despite the influence she had wielded, and, when Jenny asked why the 'Iron Lady' was not involved, she was informed by Professor Wostenholme that she lacked the vision. She had scorned her invitation, turning away from "this ill-conceived venture", as she had apparently called it.

Jenny was reminded that subsequently, and surprisingly, Margaret Thatcher had been ousted from power in late 1990 in what could have been labelled a coup. "Hardly a coincidence, shall we say?" the professor said with a wry smile, putting his finger to his lips in a gesture of secrecy.

Those attending the Bilderberg conferences consulted with Jenny on the positions they might take on issues of national and international law. She had a brilliantly analytical legal mind, and even if she did not know the answers, she would find them, often presenting a strategy to overcome democratic obstacles. She began to seriously question her work, which increasingly involved handling matters that resulted from the misdemeanours of others.

34

The Unforeseen

2nd August 1990

Peter was awoken at 4.30am by the house phone, which was ringing incessantly. His tired mind was shocked into focus by what followed.

"Peter, it is Amer. I am in Dasman Palace in Kuwait City with the Emir's brother. My God, we need help." He sounded desperate. "It is unbelievable, but we are under attack. They are shooting at us from the air and on the land. They started in the early hours."

Peter was bleary-eyed, hardly grasping what was being said. "Amer, who is attacking you?"

Then he heard the sound of gunfire as his Emirati business partner stammered back, "The Iraqis; they are at the gates of the palace, God protect us. Peter, you have influence – please, my friend, tell everyone you know what is happening, tell the world, because people are dying here. Thanks be to Allah, the Emir has escaped, but we remain trapped. The city is on fire, we can hear screaming... We have many calls to make; I must go."

The phone crackled and fell silent. The sheer surreal nature of the call paralysed Peter for several minutes then he checked his Psion electronic organiser and dialled.

After a few rings, a brusque voice said simply, "Ashford."

Peter was shaking as he began to try to explain his reason for calling.

Major Ashford had developed a respect for him since their first meeting. They had occasional contact, during which Peter would consult on investments and those currently preferred for opportunity. On a recent visit to his offices Ashford had said, "You are performing well, Peter, and it has not gone unnoticed. The type of work I am involved with ensures that stability is assured and that we do not surrender to extremes. You see, Peter, we learned much from the 1930s when many of our elite succumbed to the temptations of communism, or indeed the seduction of the far right or totalitarianism. Some of my best colleagues from Oxford were later branded as traitors, and yet, you know, they were only doing what they believed was right. I want you to know that we recognise what you have done in this city, which is helping to maintain a healthy stability. For that reason, my people will protect and look after you as far as we can; but, my dear chap, you must play the game by our rules. You may call the special number I have given you if you are in any trouble." Despite the cold manner in which he normally communicated with Peter, he softened with a final parting: "We look after those that help us, and so you will always have a lifeline if you need it. That is our gratitude for helping your country. You will be surprised how effective my team can be, and we reward loyalty, so, if you are ever in a crisis, contact me." They shook hands and Peter felt an uneasy reassurance from the protection offered. He had never called the number until now.

"Major Ashford, I don't know who else to tell, but I have just had a call from the royal palace in Kuwait; they are being attacked by the Iraqis and their situation sounds desperate."

The major cut in brusquely to check Peter's source, then told him to say nothing to anyone until he heard back from him, which he promised would be within the hour.

Peter heard nothing for the next two anxious hours, during which he paced the long corridors of his home, as he tended to do in moments of anxiety. There was nothing on BBC *Breakfast News* when it came on air at 6.30am other than a passing reference to an Iraqi build-up of forces on the border with Kuwait. However, at 7am, Nicholas Witchell passed over to Jill Dando for some breaking news from the Gulf. She announced solemnly that thousands of Iraqi troops had crossed the border into Kuwait backed by tanks and artillery, with reports of heavy casualties on the Kuwaiti side. There was nothing about the attack on the palace but only reports which were sporadic with unclear speculation in terms of what was happening in Kuwait City. Peter had tried calling Amer back on his mobile phone but there was no connection.

At 8am, Major Ashford called and said they were trying to obtain more news from both Iraqi and Kuwaiti sources. He reassured Peter that it was unlikely that the Iraqis would wish to harm the brother of the Emir and, even less, a relative of the Maktoums of Dubai. "We have spoken with those in Iraq who have influence and warned of dire repercussions for anyone harming the Emir's family or Amer Al Maktoum. I am informed that this message will be secretly communicated directly to the commander on the ground but, I must warn you, Saddam Hussein is unpredictable. He has been known to shoot members of his council for simply voicing an opinion. I am hoping that we are in time here; we are doing our best, Peter, but everyone in Iraq is terrified of Saddam, even in the highest places."

Whilst Peter was desperate for information regarding Amer, he also had a sickening sense of overwhelming personal financial catastrophe. He tried not to dwell on such callous, materialistic thoughts, but could not escape the stark reality that eighteen months previously he had committed nearly £1.5 million for a major Gulf investment, into which Jonas had invested a similar amount. Peter recalled the moment that they had signed the contract to release funds for the Al-Mughamara Tower project on the west side of Kuwait City. This was a venture to create a tower of commerce containing businesses and apartments. The investment would give them a nominal stake of 25% in the venture, but with overall control because the Kuwaiti royal family took a compulsory but non-participative investment. They had discussed with Amer the stability of the region and he had assured them that there was no prospect of conflict in the Gulf affecting the UAE or Kuwait. He reminded them that Kuwait had been an ally of Saddam Hussein in the Iran–Iraq conflict. Their partnership had helped ensure the stability of the region which had been threatened by the extremism of the Ayatollah Khomeini, the leader of Iran, who had openly stated that he would bring revolution to Kuwait. Amer further pointed out that the oilfields of Iraq and Kuwait were close to one another. This alone gave insurance, because destruction of one would potentially affect the other.

By 10am, Peter was in his office and had placed a call to Texas in an attempt to discuss the situation with Jonas, but it was 3am in Dallas and there was no response. He began to feel an enormous isolation, as though he had lost a shield and was exposed. It was that insecurity that had first driven him to seek financial success. In his work at Granvilles he had become insulated, as if he were writing his own story. He was the author, and could write the next chapter. This was the first time he felt that he had lost control. His mind drifted to the last major emotional trauma in his life; twenty-one years before, when he had resisted pursuing a life with Jenny. That was so long ago, and for comfort he sought to recall the way she looked, the sound of her voice, her scent, but was surprised that so much now evaded him. He dismissed such thoughts with his mantra *That was then...*

In truth, he felt he was in a situation with little possibility of escape. He had overstretched his company's assets to finance a deal based on an assessment that it was safe in Kuwait. Jonas and he had invested almost half their total speculative monies in a development that promised an even more attractive return than Dubai, where they had invested the remainder. There, they had seized an opportunity to invest in the redevelopment of a sports centre into a prestigious playground together with some housing for the massively growing expat community.

Suddenly he had the haunting realisation that he had not even considered Amer's safety for an hour. He was the smart Westernised Arab who had welcomed them and trusted them. He had introduced them to the royal elite, exercising his influence; and, as he often mused with a wide smile, "We are oiling the wheels – or, in my part of the world, watering the camel." They were similar ages and had become more than business partners, sharing stories of their very different backgrounds, comparing Peter's tough early life with Amer's privileged upbringing that had enabled him to attend public school in the UK. They had gone up to university in the same year, although Amer had been admitted to Oxford. Peter genuinely thought of him as a trusted friend, with whom he had enjoyed an open, warm relationship. Amer was far more comfortable with Peter than he was with Jonas, whom he considered slightly crass.

They had dined together regularly, and one evening he had showed Peter secret maps and artists' impressions of the unbelievable metropolis of Dubai that was being planned and already under construction. They had been in the Dubai Hyatt Regency Hotel, which by now had become a regular sojourn, and Amer proudly stated that his family had very strong ties with the British reaching back to the First World War. Their conversations stretched late into the night as they debated history. Amer's great-grandfather had fought with Prince Faisal and the legendary T. E. Lawrence of *Lawrence of Arabia* fame. Their aim was to create Arab states despite the imperialist ambitions of the great powers who, Amer said, had deceived them, betraying Arab trust. Britain and America had posed massive challenges to their economic survival, fostering a growth in Arabic nationalism. This strategy, Amer claimed, rebounded with the ascent of the Arabs' oil-producing power in the 1970s, leading to massive hikes in prices, wealth for the Arab nations, and an oil crisis in the West. Peter and Jonas's partnership with Amer had been potentially fruitful, offering extraordinarily promising returns in a region experiencing breathtaking growth.

Peter's thoughts were interrupted by his phone, and in seconds his old friend was speaking to him in a strangely calm manner.

"Well, my old buddy, looks like we have one almighty screw-up goin' on down there. I thought that Saddam was all hat and no cattle after the last shindig with Iran. That guy just loves war!"

Peter spoke of Amer and his concerns about his safety, and was reassured by an unruffled Jonas.

"He's well connected, and that mad Iraqi son of a bitch would be crazy to hurt a Maktoum. We got a building there, Peter, so the development may go on hold, but we gonna kick Saddam's butt. Hey, a little delay but let's just concentrate on gettin' our friend out. President Bush has told Saddam to get his ass out of there, and I just seen Mrs Thatcher on TV. She ain't havin' it either, so looks like military action, boy. We just gonna have to ride it out."

That night on ITV *News at Ten*, Peter watched Trevor McDonald broadcast that Saddam Hussein had stated that any attempt to remove Iraqi forces from Kuwait would result in major conflict. He had issued a statement that Iraq would make "great fire eat up the aggressor, and blood will be their cost". There was speculation about Iraqi weapons and their capabilities.

At 6.30 the following morning, after a sleepless night, Peter was awoken by his mobile phone's incessant ringtone.

"Peter, this is Major Ashford. I am afraid it's bad news. Our man in Baghdad tells us that the Republican Guard took Dasman Palace yesterday. Their commander is a Saddam loyalist and unreachable to us. We are informed that the Emir's half-brother, Sheikh Fahad Al-Sabah, was shot and killed defending the palace, and that Amer Al Maktoum also died during the attack. I am very sorry."

Peter left the bedroom, walking slowly into his lounge where he collapsed into an armchair. He found it impossible not to sob as he felt the fog of isolation surround him yet again. Amer had been there attempting to resolve their building issues, but this...

Oh dear God, Peter's inner voice cried out. *Please, no, dear God, please...* He found himself staring down his lawn in a surreal awareness that all was normal, but it wasn't.

Barbara entered the room and moved towards him, sensing his grief, and put her arms around him. He felt incredibly cold and then a numbness enveloped him. He knew he needed to shut off, as he had learned to do as a child, and hide from anything that could threaten his world.

24th February 1991, 1pm

Peter was in his car, about to listen to the news headlines on Radio 4's *The World at One* before heading into a meeting with his co-director Tommy Wilson to discuss the impact of the Gulf War on their investments. There had been much speculation about damage to Kuwait City, and his stomach tightened as the radio time bleeps introduced the news programme. He was parked in the spot reserved for him in the courtyard at the rear of the Granvilles building on Rodney Street. He had been gripped by the news coverage of the Allies' fight against Saddam Hussein in Operation Desert Storm. The fast-unveiling events in the Gulf were preceded each day by briefings from General Norman Schwarzkopf ('Stormin' Norman'), the more genial General Colin Powell, and the dashing British General Sir Peter de la Billière.

Peter listened intently as James Naughtie introduced the headlines, grimly announcing reports from Kuwait City that the

Americans had attacked a number of targets in air strikes. It was also reported that the Iraqis were destroying buildings as part of a 'scorched earth' policy. There were reports of extensive damage to buildings in the west side of the city. That was in the area of the Al-Mughamara Tower. Peter's thoughts were in turmoil as he left his Jaguar and walked slowly towards the offices that had represented his dreams and aspirations for the past eighteen years. He was shaking inside as he entered, attempting a smile to the receptionist.

At 2pm, he entered the meeting room and was surprised to see Tommy Wilson accompanied by another man whom he faintly recognised. Tommy looked grim as he introduced one of the senior partners from the company auditors. "Peter, I'm sorry, but it's time we faced reality: we are in the shit."

As a formal opening, Peter thought, it lacked some etiquette, but in those few words, Tommy had summed up their position perfectly. The company's assets were at stake and, if their worst fears were realised, they could even be insolvent. Even if the building into which they had sunk so much survived unscathed, because of the Iraqi invasion and Gulf War, it had been six months since any work had been carried out on its development. They equally recognised that following liberation, which appeared certain, there would be a period of reconstruction which would last months, if not years. Peter did not need to listen to the dreary explanation given by their accountant. He had to acknowledge the obvious, which was, he conceded, that he had personally taken the decision to make an ambitious investment and, as a result, the survival of the business was at risk.

As he listened to the legal position being explained, part of his mind drifted back to his old father figure and mentor Rubin Granville. How had he let himself fall into this mess? How could he have placed in such jeopardy his future in which he had invested so much of his life? Even worse, in a way, he felt he had put Rubin's legacy at risk. He felt crushed and overwhelmed by it all, until the accountant's sharp words came into focus: "You need, as directors, to consider your own positions, because to trade insolvent is a criminal offence."

Then came the bombshell from Tommy. "Peter, even if the tower survives, it is unlikely that we could sell it and recoup our money. I have to inform you that I have found people who will back us, but it will be at a price, and that will be the majority of your shareholding. I have to protect the company and my position. However, I value your skills, and I want you to stay on as a director, at least whilst we evaluate the position."

Peter realised then that he was effectively being removed in a coup. What was hardest to swallow was that it was by the one who had always shown that he had neither the skill nor the acumen to create the opportunities that Peter had exploited and from which the company had flourished. He knew why he was being retained: because of the highly lucrative work he was still doing in tandem with the government on regeneration and investment. His fragile hope was that the tower had suffered no damage, and that its value would be maintained.

After the meeting had terminated, he reflected ruefully that, only three months previously, Mrs Thatcher had suffered a similar fate when two of her former trusted colleagues created the appetite for a coup which resulted in her downfall. Julius Caesar's words to his betrayer haunted him: *Et tu, Brute?* He knew they were in trouble, but this, this he could not stomach.

"God, what a world of bastards," he greeted Barbara with as he returned home.

35

Pragmatism

Wednesday 20th March 1991

Major Ashford phoned in response to Peter's call, placed the day before, requesting news about the Al-Mughamara Tower. Peter was in a no man's land after the meeting with Tommy Wilson the previous month. Whilst still nominally the CEO or managing director, the investor framework being created to rescue Granvilles meant he would no longer be in control. He wanted to establish all remaining options before he was forced to surrender control of the company, which made any news from Kuwait pivotal. As he took the call, he was almost resigned to the inevitable.

"Peter, Richard Ashford. I have news."

Although Peter was surprised by Ashford's overfamiliar greeting, using his Christian name rather than his rank, it did have the effect of making the discussion a little less formal.

"Our man on the ground has seen the tower, or the remains of it. I regret it took a direct hit in the US aerial bombardment as the Iraqi brass had taken refuge there. When they, or what was left of them, moved out, they ordered its destruction. I'm sorry to tell you that whilst some of the structure can be rescued, internally, the damage is severe. I am authorised to communicate to you in strictest confidence that the Emir of Kuwait will retain his investment relationship with you, but he will make no financial commitment. He has made it clear he will only deal with you on this matter, and will appoint a new representative to liaise with you directly on his behalf. That is, if you wish to restart the development. Whilst the Kuwaitis are seeking to reconstruct, money will be an issue in the short term, as I expect it will be with you."

The major informed Peter that those who needed to know were already in possession of the facts regarding Granvilles' impending financial difficulties. The call was encouraging in that Major Ashford assured him that those who took the decisions had confidence in Peter's abilities and saw no reason to make unnecessary changes. "Be assured, Peter, pressure will be applied appropriately; we never leave such matters to chance."

Curiously, after the call, Peter felt a little more positive, realising that, despite everything, if the new management team at Granvilles wanted to continue with the Gulf investment, they would need him.

Two days later, he was sat in his office when his secretary rang through to say she had a call from Westminster from someone who "sounds very smooth".

Michael Heseltine warmly reintroduced himself, saying that he had been appointed by Prime Minister John Major as Secretary of State for the Environment. He wished to examine progress on Merseyside, and added that he had been fully apprised of Peter's position. "My dear chap, we like to remain loyal to our own, and I believe your cooperation has been very thorough. I think I might make it plain that we believe our initial choice was excellent, and we would wish you to continue."

Peter's spirits rose a little after the call, and a few days later papers arrived, as they had done previously, consulting him about development prospects in the dockland areas.

The following week, he was invited to attend what was euphemistically called a 'board meeting', which was a little over the top as only he and Tommy Wilson held directorships. He was introduced to two men he had never seen before from Wentworth Holdings, an investment organisation . There was a superior air about them, as if, he thought, they were about to treat him with derision.

The larger of the two men, reeking of cigar smoke, rose and shook Peter's hand brusquely before addressing him. "Mr Chainey, my name is Eugene Franklin, and this is my financial associate, William Marsden – call him Bill. We will cut to the chase; I think we may be able to assist you, and I think we have arrived in the nick of time." He was a portly man in his late fifties, with slightly bulging eyes in a ruddy face and dressed in a pinstripe suit. Bill Marsden was shorter, wearing a navy-blue suit, with receding hair, tinted glasses and piercing blue eyes. He smiled briefly but gave Peter the impression that this was not a well-used facial expression.

The atmosphere was strained as he listened to their terms. Peter was to surrender his shareholding, retaining 4%, whilst Tommy would hold 20%. Eugene stated that they wanted Peter and Tommy to retain an interest in the business and remain directors. "We see your 4%, shall we say, as insurance, Mr Chainey; we want you to be comfortable running the business and reporting to us on a monthly basis. Bill here will oversee matters, becoming an invisible asset to you in your offices."

Peter decided to let them see that he was not a total pushover, nor would he ever be taken advantage of. "Gentlemen, I'm delighted to welcome you. My insurance, shall we say, is based on two factors. First, Her Majesty's government has appointed me to assist with inner-city development and investment, and that is not dependent upon me being a director of Granvilles. Second, my friend the Emir of Kuwait has graciously indicated that he wishes to deal exclusively with me on all matters relating to redevelopment of the land on which we were building the Al-Mughamara Tower. I believe, therefore, that we are perhaps mutually insured, so to speak. My shareholding will match Mr Wilson's, if you require my cooperation."

He saw the grimace on Eugene Franklin's face and, for a second, enjoyed just a twinge of victory; a feeling he had not had for some time. His shareholding was increased to 15%, whilst Tommy's was reduced to the same percentage, which softened the blow.

By the end of the meeting, Peter had already built up a distinct dislike of his new business associates, but he had to take a pragmatic view and accept the sacrifices. As he drove home that evening he felt a gnawing emptiness inside. His uncomfortable reality was that he was no longer free, but trapped inside a cage in which, ironically, he needed to remain to retain his standard of living. This was not the life he wanted, nor that which had given him refuge for so long. The die was cast.

As the years passed, board meetings with Wentworth Holdings became a polite war of attrition wherein Bill Marsden would ask Peter searching questions as though cross-examining him. Eugene Franklin assumed the role of ebullient chairman, smilingly pouring oil on troubled waters whilst making key decisions over which Peter often had no real say. He felt increasingly emasculated but comforted himself by viewing his time at Granvilles as a means to an end and no longer a vocation.

On hearing of his predicament, Jonas, who had weathered the loss in Kuwait more easily based on his considerable assets, told Peter that he felt responsible for his misfortunes. He offered his old friend a position in his expanding business, which by now had stores right across the USA. Whilst Peter was immensely grateful for the offer, he could not accept. His roots and loyalties remained firmly in Liverpool, where, at very least, he was making a difference with his development strategy. He was concerned, however, about the prospect of a change in government affecting his work, as Labour's popularity soared under the leadership of the reforming newcomer, Tony Blair.

Major Ashford confirmed this in a phone call in January 1997. "Peter, there may be change coming. After the general election this year, it is likely that we will have a government under New Labour." The Conservatives had been in power for eighteen years but, under John Major, they had become a minority government. They were now riven by infighting, with allegations of corruption and divisions over Europe. Ashford explained that the arrangement which had been in place for the past fifteen years would have to cease. In reminding Peter that their conversations had never taken place, he made it clear, although stressing that he was sure it was unnecessary, that there would be "consequences" if official secrets were breached. "Your sensitive management of the areas we have entrusted to you has not gone unnoticed in the highest places, which may one day assist you. For my part, Peter, I wish you good luck. I am retiring from active service, which is probably a good thing as I'm not convinced that this new broom will sweep clean at all. I have genuinely enjoyed our association but, damn it, I'm seventy-seven years of age and I wish I wasn't. This may be the last time you hear from me. Take care, and I mean that."

As the line went dead, Peter's thoughts were with the person who had given him direction; often unwanted, but always with good reason and now, after a lifetime of service, Major Ashford had become an old man who would no longer exercise influence. That night, before Peter went to sleep, he expressed his silent gratitude to the major for his input over the years, and his help during the recent tough period. He had given reason, justification and an element of security to decisions which had not always been easy for Peter to act upon.

After the election in May, his official work advising government on redevelopment ceased. That month, Jonas contacted him, saying that he wanted to shift his investments away from property into the new 'dot-com' area. The call, when it came, surprised Peter as he had had little contact with Jonas in the two years preceding, other than brief faxes dealing with issues on the properties they jointly held in the Gulf.

Jonas's UK investments had performed well but, as he stressed to Peter, "This internet thing is really something, man; we gotta be in there. Talking of which, we should be communicating by email. We are dinosaurs, Peter – hell, you seen this tech shit? We can buy, sell, communicate, and do just about any business stuff on the web." He impressed upon Peter that they could work together on taking the proceeds from the sale of Jonas's property portfolio handled by Granvilles, and direct them into an internet enterprise strategy. He asked Peter if he would head up a new investment business directing funds into internet ventures. It was an offer that he welcomed, seeing it as a way out of his increasingly restricted role in Granvilles.

Peter was taking a risk because his new role breached a legal undertaking given to Granvilles. He had a duty to dedicate the whole of his time to the company, and have no outside business interest when the shareholding was restructured. However, the risk was just a touch irresistible and appealed to his rebellious side, which he had never subdued. Within a year, the strategy suggested by Jonas had borne fruit, with Peter sitting on a Business Angels investment panel. This was an organisation which invited investors to events at which hopeful entrepreneurs made presentations seeking capital for budding ventures. Peter began selecting internet-based businesses, concentrating on online retail ventures. Two of the projects in which he invested were soon delivering a return massively in excess of projections; one in clothing, and the other in hardware.

"Hell, Peter, I knew I could trust your judgement from the time I saw you bumming sun hats and ice cream back on those beaches in 1969," a delighted Jonas joked during a call in late 1998.

Whenever those days were raised, even after nearly thirty years, Peter's stomach would tighten and his mind drift, seeking reasons and finding few answers for the emptiness he knew he had once created.

By 1999, he had turned part of his home into an office from which he ran the new investment strategy for a company they set up called Investment Angels. Each month, after attending presentations given by entrepreneurs seeking capital, their portfolio gradually expanded.

36

"A Vast Right-Wing Conspiracy"

In the summer of 1994, Maria asked her mother for help as she wanted to apply for a position as an intern at the White House for the spring semester of 1995. As a second-year student at Harvard, where she was studying Politics and Philosophy, she was fascinated with the exercise of power and the people who wielded it. She had become increasingly involved in politics over the preceding three years, taking part in events organised by the local Democratic Party to raise funds and support for Bill Clinton in the presidential race. She had attended his rallies and become a firm and committed follower. In June 1992, she had watched on TV with her mother as the presidential hopeful played 'Heartbreak Hotel' on his saxophone on *The Arsenio Hall Show*. Jenny had to admit that she was drawn to Clinton's open style and easy way of talking. He appeared refreshingly honest, and when he spoke, it was like he was having a chat in your home, yet with a certain attractive vulnerability.

Jenny was reminded of a time Peter had played his guitar for her, sharing with her daughter her memories of sitting on beaches

271

in 1969, enraptured by the young man singing rock ballads of the day. Maria listened intently, as she had never before been invited into her mother's more intimate early adult life experiences.

"Oh, honey, he was so special, and he made such a mark on me; one of the most wonderful people I have ever met. I will never forget those beautiful days, but I never remember too often either."

Maria hugged her mother, seeing her holding her emotion in check with difficulty, her eyes filling.

"I made a promise to him; we called it a Covenant then. I still have it written down, although I didn't need to keep it because I memorised it. One day, sweetie, I will give it to you so you can glimpse a little of me from back then, but it was long, long ago. I have never seen him since, although I so wanted to once, but that was a quarter of a century ago."

Jenny had helped Maria apply for a place at Harvard, visiting the campus with her and showing her many of the still-familiar locations where she had once walked, and places she had visited. A word in the right place, without Maria's knowledge, ensured her admission, although as a very bright straight-A student she needed no real help. Following her daughter's request for assistance in obtaining entry as an intern, Jenny promised to pull a few strings and, after a call to Professor Wostenholme, the letter from the White House arrived a few days later. However, Maria still had to submit essays and letters of recommendation just like the other candidates. As an old family friend who was also an academic and knew of her capabilities, Wostenholme penned one of the required supporting reference letters. Maria was interviewed in December 1994, initially by phone and then at the White House. She was required to meet with a number of people in localised Federal Offices who loosely introduced themselves as security. Finally, a letter arrived confirming her appointment to the staff of the President of the United States.

This was a wonderful moment for Jenny, although tinged with some regret that her daughter was about to be exposed to the influences which by this time were causing her serious misgivings. She loved being involved with influential, powerful, people, mixing and debating issues with those at the very top, but she also recognised by now the cost in terms of the sacrifice of principle to expedience. Whilst there was no turning back, she felt a gnawing unease at the sacrifices she had made. Had idealism or materialism driven her career? She had no answers to the question which increasingly haunted her.

In May 1995, Maria wrote to Jenny on White House headed notepaper:

Dearest Mama,

I can hardly tell you how excited I feel. This is as close to power as I guess you can ever get. I am deeply involved here now in so many areas, and being introduced to people, many of whom I recognise. I have met former President Bush, who was very gracious; he kissed my outstretched hand and spoke in a deeper Texas accent than ever came across on TV which surprised me. I have met Vice President Al Gore several times, and he always makes time to say hi. You know what surprises me? That all these people are so everyday; like we could be anywhere, not in the White House. Some folks are really offhand – they guard their territory and try to protect their domains from us, and are kind of hostile – but not the President. Oh my God, Mama, I've met him at last; not just in the interns' introduction meeting I told you about in my last letter, but personally. He is incredible – oh, and a touch adorable!

Yesterday, we attended the Rose Garden, having been asked to dress for the occasion, and then drinks were served by guys in white gloves. Can you believe it? Then the President came out. He waved, then spoke briefly into a microphone, saying he wanted to say hello to as many of us as possible. He said we should enjoy ourselves like this was one of our own parties. He has such a smile, Mama, and is very engaging. He came down the line, shaking hands with each of us, then, when he got to me, someone whispered to him, and he grabbed my hand in his and said, "I have the honour to know your mother, and guess what? She speaks very highly of you." We laughed, but wow, he is amazing, and we chatted about family, my hopes, and he said you've done a great service to the United States. I was so proud of you, but kind of overwhelmed by him. This guy has some charisma, and I can tell you, some of the interns were practically swooning at his feet.

It was a prophetic statement, as within a year Jenny became involved in damage limitation regarding the Monica Lewinsky affair. Lewinsky had been an intern at the White House too, and allegations were emerging that she had had an affair with the President. Maria knew of her, spoke about it with Jenny, and gave a candid opinion on blame, but Jenny never shared that with anyone. She warned her daughter to be careful which Maria dismissed as *just ridiculous* because to her, the President was *simply adorable.* Jenny's natural instinct was protection but equally, despite her slight misgivings, she was loyal to the office she had given her life to protect.

On the 30th August 1997, she was resting in her room, watching the evening news, when her attention was drawn sharply to the headlines. "With enormous sadness, we deeply regret having to report that Diana, Princess of Wales has died as a result of injuries sustained in a car crash in a Paris road tunnel." Jenny felt immensely touched, and could not justify the depth of her feelings. Watching Prime Minister Tony Blair give an excessively obsequious, patronising speech sometime later which she found both odious and sycophantic, she nevertheless drew something from the words that Diana had become "the People's Princess".

Later, she listened as British news anchorman, Martyn Lewis, summarised how the princess had touched the hearts of millions across the world. Jenny cried not just for Diana, but recognising that she herself had lost something so precious that seemed to be represented by the shy, demure, sensitive yet driven princess. Suddenly, she was aware of time, which had stolen years and yet had failed to hide the tracks and traces of what had gone before.

That night, she retraced her steps and felt again the warm winds from the Esterel Hills waft over her, and reached out for him in her dreams.

It was in the autumn of 1997 that Jenny felt the real divide between her loyalty to the creed of her career and her role as Maria's mother. The news channels had given unceasing coverage to the President's infidelities, citing in particular his purported affairs with two Arkansas state employees, Gennifer Flowers and Paula Jones. These were being linked to the investigation by Independent Counsel Kenneth Starr into abuses of power by the office of President. Jenny was summoned to the State Department in November 1997, but this time, Professor Wostenholme informed her, he would be taking a less visible role, because these were delicate and scrutinised matters of national security. "My concern, as always, Jenny, is to protect the United States, but on this occasion we are all being watched, and we are in a 'trust no one' position. I will, of course, be monitoring and influencing events but, and I know it goes without saying, I will need your absolute discretion in all matters. There are those on all sides of the political divide who can gain from this, and, therefore, we are in an incredibly dangerous position."

On arrival at the State Department, she was met by a smart, sandy-haired man in a light grey suit who introduced himself as Colonel Samuel Ritchie and said simply that he was "with the White House". He asked her to join him for a briefing in a back office with just one small window, unlike the more palatial rooms she had previously witnessed.

Colonel Ritchie was tall, slim, and held himself erect with a military bearing she had come to recognise; men who presented as though they were on parade, even out of uniform. He laid before her some very stark facts about the current political state of the US and, in particular, the office of President. He was matter-of-fact, emotionless, as though directing a military operation. "May I call you Jenny?" he asked earnestly but with authority, before continuing without awaiting her response. "We are in a situation where the threat to the core of the leadership of this country is at stake. The House is about to launch impeachment proceedings against the President. Jenny, the truth of the matter is, the President's indiscretions are being used to discredit his office. The inquiry led by Starr is digging stuff up relating to his former business dealings in a property business known as Whitewater. This entire matter is driven by corruption and neo-extremist Republican aspirations to topple the President. We are aware that many Republicans in the Senate are distancing themselves from this, but we need a way out.

"Ma'am," he went on intently, ignoring his earlier request for an informal first-name address, "there have been no impeachment proceedings formally launched against the President of the United States since Andrew Johnson in 1868, and even then, the Senate overturned them. This time, the threat is very real, and I cannot tell you what damage it will do to our global status. Mr Starr is running out of steam and wants to get the President in any way he can. We need an intervention, Jenny, but not from the White House. This needs pressure being brought to bear, backed by cool-headed legal argument, both constitutionally and in a manner that will genuinely win over those that may require political pressure. This where you come in: we need you to impress upon those waverers who may be considering supporting impeachment that they are best served by supporting the integrity of the office of President. I am authorised to give you classified surveillance files, and you may request more to give you an edge in your discussions. These may merely give information on current views, or contain more on financial irregularities or other indiscretions. Professor Wostenholme has impressed upon me the importance of your mission, and asked that I stress to you his commitment to this. However, he will deny any involvement."

He shook her hand at the close of the meeting, informing her that others would now deal directly with her and act upon her requests. Colonel Ritchie snapped to attention as they parted. "I will probably never see you again," the younger man looked at her earnestly, "but I admire you and your work. I have, of course, now never met you." He saluted, and walked out of the office.

Jenny began work, talking to Senators from both sides of the divide, finding common ground in the need to avoid the political and global fallout that would result from impeachment, notwithstanding the damage to the strength and reputation of the USA. By January 1998, she had made significant headway, convincing waverers that their futures might best be served by not supporting the removal of the President. She had now been provided with private files that added some weight to the requests for support from those who did not wish their own indiscretions to come to light. She also directly tutored those who were to give evidence to the Starr investigation on how this should be presented.

The phone call from Professor Wostenholme at midnight on the 3rd January 1998 was a bombshell. "Jenny, we have problems: it appears that they may have definitive proof that Monica Lewinsky has been the President's mistress, and that she has given false evidence to protect him. The President himself may be implicated in the cover-up process."

Jenny's riposte was direct but not unexpected: "Jesus, Leo, can that man not keep his pants on?"

The process of 'persuasion' was given even more priority and urgency. The saga of schooling witnesses was stepped up for those giving evidence to Kenneth Starr. During 1998, Jenny's work had resulted in a number of senatorial indiscretions being made public, which added strength to her persuasiveness in dealing with others. Throughout that year, she held discreet meetings with both Republican and Democratic Senators, obtaining endorsement for the office of President, if not the man holding it. Following the vote for impeachment in the House in December, she awaited the Senate's critical vote in February 1999 which finally saved the President.

Although her endeavours had paid off, something had changed inside her. In the preceding twelve months, her work had been involved with legal and constitutional arguments at best, and coercion at worst. She confessed to Wostenholme in a follow-up phone call that she felt sullied by the experience. "While I know the guy lied, he's President; so he's been screwing around, but was that the limit of his sin, just covering that up? I cannot believe the office of President of the United States is under pressure just because the guy can't keep his dick in his pants. Leo, I am not proud of myself in all of this and I'm still not sure that the result justified my actions. Someone once said to me, 'We must embrace realpolitik as a weapon to defend us from idealism standing in the way of change.' I never forgot that, and we both know who said it."

Wostenholme gave a simple reply, reminding her that democracy was never easy to support, but was vital to defend. "Power is being wielded for the greater good, Jenny, and our President is a critical part of that."

She was slightly reassured that she might have acted for 'the greater good' by Hillary Clinton stating publicly, in early 1992, that her husband had been the victim of "a vast right-wing conspiracy", but it did not sit easily on her shoulders. She had met the President on a number of occasions but had never taken a briefing from him directly. In 1998, he had approached her at a White House function, saying that he had few words that would do justice to the gratitude he felt for her service to her country. Her daughter was right: he had incredible magnetism and oozed sex appeal. He had a sensitivity about him that drew her to him, and his stated desire to distance himself from the Washington elite made her want to side with him. Jenny didn't know whether he knew of her involvement in his case or whether he was just being charming, but it was just a little overwhelming.

She had indirectly assisted in the defence, and had directed a number of witnesses and defendants in the earlier part of the Whitewater Affair inquiry. At that time, she had dealt with Hillary Clinton, whom she had found utterly disarming, intuitive and engaging. The First Lady had shown that she was genuinely interested in her. Jenny found her refreshingly open and friendly, with a magnetism which drew the natural loyalty of those around her. She lit up any event with an incredible spirit and a dazzling smile. She always had time for others, and she and Jenny had chatted warmly about their student years, when Hillary had espoused many of the causes that Jenny had passionately believed in. They seldom met, but Jenny remained a firm fan and admirer – a fact which was to resurface many years later.

Following the defeat of the impeachment proceedings in the Senate on the 12th February 1998, she had been invited to the White House on a couple of social occasions, which she had genuinely enjoyed. Hillary welcomed her like a long-lost friend, chatting about their shared interest in law, but no word was exchanged about Jenny's work for the President. Whilst he had now become more open about his difficulties, he seemed strong in his conviction in the work he was carrying out. He radiated a kind of honesty, openly acknowledging "my troubled waters", and was more real for it.

Jenny somehow felt that she had been justified in the light of the Senate's dismissal of the case, due to the fact that Clinton had then become one of the most popular Presidents in recorded history. "You can't trust him, he's got weak morals and ethics – and he's done a heck of a good job," ABC News stated, summing up the views of the nation. In fact, Clinton's popularity ratings at the end of his presidency were higher than Ronald Reagan's.

37

A Sad Farewell

As the decade drew to a close, Jenny reflected on what she had achieved in global and US terms. At fifty years of age, she had grown pretty tired of all the cover-ups and the constant creativity that had to be used in judicial evidence. This had become an increasing drain, which she was determined to speak of when she was summoned by Professor Wostenholme in the autumn of 1999; or rather, by his office. He had been admitted to the Bethesda Naval Hospital in Washington DC, and had sent a message, employing the usual code, indicating that she must join him on urgent business.

On landing at Baltimore/Washington International Airport, she was met by the now customary limousine and driven the forty minutes to the hospital. There, smartly dressed uniformed men stood to attention as her driver showed his security pass, following which she was driven to the entrance to the huge white building complex. Inside the sliding doors, she was met by Marylyn, the professor's long-standing assistant who should have retired long ago, but had been retained because loyalty figured large in his priorities, as Jenny knew only too well. The slightly stooped figure in old-fashioned horn-rimmed glasses shook her hand, then sighed before announcing, "I'm afraid I have to impart difficult news, Jenny. He has a tumour in his bowel and it has spread." She coughed back a half-sob before continuing. "He has been complaining for months of stomach pain, but you know what he's like. He refused to consult a doctor, saying he is never sick and has no time to be."

In minutes, Jenny had been ushered down corridors into an area that was calmer, with less frenzied hospital activity. The floors were carpeted and smart panelled doors flanked the corridor. Marylyn led her to a double door at the end, on which a brass plaque announced, 'The Reagan Suite'. After a knock, to which there came no response, she was ushered into the room, in the centre of which was a bed from which her old friend smiled a welcome, opening his arms to greet her. She tried to ignore the various tubes and monitors attached to him, but immediately noticed the weakness in his voice.

"My dear, lovely friend, Jenny, you are such a wonderful sight. They are doing me no good here; I think they are trying to get rid of me." He coughed deeply, trying to recover his breath as he asked her, "Is the impeachment episode truly over for good?"

The question surprised her, as it had been seven months since the Senate had voted against the process.

"Jenny, I have no more to ask of you, but I have an eternal gratitude for all you have done for me, for your country and for the great office you have helped defend. I know I have been very wrong on occasion, pressuring you, but always I felt my requests were justified for reasons of national security. Hell, Jenny, I want you to understand that when I was growing up, I too had those ideals I know have troubled you for so long. My time was in the '30s and we all had such zeal then. Once, as a teenager, I even considered fighting in Spain against Franco, then joining Britain in the fight against Germany. Maybe I never had the courage of my convictions."

His voice became more laboured as he coughed, holding a dressing in front of his mouth. "But you, your conscience must be clear, because you have done what you have done to protect the greater good. I have never admired anyone as much as you, and I have loved you like a daughter, although I never had one. I never told you how dear you became to me. I think it is time you left this type of work. It saps you and draws you in, and before you know it, you will be as devious as me. I want you to find a more fulfilling, peaceful role where you no longer have to clear up the mess made by others. I sometimes think, Jenny, that we have all been involved in one massive cover-up to protect the power in this country."

He coughed again, and began to gag as he reached for tissues, which she handed him, her stomach wrenched by the evidence of blood as he covered his mouth.

"Maybe it has all been for the best. Sometimes I am no longer sure, but I really desire something for you away from what I have imposed upon you. Forgive me, but old habits die hard and I have spoken with friends about you."

Jenny knew that when the wily professor used those words, he meant that he had exercised his not inconsiderable influence to achieve a result which was always assured.

He grasped her hand. "My dear Jenny, I wanted to put in place a parting gift which it is my dearest wish that you accept before my final curtain. If you do, arrangements will be made for you to take up the post of senior managing partner at Latham Ellis Piper, operating from the Washington DC office. Ironic, because you will be nearer the President than you ever have been, but too much in the public eye to operate as before. Imagine no more politics, imagine no more me plaguing your life with manipulative intent which you saw through all along. You will be released from all I have ever put upon you to live as you may once have chosen, and the fact that I am guilty of imposing all that upon you; oh, Jenny, that torments me. I want you to escape all this and live the life you deserve, free of the burdens of state." His voice began to weaken, and both his hands reached for and covered hers. "Your contribution has been unstinting and your duties performed without question. I thank you, not just for that, but for enriching my life with your own."

He lay back, still grasping her hand, squeezing as though frightened to let go. "Once I was a powerful man, but now, you see, I am nothing. Jenny, you have been a wonderful protégée, companion and dearest friend." He looked at her, his eyes full of emotion, as if imploring her to take in the depth of his sentiments. "You know, moments like this are so important," he muttered before slumping back, closing his eyes and sliding into sleep.

The strains of Beethoven's sonatas, which had been playing softly in the background, now added to the poignancy. The professor's breathing was laboured, and Jenny was surprised to find tears in her eyes, stifling a sob as she left the room. As she was driven away, she felt a deep sense of utter isolation.

One day later, Professor Leo Wostenholme passed away. Jenny travelled to his funeral and burial in Arlington National Cemetery, which was quiet and did not attract much attention, but was attended by no fewer than four US Presidents. There were surprisingly few others there; only around thirty or so mourners to pay their respects to a man who had, for his service to his country, warranted so many accolades. The irony, Jenny thought, would not have been lost on him. She shook hands with some of those present, mainly those she had known through dealing with Wostenholme's office. No family were in attendance and she had never met any, although he had told her that his parents had died when he was young. She knew that he had never married, and that his family were originally wealthy and from Eastern Europe, fleeing after the Bolshevik Revolution of 1917.

As she stood with her fellow mourners in the light rain that October afternoon, opposite them the figures of Presidents Ford, Carter, Bush and Clinton were a silent tribute under black umbrellas. Listening to the priest deliver a eulogy summarising Leo Wostenholme's commitment to the United States, Jenny felt very alone. There was a poignant, sad pointlessness to his life in that he had achieved much in the gaze of those who knew him, but so little in himself. Was this how life was measured in public service: not by family values or who you might have been, but in platitudes hinting at a life involved in subterfuge for one's country?

As she was leaving, an old, familiar face approached, his wiry white hair and broad smile unmistakable. He always seemed to be everywhere there was a President, she thought, stifling a chuckle.

"Ms Baronio, I often hear of your extraordinary achievements, and I know of your enormous service to this nation. I have known dear Leo for most of my adult life, and I can tell you he was proud of that service. You and I once had a slight disagreement, I think, and I recall your lofty ideals. However, if I am not mistaken, I believe that in your work, you have accepted the expedience of which I once spoke to you. We are grateful to you. Be proud. *L'chaim.*" Henry Kissinger offered his hand, then smiled wryly as he turned away, to be ushered back towards the presidential phalanx that appeared to be waiting for him. Despite the extraordinary charm he exuded, his words did little to comfort Jenny.

Leo's grave marker was simply inscribed, with a notice announcing that a permanent marble memorial would be erected reading:

PROFESSOR LEOPOLD BERNARD
WOSTENHOLME
AUGUST 17TH 1919 – OCTOBER 25TH 1999
A TEACHER AND A PATRIOT
IN GOD WE TRUST

She thought of the words she had read about patriotism many years before at Harvard, from Robert G. Ingersoll, a lawyer and author whose writing she enormously admired:

"HE LOVES HIS COUNTRY BEST WHO STRIVES TO
MAKE IT BEST."

New York City
November 1999

The snow fell early that winter, carpeting the streets and giving the city a magical, cleansing facelift which somehow lifted the spirits too, Jenny thought, recalling her childhood in Atlantic City where snow had been rare. She had been summoned to a meeting by the senior partners at Latham Ellis Piper and asked if she wished to take up an appointment in Washington DC, where she would assume the title and responsibilities of a senior partner. Leo had been as good as his word, she thought, smiling at the idea that, even on his deathbed, he had been fixing things. Although the burdens he had placed upon her had been demanding, she so missed him. Sometimes she thought he had blighted her life, but the truth was, as she knew, that he had brought adventure and excitement into her work. She had had to be inventive, creative, clever and articulate in achieving her goals. Gaining a reputation as a fiercely successful defence lawyer had attracted much attention but, as her professor had said, "Too much exposure, and you become less effective in your work, for surprise is of the essence." He had conceded that she brought propriety to the cases she fought. The simple fact that she was taking them at all gave a sense that there was a case to be heard, even if the evidence was flimsy at best.

Jenny had thought hard about whether to accept Professor Wostenholme's parting gift, but a new start did have a big draw. It was the realisation of a highly successful career, and now here was the opportunity to work away from the pressures of what had often been a creative practice of law. She had long ago understood that there always had to be two sides to a case and often no clear justice. Pragmatism to Jenny meant the outcome was merited by the facts, however the facts might have been obtained. She knew her skill lay in an extraordinary grasp of evidence and recall mixed with an amazing gift for presentation, creating a cocktail of inalienable argument. Her outstanding success had contributed in no small way to supporting the institution that had come to be the focus of her energies. She had been proud to serve many administrations, both Republican and Democrat, in which inspired leadership had taken the United States to a better place but, underneath, the unease grew within her.

There was a gap in the day as the partners asked her to consider their offer. "We must tell you, Jenny, that your work has been of major importance to national security and you may be called upon again. We cannot protect you from your considerable abilities and the impression you have made upon the great and the good."

Jenny took a taxi to Central Park and wandered down to the Wollman Ice Rink. She sat watching the display of colourful play, the images blurring into a representative canvas, like those by the British artist, Lowry, whose paintings stated so much, yet with an almost childlike depiction of figures. As she sat in the freezing air, watching the warm enjoyment of others, loneliness engulfed her. Recent years had been momentous: meeting those with position and power, protecting them and their institutions. She had seen people react with concern, incredulity, then anger, often followed by humility when faced with evidence of their own human weakness. This would result in even the most powerful becoming humbly acquiescent to and complicit in the strategies she set. These were influential men of 'integrity' whose indiscretions directed their subsequent agreement to compromise their stated positions. Some had been more forthright, initially refusing to cooperate, but when faced with reality, the call, email or fax from them requesting a meeting inevitably followed. Had she lowered herself to playing a common pawn in a Machiavellian game of power and, yes, corruption?

As she watched the innocent fun being enjoyed by those around her, she felt remote from life, and in a moment of epiphany looked back at who she had been. She watched two teenagers hand in hand, zigzagging across the ice, his eyes never leaving hers. They kept kissing and laughing, and kissing again. As they skated on, hands clasped, Jenny ached inside as memories from so long ago flooded into her mind. *This is so crazy*, she thought. *I am a successful woman of fifty years of age and I'm dreaming of a person I lost when I was still virtually a child. Oh God, I lost myself somewhere too, and dear Peter, what has happened to him?* Jonas rarely got in touch now, so the conduit she had once valued for news had long gone, and truth was, she was a little frightened of reconnecting to it.

She felt distant from the laughter and screams of delight of those swaying across the ice, and reflected over the past year. She knew she had played a huge role in a historic event, effectively saving the President from impeachment. Yet her importance mattered not as she sought no recognition, no fame and no reward, although her earnings from her White House consultancy were significant; way above the considerable fees for her Latham Ellis Piper work. As she dwelt on the drama in which she had played a part, she saw empty achievement from which she took nothing apart from the initial elation of having performed her role successfully. There was no triumph; just an acceptance that she had done what was needed, leaving a residue of doubt from a rapidly receding wave of fulfilment.

She thought over so much that had sullied her life in the thirty years since she had sought to reach for her utopian dream. God, Peter had represented her Shangri-La before the denial; before she ignored her inner self's cries for freedom, convincing herself she might find security with Braden. She had sacrificed too much; it was over thirty years since she had felt like she was riding on the crest of a new wave of idealism that would deliver peace and love. How sour some of that dream had turned as 'the scene' was commercialised, the music packaged, and the slogans sold as merchandise. She wondered whether there was more hope now; yet, as the end of the millennium approached, she could not see the changes she believed in heralding a new age of optimism.

The past twelve months had been dominated by the impeachment, various wars, the bombing of Kosovo, and an unprecedented number of natural disasters. Mankind's impotence had been exposed, and humanity shaken by catastrophic earthquakes in Turkey, Taiwan and Greece, a mega storm in Pakistan, and floods in Venezuela. As if to add to the gloom on a more personal level, there had been another awful blow to a proud, iconic US family with the loss of John F. Kennedy Jr, his wife, and her sister in the plane he was piloting; then there had been the tragic death of Princess Diana which seemed to have extinguished an innocent dream. On a positive note, there appeared to be the prospect of the end of the Troubles in Northern Ireland, with peace talks partly brokered by the man she had fought to keep in office. Had she, then, done the right thing for the greater good?

She thought of her daughter, Maria, who had graduated from Harvard in 1996 and was now over halfway through a PhD in Politics and Philosophy. What kind of world was she facing? She hated thinking that her daughter would have to deal with the disillusionment she felt. She questioned how she had allowed herself to be seduced by all she had hated. Once before, she had sacrificed everything for so-called opportunity. Yet she knew she needed, as always, to balance reality with dreams, and, as the snow began to fall some more, she made her decision. Time to embrace something better. The die was cast.

On her return to the office, Jenny accepted the new post and was warmly congratulated by her colleagues. Her duties were to lead major defence cases, managing both preparation and presentation, which would require, as she had requested, more direct contact with defendants, witnesses and others involved. She had recognised that her skills in her performances in court could be improved by more in-depth personal analysis of defendants. She was determined, after the huge influence of Professor Wostenholme, to make the most of finally being in charge of her life's direction.

38

Christmas Reflections

1999
South Spring Valley
New York

In mid December 1999 a Christmas card arrived from Jonas containing a by-now-customary evocative message.

How's the hot beach-bar waitress? I still like a little good-quality grass but it's been a while since I sat on the sand, listening to a guitar.

He had scrawled that he was now investing in the dot-com era, asking her to write him 'one of those new-fangled emails' and giving her his AOL address. He finished with a little tease – 'Just in case you ever want to check him out, Peter is online too' – which he followed with another email address.

Jenny stared at this ridiculous, if not tempting, doorway to her past. Her life was on the cusp of another major change but, she had decided, that would come after the Season of Goodwill.

On the 20th, Maria returned home to spend the Christmas vacation with her parents. Jenny loved creating a traditional festive home, and so, as was customary, they had a decorated tree in the drawing room and a large one planted outside in the garden some years before, covered with coloured lights. Lanterns were strung in a line across the front of the house, leading Maria to tease them, saying that it was over the top, like the movie *National Lampoon's Christmas Vacation*. This was normally the best time of year, with a happier family atmosphere in which Jenny would try to forget the indifference she felt towards Braden and attempt to involve him in creating a welcoming home.

This year, she had also invited Matteo, her brother, and his wife Vivienne. Matteo worked for *The Washington Post* and, under the tutelage of Bob Woodward, had earned quite a reputation for well-researched investigative journalism. Matteo hugely admired his mentor for being one of the two legendary reporters who had relentlessly pursued the truth and published the story behind Watergate. He had long watched with admiration as Jenny's star rose. Whilst he knew of her work as a consultant to the White House, he had never attempted to use their relationship to obtain information or facts relating to stories he was covering. Vivienne was a History teacher at a school close to their home in Washington DC. They had met when Matteo was covering the re-election of Ronald Reagan in 1984, as Vivienne had been an enthusiastic supporter of the incumbent President.

Jenny's parents were due to join them, although Giuseppe had increasing mobility issues after developing arthritis. Now seventy-eight, he still kept a firm eye and control over his gambling businesses in Atlantic City. He had acquired a stick, which he enjoyed using in dramatic gestures or in a threatening manner if he disapproved of anything – which, Jenny mused, was pretty often. The long-suffering Gina endured his outbursts, relishing the opportunity to berate Giuseppe, but in good humour. She was five years younger than her husband, and refused to accept her age warranted any help, brushing away any offers of assistance except those she directed. In many ways, Jenny had come to admire them both as she had grown older. She knew their early lives had not been easy, yet they had forged a successful existence despite arriving after the war as impoverished immigrants. In later life they had built up a relationship which kind of worked, both seemingly enjoying their ritual spats during which Gina would despair at Giuseppe's wayward behaviour.

Jenny recognised qualities in them both which she had inherited, including her father's unflinching drive tempered by her mother's shrewd ability to evaluate issues and argue with an incisive edge. As with many Italian households, she recognised the delusion Giuseppe held that he ruled the home, when in reality he often had to defer to Gina and retreat with mumbling expletives in his native tongue. Although Jenny had emotionally distanced herself from her father for many years, he had sort of rehabilitated himself in her eyes when he stopped drinking heavily twenty years before. From a daily bottle of grappa or bourbon, he had limited himself to a few glasses of wine around mealtimes.

Christmas dinner was a traditional event, and a time when they would reminisce about the year that had passed and reflect upon what lay ahead. Inevitably, the conversation now turned to the year's major news story and the events in Washington surrounding the impeachment process. It had all started as they considered the worthiest recipients of a family toast. This custom had started many years before in the Baronio household. It had once been the cause of a major family row when, to Jenny's horror, her father had proposed President Richard Nixon; a step too far for her outspoken liberalism to take. They had ended up shouting abuse across the table, the occasion spoilt, but these days family tiffs were always over quickly and forgotten.

For the nomination of the 1999 Baronio toast, Jenny went first, stating that the recipient most worthy of their recognition was Nelson Mandela, who had stepped down as South African

President that year. He had, she said, been an inspirational legend who had set an extraordinary example by establishing a reconciliation process between those involved in supporting apartheid and those who had fought to overthrow it; this despite being imprisoned by the state for twenty-seven years.

This nomination drew applause from her daughter and her mother, whilst Braden muttered darkly, to an approving nod from Giuseppe, "Yesterday's terrorist, tomorrow's hero."

Gina proposed that they toast the marriage of Prince Edward to Sophie Rhys-Jones. The wedding, she said, had been wonderful; and the bride, "*lei era così bella... bellissimo*". ('She was so beautiful... ravishing.')

"*Sì, she avere le mani in pasta* ['Yes, she has her hands in the dough']," replied Giuseppe, prompting a swift single finger gesture from his wife. Unchastened, he stood up, raising his glass, and announced that he wished to toast Gina for being the most unreasonable woman a man ever had to put up with but "*La amo.*" ('I love her.') He beamed as she told him to sit down before he looked even more stupid.

That left four further nominations, and Jenny felt the tension rise even before Braden spoke.

"I nominate Kenneth Starr, the only man in Washington who has had the guts to stand up to President Clinton and the establishment – and, Jenny," he looked directly at her with cool, mocking derision, "that should suit your lifelong campaign, I believe, to challenge those in authority for the greater good."

She felt her anger, but quelled it in an instant, refusing to credit him with any reaction other than an aloof smile.

However, her daughter was a true Baronio with a passionate spirit, and was not inclined towards polite ripostes. "Papa, you are so full of shit, you hardly deserve a response. Our President is a great man, an inspirational leader, and an achiever deserving of better than you will ever understand. You know why? Because all your life you have derided anyone who has truly stood up for a principle. It's people like you and your Republican friends who have tried to oust the President because you don't care one jot for democracy when the people vote in a committed reformer. That frightens you, because it means change. President Clinton is a giant of a man, championing peace, healthcare reform for the poor, and civil rights. Those are issues my mother stood for which you have always mocked. You are so small-minded, I am ashamed to call you my father. I propose a toast to President William Jefferson Clinton. Here's to you, Bill!"

Braden walked out as Gina attempted to calm Maria down.

After a few uncomfortable minutes, Giuseppe raised his glass. "I give a toast to democracy, because when I was growing up, we dared not speak our minds about Mussolini. We are lucky to be able to disagree."

Maria apologised to Vivienne for raising her voice about Republicans, pointing out that she was not really partisan. In any event, she acknowledged that many Republican Senators had voted down the impeachment process, thereby effectively supporting President Clinton. Vivienne smiled graciously, saying that she hardly dared now to give voice to her chosen nominee, Mikhail Gorbachev, who she said was a visionary responsible for both transforming Russia and helping to free Europe. This brought smiles to the room, defusing the atmosphere.

Matteo added that he proposed that they toast Pope John Paul II, "because he is the unspoken force behind the downfall of communism in Eastern Europe, and a man dedicated to peace and freedom. He is one of the most remarkable men I have covered in my entire career. He has championed human rights, civil rights, the poor and the needy, while opposing the death penalty." He raised his glass and all applauded, before affirming the nomination with nods of agreement and rising to join him as he uttered the words, "To an inspiration to the world: His Holiness, Pope John Paul II."

The family finished their dinner without Braden, enjoying the conviviality. As laughter replaced the tensions from earlier in the evening, Jenny admired her daughter's outburst, which reminded her of her own battles with her father many years before. As the evening drew to a close, she stayed downstairs by the open log fire she loved so much, reflecting on a dream from long ago. Why was it that whenever her life hit a crisis she was drawn backwards, instead of seeking new answers? She poured herself a large cognac; then, sitting cross-legged on the floor, which she had not done for a very long time, she resolved two things: to get rid of Braden, and to cross a bridge she had not crossed for some time.

Just before she went to bed, her mind wandered, and as she was drifting, warmed by the cognac, she heard the sounds of gentle surf just yards away as the scented breeze caressed her.

23rd December 1999
Liverpool

Peter watched as the unusually heavy flakes of snow rapidly covered his garden and, in minutes, carpeted the entire view outside. The sounds of the *Moonlight Sonata* drifted gently through into his consciousness as he settled to analyse the figures turned in by his latest investment. The new venture was designed to link those in business through a self-perpetuating, growing network. Early indicators were outstanding, with a significant take-up on the low-cost platform that had been designed to give career details, skills and a message box. Premium-membership benefit packages were being taken up fast, whilst advertising interest was growing.

Both founders of the networking website were twenty-two years of age, and at a recent Business Angels event each had taken a turn in explaining how the World Wide Web was going to transform "the way we all behave". Peter had watched as they lost their audience by displaying little charisma, but his attention was drawn by their chart showing potential user growth on a website that had only just been launched. Within a year, they estimated that users would have expanded from the current two hundred by over a thousandfold to a quarter of a million. There was little competition for investing in their idea, which required £175,000 for a shareholding equating to 20%. It was relatively easy for Peter, with his business skills, to persuade them of the unrealistic nature of their investment profile, and he rapidly obtained agreement that IA (Investment Angels) would invest the money for a 51% holding.

This was typical of Peter's successes in his growing investment portfolio in an area in which traditional investors were missing out. He was staggered by the transformation the internet was bringing about; changing buying trends and overturning business-model expectations. Music was being downloaded via Napster, not bought in shops; hotels were being booked online; online auction sites were being launched, creating a platform on which anyone could sell; and most homes now had a PC. Peter had bought his first computer – a large, bulky box, screen and a keyboard running Windows 3.1 – only five years earlier. He recalled one of his nervous new business partners enthusiastically presenting his case: "I want you to imagine the market potential, Mr Chainey, with a 5,000% increase in internet users projected in just eighteen months. Mobile-phone owners will be able to access the web in the next year, and estimates are that users of these phones will then increase by 1,000%. We are talking meteoric growth!"

Peter and Jonas could hardly believe their commercial success, carried on the life-changing technological tidal wave that was engulfing the world. On that night, as he watched the snow thicken, Peter reflected on the price of his ongoing success which, right from his adolescence, seemed to have stolen so much from him. He had lost his dear friend and colleague in the Gulf only nine years earlier, for which he still carried guilt. He regretted that he had never told one of the greatest influences on his life, Rubin Granville, of the genuine love and affection he had felt for him. Emotion still did not come easily to him; it had not been an option in his childhood although he had opened up briefly in his early adult years, but, as he so often repeated, that was then and this was now.

His almost ruthless pursuit of his business goals had cost him dearly, for he had missed out on having children and, more recently, separated from Barbara after seventeen years. They had never developed the closest of relationships but it had worked for them, although she hinted many times that they needed to think seriously about a family. It wasn't that he didn't want children; it was just that he thought he wouldn't have enough time for them. She had studied to be a teacher and taken up an appointment in a school close by. They were comfortable financially and she concentrated her energies into her school, spending hours outside lessons in extracurricular activities with the pupils. When they were home together, Peter invariably had business issues to look into or meetings to plan. They rarely argued, and actually liked one another.

It was Barbara who awoke one morning in 1999 saying out loud, "You know what, I like this man, but I don't love him." As she said the words, the epiphany followed that there had to be more than this in her life. It wasn't that she wanted another man; she just wanted to live a little, and life had sadly passed them by without her realising to what extent. She did not think she had wasted her years, just that it was time to move on. She harboured no blame or anger towards Peter. That Saturday, as the moment came to her, she realised that he was a wonderful man, just not for her. By the time he came home that evening, she was ready to speak with him. He, unsurprisingly and typically, she thought later, just nodded and acknowledged that what she had surmised was true. He had no rancour, nor any undue sadness; just a recognition that his life needed to change too. He readily admitted to her his failings in being too busy to spend time with her, which he knew hadn't been fair. They hugged that night, and made love, which seemed somehow natural as they felt closer, having shared the truth, than they had felt for too many years.

No solicitors were involved, nor were they needed as they sat together over the ensuing weeks, dividing up the possessions that both wished to keep. They were quite smug as they announced to those they knew their decision to genuinely remain friends, which they managed to do. Bizarrely to many, they continued to meet and socialise together and, as Peter smilingly admitted, they probably enjoyed a better relationship apart than together. He began to rediscover books which he had had no time for since his student days, and the pleasure of immersing himself in a fantasy world brought back the comfort of his early years and a calm he had forgotten.

As he watched through his windows, mesmerised by the snow falling lazily, late that December evening, the flickering flames of the log fire sending uneven shapes dancing across the room, he pulled himself away from the thoughts that haunted him. *I am content really, and have much to be content about.* Yet, he knew then that his contentment betrayed the fact that there was so much more. Tomorrow, he would join his parents to celebrate his first Christmas in many years as a single man, and he felt something was missing. He began to think of ways in which he could change in the New Year, but knew he probably would not follow through with any of them.

Still, the approaching millennium heralded a new start; although, many warned, it might also bring Armageddon or the end of the world as we know it because of something called the Y2K bug. As computers were forecast to crash because of the forthcoming change in date format in the year 2000, alarmist predictions abounded that planes would fall out of the sky, systems fail, and countless records be lost for all time. However, a programming expert Peter knew had reassured him that it simply would not happen and that, where problems occurred, they could easily be resolved. As usual, a market opportunity had been created out of a semi-myth, and millions were being made for supposed Y2K fixes. Whilst critical of the ethics behind this,

Peter wondered whether, in reality, his own career had been any more honourable.

He reached into a glass cabinet, pouring himself a large Scotch, before settling into an armchair to read *Jonathan Livingston Seagull*. He was flying free, wafting on a warm breeze above a beach he once knew, as welcome sleep engulfed him.

39

The Millennium

Peter had spent the evening alone; the symbolic nature of New Year's Eve had long passed him by. He heard fireworks, and had watched other world cities celebrating on TV. First there was Sydney at lunchtime UK time, then later New York, Paris and London, with breathtaking pyrotechnic displays, each doing their best to outdo the others for the millennium.

He was about to retire to bed, but thought he would check his email to catch any messages from family or friends. He remembered somewhat wistfully his recklessness many years before – the parties, the music, and an awareness of being part of a new era. He wasn't a natural partygoer but had loved the few he did attend, especially at university. At that time, he was driven by a need to make a difference. His generation had been part of a new permissive society that had rocked the foundations of the post-war establishment still fighting in vain to re-establish traditions which Britain would no longer accept. There would be no return to the

299

dogma of a class system, although some clung obsessively to labels of working, ruling, middle and upper middle class as if they gave them an identity. Peter had joined those who reached for freedom before retreating to the real world he now inhabited. Long ago, life had been his to grasp, but now it felt like he was grasped by the life he had created.

"You've got mail," announced the feminine electronic voice from his computer. He clicked on the AOL icon to see a list of messages. One title stood out, and that simply said, 'Our Covenant'. He visibly started, and felt a tremor, hardly daring to move the pointer towards the message, yet he could not ignore it. He moved his mouse tentatively downwards; the message was probably nothing and from another source... yet he knew few people who regularly used email other than the younger members of his family. He had been receiving New Year faxes all day from friends – various cartoons, mostly of a somewhat rude variety and satirical at best. Peter was held by the email title and, as he stared, was tempted to ignore it. Perhaps it could wait until morning... but he was drawn back, drawn deeply, drawn in a tremulous, ridiculous way, hesitating as though frightened that it would not be from the source he hoped, or that it would be. *My God*, he thought, *I am fifty-two years old – what am I doing?* Finally, he hovered and clicked; the words jumped out at him and his heart pounded.

Hi to you, all the way from New York City with a message of love and peace from across the pond. I could not let this iconic moment in time pass without revealing a secret to you, but never tell anyone or my reputation will be ruined... perhaps for the best.

My beautiful man – for that, oh, Peter, is what you have always been to me over so many, many years, giving me such strength when I was at my weakest – crazy though it may be, as the years passed, our memories have flooded light into the darkest areas of my life. I do not know what drives me to tell you this after all this time, and as a grounded woman with a successful career, I question myself. Maybe past memories are cathartic because they take us back to a fairy tale that time has allowed us to enlarge, or maybe there is truth in the notion that our innocence made our world more wonderful before we were contaminated by reality and pragmatism – God, I hate that word.

I am writing this at 5pm and will time clicking 'send' to reach you on the stroke of midnight UK time, opening the new millennium. I hope your computer has not imploded because of the Y2K bug, or you may never see this.

Forgive me, Peter, but I need to open up to you despite the chasm of time, because my memory has bridged that gap tonight. My soul aches to tell you what I have hidden from all those around me, and often from myself for far too long. I should not walk backwards but at so many points in my life, I have been back where we started, hearing your voice, and slipping my hand into yours. I seek nothing by telling you this, but I would not forgive myself if I did not.

Thirty years ago, I met an amazing guy that rocked my world and I fell so in love with him. Even now, I can recall your touch and it sends shivers down my spine. Every dream I had was fulfilled by being with you, and my joy was in sharing every moment with you. It was like the corniest of Hollywood movies; like you were my Omar Sharif and I was your Julie Christie – remember that incredible movie, Doctor Zhivago, in which they too were separated from one another? Except our separation was real – oh God, so very real – and remained so after we parted. I reached for you then, as I have done throughout my life, cherishing all we had as though it was sacred to my being, which it was and remains to this day. I ran from my feelings, burying them in my work; I guess I needed something to pursue, and that gave me a relentless drive in my career.

I have become more and more aware of a terrible realisation — that I have betrayed too much along the way and you probably would hate all I stand for now — but somewhere, somewhere deep inside me remains the girl I once was, with the purest of ideals and the impurest of all you so beautifully released in me. I still have ideals, I think, buried someplace, and I have wishes that I never dare admit to, but I bless the memories we created for daring me to even think about doing so.

Sometimes, as now, I recall my Covenant, given with such an innocent belief in us which drove my words then, and drives them now. "You are my rock of life, for you, my joy, are my revered foundation; you are my river upon which reason flows; you are my mountain of strength; you are my calm sea; you are the sky that I reach beyond; you are the wind in my hair, the soft breeze that breathes upon me; you are the heaven we reach; you are the wild, tempestuous storm of passion within me, yet you are the stillness within my quietest places."

I am still on the beach, my baby. Welcome to the new millennium.

Jenny x

Peter sat back, and he felt her in that moment; he could sense her, smell her, taste her, breathe her. He could see the view from their tent, pitched just back from the shore of Grimaud beach, and the sea shimmering, stretching endlessly before them. Long days beckoning their laughter as they ran into the waves early in the morning, before returning to immerse themselves sensuously, nakedly in each other's arms, kissing deeply. They were making love in the first light of dawn, her soft cries as he reached for her, the sound of their passionate unity swallowed by the cascading of the waves returning again and again like those of their release.

He was in a forgotten yet evocative trance, and suddenly realised that over an hour had passed. It was nearly 2am and he found himself checking the time in New York; he just wanted to connect with her, and think of where she would be, day or night. It was 9pm there on New Year's Eve, and he wondered about her and what she might be doing. Had she a family commitment? Was she planning a night of celebration? Should he even consider any thoughts that he was denying and, clearly, he should not go there, should he? Then, fingers hovering, in an unusual act of recklessness he clicked 'reply', embracing the delicious thrill of his impulsiveness. Why not? After thirty years, wasn't it time to be free from his constraints for once? He thought for a minute before writing:

My dearest Jenny,

I can hardly write this without emotion overcoming me, despite all the years that have passed between then and now. I thank you for your words, which have echoed down to me. It is over thirty years since I last saw you, although I have never forgotten you, nor the incredible experience we shared, and the love that became our joy.

You played such a wonderful part in my early life, and I too have replayed our moments together over and over. I cannot believe it but I am now fifty-two years old. I no longer have long hair and I'm afraid it is a little grey at the edges, but I like to think I look distinguished. Oh, and the beard has gone too, and the sideburns which I think we might once have referred to as cool!

It is nearly 3am here and I do not know why I am writing except to say that all we experienced then was so incredible. I suppose we would have called ourselves 'groovy', and I know my experience with you was 'totally way out of sight'.

Of all I treasure from those amazing times, I remember, as yesterday, how beautiful you were when we exchanged our

Covenants. The words we gave to one another were like sacred vows which I cherished then and have always valued, despite returning to reality. Jenny, were we running away from a heaven we could have made if only we – or I – had had the courage? I think I shoulder more responsibility than you. I carried that guilt for many years, but it drove me forwards with a ruthless determination to succeed. I remember once I was a dreamer, and often wish I could still find that person. I too have betrayed so many of my deeply held beliefs as life has presented me with choices, many of which I feel ashamed to have made. What happened to the convictions that I once held? I sometimes wonder, yet I still cling to a sense of purpose or justice in what I do… or maybe that is a delusional effort to placate my guilt.

Jenny, I can't recall all I once said to you in our incredible Covenant, because I ran away from those words, but I still have them, rolled into a scroll. Call me an old romantic, but mine is kept with yours, tied with red ribbon. Hey, you know what – I'm a hard businessman, yet I still treasure those words, locked by a bow I tied and which I have not undone in twenty years. I do remember one part of my Covenant which has always stayed with me, and always will because it sums up not only what we held dear but part of what we celebrated during that far-off Summer of Love. These words are engraved on my soul, and I have, dear Jenny, never shared anything like them with anyone else. Do you remember? "I shall never deny you or all we have and all that we have discovered within us. I pledge that I will always love you, and that is my bond I give to you."

And so, on this first New Year of the millennium, I send you my Covenant once more as a testament to two young people who once found the meaning of their lives, but then did not have the courage to hold on to it. This will remain our secret, but maybe, one day, I will untie that bow that has restrained my words. You lit up my life once, and I so hope that you have found another with whom you can share a loving relationship. I have often thought we were saying our final goodbyes; yet we have reached out for one another at moments in our life. Many of those times you may not know of as they happened in my quietest places, but I now know from your words that you have also reached for me.

The memory is in the story we started, yet never reached the end of, or even dared to go beyond the first chapter. And perhaps that is where the preciousness that only we know should remain: locked in the embrace of our thoughts. I once gave you a Covenant, and it remains but has never been called upon. I know I will respond if ever you need me, but that should only be when we dare to recognise that we cannot live with our reality, and need to reach beyond and seek a dream. My lovely Jenny, we have a memory within us which we should keep sealed by our Covenant.

My parting admission to you, and my confession, is that I have never forgotten and will treasure always the highs we reached then, which I never reached again; they have been the only living poetry in my life and I do not have the courage to wonder whether the last verse will ever be written.

Goodnight, forgive the inadequacy of my words (I am a Scouser), and bless you always.

Peter x

He read and reread the message, not really understanding why he was hesitating, then with a rash finality clicked 'send', immediately wanting to retract his words but happy that he could not.

It was not until after midnight that Jenny returned to her computer screen, having forced herself not to keep checking to see if she had received a reply. Her excuse to herself for accessing her emails was that she might hear from Maria, who had gone over to visit friends in Boston. Braden was occupied at his golf club in a newly elected role as director of entertainment. This gave him yet more status in the little life he occupied, she thought, instantly regretting that dismissive cruelty.

Jenny had become happy in her skin, enjoying her independence with more time for herself, and knew that she was on a course to free herself from the constraints of her marriage. That night she had spent the evening watching celebrations unfold across the world, and in a bohemian gesture had opened a bottle of champagne. She had childish urges to run to her PC and see if she had mail, but… she resisted. She felt a kind of elation that she had dared to cross a self-imposed barrier with an email she knew it was impossibly rash to send, but rejoiced in the sending. Her impulsiveness had created within her an excitement coupled with an anxiety that her words would be ignored or rejected as being ridiculous. Why had she reopened this door yet again? Was the past illusory or as vivid as the love she had never let go?

At 11.30pm, she watched *New Year's Rockin' Eve*, or *NYRE*, on ABC as she had done for years. God, she was so tempted to check her mail. As usual, Dick Clark was in his iconic role reporting the *Ball Drop* from Times Square, and she smiled as he had become almost a parody of himself because he was so linked with this annual event. Watching the drama of New Year helped her to dwell on something else, distracting her from dashing to the office where her computer lived.

As the brightly lit, sparkling gold-coloured ball began its annual drop, she felt a flutter of youthful excitement and exuberance that she had not experienced for many years. She watched, still fascinated, as the ball descended off the Times Building, as it had done since 1907, in the last minute before midnight. Then, as it dropped the final few feet into a huge 'Year 2000' cradle, thirteen cannons blasted 3,500 pounds of confetti to flood the delighted, cheering revellers. Prepared for this moment, she reached for her glass of Veuve Clicquot and lifted it with the words, "To my ice-cream hippy – in the words of the song, *I will always love you.*"

Then, despite being deliciously shocked by her own behaviour, she poured herself another, pausing momentarily to listen to the pipers playing 'Auld Lang Syne', followed by Dick Clark saying, "You would not find happier people in the world outside of New York City."

She left the room and, moments later, shrieked with delight as she saw an email from Peter Chainey in her inbox, waiting to be clicked.

As Jenny read, she could feel him next to her, almost speaking the words, and by the end, tears were trickling down her face. She knew, he knew, and that night, their Covenant was re-established.

40

"Disbelief... Terrible Sadness... and Anger"

Tuesday 11th September 2001

Jenny had arrived at 7.30 that morning on the 6am United Airlines Flight 71 from Washington Dulles International, having travelled from her home for a meeting at her former New York office. Senior partners had arranged a strategic meeting to consider her proposal for a new initiative in defence management strategy.

She had moved to Washington in June the previous year, having commenced divorce proceedings against Braden on the grounds of adultery. He had put up no fight. In fact he was relieved, as it left him free to pursue his hitherto clandestine relationship with a sales executive working for his insurance office. Jenny had suspected his infidelity for some time, and when she finally discovered a message on his cell phone containing evidence of an affair, she almost welcomed it. This gave her the clear grounds for divorce that were required in New York, which did not accept no-fault actions. For Jenny, the year 2000 had given her an impetus and a determination for a new start without any encumbrance from her past with Braden, which no longer had any relevance to her present. Christmas 1999 had been the final straw, but she was not sorry in that it gave her a clarity in the way she viewed her marriage. Maria agreed that divorce was for the best, saying to her mother, "I can't understand why you stayed with that schmuck for so long."

Jenny had vacated the matrimonial home, moving to Washington DC and taking up residence in Barnaby Woods at 31st Street Northwest within a half-hour drive of her office. It was smaller than her previous residence but she loved its proximity to her workplace, the seclusion of the tree-lined neighbourhood, and the luxury of having a sizeable home office in an extension above the large garage.

The Washington offices of Latham Ellis Piper at 505 9th Street Northwest had a sober atmosphere, complete with white classical-style pillars in a palatial reception area, and grey polished-marble floors. As she had waited to be greeted on her first day, she had noted, with some surprise, that there was a large painting of Sir Winston Churchill staring down at her. *There always seems to be a link between the United States and all things British*, she thought, smilingly reflecting on the extraordinary connection she had felt with one person from England all her adult life.

As she took up her new position, she recalled the irony of Professor Wostenholme's remark the last time she saw him that she would be closer to the centre of power than ever. The offices were just four blocks from the White House. There was a constant stream of visits from White House officials, Senators, Congressmen and Ambassadors, whilst the presence of other well-known personalities was not a surprise but part of the accepted routine. Her office was no less opulent than the rest of the building, bathed in the light of an enormous crystal chandelier, with polished mahogany floors and a number of Persian rugs. Her desk was a large semicircle which wrapped around her, and her seat a generous leather chair with full, padded arms. She reflected that she enjoyed these trimmings, which would have been the envy of many in the White House. Certainly, her office was more spacious than most she had visited there, and also included a well-stocked bar, which she found somewhat ostentatious. She absorbed herself not only in casework, but in reorganising management policies inside the firm. For the first time, she barely noticed when George W. Bush was elected to office on the 7th November 2000.

On this September morning, Jenny ordered a cab to take her to Washington Square Park, where she often liked to visit and reflect. The sky was a crisp, crystal-clear blue, almost autumnal, yet warming by 8am with just the trace of a wispy moon still visible in the slight haze over the iconic Manhattan skyline. She sauntered towards the historic Washington Square Arch, based on the Arc de Triomphe in Paris, commemorating the inauguration of George Washington a century before it was built. This was a bastion of tranquillity where she liked to sit and clear her mind, free to explore some precious, private thoughts away from the pressures of her heavy schedule. She loved wandering the curving pathways outlined by plantings and interrupted by small, meandering meeting places. Here artists gathered, showing their work with an abstract nonchalance, and musicians explored their blues, expressing themselves freely in a somewhat bohemian contrast to the symbols of capitalism which overshadowed the park. Yet, she mused, had this beautiful place triumphed by surviving and thriving despite the overbearing centre of commerce attempting to dwarf its symbolism?

She glanced at her watch: 8.46am. That gave her another peaceful hour before she would have to catch a cab to the office to face reality in a 10.30am meeting.

Then she heard, rather than saw, the approach of an aircraft, suddenly imposing and with ever-increasing volume; at first, the familiar far-off jet engines, then a growing intensity of sound bringing an alarming awareness. Her fear grew as the noise increased to a roar, her head turned upward as a flash of silver caught her eye, streaking past, the sound escalating to a deafening high-pitched scream. For a split second she thought it was wrong to allow aircraft to fly so low; then came the rapid, horrific realisation as she followed the plane's path. "My God, my God, oh no, no, no, please no!" Her voice was drowned by the shrieking engines, and she felt an unimaginable terror.

A second later the impossible occurred: she saw sunlight catch the wings, jarring every thought as the aircraft tore into the wall of the North Tower of the World Trade Center, swallowed in a huge flash and a cloud of smoke. The boom seemed overlong and shook the earth, echoing violently as she heard screams from those around her and, wide-eyed, she dropped to the floor. The sound ceased and all she could hear were the cries of others, terrified and shocked by the awfulness of what they had seen. Glancing around, it was as though the very Angel of Hell had swooped, wreaking fear and spreading havoc. She raised her eyes back to the tower and could see a black rip in its structure from which a huge pall of smoke with flame at its base was reaching to darken and contrast with the clear blue sky beyond. She felt sick, then wanted to scream but could not; shocked by the unreal, petrifying awareness of the horror she had witnessed. She shook uncontrollably.

In a daze, she began to walk out of the park in the direction of the terrible tragedy she could not accept must have occurred. There was no reason in her decision, yet many others were slowly moving in the same direction, some sobbing, whilst others held their arms out to offer comfort. Suddenly, there was an overpowering smell of aviation fuel, like being at an airport, only much stronger; she wanted to hide but wandered on, without really registering why. Sirens began to wail, and she was vaguely aware of police and fire service vehicles passing her with flashing lights. Her eyes were watering but she was driven to continue following and being followed in a line of people, although some they passed were standing rigid, just peering toward the tower or crouching down with their heads in their hands.

They had walked around six blocks, reaching Spring Street, when the sound of an aircraft could be heard again, increasing until a whining, whooshing noise filled the air. As their eyes raised, the sky exploded in front of them in a ball of hellish flame, showering streams of burning debris that arced in every direction. Screams filled the air, and Jenny found herself on the floor, not knowing what was happening, as the thunderous, deafening explosion shook the ground. She could not conceive the unreal feelings that overcame her for no part of her was prepared nor could comprehend. For minutes she sat, with others, many sobbing inconsolably, then she got up and continued walking towards the smoke, aware that both Trade Towers were on fire. She had no understanding of why or any normal sequence of thought; she was just driven on aimlessly. There were shouts that New York was under attack and missiles were being fired across the city. Paper rained down on them, fragmented pieces fluttering majestically, contrasting with the huge clouds of smoke billowing violently from both towers. She was crying, yet every instinct now was to help in any way she could, so she forced back her tears. Smoke began to hang heavy over the buildings, and the constant sirens of emergency vehicles were curiously welcome in the darkness descending on the city.

As she walked closer to the Trade Center complex, she could see roads cordoned off; then she reached a small car park off Chambers Street, where an attendant had a portable TV on a small table outside his shelter. She paused to watch a CNN report that the Pentagon had just been hit, and that America was under attack. Jenny watched in disbelief as the anchor, Aaron Brown, grimly reported on what she was witnessing in an unwavering voice, despite describing the events as "a grotesque sight". She felt as if she were in a surreal drama, yet one which CNN was verifying, and then her reaction was a desire to hide or seek refuge from the horrifying reality. Grimly, the reporter told of the attack on the Pentagon, with much loss of life. Jenny began sobbing, convulsing with grief and emotional trauma. As the smells of kerosene and burning became almost intolerable, she watched the footage change to President George W. Bush. His calm, sober delivery was strangely reassuring, as though bringing some order to the mayhem surrounding her. "May God bless the victims, their families, and America."

She realised it had only been forty-five minutes since she had first become aware of something terrifyingly wrong, and felt like she was caught in the crazy depths of tormenting evil. Someone put their arms around her, and then someone else, as they sought consolation, reassurance, or meaning in what was happening. She wandered the streets for some minutes, wondering what she should do, and time allowed her to gather some attempt at rationale; but before she could fully recapture her composure, the nightmare deepened.

Drowning the wailing sirens, there came a rumbling, thundering noise, almost like that of an approaching train but so much louder. Looking up, she saw the top of one of the towers collapse and descend with a horrifying sound, then another massive explosion. Fear gripped her afresh and she ran, with crowds of others, away from the direction in which she had been walking. Stopping momentarily and turning, she saw a tidal wave of thick smoke and dust flooding towards them. Panic gripped her as she ran, tripping, then rising again before sheltering in a doorway.

The door opened, and she was pulled roughly inside, gasping for air. A wet towel was placed over her nose and mouth, and an Italian voice urged her to "*Respira lentamente.*" ('Breathe slowly.')

She muttered, "*Grazie*", and thought how ridiculous it was that she should be conversing in Italian in the middle of New York City. Her eyes were stinging, her breathing laboured, and she muttered further weak thanks as she drank from a proffered water bottle. She looked down and wondered where her shoes had gone, and then a terrible noise and a rumbling shaking of the ground became what seemed like an apocalyptic earthquake.

The last thing she heard was an agonising scream. "Oh please God, no, not the South Tower too! Oh please, oh no..."

A soft hand on her brow gradually raised her back into consciousness. She was in a bed, a mask over her face. Her eyes were streaming and smarting as she tried to see.

She was gently informed by the reassuring voice of a nurse that she was in St Vincent's Hospital. "You were picked up by one of the ambulances cruising near the WTC buildings after the towers collapsed. You were so lucky you weren't closer, there have been many killed and injured on the ground, but oh my God, all those caught inside... I just can't imagine." The nurse's voice faltered, breaking with emotion, and Jenny found herself holding her hand, each taking comfort from the other as they tried to deal with the burden of all that had happened. They shared what they knew and what Jenny could recall. The nurse told her of yet another terrible tragedy involving a fourth hijacked aircraft which had crashed in Pennsylvania. They put their arms around one another as they cried and then prayed together.

Jenny was gently and sensitively interviewed by officers from the NYPD, who asked her for names and numbers of those they could call to inform them she was OK. A doctor appeared and applied some drops to her eyes, reassuring her that she would be fine but would suffer from bronchial difficulties which might impair her breathing for a few days. There was such humanity all around her, and TVs were wheeled in to the temporary emergency medical centre set up within St Vincent's showing news of was happening not only in New York, but across the country. Throughout the day, as medical staff attended to others in the beds around her, there was a sense of fellowship as they witnessed story after story of heart-wrenching sadness mixed with the triumph of human spirit. There were extraordinary accounts of selfless sacrifice, bravery, and simple acts of humanity which touched the soul. Jenny marvelled at the incredible dedication of the police, fire service and medical crews, all of whom were working under unbelievable duress, many knowing that colleagues had paid the ultimate price for their service to others. She witnessed ordinary people exhibiting extraordinary kindness in the care they gave. As the day's terrifying realities unfolded, she took comfort from the beauty of love and compassion so freely given and shared.

At 8.30pm, she watched as President Bush addressed the nation from the Oval Office of the White House, and the reassurance of national togetherness was overwhelming. At that moment, he earned her respect not only for the dignified way in which he delivered his words, but for the utter sincerity and sensitivity she sensed in him, as though he were speaking to her directly, and yet he was reflecting the grief of the nation.

"Today, our fellow citizens, our way of life, our very freedom came under attack... [These events] have filled us with disbelief, terrible sadness, and a quiet, unyielding anger. These acts of mass murder were intended to frighten our nation into chaos and retreat. But they have failed. Our country is strong. A great people has been moved to defend a great nation... Tonight, I ask for your prayers for all those who grieve, for the children whose worlds have been shattered, for all whose sense of safety and security has been threatened. And I pray they will be comforted by a power greater than any of us, spoken through the ages in Psalm 23: 'Even though I walk through the valley of the shadow of death, I fear no evil, for you are with me'... None of us will ever forget this day, yet we go forward to defend freedom and all that is good and just in our world."

Jenny felt a pride in the giving from others she witnessed around her, and she was deeply and profoundly moved. A quiet serenity washed over her, despite all the horrific chaos of the day, and she surprised herself by recalling the words she had written to Peter in December 1999: 'I should not walk backwards but at so many points in my life, I have been back where we started, hearing your voice, and slipping my hand into yours.' Today was one of those points in her life when convention had little meaning but honest, open sharing, even with oneself, could mean so much more.

She reached for her laptop, musing it was curious that she had kept hold of that, yet lost both her shoes. She was amazed to be informed that she could connect to the internet via a wire to her computer from a central modem. Communication online had, thankfully, been part of the disaster planning for catastrophic events. She began to write, without understanding the reason why but driven by a powerful, primeval instinct.

My dearest, beloved memory,

I know that we have too often said our goodbyes, each time believing it to be the last, but today I have faced a terrifying truth and witnessed the results of such depraved acts of inhumanity that I am barely able to believe 'the evil that men do'.

I am writing this from a hospital bed in midtown Manhattan, just over three miles from the greatest tragedy I have ever witnessed; one which I cannot comprehend and can scarcely conceive. No one should ever witness such evil, nor would I ever wish to again in my life. I find it hard to even imagine, for it is beyond what I am capable of understanding or wish to make any sense of. I cannot absorb the suffering of today; not only of those in the aircraft, in the Twin Towers, or at the Pentagon, but the shadow of sadness that will fall across hundreds of thousands, those who will be traumatised by personal grief, and the millions across the world who will be affected by the betrayal of all that represents any kind of civilisation.

I am OK physically, apart from dust inhalation as I was only a few blocks away from the towers when the tragedy struck, but I have been shaking uncontrollably on and off, which I am told is delayed shock.

I feel as though a great evil has been released upon us, which seems so very far away from the dream we wanted to

*imagine when our innocent hopes were to shape a new world.
We sought a vision in which love and peace would triumph,
led by poetic phrases, idealistic thought, music, and youthful
passion. I have watched for decades the horrors inflicted by
man during Vietnam, the terrorism of the '70s, apartheid,
Beirut, Northern Ireland, and the ongoing injustice in
Palestine. Then there are the Balkan Wars, genocide, ethnic
cleansing, the Gulf War, and the inequalities of a civilisation
that still lets famine blight millions of people's lives. Yet I have
also seen hints of what we sought in those beautiful thoughts
we shared; beacons of light that have shone hope where there
was none. I remember the wonderful coming together in the
Live Aid concert raising money to combat famine, which I just
loved, where inspiration was led by music. I have seen some
positives with the end of the Cold War, the inspirational Nelson
Mandela, growing awareness of human rights, and new hopes
for peace in the Middle East. Today, however, I despaired, but
I have also witnessed compassion and selfless giving that show
the real depth of love that we have the capacity for.*

*So once again, I have reached back through the years to
help me understand an uncertain tomorrow, and although my
today has been shattered, I reach for a future still buoyed by
the spirit of love. I have never been deeply religious but today
I prayed, and I know that in the depths of hopelessness, we
can always find hope again if we have the courage to reach for
it. Tonight I will cry and think of the lives that should have
been lived and the loved ones lost; I shall try to make sense of
a world that has the capacity for evil beyond comprehension,
and acts that go beyond the barbaric.*

*I have never shared my deepest thoughts with anyone
apart from you, and that was because of the amazing bond
between us that resonates within me to this day. I want you
to know that I opened my inner soul to you, and that, despite
all that has happened in my life, I am still, somewhere inside,*

the nineteen-year-old girl who fell in love with an incredible man a lifetime ago. Somehow, I have allowed so much of what was precious in our beliefs to be sacrificed to expedience. That wretched word has excused too much, and is so easily used to rationalise abuses of power and principle. Today, I feel ashamed of my life because I have been close to thousands who have lost theirs and probably deserved them far more.

The experience of our togetherness remains a beacon lighting up some of the darkest corners of my existence. By telling you this I seek nothing other than to share, once again, my thoughts with you. This day represents one of those times which make me dwell on the thought of some day touching you again. I hope we can reach out, as we have thankfully done before, without any expectation; but I count myself lucky to savour a memory for a lifetime – one which is so very evocative today.

One day, I so hope our paths cross, so that I may again look deep into your eyes and say these words to you: "I so loved you once, and have carried that love with me throughout my life as one of the most beautiful, precious gifts that Providence has given me." Bless you always, and pray to God for a future devoid of evil. Tonight I will pray for humanity, love and peace. I seek, with tears, hoping for a better world.

I Covenant to you that I will hold you in every season of my life: my wonder at the spring, my sun shining in the summer, my forever in the fall, and my warmth in winter. I shall never leave what we have together, and wherever I am, I shall always return upon your call.

Forever,
Jenny

Even though I walk through the valley of the shadow of death, I fear no evil, for you are with me.
(Psalm 23:4)

41

Finding Solace, Seeking Peace

12th September 2001

Peter arose at 4am from a fitful sleep in which he had found little rest after the horrifying events he had witnessed on TV the day before.

He had had a working lunch with Benjamin Weiss, the chair of one of his oldest investment groups and a close compatriot of Rubin's, at the Adelphi Hotel. As they left the restaurant, they noticed a crowd gathered around the TV mounted on a stand in the reception seating area. Their pace quickened as they heard an anguished cry from one of those watching. They stood transfixed as they observed the iconic Twin Towers of New York City with smoke billowing from both, joining in a hideous black cloud.

"Oh my dear God," Peter gasped, as someone turned, saying that two aircraft had hit the World Trade Center.

As the events unfolded, TV news reporters struggled to find words that could do any justice to the shocking, catastrophic scenes, many clearly attempting to suppress emotion as they faced such immeasurable tragedy. Suddenly, cries broke out as they could see people hanging out of the buildings; then it was reported that some were jumping from upper floors or had fallen. Transfixed by the dreadful spectacle, their instincts urged them to turn their heads away in disbelief; yet the terrifying events were awfully live with terrible clarity, like some disaster movie, but so horrifically real. A tear ran down Benjamin's face as he muttered, "God will never forgive this."

Peter and Benjamin stayed for thirty minutes and joined in the cries as they realised that the South Tower had collapsed in a swirling morass of smoke and debris. Then they walked slowly from the hotel, Benjamin holding on to Peter for support and comfort; then, solemnly, he shook Peter's hand, covering it with both of his before embracing him. "We are witnessing such wickedness in this world; today we have seen the face of evil, the like of which, after 1945, I thought we would not witness again." He shuffled away, shaking his bowed head, and was met by his chauffeur.

Peter felt a terrible, haunting connection with all he had seen, as though he was there, sensing the fear, hearing the noise, with such vivid awareness it disorientated him. His mouth felt dry, his eyes were smarting, and his heart was thumping. He was not only alarmed by what he had seen but, inexplicably, felt he needed to escape from it. His face was clammy as he sat in his car, and then he was breathless; he tried to take deep breaths but felt a growing tightness in his chest. He thought he must be suffering from a panic attack, and resolved to return home. Calling the office, he suggested to Tommy that they should close for the day as a mark of respect and, to his surprise, his colleague immediately agreed.

Peter drove slowly home, he was still short of breath with a soreness in his eyes which he did not dwell upon further until years later. He watched the constant news bulletins, each featuring even more graphic content and witness reports. By 11pm, he felt exhausted, yet sleep eluded him as image after awful image of the day's events seared into his mind's eye. Then, as he drifted from one nightmare to the next, he became aware of an unmistakable scent as a soft breeze blew over him, and he was back amongst the mimosas, reaching out for a hand which grasped his own. A calm descended, and he allowed the dream to swallow him.

On the early morning of the 12th, he saw the first shards of light herald the dawn, gradually clearing away a low mist coating his garden. As he watched from his lounge, his thoughts drifted to the thousands who had lost their lives the day before in such unimaginable circumstances. His chest, which had remained tight into the late night, had cleared; but his eyes were still sore. He could not bring himself to look at the television any more. The images he had witnessed the previous day were already too sharp, haunting him.

He wandered aimlessly into his study, glancing briefly at his PC, and decided to check the headlines. As he did so, he noticed his AOL icon flashing, informing him he had email. He clicked and jumped as the name 'J. Baronio' leapt out at him, and knew somehow, even before he read a word of her message, that she had been affected, that her life had been in danger. His heart pounding, he opened the email and felt her reach for him as he absorbed, rather than just read, her sensitive words that were somehow wonderful despite the terrifying subject. As he took in all she had written just a couple of hours before, he felt a connection between them beyond anything he had experienced since the day they parted. He printed out the email, reading it over and over again, then in a flood of revelation and defiance of his 'That was then, this is now' mantra, he went to his garage. There, he sought out the small trunk in which he kept important documents finding the box tied with red ribbon. He slid back the lid to reveal the scroll, also wrapped in the ribbon that he had taken from his mother's needlework box over thirty years before. He held the paper for minutes, remembering, before tentatively pulling the bow open, allowing the ribbon to fall and the pages to unfurl just slightly.

Immediately, he recognised Jenny's neatly spaced writing, recalling her copying the words carefully, sitting cross-legged in the shade of the open flap of their tent. He gently took the rolled-up paper and unravelled the years. First, he read his own words to her, and waves of sadness yet warmth too flooded over and through him, evoking feelings from that September day in 1969 that he had only briefly touched upon over the intervening years. As he read his Covenant, and read it again, he took comfort from the memories it released within him. He then read her Covenant to him, and was unable to hold back tears not of sadness, but of emotion he had tried to suppress for so long. Whilst the ribbon had remained tied, he had filed away his Covenant, pursuing the life he had wanted; but now it was untied, his thoughts were no longer constrained. Surprisingly, he actually felt quite positive and empowered by the experience. He began to write.

My love, for that is what you have been and remain in my life, although I have hidden from you these many years... or did I hide from me?

The events of yesterday have been the most horrific I have ever seen; yet you were there, and you must have been so incredibly traumatised. My heart reaches out to you, and I only thank God you were not seriously injured. After an event of such tragic ferocity, my words will be inadequate, but I hope you can sense the depth of feeling within me.

Nearly two years ago on New Year's Eve, I allowed myself to open to you my inner thoughts that I so often deny myself before turning away to face reality again. The paths we chose in our early lives have probably contributed to the success we both enjoy now, and so, as so often happens after momentous events, we question ourselves and then turn to the past for answers.

The truth is, though, that I have no answers and have often thought of the choices I made which do not reflect the idealism I shared with you. I do not think I am a bad person, but I chose to lead a life in which I sought out opportunity, reaping the benefits… but at what cost? Some may say I have exploited my position, and that is an uncomfortable thought I try not to dwell on. Facing the consequences of decisions we make is never easy, but I never regret the decision we made to be together in the dream we once created, and that stays with me.

Tonight I undid the ribbon that has safely wrapped up our Covenants, and dared to release many of the words I had for too long forgotten. Despite the catastrophic and tragic nature of the events that have invaded our lives in these past hours, I have drawn serenity from our words written all those years ago. They reflect a precious beauty that we were so fortunate to share and explore together. In these past minutes, I have taken much comfort from reading and absorbing our testaments to our love. The words might seem to belong to another life; yet, from reading them, I know and instinctively feel that they are so much a part of us, and will remain a part of us.

My Covenant to you is still there, as it always will be until a time comes when either or both of us decide we wish to be released from it; a time I hope will never come. Our Covenants will always bind our spirits, for they were created in the purity of the love that we discovered. The words we exchanged then still resonate now, and, despite the distance of years, I can readily repeat mine which I have revisited today: "I Covenant that my life will remain open to yours for all eternity…" They are from another time, but I am just as certain now that I will never turn away from you.

I previously wrote to you that I know I will respond if ever you need me, but that should only be when we recognise that we cannot live with our reality. We have a memory within *which we should keep our dream, and our Covenant. I will always do that.*

From these tragic days, I hope our lives are blessed with a better future; one which fulfils the hopes we once shared for a world full of love and peace.

I yearn to hold you not just for this moment, but for all time; not for any one reason, but for all reasons; not for myself, but for ourselves; not just for this life, but for our forever; not to seek you, but to find you; not to understand, but to wonder.

Bless you always.

Peter xx

As he clicked 'send', he sighed in realisation that he was not saying goodbye; nor did he now think they ever would. He knew he did not need her and was not seeking anything from her, but he could not deny that he might want her. He sat watching the maturing trees he had planted ten years before sway in a fresh wind, their screening giving the privacy that he had always savoured, and shielding his world from the outside. Time had changed so much, yet in many ways everything was as it had always been. He closed his eyes, imagining; an escape that books had once given him was now fuelled by memories.

In the years following, they both took comfort from the fact that there was no need, no regret, no sadness, no pain from where they had once been. There was only a shared acceptance that a Covenant existed between them that neither restricted them nor committed them, but within which there was a bond, a lifeline if it was ever reached for. After 9/11, they did not feel the need to seek one another, although they knew they were still bound by their joyful Covenant. Theirs was a union that required no connection; that demanded nothing but gave everything.

42

A Question of Conscience

Friday 14th February 2003

"We have met before, Ms Baronio," the smartly dressed officer announced as she admitted him to her office following an urgent message in a code she had not encountered since 1997.

She remembered him as a White House Attaché Officer from the time when she had assisted with the impeachment issue in 1999. General (formerly Colonel) Ritchie had even more bearing now, with his chest covered in medal ribbons and grey creeping into the blond hair she recalled from their previous meeting. He looked every inch the film-star version of a special forces officer, and addressed her with customary seriousness.

"Ma'am, I have been asked if you would agree to a meeting at the highest level to discuss issues of national security."

Jenny knew she did not need, nor did she desire, further involvement at 'the highest level'; yet there was an irresistible temptation in returning to the centre of power. She told herself that she no longer needed this, before surrendering in a sombre tone. "Then, General, you had better fix an appointment as I have a very busy schedule. Who am I to meet with?"

The answer she was given filled her with apprehension tinged with excitement. Secretary of Defense Donald Rumsfeld, she knew from experience, was a wily and ruthless man. She had first had brief dealings with him in 1977, six months after he had relinquished the post he now held for the second time, when she was still assisting with the Watergate mess. He had informed her, at a reception for the newly elected President Carter, that her work was important both in ensuring that justice was done "in the best way" and in protecting the office of President. "I still have influence," he had remarked with a Machiavellian smile. "These people in the White House just love a Midwesterner country boy from Illinois keeping them on their toes."

Subsequently, in the 1990s during her visits to the secretive 'conventions of peace and understanding', she had seen him rubbing shoulders easily with leaders and those of influence from all over the world. He had a ready, infectious wit which got him results. She had watched him reduce a room full of Russians to fits of laughter, dissolving suspicion, then opening frank conversations in which he was respected and listened to. Equally, she had attended covert meetings at such events where discussions took place regarding potential military or intelligence operations against those Rumsfeld had been socialising with minutes before. His disarming nature cloaked a man who achieved his goals with a ruthless efficiency.

Here I go again, she thought to herself as the limousine took her through the Northwest Appointment Gate to the West Wing of the White House and down the surprisingly short driveway to the entrance porch. Two armed marines were standing outside, and as she approached the doors they jumped to attention.

On entering, she was met by a smiling General Ritchie, who brusquely shook her hand before ushering her into a side office for a pre-meeting briefing. He informed her that the day before in Rome, there had been the largest demonstration ever recorded against potential military action against Iraq, involving over three million people. He went on to tell her, in a terse, unemotional tone, that the day before that, on the 12th February, the UNMOVIC (United Nations Monitoring, Verification and Inspection Commission) had reported that there was no evidence of weapons of mass destruction in Iraq. The leaders of allies such as France, Germany and New Zealand had voiced opposition to military action and, he concluded, "We are in a position whereby the legal legitimacy of our actions, and the policy spelt out by the President, are being called into question. This, ma'am, is I believe where you come in."

Five minutes later, she was led down a long corridor with polished floors and white columns on both sides, then through large double doors into an office which was thickly carpeted. Seated at a surprisingly small but beautifully ornate antique desk was an easily recognisable figure. His immaculate shock of neatly parted greying hair; signature round, frameless glasses; pinstriped suit and broad smile announced that she was in the presence of the Secretary of Defense. Donald Rumsfeld was charming, witty and engaging as always, but there was an air of cool detachment in his bearing. The end, in his world, clearly justified the means, and this meeting was to confirm just that.

"If I can call you Jenny?" he began, his hands extended in an open, customarily disarming gesture. "We have much to be grateful for in terms of your service to this country, and we need to consult you again, quietly, away from those who may question. To put it succinctly, Jenny, we know we can trust you."

He leant forward over the walnut desk. "The only way we can take military action against Iraq legally and with UN backing right now is if they have WMD. The truth is, we know they haven't got any, which leaves us in a pickle. The Brits have convinced their Parliament of the urgent need to act, using WMD as a pretext. My concern is the integrity of the United States and the position of the President when we go in. Saddam Hussein is finished, Jenny, but we need to convince the international community that we're doing the right thing. Furthermore, we must carry our own Congress and Senate with us. You have experience of influencing decision-making and we want to seek your input here."

Jenny recognised, once again, that it was the manipulation of truth that the administration needed, backed by her experience of effective 'lobbying'. Sighing deeply, she quoted from Shakespeare: "'I am in blood stepped in so far that, should I wade no more, returning were as tedious as go o'er.' The truth is, I have no desire to wade more. Mr Secretary, I will assist, but only in drafting words and statements. My opinion is that you must not concentrate on WMD, but begin by giving a wider context. Then, when the truth outs, which I know you men of power hate, you can use your statements made now as a cover to hide your intent – which, Mr Secretary, is a regime change, is it not?"

Two days later, the White House issued a statement:

The coalition aims are to disarm Iraq of weapons of mass destruction, to end Saddam Hussein's support for terrorism, and to free the Iraqi people.

Over the ensuing days, Prime Minister Blair began to disassociate himself from the weapons issue, despite that being the legitimacy justifying his request for parliamentary support for military action. As Jenny listened to his words on the news, she felt a pang of guilt, recognising her own authorship of what she knew to be a complete misrepresentation of the truth. Her hand was behind a deception not only in the US, but in the UK too. It was a moment of harsh self admission as she recognised that she was no longer involved in protecting the integrity of the office of President of the United States, but complicit in the corruption of that office based upon an agenda set by others.

In June 2003, a package arrived by courier at her office, with the White House emblem on the front. She opened the large padded envelope to reveal a silver frame in which was a portrait of a smiling George W. Bush in front of the Star-Spangled Banner. Hand written along one corner in blue ink was the message 'America thanks you, and I extend my deep gratitude', by the side of which was scrawled the President's signature. She recalled a previous President awarding her in just the same way. Her instinct was to smash the frame, which seemed to represent the hypocrisy that taunted her conscience. Then, with a shrug, she thought she may as well hang it with the others in her rogues' gallery. "Why the hell not?" she said ruefully out loud. "You all deserve one another." Then, switching her glance to a couple of them, she had just a flash of contrition.

In late 2005, Peter was surprised to receive a call from Major Ashford, from whom he had heard nothing for over eight years. A familiar yet shaky voice spoke to him.

"Hello, Peter, Richard Ashford here; a voice from the past but, you know, in our department, we try to retire and then find we can't. I am now eighty-five years of age, still playing soldiers and bloody well enjoying it; beats a nursing home!

"I am calling as we need you to get the investment strategy moving again which under this lot has lost impetus. After the election result this year, Blair will resign and Labour will become unelectable. We need to prepare now for building the future; planning with no loose ends and all that. A list will be delivered to you by courier of the people we want involved in a number of secret investment opportunities which will be created."

He had the energy of conviction in his voice, but less of the strength of the commanding figure who had sought to have a word with Peter in the council buildings nearly twenty-five years earlier.

"Despite the Tories not holding one single seat on Liverpool Council, we have a network of people we can rely on to apply the necessary pressure. We know investors will be guided by you in terms of targets, and I'm going to give you key strategic building projects where your bids will succeed. It is critical in the coming years that left-wing interests do not take credit for the successful regeneration of the city. Blair out and Brown in is a godsend."

There was some elongated coughing at the other end, interrupted by polite apologies. Then Major Ashford continued. "You are a good man, Peter, and I know we have asked much of you. My days are becoming less assured and not even my lot can stop the march of time. For that reason, and as someone I trust who is not involved with my associates, I want to tell you something as I need to relieve my conscience and warn you of how dangerous it is to speak out." There was a pause, as if Ashford was fighting within himself. "We all knew in Intelligence in 2003 that there were no WMD in Iraq, and we did brief those in senior Cabinet. The Iraqis got rid of all their big stuff in 1991. It was all bullshit to do with power-broking between Blair and the Americans. The worst thing is, it resulted in us going to war under a false pretext, but that's not all I want to get off my chest. On a more unacceptable level, even to a hard-headed soldier like me, there was something else. Someone died, and my lot, with my involvement, helped cover it up. Why? Because the poor chap was going to come clean to the press about the crap being spun about WMD. I feel complicit in something I fought against all my life."

There was a long, tired sigh, ending with more coughing. "I never saw anything carried out so blatantly since the Cold War. I don't know why I am telling you this, but maybe the world needs a little more truth. You know what, Peter, I have always hated politics but I despise liars even more, especially those who pretend to be principled. Never trust those in power, because others may be pulling the strings. Influencing power across the world, Peter, are some of the so-called greatest minds of our age, many unelected, and others who have held office. They meet secretly and decisions are taken behind closed doors. There is even one involved, yet hidden, right at the heart of our nation's most revered institutions.

I knew him as a young naval officer in the 1940s and he is well intentioned, but bloody ruthless.

"I've already said too much." Ashford paused for a moment before uttering some final chilling words. "Be aware that they look after their own, and that includes you... but only if you never breathe a word to anyone. You now know what they can do and what they *would* do to me if they knew that I had informed you. By the way, I never told you, did I? I was born in Liverpool and, even worse for you, I supported Everton FC. Goodbye, and be careful, my old friend." There was a chuckle, and he was gone.

Peter never heard from Major Ashford again. From time to time, he would receive a hand-delivered package containing details of property or land which was to be developed or sold, or for which tenders were invited. He could choose to either invest or alert those who were on the 'approved' list. His conscience questioned whether, in truth, his motivation was lucrative reward more than contributing to the regeneration of Liverpool.

Increasingly, he felt unease at having allowed himself to be corrupted, and wondered how, or even whether, he could escape. There were now so many times when he reflected on the intimacy he had shared with Jenny in the wake of 9/11, and that reassured him that a door was still there.

43

Always and Forever

15th September 2009

The message was delivered by hand to her office, requesting her presence at the White House… only this one was very different. On the envelope was a simple phrase – 'Issued from the Office of the President of The United States' – underneath which was the White House crest. This time there was no code and no high-ranking military escort, but inside the envelope was an invitation, on a card edged with gold, at the bottom of which was a handwritten signature next to the presidential seal. The words were simple:

The President of the United States would be honored if you would accept the Presidential Medal of Freedom with Distinction in recognition of outstanding service and dedication to your country; an award which has been endorsed by no fewer than five US Presidents. The award will be presented at a ceremony which will be held at the White House on October 30th 2009.

The invitation was signed, simply, 'Barack Obama'. She stared in a distant, abstract way at the odd, almost cartoon-like rendition of the 'O' on his name, which sort of reminded her of an image of a gyroscope.

Minutes later, the phone buzzed and her secretary announced, with breathless excitement, "Jenny, it's the President of the United States." She then added, with a suppressed giggle, "Will you take the call or shall I say you are too busy?"

Jenny sat at her desk, feeling like she was in a surreal place, outside of reality, picking up the phone handset which she rarely used. Her heart pounding, she heard the words, "Jenny, forgive the informality but this is Barack Obama; how you doing?"

She was, for once, hardly able to speak, almost whispering, "I'm fine, Mr President."

He sounded warm, like a neighbour, as he congratulated her and asked if she could make it to the White House as it would be an honour to confer the award personally. He apologised for interrupting her busy schedule and said he looked forward to meeting her, especially as he had heard she had a great gift with words. "A skill I have tried to master," he said, with a touch of affected modesty.

"Mr President, for once, I guess you have caught me off guard, and I declare, sir… I confess that I am a little lost for words," she managed.

"Then, Jenny, it appears the old skills I learned as a lawyer to wrong-foot my opponent still work. I'll be seeing you." And with a chuckle, he was gone.

The doors to her office opened and applauding partners and staff entered to congratulate her with champagne.

Six weeks later, she entered the Oval Office, accompanied by a marine officer who saluted smartly before closing the doors. She was watched proudly by her parents, her daughter Maria, and her brother and his wife as she walked towards the smiling, dark-suited, immaculately dressed President. He arose from his desk as soon as she entered, then shook her hand warmly, introducing her to Michelle Obama, former President George W. Bush, and Vice President Joe Biden. Glancing sideways, she noticed, standing with a couple of other White House aides, the grinning face of the irrevocable Henry Kissinger, who shrugged his shoulders when their eyes met, as if in an apology.

The President raised his hands solemnly, turning to the small gathering. "There are some who merit this honour through some great single act, but Jenny Baronio has served her country with unswerving dedication through no fewer than six presidencies, helping to support and protect the institution of President of the United States. She has carried out her duties often quietly and with little recognition. Today, we want to give her that recognition; we openly recognise her achievements, which embody the noblest of endeavours: that of serving this great nation of ours, selflessly and while upholding the highest values of integrity. Jenny, please step forward."

She moved slowly towards the President, welcomed by his warmth and natural charisma.

"Ginevra Maria Baronio, it gives me enormous pleasure – and indeed, it is a privilege – to present and bestow this well-deserved honour, the *Presidential Medal of Freedom with Distinction,* upon you." The President placed the blue ribbon, edged in white, around her neck with a measured dignity, allowing the white pentagon surrounded by gold eagles with stars in the blue centre to lower gently. He then bowed and shook her hand.

An overwhelming feeling of unreality, accompanied by profound pride, swept over her. There was applause as she shook hands with each person present before embracing both her parents. Her father Giuseppe, now in a wheelchair, attempted to rise. "*Mia principessa,* I am the proudest father in all of Italy."

She gently admonished him, to relaxed laughter, "Papa, this is not Italy; you are in the White House."

"Oh, Mama, I am so, so proud of you." Maria flung her arms around her. "I have come to admire you so much for your dedication to making our world a little better. I have modelled my whole life on yours."

That meant so much to Jenny; an affirmation from the daughter whom she had loved and planned much of her life around. It all seemed, however, a little bizarre that she was in the White House with the President, yet able to share a wonderful connection with her family simultaneously.

Michelle Obama spoke quietly to her. "You have a beautiful daughter who loves you. I was worried when we came here – I thought the White House was no place for a family – yet now I now treat it as my home; I make dinner for Barack, and we often chat about the day with our daughters, like a normal family. It's all a little crazy, but you know what, doesn't the normality make it a little reassuring despite the theatre?"

The setting was more than a little theatrical and surreal as Jenny stood by her family in the iconic Oval Office, surrounded by some of the most powerful people on the planet. There was something inevitable about the smiling figure of Henry Kissinger approaching her. "My congratulations go without saying, and well deserved." A pause, with a sidelong, quizzical look. "I seem to recall, Ms Baronio, that you once admonished me for espousing expedience. Yet, you might appreciate the irony of being given this honour. Did you accept pieces of silver to support an institution when you had reservations about the morality of doing so? My question would be whether your prosperity has resulted from expediency or commitment, or maybe both?"

Jenny had always relished being challenged, and retorted, "My integrity has lain in diligently carrying out my work, which has resulted from the poor judgement or mistakes of others. As a result, I believe the end justified the commitment."

Kissinger smiled again. "I never joust with a lawyer, and certainly not one of your reputation, but in Hebrew, 'prosperity' can mean peace, completeness, safety, health and satisfaction. So, maybe you *have* prospered? You see, I am better at questions these days, but I often find that, in proposing answers, others I advise find a better way." After this parting remark he wandered over to talk quietly with Vice President Joe Biden.

As they shared wine served by smartly dressed waiters in white jackets, the President broke away from his staff and took Jenny to one side. "Your reputation lies in saving many a difficult situation. I am only thankful I have not required you... yet. Practising law is one thing, but mixing it with politics is quite something."

She was disarmed by his charm and felt utterly relaxed talking to him, sensing in him a warmth and sincerity she had rarely experienced in her dealings with the White House. "I have to say, Mr President, my life's path is not without many questions, and I often worry I sacrificed too much of my self-esteem for what I perceived to be a greater purpose. I am honoured today, but I hope the personal cost justifies the end result."

Barack Obama looked at her earnestly. "You know what, Jenny, every day I ask myself a similar question, but if I hadn't sacrificed a little of what is important to me, I couldn't make the difference needed, and that is what I'm here to do."

She felt an openness and sensitivity in this tall, imposing man and his genial nature. "The question I ask, Mr President, is whether my work has been protecting the integrity of the institution of President or protecting the office from the man who occupies it? I am an old hippy and I once believed in simple philosophies like love and peace."

Obama laughed and took her hand. "Hey, you want to know something, Jenny? I've smoked marijuana, but don't tell anyone."

They both laughed then, sensing a genuine warmth between them. For once, Jenny felt relief that this was a presidency that would not need her, and she was right.

That night, as she drifted, she was drawn into Peter's waiting arms as the sound of the surf surrounded them.

On the 31st May 2009, Peter celebrated his sixtieth birthday quietly with family at his home. It was a Sunday, and he was expecting his parents, who were being brought over by his cousin. He had woken with an unease, looking back over his life. He felt increasingly disillusioned, recalling his formative years when, inspired by the age he lived in, he had relished the thought of a future in which his generation were going to change so much. Now he had become part of the very system he had pledged not to be part of.

When he heard the car on the gravel drive, he went to the window and watched as his parents were slowly helped out. He flicked the switch on his CD system for Glenn Miller to start playing 'In the Mood'; a favourite of theirs. Jim and Rose were now in their eighties and utterly devoted to and reliant upon each other. Jim had a stick which he affected was not needed, whilst Rose walked unaided but with a stoop; something, Peter reflected ruefully, she never would have allowed in him as a child.

Jim greeted his son with a handshake and an affectionate pat on his upper arm. Rose gave him a hug, which had been unknown until around ten years earlier. It was as though in later life she was taking comfort from expressing the affection that had been alien in the background from which she had come.

"Bloody hell, Peter, what's goin' on with that gobshite Brown?" his dad started, hungry for the political debate which had become a signature event whenever they met. "He's a friggin' armchair socialist."

This earned him a swift rebuke for swearing from Rose. Peter had come to admire his father, developing a closer relationship with him in adulthood than he ever could as a child. Jim was proud of Peter's achievements now, admiring his son's break away from his working-class roots. He retained a staunch loyalty to the

Labour Party but they both agreed, from differing perspectives, that the working class had been poorly served by government.

"I thought Blair was a waster, but this man Brown is hopeless," Jim continued relentlessly. "He has no charisma. Nice man, wrong job. He says he is tackling the MPs' expenses scandal – well, good luck with that one. He's led the country into deeper recession, failed to inspire, and lost the support of the working man. Now that young David Cameron; there you have vitality and spirit. I think I'm in danger of becoming a bloody Tory. We need another Margaret Thatcher – now, *there* was a real woman." This drew a playful slap on the back of his head from Rose as he sipped his schooner of sherry, which had become a favourite in recent times.

Peter's cousin Michael had slipped an album into the stereo – *Hits of the Hippies* – and as Janis Joplin's haunting yet melodic voice drifted to them he asked Peter what it had been like back then. As the music carried his thoughts, Peter related that it had been a time of amazing emancipation, but that it had been betrayed by those who sought to profit from it. The room went quiet as he opened up in a rare moment of emotional recollection.

"In 1969, I met one of the most wonderful people I have ever known; a beautiful person who filled my head with dreams I lived for three wonderful months. I fell in love with her, and she with me. They were the happiest days of my life; we were carefree and celebrated our own Summer of Love in 1969. I have never forgotten her; her name was Jenny, and I shall always treasure the time I was privileged to share with her. I live with regret for what might have been, and have done all my life since we parted. We separated so that we could pursue so-called normal lives and build our futures. I know it broke her heart, and it affected me massively. I have never spoken of this before, and I will not do so again." The last words were said with a quiver in his voice.

As his parents left that evening, they both looked closely at him, his mother saying, with a half-sob, "God bless you, Peter. I should have spoken to you back then; I'm so sorry."

His father clasped both hands around his son's. "I had no idea, lad. I never was any good at showing it, but I have loved you as best I could."

After they had gone, Peter went to the mahogany cabinet in his lounge and pulled out the scroll of paper he now kept there, still wrapped around with red ribbon. He read the words, written an eternity ago, trying to absorb who he had once been. In some ways they were more relevant to the person he felt he was becoming again or the person he had never really left behind. Those days had been a utopian fantasy; yet he longed to be there again, rediscovering his youthful exuberance. He drifted to his laptop, just knowing that he needed to, and wrote:

My dear, beautiful hippy chick,

I just thought of you, as I so often do, and could not sleep without sending these words: "I Covenant that my life will remain open to yours for all eternity, and that I shall never deny you or all we have and all that we have discovered within us. I pledge that I will always love you, and that is my bond I give to you."

I ask nothing, seek nothing, but wanted you to know everything.

Until we meet again.

Forever,
Peter x

Before he went to bed two hours later, he sensed her reply before he read it.

My gorgeous beach bum,

I think of you always, and life will no longer dim my thoughts; they shine with the sharing of our secret which has lasted forty years. I think one day we will kiss again, and I long to melt once more in your arms. Until the time comes, "You are the wind in my hair, the soft breeze that breathes upon me; you are the heaven we reach; you are the wild, tempestuous storm of passion within me, yet you are the stillness within my quietest places. I Covenant to you that I will hold you in every season of my life." In the Fall of my life, I await our moment.

Goodnight, always and forever.

Jenny xx

44

The Final Curtain

When the discovery was made, in February 2018, of Peter's investments outside Granvilles, an urgent meeting was convened. He entered the boardroom to be greeted by cool, aloof faces. As he had expected, Tommy Wilson was there, his thin, silver hair now receding, wearing an almost triumphant look, together with the chairman, Eugene Franklin, and Bill Marsden. Over the years, Peter had suffered their control over the domain he had once cherished as his own, and had worked with them, but with little respect for their input.

"Peter, I think we have a problem," Eugene began, somewhat sardonically.

Peter was reminded that, when they had come into the business, he had agreed that he would have no outside interests without written approval from the board. His internet investment work had been discovered when a young entrepreneur who had pitched to a Business Angels meeting had applied to Granvilles for a job and been interviewed by Tommy Wilson.

There had been an inevitability about this moment, and Peter was surprised that it had taken so long to happen. He had already decided that, at sixty-nine years of age, he no longer gave a damn whether he stayed with Granvilles or not, and it was only habit that kept him there. As the chairman's voice droned on, feeding his own ego, Peter's mind was elsewhere. He did not need his job as his portfolio with Jonas now gave him a six-figure return each year. He had little stress since reducing his working hours some years before, and still loved to dabble in the property market, although the investment guidance in sealed envelopes had ceased to arrive when the Conservatives came to power, which he kind of missed. Under Prime Minister David Cameron, there had seemed to be more stability in the country, very unlike the turbulent days of the early '80s when Peter had first become involved in the transformation of Liverpool.

In 2016, he had been sorry to see Cameron's government go, but knew that a referendum on Britain's membership of the EU had been the right step to take. There was an increasing frustration in the country that too much power had been ceded to an undemocratically accountable Europe with excessive bureaucracy. Peter was not surprised by the people's vote to leave, and felt that, for once, democracy was triumphing over political dogma.

These were historic times, and the ongoing debate over the future of the country after Brexit, together with the extraordinary, chaotic scenes in Parliament where there was little agreement or common ground, made Peter re-evaluate his own direction. He had already decided that it was time for a new life; and, smiling to himself, felt that his mind now was no different than it had been when he was a heady twenty-year-old selling ice creams on the beaches of the Riviera.

Peter had negotiated a part-time contract with Granvilles ten years earlier; ostensibly to take partial early retirement, but the reality was that his growing external investment portfolio required more input. He and Jonas had put together a strategy which suited them both, requiring minimal input to gain maximum return. They sought out smaller internet entrepreneurs who could develop and manage themselves, with financial monitoring from Peter. As he sat musing over the total value of his portfolio, whilst Eugene continued pointlessly, he had an urge to flick something at him, like he had sometimes done to the teachers when he was at school. Peter had always had a mischievous streak, and he was finding it hard to restrain a boyish impulse to bring the entire fiasco to a close, asking himself with an inner chuckle how his career could have plummeted so far from being an ice-cream vendor.

"…and so, Peter, we have concluded it would be appropriate for you to resign."

As he listened to those words, Peter felt an elation, as though a burden was lifting off his shoulders. The thought of being free from work actually had appeal; it had been a long time since he had lived with little or no responsibility.

"However, we will honour dividends to the end of the year if you agree to undertake a final mission in Dubai."

Peter made a decision that day to revisit the idiom that had dogged his life for too long, 'That was then, this is now'; changing it to 'What was then, lives on now.'

September 2017

The day the unmarked message was delivered to her by a courier was one she had pretty much anticipated would come. This was because Washington seemed to be in some disarray, and had become pretty weird in the past year; far more so than during previous transfers from one President to the next. She had watched the election campaign with mounting incredulity as Donald Trump played to the electorate, pandering to what she perceived to be the basest of instincts. A prospective President acting with such vitriol towards his opponent was one thing, but watching him leading chants of "Build that wall", citing a threat to national security from Mexico, had dismayed her. She had felt genuinely sorry for Hillary Clinton, whom she had known for many years and who, she thought, deserved a better opponent. Trump constantly wrong-footed her, not through skill but with behaviour that was utterly outrageous. After his inauguration Jenny had become increasingly concerned about his controversial decisions and contentious policies. These caused divisions in government and inside the Republican Party, and a deeper rift between the two main parties. There was no longer any kind of consensus politics, with Democrats being alienated and individuals personally insulted by the President. His mocking derision of Senator John McCain, a man in poor health who had been a patriot and a conviction politician from Trump's own party, appalled Jenny. She worried that the institution she had helped protect all her working life might be tainted not by political circumstances, but by the holder of the office.

She was not surprised, therefore, when she was asked to go to the State Department, via a coded request used to denote issues of national security. A plain envelope was delivered to her inside which was a simple briefing:

We will require your advice and opinion on the gravest of issues: the impeaching of the President of the United States.

There was no signature or evidence of the source, nor even an indication of whom she was to meet; only a date, a time, and a conference suite number.

In recent weeks, Jenny had made no secret of her views, as had been the case all her life, expounding her dismay to both Republican and Democrat friends that the country was being led into turbulence by the Trump administration. At a recent dinner, one Senator had listened intently before drawing her to one side. "We may need your help, Jenny. If you are called, are you prepared to join a movement for change?"

She had thought for a moment before dismaying herself by saying, "I want the best for the United States, and for that reason, I cannot join you, but I will help."

On arrival at the State Department, she was ushered to a ground-floor room in which a rectangle of tables had been arranged, around which thirty or so people were standing. As she walked in, she was greeted by a familiar face of General Samuel Ritchie, who was in full uniform, impressive as ever, his lines of ribbons giving him an air of experienced authority and sober credibility. He shook her hand brusquely before bidding her to sit by him as they faced the delegates. She recognised a number of them, including some of the big hitters from the Washington scene such as Senators and Congressmen, and one person sat to the left of Ritchie was definitely CIA. Coffee was served, adding banal normality to the drama of the unfolding events; a ritual she had seen so often before.

General Ritchie rose to his feet. "Ladies and gentlemen, we all know why we are here, and we are joined by an esteemed guest who has a fearsome reputation as a sharp, no-nonsense lawyer with forty years' experience in dealing with White House affairs." Then, with a wry smile, "And I don't mean those that President Clinton may have had."

A murmur of polite laughter broke the tension.

"We, in this room, represent many who are united today as Republican and Democrat, military and civilian, secret service and law enforcement, lawyers and staffers, because we may have a national crisis. Together, we are faced with an unprecedented situation: we must consider questions regarding the fitness of the President to hold office. Today we must seek answers, and we are here to brief others, all of whom love America as we do, but there is an inalienable unity in our need to consider those answers. We are not conspirators, but patriots faced with a situation our Founding Fathers, in their wisdom, anticipated, and we need advice not only legally, but strategically." There was a hushed silence as he paused, before saying quietly, "We are here to consider the impeachment of the President of the United States." He then invited Jenny to give her observations and advice on a direction, together with the legal obstacles involved.

Jenny began by giving them some basics to put them at ease. "First, may I reassure you all that none of you may be indicted for treason, because you are not levying war against the United States or adhering to its enemies. Take comfort in the fact that you may only be guilty of sedition… which is a grand felony."

Laughter ensued, following which she informed those present that she would not and could not have any part in potentially damaging the very institution she had worked all her life to protect. However, she was prepared to give legal advice and would do so in total confidence to anyone involved in any actions causing concern, together with the potential consequences. She counselled that in the event that investigations revealed irrefutable evidence of wrongdoing then impeachment was viable, but only with cross-party support. If Congress voted for impeachment, it would be a pyrrhic victory if it was along party lines as it would, inevitably, be overturned in the Senate. To the public, she warned, this would then be viewed as no impeachment, strengthening the President's position and, possibly, his popularity for standing up against Washington power brokers. She had already been briefed on clear evidence that the President had colluded with the Russians both during the presidential campaign and beforehand. However, the source of this evidence could not be released because the informant was, at the time, a close associate of Vladimir Putin. Jenny advised that any investigation should not just concentrate on the President, as evidence of collusion would emerge from those around him.

She stated that she had already had discussions with the former FBI Director Robert Mueller, who had confirmed that he had evidence of offences being committed by many of those working for the President. Her advice was to obtain confessions via plea bargaining in exchange for securing information on the President's direct involvement. Whilst he was adept at covering up his tracks, he was vindictive if those close to him expressed opposing views. Hence, he had made many powerful enemies, such as the man whom Barack Obama had appointed Director of the FBI, James

Comey. However, Jenny warned, for any motion to carry the majority of the Senate, it was critical that any evidence used be classed as major wrongdoing, or the Republicans would close ranks and oppose the action. She cautioned against attempting to use the weapon of sexual scandal. Whilst the Russians had evidence of impropriety recorded in a Moscow hotel, she pointed out, "As recent history shows with the soap opera *Bill, Monica and the Interns*, America forgives those who can't keep their pants on."

She concluded her briefing by stressing that it was unlikely that the current investigation led by Mueller would unearth direct links between actions by the Russians and the President. The power would lie in the extraction of more information from those being indicted. When vulnerable, the guilty talk, and are only too ready to implicate others. In a final warning, she stated again that any attempt at impeachment viewed as partisan would fail. "Integrity has a place, but believe me, I have learned to my cost that expedience and pragmatism are more powerful."

After taking them through the necessary constitutional processes, she finished with direct advice that reflected the answer to the question she had posed throughout her life: "Go for the man, not the institution; if his sins find him out, the institution is greater than he and will ultimately bring about his downfall."

It was the last time she would ever allow herself to accept an invitation back into the centre of power, from inside or outside the White House. As divisions in the political sphere increased, Jenny thought back to a less complicated time when she had been driven and inspired by so many beautiful ideas. A door had once been left open to which she was now drawn. She faced a future from which freedom from her present beckoned.

45

Free at Last...

Her dress, on that beach, was white and diaphanous, and the outline of her body was seductively silhouetted in the shimmering sunlight. She tossed her head, her soft, flowing hair cascading down her back; her mischievous, teasing eyes were captivating. An intense look – "I love you" – and she danced away; his hand reached out... Suddenly she was fleeing along the sand, laughing as she sprinted from his outstretched arms, daring him, taunting him, then holding him. Back in the tent, she lay before him, her long dark hair framing a cute smile, welcoming him back into her arms as the sound of the sea on the shore whispered to them only yards away...

Peter awoke, and knew that it was time to break free. Despite trying to dismiss his feelings as irrational, they flooded his consciousness, breaking like waves, gently, softly awakening his soul. The music from earlier, 'Where Do You Go To (My Lovely)?', played within him; but in his mind, it changed to 'Where *Did*...?'

His thoughts turned to the following day's schedule and the futility of his position. He looked through the window at the lights of central Dubai, and faceless buildings stared back with dispassionate derision.

When you're alone in your bed...

He visibly shook and stood up, attempting to wrench his mind back into focus. The music, the vision, the emotion swept over him again, returning like an ocean wave. His tablet was blinking at him but the message was a faded irrelevance.

Tell me the thoughts that surround you
I want to look inside your head, yes I do...

His prized Rolex and his immaculately pressed tailored suit were set out but suddenly seemed immaterial, and he almost resented them.

Your loveliness goes on and on, yes it does...

Unable to sleep, and in an attempt to push some logic into his thoughts, he pulled open the case containing the property sale agreements he needed to peruse before his meeting the following day. Disposing of the property Granvilles owned had been a sobering experience as the values had plummeted in an unexpected slump, wiping 25% off the anticipated return. But he just did not care any more. What had it all been about? Wistfully, he looked back at where he had been in a time before career, investment, stress, reports, borrowings, share valuations... and, yes, before he had let his life be corrupted.

Their tent was pitched just outside Le Lavandou; the scent of mimosas was intoxicating. She pulled back the tent flap, laughing at him. "Peter, you are just the cutest beach bum I ever saw, and I love you – will you be my forever?" As he looked at her, he knew their unity was infinite.

Finally, he made a decision, shocking himself with the audacity of it, despite a nervous ache of anticipation. Yet somehow he sensed she was waiting. Reaching for his phone, he hesitated, then said out loud in a slow drawl, "Hell yes", before calling a Texas number.

"Hey, Mr Cronkite, how's you doin', man?" Jonas's voice and demeanour were the same as ever.

"Love and peace to you, man. Jonas, I need Jenny's number; it's crazy, but I want to call in our Covenant."

Jonas's response was a pause, followed by a long, whistling sigh suggesting that this moment was not entirely unexpected. "Jesus Christ, Peter, what took you so long? You left it a frickin' lifetime. You been drinking, boy? If you have, you need to go back to sleep, capeesh; and if you haven't, well, hallelujah, I think I need a goddamn whisky."

Peter's tone was profound and urgent. "You were there, Jonas; I am reaching for a dream, but I made that Covenant, as she did to me. It is time, before there will be no more time."

Suddenly, Jonas was excited by the whole idea. "Peter, wow, this is a crazy, incredible thing you doin'; so damn crazy it is, like we used to say, just way out of sight, man. Hell, I need to roll a joint." He gave Peter her mobile number, parting with, "Hey, good luck, y'all. Far out, man, just far out."

20th May 2018, 4pm
Four Seasons Hotel, New York City

Jenny had finished preparing the case but her normally focused mind was interrupted, disorientated, distracted. She lay on the bed, and as her mind drifted, she was transported away, opening to the warmth of the dream that welcomed her back, bound by a truth she had never denied.

Back on the sands, she waited for him, watching his slim, taut body and smiling face as, dressed in gorgeous white jeans and a frill-fronted shirt, he walked towards her. A gentle breeze caressed her, and her thoughts reached for him. The words they had spoken and shared had never left her; nor had their afterwards in the lamplit room, the flame of the lantern dancing on the wall as they reached for one another, with chords of easy music echoing off the walls from the streets below...

"Oh my God," she whispered rapturously as she awoke, still holding him, recoiling from yet adoring the heavenly dream that had stolen her away. What had happened to him? Where was he right now? The passion – oh God, nothing had ever compared since. She admitted, even confessed, that she had never again given herself so totally, so beautifully to anyone. Now she remembered their hidden, secret sin with a wicked inner pang; just by looking intensely into his eyes and crossing her thighs she could reach an orgasm of overwhelming intimate joy, wrapped within her love. Her feelings were beyond expression, and she rejoiced in them.

Smiling inside, she tried to dismiss the thoughts that drew her from her conscious self, but her awareness floated languorously, focusing upon images, and the dream drew her in more deeply as the words of a song from that time played to her: 'Wild Thing' by the Troggs, which resonated as she felt her heart sing. She so needed to 'know', whether her dreams of love were 'for sure'. She knew the answer, which taunted her.

Jenny turned her mind to the case she needed to defend, trying in vain to force away the thoughts that surrounded her in her bed as trivial distractions, but which, somehow, seemed so powerful. What the hell was she doing there, defending this schmuck? Had her client known that he was flouting internal revenue laws when he moved $40 million US into the Caymans? She knew the answer to that too, and it haunted her.

She could hear Peter's wonderful voice as his warm brown eyes looked directly at her, hand on hers, his words mesmerising as the warm wind wafted over them, wavelets lapping the white sand, whilst nearby trees gently rustled and swayed. "I Covenant that my life will remain open to yours for all eternity…"

On a crazy impulse she reached for her iPhone, but then thought that this was getting a little too crazy… yet she felt something tangible drawing her in. *I can dream some more forbidden dreams*, she thought, and lay back down, reaching for him again as she let herself drift and break free, recalling his gorgeous body, teasing eyes and soft kisses. Her mind lifted her to the heady place she so vividly recalled, with flowers in her hair. She felt very aware, sensuous, languid, and was shocked to find she was aroused, imagining, wandering, recalling; every part of her body yearned, sensing that somehow he knew as she knew. Drifting, she could see him waiting for her, his arms open. She reached for her phone again… then it rang.

Her heart thumped. "Hello," she said shakily, "this is Jenny." She just somehow knew, even before he spoke, and she was trembling.

"*Eskimo Glace et chocolat, demandez les.*" The deep, still familiar voice echoed from the past to the present. She felt him in those first words, and shuddered with the shock.

"Peter? Tell me… oh no, really?" she gasped.

"'Oh no'? Now that's not quite the greeting I expected off me hippy chick."

"Peter, I do not believe this – really? I was about to get your number off Jonas. Oh my God, how incredibly wonderful. All these years, all this time. I have dreamed of this, I so wanted to speak again, even just once; I so, so wanted…" She began to sob.

His soft voice surrounded her. "Hey, you haven't even bought an ice cream yet. Well, maybe you should just run across the sand in your bikini and see what I've got." He sounded so familiar to her, with that strange, warm English accent that she always associated with him whenever she heard anyone from Liverpool speak.

"I don't think you would want to see me do that now; I'm not the girl you knew. I grew old, Peter, but in my heart, you have always been my Peter Pan. My hair is still quite long but I always wear it up now." God, she hated those last words; they sounded so pointlessly ridiculous, but she was more nervous than she could ever recall being.

"But, Jenny, I *do* want to see you, even if it is our last time, because you have been my Wendy and perhaps we should journey to Never Never Land. Can you fly?"

Her words stuttered out before she could stop herself. "Yes, I can... I mean, I can fly, I think, and yes, God forgive me, I do want to see you."

The die was cast, their chatter growing in confidence as they talked. An hour went by, then two, and still they spoke, drinking in each other's words. Their stories filled the empty years with an inevitable, unstoppable attraction, both of them wonderfully finding that they really did connect, despite the lifetime that had intervened. Their laughter was easy, and their words flowed. Finally they decided – crazily, but beautifully – that it was time they revisited their haven. They agreed a date for Sunday 17th June 2018 in Port Grimaud, time to be confirmed. Her heart sang; she sang. He felt unbelievable because he knew he could fly. They were as nature itself, and, having forced their lives to intervene, they were daring a return to where it all began – to where their instincts drew them.

She was his life's dream and he was hers. They ran naked down the beach of Brégançon, and laughed that President Pompidou might be watching them from the windows of the private palace across the short stretch of water overlooking the bay. Then into the ocean, swimming, turning, diving, eyes meeting, arms reaching, legs encircling, their passionate cries welcoming a new dawn.

Thursday 14th June 2018, 8.30am
New York City

Jenny stared out from her room on the ninth floor of Manhattan's Four Seasons Hotel, across Central Park to the Hudson beyond. This was the third part of the court hearing regarding her client's tax avoidance; a case she had accepted reluctantly, and only because Senator O'Brien had called her, seeking a favour. She no longer felt part of the old ways, and had no desire to be a part of them. Her life had a new direction, without direction, and she loved the sheer thrill of it. She felt utterly liberated from the constraints that had bound her, recalling how she had felt before reality had intervened and interrupted her idealistic innocence. Adrenaline mixed with a growing certainty began to guide her thoughts mischievously. Then, her mind made up, she descended into the lobby with its towering ceilings, marble floors and giant pillars, asked the bellboy to hail a cab and, with her two bulging briefcases, left for the Manhattan Law Courts, wondering whether her life had always been leading to this moment.

1.30pm
Titanic Hotel, Liverpool

Peter crossed St James Road, glancing briefly down the hill to the River Mersey; so different now from the gloomy sight of his childhood which, like his life, had been transformed. Now, smart, fashionable shops and restaurants lined the Albert Dock, whilst the chic promenade by the Liver Buildings rivalled any waterfront in the world. Contributing to the regeneration was one part of his life's work that he took some pride in.

He walked to the stylish Titanic Hotel, formerly the offices of the White Star Line, where he had been summoned to a meeting. He paused for a moment in the doorway, looking up to the railings of a balcony from which he knew that in 1912, executives of the White Star Line had shouted the latest news of the Titanic disaster to the crowds below. That made him put in perspective how small his decision was but he wondered whether he would now meet a tumultuous outcome. However, he felt driven and he knew he had more purpose now than he had had in a very long time. With renewed resolve he strode through the iconic round reception, taking the lift up to the smart suite on the second floor, and in seconds he was before the board of Wentworth Holdings.

"So, Peter," Eugene Franklin looked at him over thick-lensed half-moon glasses, his portly frame restrained by his silky grey business suit, "have we your agreement to sell your holding to us for the amount put forwards and for your immediate resignation? As you know from our previous discussion, if we don't reach agreement now, your holding will be diluted and lose value over time, and your position here will become, shall we say, untenable."

The chairman leant back, nodding knowingly to the four other people in the room: two from Wentworth's, and Peter's associates in Granvilles, Tommy Wilson and Bill Marsden. They appeared odious to Peter now and he looked at them with utter disdain. The chairman seemed unimposing, rather like the Fat Controller from *Thomas the Tank Engine*, Peter thought with a smile.

"Mr Franklin," he said, "I have thought hard about this and, notwithstanding the generosity of your paltry little offer – doubtless rather like the size of your mind, your ethics, and maybe even your manhood – I would like to tell you all to stick that offer, as they say here in Liverpool, where the sun doesn't shine. Good afternoon, gentlemen, and fuck you all." His triumph complete, he reached for his former life and shouted back, "I'm going to sell ice cream on the beach."

9.45am

New York County Courthouse, Foley Square, Manhattan

"Ah, Jenny," Calvin Rochsteiner purred to her as she entered the briefing room inside the court building. She was repulsed by him, with his overbearing, dominating nature; swept-back black hair; and shiny, immaculately tailored business suit, the shirt cuffs sporting somewhat vulgar gold and diamond cufflinks. Rochsteiner beamed at all he met with a slick, self-assuredness, propped up by the sycophants with whom he surrounded himself. "I trust you are well prepared to deal with the government's gross interference in my affairs." He smiled with overly whitened teeth.

His assistant, sitting next to his boss, smiled benevolently at Jenny through darkened glasses and asked, "Ms Baronio, may we see the final transcript of the defence so that we might, er, adjust as necessary?"

She looked down at him with unusual disdain. "That will not be necessary; my preparation is meticulous."

His reaction was to commence a protestation, but he was silenced by a wave from his superior.

Why had she dedicated her life to defending and helping so many lowlifes when she had had such fabulous intentions? She wondered whether she really had made any difference for the better. The past weeks had prompted so many questions, but in a way, they no longer mattered to her, because she was recapturing what she had lost.

As they entered the Court, she imagined music from a former time playing in her head telling her that the answer was *blowing in the wind*. She could see Peter waving to her across the sand, his long hair flying in the soft breeze. Right now, she grasped where the answer lay.

"All rise."

The stark words cut into her drifting consciousness; was she really going through with this? *The People versus Rochsteiner* – the truth of that case title resonated with her, and she knew this was the time, her time, and that the time was now. When invited, she stood, placing one hand on the edge of the lectern and retaining the other for gesture, which she relished making good use of in court. She was aware of her client's eyes drinking in her every move with a self-assured arrogance. "Your Honour," she declared loudly, defiantly and confidently, watching Calvin Rochsteiner's smiling face, his demeanour reflecting his utter belief that his dollars would decide the outcome, "Your Honour, I am an attorney, I believe, with some standing in my profession, and I take great pride in my position today, acting as an officer of the court. I have a responsibility, do I not, to see that justice is properly and judiciously managed?"

Rochsteiner's shiny round face was nodding with a confident smirk.

"Your Honour, I have looked into my client's affairs and the only conclusion that my client would expect is that he is found not guilty of the very serious charges he faces."

She could see him nodding even more vigorously.

"But, Your Honour, you will note that I used the term '*would* expect', not '*should* expect', because it must be supremely material to this court that justice is upheld. It is for that reason that I can declare, quite openly, candidly, and without any doubt whatsoever, that my client is guilty as charged. I can therefore no longer represent him, as I believe that justice should take its course."

There was an audible gasp in the courtroom, followed by increased muttering, and Jenny watched Rochsteiner's face turn white, then redden with anger. She sought leave of the court and, as proceedings were adjourned, left the building feeling, for the first time in years, that she was free at last.

46

Never Ending or Beginning

Monday 18th June 2018, 7.30am
Port Grimaud, Côte d'Azur, Southern France

Peter stood on the balcony of the Hôtel Plage des Rêves, mesmerised by his memories and transported to a former time, unmoving until he felt her soft arms around him. He turned to her, their eyes drinking one another in, tears falling in unison down their rapt faces.

"I love you, I love you – oh my God, Peter, where did we go to?" Her whispered choke was filled with emotion.

Peter held her to him, and she buried her head in his shoulder, their thoughts escaping to a faraway place, watching, remembering, drifting so distantly, yet joyfully in their awareness of their now; this was their time and they had seized it.

They had arrived in Nice the day before, but their yesterdays, todays and tomorrows had lost all meaning in the timeless bliss of their reunion. He had waited two hours for her flight, remembering vividly his utter emptiness so long ago as they had parted, each walking away from a dream they had created into lives they attempted to embrace. As the screen displayed the arrival of the 13.50 Flight B0241 from New York Newark, his heart leapt and he felt surprisingly nervous. It seemed an age before the passengers began to filter slowly through the arrivals doors.

When he saw her, he was filled with an excitement and euphoria he could scarcely restrain. Her dark hair was shorter now, yet still reached her shoulders; her looks were unmistakable, different yet so wonderfully familiar and, he smiled, those pouting lips still irresistible he had so often seen in his dreams. Jenny was wearing a long white jacket over a silky pink chemise, together with black pants which had an alluring sheen. He admired her open gold shoes, their chic heels showing that she had real style, in contrast to his open-necked denim shirt and matching jeans. She was older, but so very beautiful, with features that had carved themselves on his memory and which remained as exquisite as he had remembered.

As she turned the corner, her eyes met his, then, dropping her bags, she cried out, "Peter! Oh my God", before running to him and wrapping her arms around him. Her sobs were unstoppable, and she held him tightly as though frightened to let go. Finally, she looked him straight in the eyes. "So what took you so long, hippy boy? It's very rude to keep a girl waiting."

Their first kiss was as natural to them both as it was surprising, compressing time in the eternal union that they knew was theirs. They sensed a passion they had both only known once before in their lives, and exited the airport arm in arm as Peter dragged her case to the waiting hire car.

Oblivious to their lives in between, their intimacy is intense as they look across the bay, little changed in fifty years, their thoughts reeling, yet with the calm, triumphant acceptance that they had sought, savoured and found. They kiss, and feel the years slide away, time collapsing them into a place they had hidden from yet treasured all their lives.

Peter points out to her the old shutters of what had once been La Cave de Grimaud –now Le Cafe de Venice, but it would always retain its original identity to them. This was where Monsieur Le Fèvre, the very rounded *propriétaire*, had first serenaded them with his accordion. They laugh, remembering him singing 'That's Amore' in a very French accent as they had drank glass after glass of Ricard until their heads swam and their joy in one another was wonderfully amplified. Monsieur Le Fèvre had told them, "*Vous êtes amour, mes chers amis; ce sera pour toujours.*" ('You are just love, my dear friends; it will be for always.') Those words now echo across half a century binding them to this moment.

They kiss again, so aware of the nature of being, then they hold hands, her head resting on him, as their eyes take in the view across the vista of the shimmering sea. St-Tropez Bay stretches before them, the warm breeze gently caressing them, wafting the scents they never forgot, stirring their senses adding to their haven of contentment. They gaze over the sparkling Mediterranean, their thoughts transporting them back, and words are understood yet unspoken in the silence of their togetherness. Their awareness of each other is overwhelming yet peaceful in the stillness of this experience where time is no longer relevant. They are lost within a remembered happiness that is as joyful now as in the days of its creation. They are back inside the hopes born so many years ago, rekindled in their waves of love and desire.

Jenny is held by a sense of eternity and timeless serenity, never wanting anything to change this moment. Returning to the bed, she lies there, watching him on the balcony, trailing her gaze over his nakedness, marvelling at how well proportioned he is. He still has a gorgeous body, and she admires his profile and shapely, defined legs; she feels a passionate yearning again, giggling at her unashamed wantonness. At her age, she thought, how deliciously inappropriate it felt to be naughty, but still crave more. She looks down, pulling the sheets over herself, trying to conceal the changes time has made to the body she was once so proud of. Scarcely noticing Peter returning to her, she melts, surrendering, as he gently removes her hand from the covers before pulling them back, exposing her. He leans forwards, his eyes on hers, as ever so lovely, and kisses her shoulders, his tongue sending delicious shivers through her, evoking memories. Her arms encircle him. As their warm limbs wrap around one another, they lie together as one, seeking a profound connection which is returned in their deep embrace. She abandons herself to waves of ecstasy coursing through her as she cries out again and again, embracing heavenly heights which he too reaches, breathlessly whispering to her.

Peter holds her head on his chest, slowly stroking her hair, experiencing a profound tranquillity and a natural belonging. It was as if he had returned to a place he should never have left. He could find no logic in the decision they had made to meet, but nothing made more sense. He had lived his life making logical decisions and had lost himself in the process. This moment was, by any practical judgment, so wrong, but he also knew that it was so right. The fairy tale of the girl who in a different lifetime had run to him across the beach had become real. As he drifts into a restful, blissful doze, he mutters his changed mantra to *What was then, lives on now.*

She is unable to justify all that has happened, nor would she wish to; rapt with their daring to seek and their acquiescence in that dare to turn the clock back. The need had seized her and brought her to him, for he had invoked their Covenant: *I shall never leave what we have together, and wherever I am, I shall always return upon your call. I love you.* Her certain sense of yesterday is her uncertain signpost to her tomorrow, with all the in-between shrunk to a relevant irrelevance. She sees the images and listens to the sounds of her life as her eyes close and she drifts on a serene current to a heavenly, welcome unknown; her past has become her present and her soul rejoices. She giggles like the nineteen-year-old she was when they first met. *I am successful*, she tells herself, laughingly demoting the 'am' to 'was'– but the 'am' had been such a bummer because she had escaped to where her dreams had never left.

As if there had been no life between, their Summer of Love drew them back; back into a beautiful book that their words, actions and intimacy were writing, or rewriting. Their Covenants light up the future from an ethereal past. They drift into a dream they have created, dancing to the eternal dance of destiny, content within their perfect serenity, having sought and found their love and peace for always. Echoes of their circle descend in the words of a song – long forgotten, but to which they have returned upon their ever-spinning reel. There was no ending or beginning because it was and always would be in the windmills of their minds.

Round like a circle in a spiral
Like a wheel within a wheel
Never ending nor beginning
On an ever-spinning reel

Like a snowball down a mountain
Or a carnival balloon
Like a carousel that's turning
Running rings around the moon

Like a clock whose hands are sweeping
Past the minutes of its face
And the world is like an apple
Whirling silently in space

Like the circles that you find
In the windmills of your mind

Like a tunnel you can follow
To a tunnel of its own
Down a hollow to a cavern

Where the sun has never shone

Like a door that keeps revolving
In a half-forgotten dream
Or the ripples from a pebble
Someone tosses in a stream

Like a clock whose hands are sweeping
Past the minutes of its face
And the world is like an apple
Whirling silently in space

Like the circles that you find
In the windmills of your mind

Keys that jingle in your pocket
Words that jangle in your head
Why did summer go so quickly?
Was it something that you said?

Lovers walk along a shore
And leave their footprints in the sand
Was the sound of distant drumming
Just the fingers of your hand?

Pictures hanging in a hallway
Or the fragment of a song
Half-remembered names and faces
But to whom do they belong?

When you knew that it was over
Were you suddenly aware
That the autumn leaves were turning
To the colour of her hair?

A circle in a spiral
A wheel within a wheel
Never ending nor beginning
On an ever-spinning reel

As the images unwind
Like the circles that you find
In the windmills of your mind

('The Windmills of Your Mind'
Sung by Noel Harrison, 1968)

About the Author

Christopher Kerr was born in Bedford, but has lived in a variety of UK locations, mainly in the North West of England. He has become a fiction writer after a varied career as a civil servant, marketing executive, sales trainer, and entrepreneur.

He now concentrates on his writing which fulfils a lifelong ambition. This has become a passion and one which he describes as "a creative labour of love" (on most days!)

Christopher's debut novel, *The Covenant*, is a human drama story set against a background of contemporary and historical real-life events posing many poignant life questions.

His professed wish is that readers find his work thought provoking, compelling and enjoyable.

Christopher lives in an idyllic village in North Wales, enjoying welcome peace and tranquillity, where he is currently working on his third novel.

Thanks

I would like to thank those who have read, listened, commented, and supported me in the creation of this book. That support has been particularly valuable in exploring the emotional conflict flowing from questions and contradictions in the idealism facing the main characters. This process has also helped me to reflect on many aspects of my own life some elements of which may be reflected in the story. I am enormously grateful for your input and encouragement – You know who you are.